Bare Nell

Leslie Thomas was born in South Wales in 1931 and, when his parents died, he and his younger brother were brought up in an orphanage. His first book, *This Time Next Week*, is the autobiography of a happy orphan. At sixteen he became a reporter on a weekly newspaper in Essex and then did his National Service in Malaya during the Communist bandit war. *The Virgin Soldiers* tells of these days ; it was an immediate bestseller and has been made into a film with Lynn Redgrave and Hywel Bennett.

Returning to civilian life, Leslie Thomas joined the staff of the *Evening News*, becoming a top feature writer and travelling a great deal. His second novel, *Orange Wednesday*, was published in 1967. For nine months during 1967 he travelled around ten islands off the coast of Britain, the result of which was a lyrical travelogue, *Some Lovely Islands*, from which the BBC did a television series. He has continued to travel a great deal and has also written several television plays. He is a director of a London publishing house. His hobbies include golf, antiques and Queen's Park Rangers Football Club.

His other books include *Come to the War*, *His Lordship*, *Arthur McCann and All His Women*, *The Man With the Power*, *Onward Virgin Soldiers*, *Stand Up Virgin Soldiers*, *Tropic of Ruislip*, and *Dangerous Davies: The Last Detective* – all of them published in Pan.

Leslie Thomas

Bare Nell

Pan Books London and Sydney

First published 1977 by Eyre Methuen Ltd
This edition published 1978 by Pan Books Ltd,
Cavaye Place, London SW10 9PG
3rd printing 1978
© New Lion Dealings 1977
ISBN 0 330 25427 8
Printed and bound in Great Britain by
Richard Clay (The Chaucer Press) Ltd, Bungay, Suffolk

'Tis Pity She's a Whore
John Ford

one

Even as a young girl in the West Country of England I realized that I was intended for an unusual life. In the school I was clever with words and I was pretty in what they call in those parts a 'fruity' way. I knew that one day I could become perhaps a famous writer or a famous whore. It was my spelling let me down.

From the beginning I was called Bare Nell; little Nelly Luscombe, naked and brown, her body just podding, paddling in the village stream, or squatting there, trout wriggling about her thighs. In 1943, American soldiers waiting to go to war would toss money and chewing gum to me and ask where my mother was. They would sit on the stream bank and watch me for hours, looking wistful.

Oh, my dears, I have lived a full, sexy, merry and sad life. More even than *full*. Overflowing! In the chapel in Hopewell in the South Hams of Devon, I remember how the minister used to bawl at harvest festival, up in the pulpit, throwing his arms out over the loaves and the turnips and suchlike (he was a thoughtful man who would escort nervous young choirboys to their homes on dark Devon nights). 'What bounty!' he used to cry (at the harvest festival, that is, not on the dark Devon nights). 'What bounty!' I have always remembered that. For what bounty I have known! And not just bread and turnips either.

In this life I have known, loved, lived for, lived on, lived off, laughed and cried over, many men. Most are nameless (as well they deserve to be), others, such as Lennie the Lizard of the Lounge, I would prefer to forget.

My mother used to say: 'Have no shame in your life Nell,' and I have done nothing that causes me shame. I have worn white at all my weddings and I did *not* (Scotland Yard, please note) poison Pierre Arthur Bickerstaff.

In fact I would like to clear up the misunderstanding about Pierre Arthur Bickerstaff and the way he went, before I tell of anything else in my life. Pierre Arthur Bickerstaff died by swallowing sulphur which he ate by mistake for custard powder when he was drunk one New Year's Eve. He died so close to midnight that there was some doubt about which year should be mentioned on his gravestone. He was trying to make Crème Caramel. When he was sober he was quite a good cook. His grave can be seen in Kensal Green Cemetery in London and I place a posy of seasonal flowers upon it whenever I am in that area. The headstone is very nice, with a pair of strutting birds carved on it which, considering the custard powder tragedy, is just right. Indeed, so attached was I to Pierre Arthur Bickerstaff (as I have said repeatedly at the Yard) that I have put a deposit on the next burial plot to his, so that when I go, which I hope will be getting towards the end of the next fifty years, I can lie comfortably beside him. It will be quite like old times, but quieter. I have also deposited a sum of money with Pleesum, Squeezem, Filth and Foulenough, solicitors of Bognor Regis (a disguised name to protect the innocent), for the carving of a headstone for me. It will be a lump of red Devon rock topped with a female equestrian figure and the inscription: 'She rode the horse of Life'. I made that up myself.

For a long time I have wanted to put my life on paper because so many books have been written to give the whore a bad name. The bed has been my workbench. There all life is horizontal. Nothing that has happened has made me want to change my feeling that man's goodness outweighs his badness by an important half-an-ounce. I was born and I have lived as a romantic. As a little girl I could not understand why the sun did not go down with a roar.

I was born in the front room of Number Three Chapel Cottages, Upcoombe, a village over a red hill from Hopewell, in the county of Devon. My father, who was only five feet two and painfully thin, would shout every Friday: 'I'll knock this house down with my fists.' In my first years I really believed he could do it and I used to eye him cautiously and edge nearer the front door. It also occurred to me that if he actually carried out his threat, then the cottages on either side – and those on either side of them – would fall down too, since they formed a slanting terrace down the lane to the stream. I wouldn't have minded Mr Wormy Wood on the lower side finishing up under his house, because he used to swear at my mother, but on the upper side was Granny Lidstone who was sweet and old and only had one tooth and I would not have liked anything to have happened to her. I used to go into her house and she would make me toffee apples. One day I could stand it no longer and I warned her to be ready to get out of the house at a moment's notice because my father had the power to demolish the terrace, but she did not seem very worried. 'Your dad couldn't knock down a skittle, m'dearie,' she said, ' 'specially on a Friday.'

My mother spent her days boiling other people's washing in a gigantic copper vat. To me, looking into it was like looking into the centre of the earth. She seemed like a bundle of washing herself, round, done up with string around her waist, her hair plastered round her forehead and neck, her face sweating and like tallow. When she was not washing the clothes, she was ironing them, with more steam rising about her from the iron. She spent her life in vapour. Even as a little girl, I thought there must be some better way of living. My sister Mary and I would sit and watch her enveloped by the steam as if she were a ghost appearing at a seance. Mary, who was four years older than me, whispered one day: 'I'm not going to do that, Nell, not when I get grown.'

'Me neither, Mary,' I agreed. 'I'd rather go on the streets.' I was about eight at the time. I must have heard the expression from somewhere. Mary must have been impressed by the sound of it because I remember she said: 'And me.' She never did. She went to work in a bakery.

Ah, but it was a lovely place to be a child. The little Devon hills were all around, red earth and green meadows, the lanes were deep and banked with primroses as soon as the year's first sun came out. If I climbed on to my bedroom window sill and stood outside the house, holding on to the old guttering, I could glimpse a patch of the sea. Hopewell was only a mile away but to me it seemed like a distant place. It meant climbing the hill out of Upcoombe village and then going down the other side to the creek and the place where swans used to reflect themselves in the still water. The main street rose from there to the spire of the church on the next hill. I remember now climbing from our village on a morning at the beginning or the end of the year and seeing the point of the church and a few of the taller roofs nosing up through the mist that had gathered over the small town. It was a lovely place.

The stream that ran at the foot of Chapel Cottages was never more than a few inches deep. It ran over soft pebbles, polishing them more and in summer it had giant sunflowers on its banks, growing against the walls of the chapel and the end cottages. In those days I never gave a thought to where the stream came from or where it went. All I knew was that I could see clearly down through the water to my toes. It came in fact from a spring above the village and it ran eventually into the creek at Hopewell and then down to empty into the sea.

I was six when the war began. It seemed to make no difference, except that men went off, even my father eventually, which I thought was a masterstroke on the part of our Government because, provided with enough cider, he could undoubtedly do untold damage to enemy houses and property. Nothing seemed to change except that my mother was happier with my father absent. In fact I think she believed that Hitler could not be all bad to have brought about such a relief to a hard-pressed woman.

But the village and the town, season by season, went their ways, just as quiet and slowly as before. At the small school we had gas-mask drill and we were told to save paper, tins and water. I remember going to the stream and getting water in several containers, jugs, basins and a small bucket, and saving it in the front room of the house. I expected that someone would come and collect it for the war effort but they never did. Men from the town and the village died in battle, of course, and my mother would see their names in the local newspaper and shake her head and sometimes cry for they were often the friends of her younger days. She always read about the casualties. Sometimes I thought she was looking to see if my father was mentioned.

Growing up had never occurred to me, which I suppose is very odd for a child. I was content with the sameness of each day and the everyday things it brought. Nothing seemed to change. My own changes I was the last to notice.

Towards the middle of the war soldiers began to gather in the South Hams. A few at first but then more and more, thousands and thousands, mostly Americans riding in jeeps and tanks and floating on boats and barges in the Hopewell Creek.

Even then, as a child, I thought that under their helmets and in spite of their guns and blackened faces the soldiers seemed, for the most part, young and lost and lonely. Apart from the black faces, it's the sort of look you see in brothels the world over.

Some of the women from Hopewell, and some from our village and the others around us in the South Hams, used to keep the Americans company, but the women who did not used to gossip and watch them spitefully. The women who went with the Americans had stockings and butter and gum and this caused jealousy. Sometimes there were fights in the town pub and the vicar of Hopewell began praying in the services, asking God for peace in the world and also in the town.

There were some soldiers, as I said, who would come and sit on the bank of our stream when I was paddling there as I often did in summer. I had never thought I should wear anything to cover me in the stream and apparently neither had my mother because at one time there were only the villagers to see me and they had known me since I was born. Now these foreign American young men came regularly and sat there. They were very funny and kind and gave me chewing gum and sometimes a few pennies. I showed them how I could catch trout with my fingers and they would ask me about my mother (Was she young? Was she pretty?) and if my father was away at the war.

Then one evening I had stayed at the water a bit later than usual because my mother had gone to collect somebody's washing and had remained for a gossip about the Americans, and my sister Mary had gone to work as a housemaid in Hopewell Manor. She would go straight there from school and help until seven o'clock. They gave her half-a-crown a week for that.

So I was in the stream, naked as ever, with the day drawing away over the fields towards the sea. Some flies and midges came around for the air was warm and they liked the water and my skin. I was wondering if that night I could stop in the stream later than I had ever done before (already my feet were growing dim) when down Chapel Lane came the American soldier. It was the one who had told me that he was a cowboy before they took him for a soldier. He was alone.

'Hiya, Nell,' he called as soon as he saw me. 'Kinda late for that.'

'I'm waiting for my mum,' I said as though I always waited in mid-stream.

He squatted on the bank. 'Gee, that stream sure looks good,' he said. 'Is it cold?'

'No,' I said. 'What's your name?'

'I'm the one they call Bronco, Sergeant Bronco,' he said. 'I was a cowboy.'

'You told me that before,' I remembered. 'But I didn't know your name. Where's all the others gone?'

'Gone to chow,' he said. Then quickly, 'I feel like I could just get in that stream myself, Nelly. My feet are howling like dogs. We been marching.'

He took his shoes and socks off and then, mildly to my surprise, his trousers. I wondered why he could not just roll them up, but I thought he had to keep them smart for parades.

The evening was very dim and silent around us. I did not feel afraid, only curious. Thoughtfully I sat down in the stream, letting the water rise and run over my legs and gurgle around my waist. It was such a natural thing for me to do, almost like absently sitting in a chair, that I hardly noticed the feel of the water. Sergeant Bronco looked down at me and then jogged his chin up and down as though he had come to a decision about something.

'I just feel I might come and sit down there with you Nell,' he said slowly. His face was becoming dim but I could see his eyes shining.

'Ah,' I replied with childish aplomb. 'Then you'll get your drawers wet, won't you?'

'Right,' he smiled. 'Right. Okay, I'll take them off I guess.' And he did. Right there in the stream in the evening light. He moved a little closer and I smelled some drink on him, a familiar enough sensation for a girl who had lived years of Friday nights with my father. But he was smiling his friendly American smile and he took his drawers off as naturally as he might have taken off his hat. I was intrigued but not anxious.

It was the first male organ I had ever viewed. It dangled like some sort of a third leg. I stared at it in the dusk.

'What be you calling that?' I inquired, pointing my finger carefully towards it.

'That?' He seemed quite surprised I should have seen and looked down at it as though he had never noticed its existence before.

'Well now ... what yould you guess, Nell?'

I thought it was a reasonable inquiry. I'd been asked sillier questions at school. 'Well now,' I said slowly in my Devon way. 'I think it looks like a jumbo.'

12

'Great,' he laughed, but not loudly. He lowered himself into the stream and his face changed in the half light as the water closed around him. 'Gee ... ze. This is a little cool.' But we were there now, sitting in the water, the soldier and the naked little girl. He would soon be going to the war and I would stay in the village to grow up. Around us it was nearly dark and the only noise was the sound of the late insects and the slipping of the stream.

'Jumbo,' he repeated pensively. 'That's a great name for it.' He shuffled towards me, his bottom scraping the river bed. The tail and front flaps of his army shirt were trailing in the stream but he did not seem to notice. He came to a stop only a yard away. His big legs spread open with me sitting daintily between them. Now he was close I could see his face was worried.

'Nelly,' he said hoarsely. He kneeled up, bringing his torso out of the water. 'Nelly, will you hold Jumbo for me?'

I cannot recall being shocked or even thinking it an unreasonable request. Maybe I was meant for the life I eventually led. 'Hold it?' I inquired, however. I looked down. Despite the cold water, now running in streams down his skin, the implement was still long and thick, hanging down. 'Hold it?' I repeated. 'Now what would a maid like me be wanting to hold that great thing for?'

'It's to help ...' His voice was now a pleading croak. 'It's to help in the war against Hitler.'

Even after all these years and all my experience, I still think it was the best excuse I have ever heard.

It must have impressed me because I looked down again. His legs were arched. It was hanging like a bell in a belfry, its end just brushing the stream.

'Well, I don't know,' I hesitated. 'I bain't done that before. I'll go and ask my mum.'

'No,' he replied hurriedly. 'I'm getting real cold here.' He reached forward and took my hands in his, but gently. His eyes were anchored on my brown, bare face. He was still smiling but it was a trifle fixed. I let him take my hands and felt them touch, then close around the jumbo. It was hot! I was amazed. Then further amazed as it began to grow and stiffen in the most magic way. It was like the inflating of a bicycle tyre. I thought he was performing some sort of conjuring trick (which of course I suppose he was in a way of speaking) and my big eyes grew bigger in the dark as I felt the life pushing through it. 'Sergeant Bronco,' I whispered uncertainly, 'it's moving.' I had a notion it might even wriggle off downstream.

'Sure, sure.' His voice was like grit now. 'Hold on to it honey and it won't be going nowhere.'

I should confess now that I liked the feel of it and it is a pleasure that has never left me. Its silken strength, its homely warmth, its mind of its own. I began to run my fingers over it and the small palms of my hands. It had stiffened like the stalk of a bullrush. I was amazed by its capacity for growth. The man looked all out of proportion. 'Will it get any bigger?' I inquired, pushing my face down towards it to get a better view.

'It could try,' he said. But his voice was like the last gasp of somebody being strangled. I looked up to see the most tremendous torment in his face. Instinctively I rubbed my fingers up and down. The expression tightened, as though someone was pulling together a strong bag. 'Jesus ... I'm coming,' he whispered.

'Don't die!' I cried in misunderstanding. I had genuinely thought he was about to expire and that his remark was his warning Jesus that he was on his way. My Auntie Dolly had said a similar thing before she went.

He was not dying but in the next moment he threw himself towards me and clutching my small body in his arms he crushed me to him. Ridiculously he hung on to me for a minute or more and then collapsed into the stream, his torment washed away with the innocent water. His face was running with tears. He pulled himself from the water and pressed his young man's cheek tenderly to mine.

'Nelly,' he said. 'Great Nelly.'

I never saw him again. He must have gone off to the war and perhaps he lived and perhaps he died. I promised I would keep our secret (and I have until this day) and I went home as usual, had my supper and went to bed. My mother came up to hear my prayers and I prayed especially for the sergeant, which amused and puzzled her. But I, Nelly Luscombe, knew that I had already done something to help the fight against Hitler.

'Mum,' I said before I went to sleep. 'We're going to win the war.'

*

By the finish of June all the soldiers had gone and the country-side had fallen silent. No more tanks in the lanes or guns in the streets. It was as though they had taken their war completely with them. Aeroplanes passed distant in the sky, like needles shining on a blue cloth, but they seemed to have nothing to do with us or our lives.

The Americans were missed by some, of course. By the publicans and the shopkeepers and the women they used to keep company with. No more gum or stockings, no more grappling in the alleys of the town. The women seemed lost, missing the Americans more, it seemed, than they missed their true husbands who were away fighting in some other part of the war. I left the village school that summer and had to go into Hopewell to the town school and on afternoons while I was waiting with the other children for the bus that went to the village, I would sometimes see these women, half a dozen or so, sitting on the seats by the creek where they had once sat to meet their lovers. Now they were subdued and just crouched there throwing stones at the swans. Some of the other women who were in the town would not speak to them.

Once I saw one of the lonely women hit one of the swans with a quarter brick and it took off from the creek in a terrible fright with all the other swans following it. They set out down the water towards the sea, in a long vee-formation, the air creaking out from under their wings. They looked lovely; just like bombers. But the women just sat and stared at them until they were out of sight.

Then one of them began to cry and wail. All us little children waiting for the bus heard her plainly cry: 'Oh Wilbur! Oh Wilbur! Where be you now?' And she got up and tried to throw herself bodily into the creek. The others all grabbed her and stopped her before she got to the edge, but the upset spread to all of them and another cried out: 'Oh Hank, my Hank.' And a third. 'Benjie! Benjie boy!' And before long they were all crying and wailing on the seat on the very edge of the creek. It was a very curious sight to see. I could not understand it, all howling and hanging on to each others necks like that, while we children and the townspeople stood and watched. I suppose it was the first time any of the poor women had really been in love.

But it was summer and I was a young girl. The noises of

wasps about in the faces of the sunflowers, the warmth of the air, the smell of the fields, all went unappreciated by me. All I knew was that they were there, all about me. Every day I woke early, always it seemed to the fresh sun. I dressed in one of my three dresses for school. I continued to bathe in the stream each afternoon now uninterrupted, and always naked. Now I come to consider it, my wardrobe was so sparse I could hardly have bathed any other way but nude. Not that anyone ever said 'nude' in those parts at that time. I never heard the word until I was working in more sophisticated, but still naked circumstances. In the stream I was bare.

My adventure with Sergeant Bronco had interested me, and I thought about it from time to time, but it had given me no feeling of disturbance. It was not necessary for me to go to any great effort to keep it a secret because it did not lie in my mind. I was more moved, I think, the first time I ever saw a farmer's fingers on a cow's udder and more alarmed the first time I saw a carthorse crap in the road. Many years later a psychiatrist became deeply interested when I told him these true facts.

In those summers we had three weeks off from school in August and another three weeks in later September and earlier October, so that we children could help with the harvest. That was a good time for us, in the fields with the men, really helping with the threshing and the corn. The days always seemed to be hot and red and I can smell the dust of the corn now. Rabbits and rats would run in terror from the island of grain that got ever-smaller in the middle of the field. The dogs would chase them in furious excitement and the men would often shoot the rabbits and take them home to be skinned and cooked.

The men used to bring hunks of bread and cheese and slices of onion in muslin cloth and as the day wore on they sweated more and would drink pint upon pint of rough cider. This was provided by whoever owned the field and was known in the locality as Farmer's Revenge because of the tremendous diarrhoea it caused. The men were used to it, of course, but if any of us children drank it we would soon be seen streaking across the cut field as fast as our small legs would carry us. I can still remember the awful sensation of believing that I would not reach the hedge in time and the agony of hearing the great guffing laughs of the men as I ran. The psychiatrist was very interested in that too.

What used to be worrying was that as the evening got near the men used to get very fruity on the cider and start making to catch some of the older girls and young women who were up there working with them. My mother would always come and fetch me from the field at six o'clock because she knew that the raw cider made the men feel mazed and randy. Then, to my surprise, she started coming up to the fields to work herself, bending with the rest of them and having an occasional swig of the cider flagon. It did her a real good. Her face lost its steamy look and her cheeks got brown and her eyes bright. She had always been on the rounded side, but I could see this pleased some of the men who would pause to look down her brown neck to her large breasts when she was bending and working. One day I noticed three farm men all timing their own bending so that they were upright as she bent down. It was like a sort of slow barn dance. When she realized what they were about she pretended to be annoyed but after a minute she laughed as merrily as any of them. I had never seen her like this. It was as if she felt young again.

There was a young man called Luke, big and red as a plum, with curly hair, who had bad eyes which kept him from the war. He could see my mother well enough, though, and I could see that she liked him, for they always laughed together and it was his cider flagon she always drank from. They used to make silly jokes and hoot like owls about them. I stood aside and wondered why she had never laughed with my father like that and, as well, why my father, who was undersized, should have been sent to fight Hitler, while Luke, just because he had got sheep dust or corn dust in his eyes, should be there in an English field gathering the harvest with my mother.

I was further mystified when, one noon when everyone was taking their dinnertime and the dogs were lying under the bellies of the horses in the shade, I wandered off to the far edge of the field away from the place where we were working. The corn was still standing there and I went around the edge, feeling the ears of grain tickling under my armpits. My hair and my forehead must have been just above the level of the crop. I was going to a bank of honeysuckle or something (to think I have forgotten honeysuckle) and I was sniffing the air to get a scent of it when I smelled the unmistakable stench of raw cider. Then I heard a growling laugh from somewhere ahead and then a guilty chuckle that I knew was my mother's voice.

'Now Luke Lethbridge,' I heard her whisper. 'We shouldn't be a-doing of this. These corn stalks are sore on my arse.'

I moved a yard further in the grain and I could see them wallowing. I could hear him groaning and sweating. Then, to my astonishment, a great pink, male rump rose above the corn like a whale coming to the surface of the sea. It rose and fell several times and I heard Luke Lethbridge grunting happily and my mother making sweet groans. I did not run, I wandered away, worried and wondering.

Bravery has always come naturally to me. That evening when it was getting dim and everyone was just about going home, I went to Luke and stopped him with my small hand on his thick belt.

'Luke Lethbridge,' I said, 'what were you about with my mum in the crop?'

He had fair hair and fair bushy eyebrows (very bushy, come to think of it; perhaps that's why he couldn't see enough to go and fight in the war). His face was round and red with the work. He stopped and thought about it, as though he wondered if it was worth an answer.

'Rastling,' he said at last. 'We was rastling, maid.'

'Rastling? Rastling?' I remember saying bitterly. 'How be it you take your bags off your arse for rastling?'

'It was 'ot, maid,' he said. Devon farm labourers rarely take offence. 'It was 'ot, when we was about it.'

And then he clumped away, his big boots banging the earth, his coat over his shoulder, his shoulders swaying like a farm cat heading for his wife and his tea.

The matter came to an end in a very odd way. There was another man working in the fields, a man called Daniel Pentecost, as dark as Luke Lethbridge was fair. He was short and wide, like an anvil, and just as strong. He must have taken more than one glance at my mother too because he and Luke became enemies in the harvest fields that year. When I think of it now, it is amazing the attraction that she had, rough and full as she was, for these country men.

I don't know whether my mother paid any heed to the lust,

love or jealousy of Daniel Pentecost, but he was driven to do the thing he did only because of her. Daniel had charge of one of the teams of big horses which pulled the reaper through the standing corn or the waiting hay. They still used them then, their retirement to make way for the tractors put back by the war, and they were handsome things, with bowed heads and big shoulders, pulling the farm machinery. Years later some crazy man showed me an obscene photograph involving one of these noble horses and I was so upset that I burst into tears and struck him on the ear with a three-quarters-full bottle of gin. It was no more than he deserved.

There were two horses in Daniel's team and he would drive them from his perch on the reaper (or the plough at the onset of the year) with shouts of 'Hup, Samson! Hup, Goliath! Come on ye big bastards!' He never said very much else, even at the village pub. It seemed he could only talk to horses.

One dinnertime towards the end of the harvest days Daniel sat eating and swigging from his flagon, beneath his horse's belly, like the dogs, shading himself from the noon sun. (In winter, when he was ploughing, he had been known to shelter below the horses when there was heavy rain. He was quite at home there.) I had been scampering with the other children through the hedges and the honeysuckle and returned to the place where the workers were all gathered to see at once that my mother and her lover Luke were missing. I remember how loaded my heart felt. I sat down beside one of the wagons and considered setting the corn afire. Daniel's thoughts must have been on the same subject. He rose from beneath the horses' stomachs and quietly began hitching them to the reaper.

'Ho, there, Dan'l,' one of the other men shouted. 'You no need to be startin' yet! 'Tis only one!'

'Knackers to you, Brian Brewer,' Daniel replied slowly. 'I be startin' now.'

They must have realized what he was about, because everyone stopped eating their bread and cheese and the cider was stopped on the way to men's lips. The women and children grouped closer together as they do in a crisis. But I stood apart from the others and watched him tut and turn his horses off to the fringe of the grain where he had been cutting before dinnertime. The reaper turned over quietly behind him.

'Ho, Samson! Ho, Goliath! Come on ye big bastards!' he

called and leaned forward like the captain of a ship searching for something ahead.

He had gone right to the distant side of the field before I, in my childish way, realized what mischief he was about. If the others knew truly what it was, then they still did not move, but stood like stones watching him. Then it came to me. He was heading those horses and that great whirling reaper for the hiding place among the grain of my mother and Luke Lethbridge. 'No you don't, Dan'l Pentecost!' I suddenly cried. 'Don't you go a-cutting of my mother!'

I started to run screaming across the stubble. The stalks cut my ankles and my legs as I ran. There was a long gap behind me and then something released the others from their trance and they all started to fly after me. It must have been a rare and curious sight to see us all charging across that stubble, me half-naked at the front, women with skirts up, men stripped to the waist, ploughing on with their heavy boots, following, and a long tail of excited children, eager for the sight of blood, coming along behind.

Luke must have been giving my mother a good seein'-to, because they did not hear the approach of the horses and the reaper and they did not hear us shouting. Our agricultural training was such that we ran in a broad angle around the edge of the uncut grain, not daring to go through it, or knowing that it would be too thick to penetrate.

Daniel and his horses moved on. I was running like I had never run and yelling in my piping little voice. Daniel heard me and turned in his seat. Then he looked forward again and urged Samson and Goliath, the big bastards, on with further relish.

They say it was Goliath that stepped right in the middle of Luke Lethbridge's back. It was certainly Goliath that reared up first, bringing the other horse up with him in the shafts. Like some daytime demon, Daniel tried to urge them on so the blades of the machine he was trailing would pass over the couple in the grain. As it was, the horses nearly accomplished his wicked plan for they flew up and then plunged down. But they had slewed to one side and Luke and my dear mother just escaped the full weight of the iron hoofs, which can give you a nasty knock at the best of times.

Daniel got himself down from the seat of the reaper and took off across the fields; nobody chased him. They say he was crazed. They say he reached Exeter the next day and joined the Navy.

The villagers got hold of the horses and then lifted poor Luke from on top of my mother. It was a strange sight there in the sunny field. He was without his trousers, and right in the middle of his back, like a blacksmith's sign, was the imprint of the great horseshoe. My dear mother had been pressed several inches into the field and actually left a hole when they pulled her out. I had feared she might be bare. She was not but she might as well have been. Her skirts were up and her drawers were down and her breasts were bulging fully out of her bodice like loaded goatskins. Nobody seemed to be able to do anything about it so I pushed my way between them all, the staring fools, and heaved her breasts back where they belonged and pulled her skirt decently down.

'God bless you Nelly, darling,' she gasped, opening her troubled eyes. 'Your mother was just having a rest.'

One odd result of my mother's injuries, which were not very serious (neither were Luke's. A lot of local men said coarsely that he had got the horse to help him 'get in'), was that my father was given compassionate leave from the war to see her. It was the only bit of compassion he had ever had anything to do with.

He turned up in his army clothes and it turned out that he had not actually been at the war at all but somewhere like Aldershot. In a cookhouse. He had soup on his trousers. They had not bothered to give him much of a uniform and he arrived looking like a furtive whippet, his tunic collar miles too big. Nobody told him what actually happened in the cornfield, or if they did he had too much caution to get tangled with big Luke, and all he did was mutter some words of sympathy to my mother and pat myself and my sister Mary on the head. He had funny, heavy hands for such a weedy man and his patting always hurt like someone hitting you with a piece of wood. At times this sign of affection set us both crying, which made him surprised and often very angry.

It did not take him long to find his way from the house and smartly up Chapel Lane to the pub. We watched from the cottage windows and saw his comical figure going jerkily up the cobbles, the uniform seeming to hang in heavy layers about him. He came back brimming with cidar bombast and threats. One of his threats was nasty and very dramatic, since he made it clear that he now had the power to blow us all up. In the past his promise had been to tear down the house with his hands, but the army had now taught him how to explode it. Before our alarmed and helpless faces – Mary and I were crouched against the kitchen table and our mother was sitting white as her own washing in the rocking chair – he proceeded to make preparations for the disaster.

It seemed enormously simple. From his army pack he produced a metal oblong box, formed by two army mess-tins (although we didn't know they were mess-tins), one fitting inside the other. He placed them carefully on the table and we stared at them.

'TNT,' he said. 'Explosives.'

'Percy,' my bruised mother said from her corner. 'You mustn't frighten our little girls like that. Or me.'

'I'm going to blow us all up,' he said, hardly turning to her. He smiled his ghastly cider-stained smile in our faces. 'It's something I've always wanted to do.'

There didn't seem much answer to that, but I tried. 'Daddy,' I said trembling. 'You'll be disturbing Granny Lidstone next door. And her'll be in bed.'

'Her'll soon be out of it, the old cow,' he replied wickedly. His teeth were so rotten and he had that fearful smile. He looked around at us, to see, it seemed, if we were paying attention.

'TNT,' he said again. 'Packed solid with it my dears. Now the fuse.'

He took from his pocket what looked uncommonly like a bootlace – and was in fact a bootlace – and this he deliberately dipped into the paraffin of one of the two lamps we had in the house. 'The fuse,' he said, holding it up like a conjuror.

'Percy.' My mother was shaking. She was trying to get out of the rocking chair. 'Percy you must not blow this house up. You've had too much scrumpy.'

He turned and gave her an easy push which sent her back into the chair and the chair to rocking. 'This is my house, you are my wife, and these are my little maids,' he said smugly. 'I'll

22

blow them up if I like. And I ain't had too much scrumpy. It's like mule's piss at Aldershot.'

None of us had tried to escape. It was as if he had mesmerized us. But now, to give added effect, the swine went up to the kitchen door and locked it with great show. He grinned like a pantomime demon around the table. Mary put her hand out and held mine. 'Now ... the matches,' he said.

'Percy, mercy. God help us,' moaned mother.

'You'll be with God in a few minutes,' he said, smug as ever. A thought struck him. 'On the other hand we ought to tell him we're on the way. Let's have a prayer.'

The lousy bastard made us kneel and we prayed in faltering voices for our everlasting life. Mother tried to put in a word about saving us from the bomb, but dad turned quickly and slapped his hand over her mouth before the message was half out. When we had finished the prayers he grinned around at our faces and then said again: 'Matches.'

He struck three before he got one alight and I swear he was doing it purposely to prolong the agony. His bomb was sitting on the table with the bootlace fuse hanging from it like a wet tail. While he was fumbling about with the matches I pushed it across the table towards him but he saw me and pushed it back again. Mary began to cry and I joined in and then my mother began to howl louder than any of us.

He carefully lit the third match and put it to his fuse. It flared up with a blue flame and travelled slowly, but fast enough for us, up the length of the lace towards the mess-tins. We all stared, our eyes bright with fear, I should think, in that lamplight. Then the flame reached the bomb. We clenched our eyes together and Mary almost broke the fingers of my hand.

'Bang!' shouted my father. We all screamed and fell down. But we were not dead and lying there it crossed my mind that he had been up to his sodding tricks again. Trembling we got up and looked over the edge of the table. He was sitting grinning. He opened his bomb, taking out some cheese sandwiches and began to munch them. What a bastard.

two

The school at Hopewell was down an old cobbly street and then up again to where the playground was slanted on the side of a hill, a good place for roller skates, cart-wheels and sliding on frosty mornings. At the bottom of the playground incline was the school wall and often, in all seasons, children were sent to the Cottage Hospital after colliding with the wall.

From outside villages the pupils came in by buses to school. My memories of the place are of droning voices chanting out multiplication tables into close summer afternoons, of the smell of floor polish and cabbage, blackboard chalk and the various country smells brought in by the children and the farms. In class I sat next to a boy called Bertie Hannaford who reeked of pigs. It was not his fault – as he told me tearfully when I complained about it – because he had to work in his father's sties before setting off for school each morning. I think this crisis between us sparked off our love affair. It made me sorry to think of him wallowing in all that swill on early mornings, and, fighting every inch of the way, I forced myself to sit even closer to him in class, in assembly and even at the tables at dinnertime when all the other children would keep themselves as far away as possible. He was eleven and I was ten.

After we had realized we were in love, we would walk hand-in-hand from the school, his palm as soft as mine (the result, I suppose, of dipping it daily into pig buckets), and the most terrible foul stench coming from his simple clothes. I kept promising to kiss him and, when I could put it off no longer, I took a deep breath and almost staggered into that first, and as it happened, last kiss. It was not the piggy nature of the kiss, or the boy, that stopped the romance. In fact he kissed very well, powerfully and with a certain amount of gnawing, surprising in a young lad like that. I suppose that might have come from watching the pigs too.

No, the thing that stopped our affair was the result of his male desire to show off. Only a few minutes, in fact, after that first kiss, while I was still gulping for air, he picked up an acorn from beneath the tree under which we had romantically embraced.

'Oi can put this right up my snout,' he said, beaming with simple vanity. 'True as true, oi can.'

Even at ten I remember feeling unimpressed at this bragging. Putting an acorn up a nose seemed to me to be both stupid and the sure sign of a big nostril. Years later a man tried to tell me he could put a pigeon's egg in his ear and I could not find any interest for that either.

'Don't you bother Bertie Hannaford,' I said. 'It don't make any odds to me whether that acorn goes up your snout or not.'

'You don't think oi can do it,' he grunted. 'But oi can. Sure as shit oi can.'

'Oh go on then,' I sighed, 'Bertie Hannaford.' I sat down under the tree, putting my elbows on my knees. Just to make a further impression he started to do some kind of what you might call limbering-up exercises, running around in tight circles, his thin legs like sticks out of his ragged, baggy shorts.

'Why be you a-doin' that, Bertie?' I asked him. By then I must have begun to wonder what romance I had seen in him in the first place.

'Oi be getting a sweat on,' he replied, still whirling about in little rings. 'If oi get a sweat on then 'ee slips up easier, don't un?'

I cupped my chin in my hands and watched him, feeling very dull. It's a mood that has come over me many times since, for I never have been able to like men who show off. Eventually his whirling slowed and then he stopped, standing, panting. The smell of the sty came from him in strong waves.

'Now,' he panted. ' 'Ere goes.'

He held up the big brown acorn for me to see. I nodded and sat watching. 'Da-ta-taaaa ...' he imitated a sort of fanfare, then, first squinting down at the acorn, pushed it up his nose. I was surprised how easily it slid up there. It bulged underneath his skin making him look as though he had a boil or a growth.

'There then,' he said proudly, spreading out his hand like some act in a circus. His voice sounded strange. ' 'Ow about that, Nelly Luscombe?'

'Ever so good,' I answered, then quite impressed by the performance. I paused and looked at him standing there. 'Now let's see you get it down.'

He laughed what was supposed to be a reckless laugh. 'Oi'll

get 'ee down, all right,' he reckoned. 'That bain't any bother for oi.'

He put his thumb to the outside of his nose and pressed downwards. Nothing happened. Then two fingers also pushing down. The acorn stayed up there. Then two fingers pushing down and one from the other hand up inside the nostril. Nothing came down. Slowly he turned towards me with terror in his face.

'Oi'll be fucked,' he trembled. 'It be stuck!'

Stuck it was. We tried everything, pushing, pulling, trying to lever it out with his penknife. I even thought of banging him on the side of the nose with a stone to try and splinter the acorn, but he backed away just as I was about to hit him. He burst into tears and I had to take him back to school. We were late for the afternoon lessons and the teacher, a sharp, short-sighted woman, yelled at us and made us sit down at our desks. All the other children began to snigger. Bertie was still sobbing but the teacher purposely took no notice of him. She went on with the lesson. My hand kept half going up and down again but she ignored me too. Then Bertie howled dramatically. 'Oi be dyin'! Oi got an acorn stuck up my nose.'

She became very angry because she thought at first that he was playing-up, but then she saw the swollen and bruised nose and the blood around the nostril and she bent down and had a look. She went to get the headmaster who had a further look and eventually sent for the town ambulance. Bertie was taken to the Cottage Hospital where they got the acorn down and sent him home.

Somehow the business had irritated me and I decided I had been wrong about him. I realized I could never love anybody so foolish as to put an acorn up their nostril and not be able to get it down again.

In country places like that they look on children, or used to look on them, with the same sort of quaint mind that they would on livestock. A boy might have a good eye for a furrow or show promise in the making of a fence; a girl would be considered in the same way, as something useful, or something that would be useful one day. I remember going to a harvest supper and dance, making myself look all shining and pretty in a red dress with a white frill at the hem. I had lovely full hair and a pretty face and brown arms and legs and the beginnings of the bust that was to make me famous. At the dance I knew some of the boys and more of the men were watching me. My mother dropped her purse and I purposely bent over from the waist to display all my rounded parts and healthy legs. Behind me I heard two farm men discussing the view.

'Ah,' one of them said, with Devon slowness. 'That little Nell Luscombe be growing fast. Won't be long afore 'er'll carry a couple o' good churns.'

They were great nights, those. The harvest supper and dance, the Christmas supper and the Easter Barn Dance. I remember them better than all the grand events of later years. The war was far away outside the walls of the village hall and inside all was rosy and comfortable, with enough to eat and drink and with all sorts of dancing and the village people doing turns on the stage. Even the local gentry would come along. Sir Waldo Beechcroft, his wife, Lady Martha, and sometimes their idiot son Parsifal. Parsifal was a poor young lad, mazed as they said locally, who turned the same hollow ghastly smile on everyone.

Rumours were put around that he sat for hours in Sir Waldo's barn flipping beans in the air from the end of his erect penis, a story I later found to be correct. Lady Martha talked to herself a great deal and was said to be in direct communication with ghosts. Her other son, who was sane, had been killed in the battles in France.

Sir Waldo was then in his late fifties. He was thin and hairless and had a long damp nose. It was rumoured that he liked wild dancing and young girls. It was his nose that drew my eyes. It seemed to start high up on the baldness of his head and descend like a long toboggan run. Fascinated I stared up it while we were partners, for we had come together in a progressive barn dance, the Lord and the little girl.

'Now who are you, gel?' His voice seemed to fall down to me.

'Nelly Luscombe,' I said. 'From Chapel Lane.' I thought I had said it in my normal voice, but perhaps I had whispered it because I was shy (although I doubt that) or perhaps the village band's music was too loud. Anyway he called down that he had not heard me. He asked me again. But he still did not hear. So he put his hard arms around my waist and lifted me up to him. I ended up with my legs around his thin ribs and his hands making a seat for my bottom. Everybody laughed at his kindness and liking for children.

'Now *who* are you?' he repeated. 'Pretty.'

'NELLY LUSCOMBE!' I bawled in his face. I heard the consternation of the villagers all around me and I heard my mother squeak over everybody else. But Sir Waldo pretended to laugh sportingly (the laugh shot down his nose too) and put me down to the floor again. I was glad of that.

'When you're a bigger girl, Nelly,' he snorted, 'you must come and work at the house. You'll like that.'

I was not at all sure that I would like it but I said a proper, grateful 'thank you' to him before he moved on to the next partner. My mother took me home that night and we walked, with my sister Mary, along the moonlit road. My stream was lying all silvery at the foot of the lane and owls were about in the roofs. My mother was upset.

'Nell,' she said as we went up the lane. 'You're a wicked girl.'

'Why am I, mum?' I asked surprised.

'You should never, *never*, shout in the face of the gentry,' she said. ' 'Tis not proper.'

When I think now of all the faces of the gentry I have shouted at, and worse, I have to laugh. But she meant it, poor creature. She did not know any better.

When I was very young I attracted the red eye of many an old man, when I was in my early twenties it was the middle-aged husband who wandered my way, and now I am casually coming to middle age myself it is the young men who find me to their liking. It is strange how the fancies go.

The headmaster at the town school was a gentle, eccentric and grey man, Mr Bunn, who in attempting to bring home to us in that peaceful place the fact that there was a war on would sometimes walk about the school wearing a gas mask. One day, in assembly, he insisted that all the other teachers wear their gas masks on the platform and he read the lesson from the Bible and said muffled prayers through the black piggy snout of what he called his respirator. The children began to snigger and then, for we could not help ourselves, laugh outright. The school was in uproar. The next day he made us all wear our gas masks through assembly. We sang 'God has blotted them out' and it must have sounded very strange. It was also very difficult and some children fainted. Mr Bunn said it was all to make us aware of the war.

Mr Bunn should have retired long before but because of the shortage of teachers in those times he stayed on. But he became increasingly unusual. Even further obsessed with the war effort he had his pupils ranging the countryside gathering wastepaper and old tins and other rubbish he imagined would defeat what he called the Hordes of Hunland. None of this salvage was ever collected and it stood like a giant rubbish dump in the school playground for months until the sanitary authorities removed it. He encouraged us to Dig for Victory and could be seen himself, far into the night, digging up old waste pieces of ground, apparently thinking that they would be useful for growing food. The vicar had a battle with him when he wanted to start digging up the churchyard and one summer evening he stood beside the bowling green, grinning and holding a garden fork. The police were called to warn him.

One Christmas Mr Bunn wrote a nativity play for the school which caused controversy because it included the figure of Hitler who arrived in the Bethlehem stable with the object of putting Jesus down and was attacked with a sickle by the Virgin Mary.

For me the idea seemed to be exciting and I was the first to volunteer to play Hitler and when this was rejected, put my hand up for the second-best part of the Virgin Mary and was accepted. My mother was very pleased when she heard the news (she had some belief that anything like that gave you credit with God). She was puzzled and doubtful about the inclusion of Hitler but, since she accepted unquestioningly every decision made by authority or by anyone socially higher than herself – which was almost everyone – she reasoned that it had to be all right. She offered to make me a Virgin Mary outfit from a pattern but Mr Bunn said they had suitable costumes in the school store and it was with the object of seeing if they would fit that one afternoon he called me from class.

He was a nice, feathery old man, I thought, although that day he was upset because some boys had written 'Mr Bunn is a Hun' on the school lavatory wall. I was content to follow him to the storeroom and even to hold his friendly, shaky hand for the final part of the ascent up the school stairs.

'There,' he breathed when we had finally reached the storeroom. He closed the door behind us. It would give us more space that way he said, more leeway. I couldn't understand why space was needed to be fitted out with a few flowing bits of cloth, but I did not ask. He turned his face around the shelves. It was not a very large room but it was stacked with school junk. Eventually he said: 'Ah yes, Nelly. There it is. The Virgin Mary.'

There was a box on a high shelf and he said he could not reach it. He would have to go and fetch a step-ladder.

'Don't, Sir,' I said helpfully. 'I could reach it. If you lift me up.' I must have been a dirty old man's dream. I was always being lifted up.

Mr Bunn seemed amazed and delighted by the suggestion. 'Now I would never have thought of that,' he said, looking cheered. 'Let's put a chair up against the door so nobody comes in unexpectedly and knocks us all over like skittles.' He got a chair (it was then I began wondering why he didn't simply stand on the chair as he had to go and fetch one anyway) and fixed it under the door handle. Wheezing a bit he crouched down and I climbed on to his old shoulders. The first thing I felt were the bristly grey hairs at the back of his neck sticking into the skin of my legs.

'Upsidaisy,' he growled jovially as I rose in the air. He held me just above my podgy knees. I did not know the exact box which contained the Virgin Mary outfit and he seemed to have forgotten, or lost it, so for a while we waltzed back and forwards, with me jogging against the nape of his neck. I could feel him beginning to sweat. It was very odd being like that in that small, tall store-room.

But he was quite elderly and I think the weight and the strain of one thing and another weakened him because after about five minutes he saw the box we needed and I managed to take it from the shelf. He lowered himself like a giraffe and I climbed off his neck. I rubbed the sore parts of my legs.

'Now, let us see,' he said, opening the box. 'One Virgin Mary costume. That's it.' Out came a white silk dress and a blue robe with a cardboard halo which had been worn by generations of girls on the school stage. The same costume, without the halo, was used for the May Queen when we had the maypole dancing in the summer.

'Let's see if it fits,' he said cheerily. I put the costume up against me, but he said I ought to take my dress off to make sure it was right all round, and I thought there was nothing improper about this. After all, he was the headmaster. He made a fuss about undoing the buttons at the back of the dress and I had it off in two wriggles. I stood there only a little embarrassed, in my drawers and vest. Mr Bunn hinted that it might not be wise to mention this to my mother, although, I am sure, her only thought would have been to thank heaven that I was clean underneath, as she used to say.

'Oh dear, oh dear,' he said. 'Your legs are very red.'

' 'Tis the hairs on the back of your neck, Mr Bunn,' I said boldly. 'They're stiff as a hedgehog.'

'Oh dear, oh dear,' he said again and sportingly rubbed the red parts, briskly like a football trainer. He did this for some time and then looked up thoughtfully. 'It's time I had my gas mask drill,' he said. 'I don't suppose you've got yours, Nelly?' I admitted that I had not brought it. 'Never mind,' he said forgivingly. 'I'll have my practice and, so that we won't be wasting time, keeping you from your lessons too long, we'll say a prayer for God's blessing on our King, our Country, and our Nativity play and your part as The Virgin Mary.'

All this, coming from Mr Bunn, sounded not unreasonable to a girl only just ten. I watched him put his respirator on and take a few practice deep breaths. Then he knelt by the side of a large tin trunk and motioned me to join him. We bent there, next to each other, the old man in his gas mask, the girl in her vest, and prayed for all the things he had suggested. When we eventually rose he took off his gas mask and his face was covered with sweat. But that seemed to be it. I put the dress and the cloak and the halo on and took them off and replaced them with my own dress and in no time I was on my way back to the classroom.

Then, when almost at the door, I realized I had left in the storeroom an exercise book which I had carried from class. I went back and opened the door. He was sitting, crumpled, head in hands, shaking his face back and forwards. And he was crying, really crying and repeating to himself: 'Bunn the Hun. Bunn the Hun.'

He did not know I was there for he had not heard me open the door. I stood, suddenly overwhelmed with sadness for him, for I could see he was in trouble although I could not understand why. I backed out and closed the door and went thought-fully back to the classroom.

Our lives went on peaceably in our narrow lane, in the insignificant village outside the small town, with not much to bother our days. Things were still done in the steady old ways. Change had always been slow and the war made it slower. Horses pulled in the fields and in the steep streets of Hopewell too; people worked long days and went home tired to listen to the news of battles far away. About us the farms and fields altered only with the year, shrugging off the seasons, and some strange olden customs were still followed. One day I saw a farmer, wearing no trousers, squatting thoughtfully in a ploughed field, testing the warmth of the earth to see if it was sowing time. What seemed to us to be exciting things happened, of course, as they do in all places. Wall-Eye-Willie, the Upcoombe simpleton, went seriously mad in the middle of August and tried to chop his mother to pieces. It took eight neighbours to hold him down while the rest of the village gathered around shouting advice and encouragement, some of it intended for Willie himself. I stood with Granny Lidstone and watched the spectacle, feeling very unhappy for Willie whose eye was the only frightening thing about him. His mother was proudly showing the people the axe with which the attack had been made, while poor Willie was gurgling under the weight of all those people sitting on top of him. The axe was quite small and one that did not look as though it could have done much damage to the outside of Willie's mother, who was the largest and hardest woman in the South Hams, well-known for her tunnel-like mouth. Granny Lidston held my hand and nodded wisely at the scene. 'They've been and sent for the Sanity Inspector,' she said.

There were other rural sensations. Farmer Swanley, who lived at Rotten Hill all solitary and in a house that fell more to bits every winter, was found dead in bed with a dead pig lying beside him. People said that he had the habit of taking the pig to bed to keep him warm. It was put around that it was a suicide pact.

Weddings and babies occurred regularly and not always in the correct sequence, the forces of nature always being stronger in those who live next to the ground. The people seemed to sense the rising of the sap. There was a field next to the Totnes road which was always full of couples of a spring evening when the urge was very strong on them. We children used to stand in the gate and count the boots and bottoms. I remember it was called Fallingfield.

But it was always death that was of the greatest interest. We would stand petrified, entranced, in the street or watch from windows as a bright coffin was taken by to the 'gravy-yard', as Granny Lidstone used to call it. It was frightening but very thrilling to know that someone you had seen walking about that very place was being carried boxed on the shoulders of those grave men. Village people loved to add titbits of fairy tale to the deaths of their neighbours. 'Oi looked out in the night and there I seed an angel standing knocking at Flossie's door. And oi thought "Ah, that Flossie will be agone come the morning", an' she was.'

The departure that caused the most interest was that of Mr Rush, a fat, rolly man who had been a sailor in his time. He died, as they said, of a disease that made you swell something terrible even after you were gone. They put him in his coffin and he swelled so much he exploded in the night in the front room of 12, Holmedale Villas. Granny Lidstone swore that she actually heard him blow up. The coffin was shattered and his wife said the wallpaper looked as though it was covered with roses.

My sister Mary would come home breathless from working at Hopewell Manor and would have to sit, absolutely bursting to tell me something, but forbidden by our mother (who always said she knew what was right and what was wrong) to tell a word. Once we had gone to bed, though, and all the lights were doused, Mary would creep out from the blankets and open the curtains to let the moon in and we would lie, curled up, stifling laughter in our bed while she related what oddness she had seen.

The Manor was often visited by people in important-looking uniforms who arrived with cars with stars painted on them. There was a lot of eating and drinking done and on one occasion an Admiral was reckoned to have dropped down the well in the grounds and to have very nearly drowned before being pulled out. Sir Waldo apparently always went around talking gibberish, peering down the chute of his nose, and indecently assaulting any of the staff whom he managed to seize unawares.

Lady Martha knitted long red scarves for Russians. When they had their dinner parties with generals and other high-ups they used to plan the battles of the war on the table and often left it covered with drawings and maps and scraps of paper scrawled with figures and secrets.

While these things were taking place at the Hall, not very far away in the barn, Parsifal, the idiot son, was enslaved by his pastime 'Oi seed 'ee,' Mary whispered to me in our moonlit bed. 'With moi own eyes oi seed 'ee do it.'

One placid afternoon just before teatime, a lost German bomber flew over the town and then the village and dropped one bomb which blew down all the houses in Chapel Lane and killed the three people who were in them at the time. Wormy Wood, Granny Lidstone and our mother.

I was on my way home from school when this thing happened and I got off the bus in the village to see the smoke and people all crowding round Chapel Lane. I nudged my way through the crowd and saw what it was like. The air raid wardens and the fire-brigade and all the rest of them were pulling and tugging at the pieces of what had been our house. Our sofa was strangely sitting there in the rubble and the fireplace and the chimney breast were still standing. People rushed and shouted. The terrace was so flat you could see my stream at the bottom of the lane.

Standing a bit apart from all the other people was my sister Mary. She was by herself, ever so still, and I went over and stood next to her and watched with her. For a long time we didn't say anything but just stared at what was going on, but not in any sort of panic or anything. It was as if we were watching men doing some road-repairing. I did not realize it was a bomb had dropped and I said to her: 'Mary, did our dad do that?'

'No,' she said, still staring ahead. 'A German bomb done it.'

The men were shouting and pulling stuff away from one corner of our house, where our kitchen used to be. At the back our dresser was sticking up out of all the mess.

'Is our mum in there?' I asked Mary quietly.

'I reckon 'er is,' she replied.

'Will she be all right?'

' 'Tis doubtful,' said Mary shaking her head. She was fifteen at the time.

'Who'll look after us?' I said.

'I'll be looking after 'ee, Nell,' she said seriously. 'So don't you go causin' me any trouble.'

When at last I went back, after all these unruly years, I went to the library in the main street by the church gates (they used to lock these during the war, it was said as a defence against enemy parachutists, something which puzzled me even as a child). Walking there again I felt sure that somebody would recognize Nell Luscombe, but nobody did. Nor did I get a glimpse of a face I might have known. I kept trying to imagine what my childhood friends would look like after all the years, trying to fix their faces on to the faces that passed me by. But the population were all strangers and nobody looked at me. In the library I asked to see the files of the *Hopewell Chronicle* and I turned the dry pages until I came to the report of the bombing of Chapel Lane on that wartime afternoon.

Because of all the secrecy of those times they could not even mention the name of our village, but called it merely a hamlet in the South Hams. The victims were named: Mrs Amelia Lidstone, aged 78; Mr Algernon Barker Wood (what an important name for old Wormy) and Mrs Joan Annie Luscombe, aged 32, the mother of two little girls. The report was almost brief, just the spare details and somebody praising the work of the air raid wardens which was strange because nobody was rescued and all they had to do was to clear the mess. I did not expect much to be in the newspaper but I expected more than that. But in those days, I suppose they did not want to encourage the enemy just when we were on the point of winning the war.

It seemed extraordinary, but the paper was full of things that were nothing to do with the war, whist drives, reports of the crops, a new vicar at some church, a dance organized by the Red Cross, plans for new drainage, cooking recipes and sewing hints, somebody wanting help with looking after some stables, a letter complaining of the poor biting quality of wartime false teeth, and another recalling the history of the Hopewell darts league. The Germans had dropped their bomb in the middle of all that.

Feeling empty I turned the pages to the following week's issue. There was a whole column about the three funerals, our mother's the last of them, written about just as though it was the burial of someone who had fallen down stairs. The list of mourners brought back names in my memory, some of whom I could picture from my childhood. One of the coffin bearers was Luke Lethbridge, her lover from the harvest field. A single sentence said that the widower – serving in His Majesty's forces – followed the cortège in uniform.

What it did not say was that my father trailed behind the coffin oozing cider, marching in his ridiculously baggy uniform and on his shoulder a shotgun borrowed from one of his public bar friends. I can see him now, like some army dwarf, striding out below that great greatcoat, his eyes floating emotionally way in front of him, with the shotgun held as if it were the funeral of the King. Over the open grave he let off both barrels into the surrounding trees, disturbing the rooks not to mention the vicar and the mourners, and then burst into gusts of tears. The bloody bastard.

Another item in the newspaper said that a collection among friends and neighbours in Upcoombe had amounted to the fine sum of thirty-one pounds, seven shillings and elevenpence and that this was to alleviate the suffering of the motherless children. It was handed to my father and, needless to add, went only to alleviate his suffering.

After the funeral, we went, surrounded by mourners, to the house of Miss Timms, a drunkard from the village whom dad knew although until that afternoon we had not realized how well he knew her. There he held court with a glass of whisky in one hand and the other around Miss Timms' waist. She was a good-sized woman, swollen by cider, and his short arm hardly came out the other side of her. Mary and I looked at each other doubtfully.

The drinks and cold meats went down the surrounding throats in steady quantities. They sat all around the walls, like a sort of shadow show, enjoying themselves and gossiping about other funerals they had enjoyed. There were some uncles and aunts and some other bits and pieces of family. One uncle, whom I can never remember seeing before or since, made me sit on his lap and squeezed me between his legs in play, which I did not like although he seemed to.

'Mind ee,' said one of the aunts in mid-guzzle, ' 'er didn't suffer. I allus thinks it be not so bad if 'ee don't suffer.'

'Naw,' said another, her face sunk in a sandwich. ' 'Ee sure don' suffer if 'ee gets struck by one of they bombs.'

'Naw,' my father agreed with a wise sniff, his mouth awash with pie and whisky. ' 'Er didn't suffer one minute.' He had made her suffer for years. 'In war,' he said, looking around like somebody essential. 'In war, people die. All the time they be dying. I know.'

' 'Ow is it you know, then?' asked my Aunt Ella, whom I liked a bit. 'Oi thought you was tucked up safe in Aldershot or somewhere. 'Ow would you know about dying?'

That upset my father. 'I be on *secret* work,' he rasped. His voice dropped like a stone and he stared around at everybody as if he thought we might all be spies. 'On His Majesty's Secret Service, I be.'

They knew him too well to be impressed. 'What is it, this secret work?' Aunt Ella demanded. 'What be you about?'

My father glowed angrily. You could see it even though the room was reverently dim. His sharp cheeks were like spiteful coals. 'I can't tell 'ee, can I?' he snorted, whirling around, sending pie crumbs spraying around the room. ' 'Ow can I tell 'ee? Not if it be secret.'

'We *all* be family 'ere, Percy Luscombe,' grunted Aunt Ella. 'There be no need to keep it from us. 'Tis my opinion that there b'aint be any secrets. You be in the army cookhouse, and don't deny it either. All the secrets you have is what goes in the bloody soup.'

My father went mad. He rushed up to Ella, throwing his khaki arms about and shooting her with pie crust. She wiped it away carefully and looked him in the eye. 'Go on,' she said. 'Deny it.'

'I be a fightin' man!' he howled. It was the whisky howling. 'I be in dread mortal danger!'

'Aye,' sniffed Ella. 'Dread mortal danger of dying of drink.'

'I got a gun! You seed my gun today! I fired 'un over the grave of my poor wife.' He stopped, fell on his knees and began to sob, pounding his fists against the sofa. He had done it so many times that it had no effect. The relatives just sniffed and carried on with the food and drink.

'Gun?' put in Uncle Herbert, who was Ella's husband. 'That

b'aint be no army gun. That were a bloody rabbit gun you had there George Luscombe. And I knows where you got it. From Jed Brown at the pub.'

My father got to his feet. 'Drinks!' he shouted. 'Everybody 'ave a drink. It's all on me.' He jumped out of the whole argument like that. He always did. And because they all knew him they didn't go on with it either. They forgot the gun and the Secret Service and all of it and set to drink and eat as much as they could in memory of my mother. Mary and I sat and watched them wolfing. Somebody gave us a pie between us, asking us not to let the jelly run on our dresses, and we had one sip of sherry each. They all got up and trooped out to go to the pub, my father and Miss Timms following behind, him with head bent almost double with grief for the benefit of the neighbours. No one said anything to Mary and me. We just stood there in the room with what they had left scattered all around us. She looked at me and I looked at her. Nobody wanted us.

three

The next day a woman with a black moustache took us to St Bernard's Institution at Bristol, a city we had only heard tell about. We did not know we were going to a place like that until we actually arrived at the iron gates. My father had said that he was sending us on a holiday and innocently Mary and I had begun to collect the buckets and spades which we had kept since the pre-war days when we had been able to go down to the Devon beaches. Helped by Miss Timms he piled up the lie, saying that despite the lateness of the year it would still be warm in Bristol and there were several good beaches nearby. We packed everything we had, which was not a long job, and set out for the station with the moustached lady who came especially to fetch us. She was a miserable-faced creature (although women with moustaches always have a hard struggle to smile) and she hardly said a word to us. But she kept staring at the buckets and spades and eventually, after we had changed trains and were on the last part of the journey, she leaned over and said meanly: 'What you be wanting with those things?'

We were amazed that she had never seen a bucket and spade and apparently did not know their use. Mary explained that they were for digging sandcastles and the woman listened for a minute, her whiskers twitching, before sniffing up the length of her nose and grunting, 'You won't be digging sandcastles where you're going.'

We came separately to the same conclusion that she was jealous because she was too old and crabby to enjoy beaches and things like that. It was only when we walked up the hill towards the place where we were going that it began to dawn on us that something was wrong. The building was outside the city in untidy fields and yet for some reason its walls and windows looked hung with soot.

For two village children grime was unknown and we stood on the hill and gazed up at the dark gates against the dark sky. The iron letters, like a black rainbow, curved against the sulky clouds. ST BERNARD'S INSTITUTION it said. Mary dropped her bucket and spade causing Whiskers to jump. The bucket rolled, lop-sided, down the hill. We had been tricked.

The first thing the matron, who was called Mrs Fagence, did was to have all our clothes burned. We were hurt about this because our mother had always kept us decent, but Mrs Fagence said they were falling to bits. 'They're only fit for the incinerator' she said. They gave us some stiff pyjamas, odd bottoms and tops, and sent us to be bathed and have our hair combed for nits.

A boy from Plymouth had arrived just before us and he was having his clothes burned too. All three of us stood stark bare on the landing; then the boy rushed naked after the woman taking his trousers to the incinerator and fought small hand to large hand with her until he got the trousers back. He hung on to them and turning away from her he started to get something from one of the pockets. The old cow smacked him across the backside leaving the print of her hand there. But he had got what he wanted, his penknife. He was crying and the woman, seeing the penknife, began to howl 'A knife! A knife! He's got a knife!'

'It's my penknife,' said the boy. 'I want it.'

'Don't you dare stick it in me.'

'I don't think it would,' he said simply, walking back towards us. 'It's not sharp enough, missus.'

This boy, David Lenny, was ten, a year younger than me. In later life he was to become my lover.

It was strange that when I first saw him he was wearing no clothes and that's the way I remember him best. They put us in the bath together and we sat opposite each other, neither of us shy, but our lives full of catastrophe, both present and future.

'I come from Plymouth,' he said. 'Where you from?'

'Upcoombe.'

He did not ask me where that was.

'My mum died in hospital,' he said next.

'A bomb hit my mum,' I said triumphantly.

'My dad got torpedoed. He got drowned.'

That was difficult to trump. But I tried.

'My dad goes on secret missions. I expect he'll be dead soon.'

'Did they burn your clothes as well?'

'Yes.'

'It's bloody terrible here,' he said.

'Yes. I'm going to hate it.'

'Me, I'm going to escape,' he said. 'That's why I wanted my penknife. I'll be needing that.'

'Can I come with you?'

'If you like.'

We stared at each other up the length of the bath. It was in the middle of a great tank of a room with half a dozen other baths in it. We had to keep our voices low to stop them echoing around. I could see he was looking at me more intently. He pointed his finger at my girlish breasts.

'Can I have a touch of those?' he asked politely.

'Why?'

'I never touched any before.'

'All right. If you're quick.'

He moved forward in a sort of studious way, his eyes on my pale blunt nipples. His fingers came out of the water and he examined each breast in turn, running his touch over the swellings, and tapping each nipple with his middle finger like he was sounding it to see if it was hollow. He had the talent for it even then and I felt the little electric thrill run from my teats down my stomach. I could feel myself blushing in the steam. Then he looked at me and grinned in the way I came to know so well in later years. He pressed the right titty harder with his finger and said 'Ding-ding.'

We both giggled, then laughed. Then another miserable woman (the place was stocked with them) came in and stared at us because she could not understand why we were laughing. 'What's all the joke about?' she said. She had been eating and she had some macaroni cheese hanging on the front of her blue overall and another bit on her eyebrow.

'Nothing,' said David. 'We was just laughing for nothing.'

Not long after we had been sent to that disgraceful place for children, I had a nasty and frightening adventure with the mayor of a nearby town and his white mouse. All sorts of dignified people used to go in processions through the home and stare at us and nod when something was explained to them about us by somebody on the staff. We used to be sitting there, munching our meal or washing up in the dormitory, dusting or putting polish on the floor. And they would troop around like groups of pigeons, most of them senile and snobbish, screwing up their lips as they inspected us, trying to smile as if they could well remember the times when they were in an institution.

After a few weeks you got used to it and you just carried on with what you were about, giving them a quick grin to order, or holding some old pigeon's hand when it made her feel better. They used to contribute to the place, so they liked to come and see what good their money was doing us.

But, even at that age, I must have had some sort of eye and taste for the glistening things of life, because when the mayor and his wiry wife, and another clutch of mumblers, were shown around one day, I looked at his chain and wondered to myself how much it might fetch in the right hands. He saw me looking and he whispered to Mrs Fagence and she called me away from the washing-up sink, telling me to wipe my hands dry. 'We can't have you wetting the mayor,' she said. I was wearing a miserable sort of striped pinafore and I rubbed my hands down that. He looked dignified, as if he was sucking his cheeks in, and his smile was like a crack in an eggshell. He tried to tempt me forward as if I was a puppy or something, holding out his golden chain with its lumpy badge on the end.

'You know I think she would like to see this,' he said patronizingly to the people around him. 'Would you girl?'

Since there seemed no chance of getting my hands on it permanently I was not over eager, but it was the richest thing I had ever seen at close quarters and I was interested, and always have been, in rich things. Standing before him just under his waistcoat I looked up at it dangling just above my eyes, without saying anything and without moving.

'You can't see it properly like that,' he huffed. 'Let's see . . .'

He glanced around in a way that hinted he was used to people running and getting chairs for him and somebody quickly brought a chair. He sat down, spread his black-trousered legs like a plump spider, and when he was all smoothed out and set, he reached over and lifted me on to his knee. All the children were watching and I sat stiffly and began swinging my head mechanically from side to side like a ventriloquist's dummy. I was very good at that sort of mimicry and it has proved very useful during my career. It is shocking what some perverted men do to helpless ventriloquists' dummies. I knew a man in Antibes, once, who had a whole cupboard full of them, all ragged and shagged, poor things.

As I sat, like wood, on the mayor's lap, twisting my head one way and then the other, the other children burst out laughing. David laughed bigger than anybody – because he was very brave and defiant for a small boy – but after joining in for a minute because they felt they had to, the grown-ups stopped and Mrs Fagence gripped my upper arm viciously and told me to stop clowning.

The mayor chortled in a pompous town-hall sort of way, but he soon stopped. It was like water running away down a plug-hole.

The grip Mrs Fagence had on my arm shot tears into my eyes. I stopped my acting and just sat there. He had put a buttery hand around my waist and now he tightened it a bit.

'Ah,' he said in his resounding official voice, like somebody talking into a chamber pot. 'So it's the mayor's old dangler you're wanting to see, is it?'

He held out the end of the chain and even at that age I could see it wasn't even true gold, just some metal done over with gold. I pretended to be fascinated by the tatty buckles and badges around his sweaty neck. I ran the chain through my hands and he explained what the coat of arms meant on the end. My eyes kept going to the tide mark running around above his collar, making it look as though his head were detachable.

He put me down eventually and after all the usual pattings and pettings they cleared off to their cars and left us to get on with the washing-up. David whispered to me that he was making plans to escape from the place and asked me if I wanted to go too. I nodded excitedly over the soapsuds. Where would we go, I wondered. Perhaps over the ocean. Perhaps to kind people who would take and protect us.

Mrs Fagence called me the next day into her office, which smelled of floor polish and wet sheets. 'Oh you're a lucky girl, Nell Luscombe,' she bawled. 'You're going to tea – with the mayor! He's sending his car. His car!' I nodded calmly.

'I hope you're grateful,' she said pursing her mouth. 'You ought to be grateful.'

After school, in a fresh, flowered dress produced from some secret store kept for such emergencies, and nearly new buttoned shoes (taken from a girl who had arrived wearing presentable clothes) I waited for the mayoral car. While I stood stiffly, Mrs Fagence gave my hair a final examination for nits and chanted instructions on eating correctly and not picking my nose. She seemed to think I ought to be all agog and nervous, but I was not. Occasions like that never did worry me. I have been led to the bed of a perverted Crown Prince without a tremor.

The mayor lived in a small town about half an hour's drive away and I sat grandly alone in the back seat of the car with the chauffeur stiff as a new boot in the front. At first I sat on one end of what seemed an enormous seat and then on the other, bright in my dress, my legs sticking to the leather. Then I sat in the middle, like royalty, balancing myself with my hands pushed out like props on either side. But that seat was made for larger bottoms than mine and I could not get comfortable. Eventually I simply stood on the seat and looked out through the little black window, poking my tongue out at two young army officers following behind in a car.

The mayor's home was heavy and quiet in the main street of the town. Outside it was covered in creepers which even fell over the windows. It had been raining and drops fell from the top of the doorway on to my dress.

I was eleven years old and I had no idea what sort of power a mayor actually had. Vaguely I thought he must rule everybody around in the town and the countryside and have many running servants, so I was surprised to find him alone in the house.

Even the chauffeur backed out and went away and I was left there with the mayor. He said I could call him Uncle Dick. He took my hand and showed me around the house which was big and boring and not nearly as warm as Granny Lidstone's was before the bomb hit it.

But after a while we went into a room where a good fire was burning and two padded sofas faced each other in front of the grate. There was a short table and a tea tray on the table with cakes and sandwiches the like of which I had never seen even in shop windows. I thought perhaps in his position he might get special rations. The sofas faced each other and Uncle Dick suggested that we placed ourselves one on one side and one on the other. When I sat down the table came just below the bulges of my knees. Straight away the dress they had given me rode up my legs. I did not think it was immodest or even important, and after one try at pulling it down, only to see it climb again, I did not think about it again but began filling my mouth with peanut butter sandwiches.

The mayor asked me if I preferred tea or milk and I said I would like milk. I saw his hand was trembling with the jug and it slopped over. He filled a cup for me and handed it across. I could see he was still shaking and I remembered being told at Sunday School about the man in the Bible who was sick of the palsy.

'Do you suffer from the palsy?' I asked politely.

His eyes bulged and he blew crumbs from his mouth and choked. Then he laughed, without any meaning, and bent over and patted my knees. We continued to sit there, facing each other across the fireside. Now he did not seem to know what to say and I did not care very much. I was craftily trying to race him to the last cream bun. He had poured himself some tea and the cup rattled again in the saucer.

'Your mummy is dead,' he said eventually.

'A bomb got her,' I said casually through the cream of the bun which I had succeeded in capturing. 'A German one.'

'What a shame. What a pity,' he sighed. 'And what about your father? He's in the army, isn't he Nelly?'

For some reason I was quite chilled he knew my name.

'Fighting in the war,' I said blatantly. 'Secret operations.'

'Do you get letters from him?' He was leaning towards me again.

'No,' I shrugged. That was another thing that had not occurred to me. 'I don't reckon 'ee knows where to write. Anyway I 'spect 'ee be busy fighting.'

'I'll make inquiries,' he said importantly. 'I'll find out where he is and make sure he sends you letters.'

'All right, if you like,' I replied off-handedly because it truly did not matter to me. And he never *did* do anything anyway because we didn't get any letters from our father.

There was another scrap of silence. Then I dropped a dollop of cream on my exposed knee and I must have opened my legs as it landed. As I flung them apart I heard a funny quick sound from the mayor. Granny Lidstone could draw in her gums and make that noise. I looked up at him to see him staring right up my legs. I could not believe it. *He was staring right up my legs!* His eyes were all stuck out and I was frightened to close my legs so I left them open. It had never occurred to me that a man would want to look up there.

'Would you like the cream horn?' I asked politely.

He jumped out of his stare. He was pink in the checks and his lips had gone all rubbery. 'Er ... no. No thank you ... Nelly,' he managed to say. 'You have it. I'll be back in a minute.'

As soon as he had gone I grabbed the cream horn and locked my knees tightly together. I had another good try at pulling the dress down over them but it was no good. He was gone a few minutes and when he came back he had got his mayor's outfit on, a long red coat with fur down the front of the sleeves, the forged gold chain I had seen before and a three cornered hat which I thought made him look odd.

'Don't you think I look grand?' he asked me, gleaming pomposity.

I must have thought about it. 'Oh yes,' I said after studying him. 'Just like Mr Punch.'

He was not overpleased with this and his face went hard about the edges. But then he put his smile back like somebody replacing a clock on a mantelpiece and walked forward, until he was standing above me, the robes seeming to block out the light like a heavy curtain. 'Feel the fur, Nelly,' he said. 'Do you like fur?'

I reached out to touch the edge of his sleeve and jumped as a small, white, pointed face nudged out of the drooping sleeve. It was a mouse.

'That's Perkins,' said the mayor. He touched me again on the legs and I moved up to make room for him on the couch. In those heavy garments and in front of a roaring fire I could see he was beginning to sweat. 'Do you like mice?' he panted. He brought the thing out of his sleeve, held it and invited me to shake its paw.

'Shake hands, Perkins,' said the mayor. 'Shake hands with the pretty young lady.'

The mouse was as reluctant as I was, but we put on a little show of shaking hands. Then the mayor took my hand, selected a finger and helped me to stroke it down the mouse's back. He seemed to get more enjoyment out of this than either Perkins or me. His face had grown very fat and florid and the sweat was oozing. I thought perhaps the chain was hanging too heavy on him.

'You're a bad lad, Perkins,' he breathed on the mouse. It did not seem to care. 'You're always escaping and running in the most inconvenient places.'

I had the last peanut butter sandwich halfway to my mouth but the uneasy feeling came on me and I stopped with it poised in mid-air. The mouse could smell the peanut butter and its whiskers were vibrating.

At that moment that bastard mayor let his rotten mouse run right up my leg. It was the most amazing and terrifying thing. Even now I can feel it making a dash for my drawers. I hardly had time to break out of my freeze and scream before the mayor in his furry robes was on top of me and grabbing at my dress and my bottom and my legs. 'Perkins! Perkins!' he was shouting. 'Come back at once! Naughty mouse!'

His weight knocked me back on to the couch. I screamed really loudly then. I could feel the creature charging about up there.

I was screeching and jumping about and the mayor was just about smothering me with the weight of his fucking ermine, and grabbing now at my drawers making out he was trying to grab the mouse. 'Perkins! Perkins! Naughty mouse! Naughty naughty mouse!'

Even now I can see me kicking back on the couch, my legs

flying about in the air, the mayor howling, sweating and grabbing all over the place. I can hear that cry of 'Perkins! Perkins! Naughty little mouse!' echoing down the years into my trembling ear.

He finally trapped it. 'Got him!' blubbered the horrible mayor. 'It's all right, Nelly. I've got naughty Perkins now.' He fumbled around under my skirt until he had the mouse firmly in his hand. Slowly he drew it out. 'Perkins,' he said, holding it up. 'Perkins, the mayor is ashamed of you.'

I had collapsed back on the couch, everything drained from me, and I began to sob.

'Don't cry, Nelly,' he said. He took advantage of the sympathy to put his hands on my legs again as he leaned over. 'Have another sandwich.'

He handed one to me and I automatically accepted it and began to bite it through my tears.

The mouse had gone back up the sleeve of the robe, having no doubt found the experience just as trying as I had. 'Perkins is a very bad mouse,' muttered the mayor. He looked flabby and deflated and I'll wager he was. 'Wherever will he get next?'

'Anywhere,' I managed to say through the crumbs and the crying. ' 'Ee can go anywhere as long as it b'aint up my dress.'

It was the later days of spring when we made our escape. David had planned it for a long time but he said, in his wise youthful way, that we ought to see what the war situation was before we went, since the authorities might think we were saboteurs or spies. But on a night in April he crept to me in the dormitory and kneeling by my bed he whispered: 'The war's nearly over, Nell. We'll make a run for it soon. You're sure you want to?'

I remember pushing my hand from beneath my blankets and it touched his worried face. 'I want to come with you Davie,' I said. I felt him bite my arm gently and then he went off between the dark beds, crouched like a dwarf.

We decided to give my sister Mary a chance to go with us but we were going to tell nobody else. Mary said she did not want to come because she had obtained the job of clearing the staff room which meant that she could eat what they had left at the table and there was a good chance that she would soon be a prefect at the school. She always was one for advancement.

It was not easy for us though. It needed a lot of bravery.

Children who had run away were caned when they were caught and they never did it again. In fact I thought that David was wavering, although he kept winking and nudging me because of our secret. Two or three weeks went by without any signal for us to go. I was impatient.

'All right then, when are we going to bunk?' I challenged him in the school playground. 'I'm waiting.'

'Any day,' he said out of the corner of his mouth. 'When the time is ripe. I'll tell you. We'll need clothes and food and money.'

The clothes were easy and the food not that much of a problem because I could pick the lock on the storeroom door in one minute ten seconds, which was faster than anyone else in the place. But the money was a different matter.

'How we going to get the money?' I asked.

'Grab it. Steal it,' he said casually.

Even so it needed something drastic finally to make us run away from St Bernard's. It happened one afternoon at the end of April when I was walking with some girls towards the boot room where the children had to clean shoes or boots ready for the next day's school. We went around the corner and there I saw Davie hanging out of the window of the Superintendent's study which was two storeys up. He was screaming in a strange whistling way, suspended from the sill, with Mr Fagence framed in the window holding Davie's wrists and shouting at his face: 'Thief! Thief! Little swine thief!'

I screamed out and ran to the base of the wall because I had some idea of catching him when he fell. The other girls just stuck open-mouthed and stared up at the sight of Davie's legs kicking above them.

'Confess!' shouted Mr Fagence. 'Confess!'

'Yes! Yes I did, Mr Fagence!' Davie yelled back.

Then it came to me that, unbelievably, the bastard man was hanging the boy out of the window on purpose. He was not trying to rescue him: he was risking his neck.

'Stop it, Sir!' I bawled up at the window. I scurried back from the wall so that I could see him and he could see me. 'Stop it. Pull him in!' I howled madly. Tears were spreading all down my face and over my mouth. 'I'll tell the bloody police! You'll be in prison for this! I'll tell on you!'

It was a rash threat, but it seemed to bring the man to some sort of sense. He glared down at my upturned weeping face but then shouted back as though he had to explain: 'A thief! I won't have thieves at St Bernard's!'

But at least, then, he started to haul Davie back inside the window, scraping his face and knees up against the ragged brickwork. I was still sobbing and shaking. I turned savagely on the other girls. 'You saw that. You're witnesses, remember!' Then I ran through the nearest door and up the stairs. The Superintendent's door was shut and locked. Wrathfully I banged on it with my fists. To my surprise it opened at once, and Davie came out, his cheek grazed and bleeding, his face ghost white, his eyes bulging like a calf's.

We stood helpless, facing each other. Nobody else was in the corridor. I put my arms about his thin body and held him to me like my mother used to hold me. He wasn't crying now but his body was stiff as if he had frozen and he would not talk, only shake his head. I began to walk with him down the corridor. We were almost at the far end when the door opened behind us and Mr Fagence, sheet-faced as well, came out into the corridor and yelled after us; 'Thief! Thief!'

My fury swamped my fear. I turned back, keeping my arm about Davie's shoulder. 'Shit! Shit and more shit to you, Mr Fagence!' I shouted. I thought he was bound to come after me, but to my surprise and relief he turned angrily, went back into the room and slammed the door. Then I could hear his fists pounding it from the other side. He was not fit to look after rats.

Gently I took Davie down to the ablutions and washed his face in cold water. He was sick in the wash basin. I took him to the toilet because he wanted to sit down. He sat on the pan with his head held in his hands. He still said nothing but eventually he drew his face up and stared at me standing by the door.

'I reckoned I'd had it then, Nelly,' he whispered. 'Thought I was done for.'

'We'll tell the police,' I said decisively. ' 'E's not allowed to hang boys out of windows. He be a cruel bastard.'

'The door was open,' sniffed Davie. 'And I thought I'd take my chance and get some money for our bunking off. I'd just got my hand in his cash tin when the sod walked in. He went right off his head. He knocked me all over the place. Then he punched me right in the stomach and while I was doubled over he picked me up and hung me out of the window. Fuck, I was so scared Nelly.'

I took a step towards him as he sat in the cubicle and put my hands on his head again. I just pulled it to my stomach, feeling its hard roundness against my belly. 'We've got to tell the cops, Davie,' I said again, looking at the pipe up the wall. 'We can't be lettin' the sod get away with that, now can we?'

Wearily he rubbed his head against my pinafore. 'That's no good,' he whispered. ' 'E told me. When 'e got me back in the room, 'e told me. If I told the coppers then 'e would reckon that 'e caught me hanging on to the window sill, like I was trying to climb out because I heard him coming. It'd be only his word against mine. And you know who'd win.'

I sighed. 'What we goin' to do Davie?'

'We goin',' he decided. 'We're certain goin' now. I got an idea.'

'What idea?'

He shook his head. 'B'aint tellin' you right now, Nell, because I need to have a shit. And a bit of a think. Shut the door Nell.'

For a moment, his head still against me, he put his arms around my legs. I could feel him trembling still. Then he sat up and began to unbuckle his snake belt. I left him there and shut the door.

At school we had been learning lessons about some peasant revolt years ago in history. The teacher always told us we could learn from history because history always came around a second time. I found it all boring and dry, but Davie, who sat in the desk across the aisle from me, seemed to pay a lot of attention. He told me he was trying to learn how to be great.

'It's us,' he said, as though finally deciding, as we walked back to St Bernard's from school. 'We're just like them peasants. We've got to revolt, Nelly, we've got to rise up against them. We'll do it tonight. And while everyone's revolting I'm going to creep in and nick the money from the office.'

It was a marvellous rebellion. We talked everybody into taking part although Mary said she would not do any actual attacking but would stay at the far end of the corridor to keep watch. 'I don't want to be gettin' myself into any trouble,' she said. She ought to have been born in Switzerland that one.

Davie planned it painstakingly. He had one boy, a little kid from Cornwall called Blackie, who was small but very clever at jumping, running and tipping head over heels. I often wondered if he ever became a clown or a tumbler in a circus. He would jump from or over anything. There was a swing bridge down by the docks in Bristol and, when we were allowed out for Sunday walks with one of the staff, he would slide off and climb over a fence and leap from one bit of the swing bridge to the other just as it was opening. He left the jump too late one day and had to be rescued from the dock by the bridge keeper. Even while they were still in the water he accused the bridge keeper of speeding up the opening so that he would miss the other side.

This acrobatic boy was put on top of a wardrobe just behind the dormitory door. He was an ugly little soul and he crouched there like one of those gargoyles, grinning and waiting.

Also on top of the wardrobe was a little girl who was a bit slow and mental. She was called Mad Martha. She was about seven and she did not remember her parents or even know where she came from. She just went around with a kind of damp smile on her face, gentle and silly, although one day she strangled three rabbits. She had just got into somebody's garden and seen the rabbits in their cage and taken them out one by one and strangled them. She was like that.

We had put her behind the boy Blackie and told her what to do. It was not difficult to persuade her to get up there because she did everything anybody asked, nodding that everlasting, mad smile.

When everything was ready Davie gave a signal and all the other children started a riot. It was in the boys' dormitory and the girls were never allowed in there so we knew that the mixture of voices would soon bring Mr Fagence to see what was happening. The children loved it, shouting and cursing and throwing things. It must have taken less than two minutes for the Superintendent to take the bait. He charged up the corridor, obviously having come straight from his evening meal because he had a handkerchief tucked into his trousers and his mouth crammed with macaroni cheese.

'Whaht, whaht, whahtsh going on?' he shouted through the food. 'Shtop . . . shtop it! Shtop it at oncsh!'

At that moment little Blackie launched himself through the

air and caught Mr Fagence square across his shoulders. He went down like he had been hit with a telegraph pole. Then all the eager boys piled on top of him. While he was kicking and choking underneath the mound I grabbed the fork from his hand which was sticking out of the side and gave it a good shove straight up his arse. I enjoyed that.

The second part of Davie's plan was still to happen. Davie stood apart from the pile of boys now entirely hiding Mr Fagence on the floor. He had calculated beautifully. Mrs Fagence had not yet arrived but we knew she would not be long. Davie eyed me and I nodded. All the girls were ready and waiting.

Along the corridor she came, the bloody old ginger harridan, bellowing and throwing her wicked arms about. She had two pieces of macaroni cheese hanging over her lower lip like devil's fangs. They suited her. At first she thought it was just a general fight and did not realize that her husband was underneath the pile of boys.

'Beasts!' she screamed. 'Animals! Stop, stop!' She began kicking the nearest boys with her pointed shoes and then bending over and belabouring them. On Davie's signal, and it had been well rehearsed, the boys rolled away revealing the smashed Mr Fagence underneath. It was as though twenty pigs had rolled on him.

'Mr Fagence!' screamed Mrs Fagence. 'Oh, Mr Fagence!'

Davie nodded to Mad Martha smiling on top of the wardrobe. She may have been dim but there was nothing wrong with her timing. She flew through the air like a fat bat, striking Mrs Fagence between the shoulder blades with the same accuracy that Blackie had shown with Mr Fagence. It was wonderful to see. The old cow pitched forward with a terrible croak and then all the girls pitched in, whooping like red indians. The boys then fell on Mr Fagence again, jumping up and down on him as if he were a trampoline. I thought they might even squash him to death but I did not care. I went over to the female pile, with Mrs Fagence prostrate underneath, pulled her handbag away from the rubble, took her purse out and the key to the office. I gave the key to Davie so that he could get at the cash box. We went quickly from the dormitory, bursting with success and joy. At the end of the corridor Mary was concealed in her watching place. It would not be long before other members of the staff would come running. Mary wanted to be clear of the trouble by then. She saw us and then looked away as though she did not want to be a witness.

'Bye, bye, Mary,' I laughed, holding on to Davie's hand.

'You'll come to no good, Nell Luscombe,' said Mary, her face still turned away from me. 'Mark my words.'

'I know,' I laughed. I think I did too.

four

It was wonderful to be free. I have always found stories of elopements enjoyable because of the excitement and the making for freedom and I suppose, young as we were, this was a kind of elopement. I really trusted Davie. I believed that nothing could go wrong with us and our plans as long as he was with me. In those days he had what you could only call a deep confidence, amazing in a boy of his age, very silent but sure.

We went on the bus to Bristol, paying our fares out of the four pounds eight shillings and eight pence, all in silver and copper, which we had taken jointly from Mrs Fagence and the office cash box. The coins weighed down the pockets of our overcoats and clanked as we moved.

On the ride down the town and through the streets, the money weighing us down like donkeys, we said scarcely a word to each other. Inside I was pent up like a balloon and I could see by his fixed face that Davie felt the same way. When he gave the conductress the money for the fare his fingers were shaking but the rest of him was in control.

We got to the bus station in Bristol and sat eating cold meat pies in the waiting room. I let him do all the deciding. It was good to have someone to depend on again. 'We got to get away from 'ere Nell, as quick as lightning,' he said. 'They'll start the police looking for us soon and we're sure and certain to be picked up in Bristol.'

'Where'll we go then?' I whispered. We were sitting on benches in a dark part of the waiting room and a bus woman from the office, wearing a cap too big for her, kept poking her head around the door and looking at us. After a bit she examined us harder and said : 'I hope you two aren't up to mischief.'

'We're waiting for the bus, madam,' answered Davie in a marvellous sort of upper-class voice. He sounded as though he'd come from Harrow instead of St Bernard's. I was astonished because I'd never heard him do that before. It was not just the high-born tone of it but it was so aloof, like someone who is used to ordering servants about. It stopped the nosey woman. I swear that she did a little half-curtsy and mumbled that she was sorry before disappearing. Full of admiration, I grinned at Davie. He just shrugged and said : 'We need a map, Nell. I tore one out of the atlas at school but it's not big enough.'

'There's a map on the wall,' I pointed out.

It was a bus route map stretching all over Somerset, Devon and Gloucestershire. All maps had been taken away when they thought the country was going to be invaded by the Germans, but now the war was nearly done they had put them back in such places as bus stations. This one was fixed behind a glass plate and was framed with wood. Davie did not say anything further. He scarcely bothered to look around. He just stood up and went to it like a cat. There was no one else in that part of the waiting room. Down the far end was a man dozing on a bench, his snores mumbling towards us.

It took less than two minutes. Davie took out his penknife, levered away the side frame and easily drew the map out. It was like a picture thief in an art gallery. I'm certain that even then he used to *enjoy* stealing things. The map was folded and stuffed in my knickers. He quite often put stolen things there.

'We'll get on any bus,' said Davie. 'Go up on the top deck and we'll look at the map there.'

Poking our heads from the waiting room we saw that a bus was just about to leave, its windows alight and its engine starting. We did not bother about its destination but just jumped aboard and went upstairs. Then, when we had started, we realized with a sickening feeling that we were going back the way we had come – towards St Bernard's.

There were only two other people on top of the bus and they were right in front so they did not see us duck low as we went by the iron gates. Davie could not resist a brief look. He prised his head up a couple of inches and looked out. I followed him.

'Christ,' I breathed. 'What we gone and done?'

Every light in the place was on and the main door was open. Two policemen stood outside by their car and an ambulance was just drawing away. The fear of the fugitive fell over me. 'Do 'ee reckon we killed them, Davie?' I said.

'Might have done,' he shrugged. We were past now and we sat upright once more. He sniffed confidently. 'But they can't hang us Nell. We're too young.'

I had some idea about making our way back to my village. It seemed the natural thing to do and one place was very much as good as another. I thought I might find help for us there, perhaps someone who would take us in and be kind and let us live there with them. I also had some strange notion that our house might, by now, be rebuilt.

The weather was warm for our journey. The first night we slept in a pile of sacks in a field just outside Bristol. They had been used for fertilizer or something and just left lying there. They smelled to heaven and back but we were tired and it was late so we made the sacks into a bed, the mattress several layers thick and the rest over us like a smelly blanket. But they were warm and we lay wearily down together.

Apart from my sister and my mother I had never slept with anyone before. It was funny because we were suddenly nervous of each other, not letting our bodies touch, lying a foot apart, a sort of no-man's-land between us. Then an owl started and there were other night noises. I began to feel afraid – I sensed that Davie was on edge too.

'Davie,' I whispered in the darkness of the field. 'Don't these sacks pong?'

'They'll do that, Nell,' he said seriously. ' 'Tis fertilizer. It makes things grow but it pongs like 'ell.'

'Davie, do you think they'll catch us?'

'Over my dead body,' he said strongly. 'Nobody's going to catch us Nell. We'll get somewhere safe.'

I felt reassured and glad I was with him. We were still lying a foot apart.

'Is there *anything* you're afraid of, Davie? Anything at all?'

I felt him half turn under the sacks. He seemed to be thinking about it. Then he said quietly: 'Lockjaw. That's the only thing I'm afraid of. Lockjaw.'

'What's it do to you?' I asked. 'Lockjaw.'

'If you cut yourself or something,' he whispered in the dark, 'it goes to your jaw and you can't move it. It locks tight. You can't speak and you can't eat. So you die. It's a killer. 'Tis the only thing I reckon I'm afraid of, Nell.'

We were silent for a while, then I moved first. I pushed myself to him and he put his bottom into my lap. My arms went about his waist and we slept.

All the silver and copper we had taken weighted our pockets down and slowed us on our journey. We dare not ask anyone to change it into notes in case two children having cash like that aroused people's suspicions. It hung down in our coat pockets like lead as we trudged on our journey.

Davie carried most of it in the pockets of his worn overcoat and it bulged out at each side and made his walking difficult. The second day after our escape we came to a neat place with a river and some rowing boats drawn up against a wooden pier. We stood looking at the boats. There was not a soul around, no sound except the ducks on the water and a breeze, pushing against a clump of overhanging trees. The sun had fallen behind some clouds and it was very warm.

'I used to go out in boats like that once,' said Davie looking at them expertly. 'All the time. I was always rowing somewhere, you know, Nell. I can do anything in a boat.'

Because I believed everything he said I nodded. It was not until that day I knew he had an unsteady side to his nature, a leaning towards what you could call romancing. 'Could you row one of those?' I asked.

'Easy,' he said. 'Dead easy.'

We stood on the bank in our hanging coats, dirty faced, I expect, although we had decided to try to keep ourselves washed since seeing a poster which said 'VD is dangerous. Clean living is the real safeguard.' We did not know what VD was or why it was dangerous, but we decided that if we were going to look after ourselves, we ought to have some sort of wash each day.

'I bet you wouldn't row me across the river,' I murmured.

'There and back in five minutes,' he boasted. 'Come on Nelly, there's nobody around.'

He gave the nearest little boat a push with his foot and it

slipped without trouble into the water. He had another quick look round and picked up a pair of oars from the next boat along the line.

'Jump in Nell,' he said. 'And I'll show you how I do it.'

The boat wobbled wildly when I stepped in but I only laughed because I did not want him to see I was nervous. He held my hand like a gentleman and I staggered to the square end and sat down, my eyes fixed on Davie. He did not seem to be completely at home, not as much as I had expected, and he had a lot of trouble getting the oars fixed. But eventually there we were, very romantic, a young girl and boy in a boat on a placid river in the spring. He pushed the boat out from the bank and gave a couple of clumsy tugs on the oars. The water came up and hit him in the face. I started to laugh because he looked so funny with his soaked face and wet hair and his head sticking out of his overcoat like a tortoise.

'Don't you make fun of me, Nell Luscombe!' he shouted angrily.

It was such a shock to hear him so quickly bad-tempered like that. I just stared at him, suddenly frightened. He saw my amazement and calmed down. 'It's just these oars, that's all,' he said in a quieter way but still huffy. 'They're the wrong size, see.' Then his face went funny and tight again and he almost shouted once more. 'So don't you go laughing.'

'Sorry, Davie,' I said, knowing my tears were rising. Then a different expression fell on his face. 'Christ Almighty!' he exclaimed. 'We be sinking!'

We were too. The bottom boards of the boat were letting water through like a grating. I cried out with fright and he started to pull wildly back to the bank. 'Pray for us Nell,' he said in a choking way. 'I can't swim.'

All children in those days were taught to pray. I flung myself into the bottom of the boat and began to ask God wildly to save us and forgive us our trespasses, particularly attacking Mr and Mrs Fagence and stealing the money. The only answer was the cold unstoppable water climbing up past my bent knees. It came up in a rush then, so that we were sitting awash with it, bursting with tears, both howling like mad, and the boat going down. The river seemed to take one last bite at the boat and then gobbled it up. Then we were in the freezing stream of it and our shouts stopped as it took our breath away. Then I saw the oar floating in front of me and I grabbed it. David did the same thing at the same moment.

'Coats,' gurgled Davie. 'Get them off.'

I don't know how we managed it but we both got out of our coats and their weighty loads of coins. The river current sucked them down. It was terrible. But now we found the oar would keep us afloat. We began to kick towards the bank which was only a few yards away. There was still nobody around. We could have drowned and nobody would have seen.

Fortunately the bank was easy because it had been made so that the boats could be launched and brought from the river. We crawled out and stood shivering and weeping on the mud. 'The money,' I howled, realizing now. 'Now we b'aint got any money.'

Davie looked thin and cold. He was like a skeleton. But he was not one to delay. 'There's a house over there,' he shivered. 'Let's go there. Say we fell in.'

'We did fall in,' I said, trying to make a little joke of it. He did not laugh.

'Come on Nell,' he said, getting up. 'We'll be freezing to our deaths.'

Stiffly we got up and stumbled along the bank of the river. The house was only a cottage, with a garden crammed with flowers and a cat asleep on the window sill. But, cold as I was, I remember how it made me stop, a chillier feeling coming over me. It was a house, somebody's home, just the same as I had had not many months before. Davie apparently felt nothing of the sort. He opened the small pointed gate and went to the front door. 'Don't say anything about the boat,' he whispered before knocking. 'It might have belonged to them.'

I shook my head, trying to get myself out of my trembling. He knocked at the door. It sounded old. Nothing happened. He tried again and then a third time. There was still no answer.

'Let's have a look around the back,' he said coolly. I sensed that he was, even then, quite capable of anything and it frightened me. But I simply nodded and followed him. At the back of the cottage was a vegetable garden and a small arched door lolling with flowers. On the whitened wall a tin bath was hanging. Davie knocked with his knuckles on the door, then banged the bath with his hand and called: 'Anybody home?'

Nobody replied. By now my teeth would not keep still

because of the wet cold all over me, and my legs vibrated so much I could hardly stand. To my astonishment Davie tried the door. It opened. He poked his head through the opening and called again. 'Excuse me. Anybody home?' Even from there I could hear a clock ticking like a sharp hammer in the room beyond the little corridor where we found ourselves. Davie strolled in. I was amazed and my hand went out to warn him not to do anything wrong. But he did not seem to feel it. He just walked in, a couple of careful steps first and then straight into the room as if he owned the place.

'Davie,' I whispered. 'Davie, we'll get caught.'

'No we won't,' he said surely. 'There's a note left here on the table. The woman won't be back until six o'clock. She left the note for her husband.'

'What about him then?' I asked. 'What if he turns up?'

'He won't,' he said, a touch impatiently. 'The note says he's to put the potatoes on the stove if he gets home before her. And she's not due until six.'

'You're very clever, Davie,' I said.

'I'm very cold, Nell,' he replied, accepting the compliment. We glanced around. 'But we can have a good time here, can't we? Let's have a look around.'

I was still doubtful. 'Be careful, Davie, whatever you do.'

'Nelly,' he said turning around quickly on me. 'Shut up.' I looked at him. I did not know whether I admired him or was frightened of him. It was the same all through the time I knew him. But he had thought of everything.

'If anybody comes,' he said, spreading his hands, 'we'll just say that you fell in the river and I rescued you and we came in here because of being wet and you being half drowned.'

'Rescued me?' I said, a bit annoyed. 'You can't even swim.'

'THEY won't know that WILL they?' he replied, almost shouting the two words in his impatience. 'Now stop worrying. Let's have a look around.'

I could still hardly believe that he was doing it. But there he was, with me trembling behind him, going through the house like a professional burglar.

We went up the narrow cottage stairs. There were only two bedrooms with a small landing and a row of coat hooks with a flannel dressing gown and a man's jacket hanging from them. Davie took them down. 'These'll do for the minute,' he said, handing me the dressing gown. Without a second glance at me he began to take off his clothes. Then he saw me looking and stopped. Although we had been put in the same bath together on the night we arrived at St Bernard's, we had not seen each other naked since. And this, being by ourselves, in somebody's house, seemed somehow different.

'Oh, all right then,' he said, sensing my look. 'Turn around, back to back. Unless you want to be going to the bedroom, Nell – in case I spy what you got.'

'No Davie,' I said, trying to sound unconcerned. 'Back to back be all right.'

We stood on the small landing, facing opposite ways, and took our cold wet clothes off. Mine were sticking to me and I heard Davie's trousers slosh on the floor. When I had taken off everything, including my shoes and socks, I just about tunnelled myself into the big woman's dressing gown. I felt better then. 'Are you ready, Davie?' I said over my shoulder before turning around.

'Ready,' he answered. 'But don't you laugh, Nell Luscombe.'

It was a job not to. He was slim and quite small and the man's jacket swamped him, coming down below his knees and the arms hanging like apes. 'It don't fit very well, do it?' he said in a sulky way. 'But there, it don't matter. There be nobody to see me – excepting you.'

'It's all right,' I said, hurt by the casual remark. 'I don't reckon it matters.'

Davie was going through the pockets. Some cigarette papers and a few ends of tobacco came out and some butt ends. 'No money,' he grumbled. 'I wonder if there's any around about.'

'Davie!' I exclaimed because I felt shocked. This was different to stealing from Mr and Mrs Fagence.

'What'll be the matter with that?' he said. 'We ain't going to get any further without money, that's for sure. Unless we can fish it up from the bottom of that river there. And I ain't trying that. So we got to see what we can get in here. Stands to reason.'

He went back downstairs and went straight to the dresser in a space next to the fireplace. There was a two shilling piece there on top of an insurance book. He flipped it expertly into his pocket. 'Come on, Nell,' he said half turning. 'Don't be standing starin' like that, you get looking.'

'Yes, Davie,' I nodded. I started slowly but he was so fast he had gone through the room before I had looked in a couple of drawers and found nothing. 'I got a wristlet watch,' he said holding it up triumphantly. 'We could sell that and here's a sort of ring. Could be gold.'

'That'll be a wedding ring, Davie,' I said sternly. 'God'll send us bad luck if you take that wedding ring.' It was very big for a wedding ring. It was probably a small curtain ring.

'God ain't sent us that much *good* luck yet,' he pointed out, dropping it into the jacket pocket. His thin shins and feet sticking out from beneath the outsized coat made him look oddly like a black and waddling duck. 'See what be in the larder, Nell. We might as well fill ourselves up.'

I went to the larder in the small kitchen. There was not much there but we took half a loaf of bread and some margarine and some cheese and a jug of milk. We sat down at the kitchen table and without speaking wolfed the lot. There were some onions and a pot of jam which we also took for our journey. It was now about two o'clock. 'Nobody'll be back for a long while,' said Davie when he'd finished the last drop of milk. 'Then they'll have to go out and get some more milk.' He laughed wickedly and I laughed too but I had to make myself.

'Why don't we go and 'ave a bit of a lie down in the bed upstairs,' he suggested. 'I wouldn't mind being in a bed for a change.'

I could not believe his nerve. 'But Davie they might come back.'

'Who's bin a-sleepin' in my bed,' he giggled.

I sniggered into my hands. 'You wouldn't dare,' I said.

'You know I would,' he replied straight away. I knew he would too. 'Listen, I tell yer, they *won't* be back. Not till five anyway. I saw an alarm clock by the bed. We'll set it to make sure we wake up. 'Tis easy.'

I nodded through my last mouthful of bread and margarine. 'All right then,' I said. 'I'm worn out.'

We went up the short stairs together. 'After,' he said, 'we'll look for some proper clothes.' We looked into the smaller bedroom. 'It's a girl's room,' I said. 'That's not going to help you much, Davie.'

'You get a bit of sleep,' he said. 'I'll still have a look around. Never know what I might find. I don't feel that tired anyway.'

'You said you did,' I reminded him. 'Only a few ticks ago.'

'I said I wouldn't mind being in a bed,' he said. 'But I b'aint all that tired. You close your eyes and I'll come and lie down in a minute.'

'Shall I get into the bed?' I wondered. I had gone to the second door and stood looking at the big downy bed.

'Get in,' he said after a second's thought. 'Might as well be killed for a sheep as a lamb, Nelly.'

'I don't want to be killed for anything,' I said. I still hesitated. It seemed criminal to get into somebody's bed. Worse than stealing.

'Go on,' he said, giving me a small push on my way. 'Get in.'

'All right. But I'd better keep this thing on.' I sniffed down at the flannel dressing gown. 'Just in case.'

'Do what you want,' he said. 'I'll keep my eyes open anyway.'

I walked into the bedroom. Its low ceiling and its bent walls made it seem, I remember thinking, like the inside of a loaf. The bed looked clean and soft. It made me feel even more tired. I sat on the edge and it curled down under my weight, soft below my bottom. There was an old-fashioned long mirror by the wall, on a stand and swivel. I moved along the edge of the bed so I could see myself in it. To my surprise, my face had gone quite brown in a few days in the open air. I pushed my hair into some sort of shape and smiled hopefully at my reflection. The dressing gown almost drowned me. I moved my leg and my knee came through the gap. I nudged it further and my leg came out. From the end of my toes to the top of my thigh. I had never thought much about legs, but now I looked at it and I thought it did not look bad at all. The terrible food at St Bernard's and the work had slimmed all my podginess away. With more curiosity, like someone unwrapping a parcel, I opened the front of the dressing gown, a fraction at a time, looking over my shoulder first to see if Davie was around. I could hear him moving in the house but he was not near the door. I let the dressing gown drop open.

My body surprised me. I had not seen it in a full length mirror before. My breasts were really ripening, pink and full with their small blind nipples showing against the young skin. I glanced up at my face and I saw that I was blushing. Tugging the dressing gown around me I moved away from the mirror and pulled back the cover of the bed. But I could not resist going back to the glass for another look. Davie was still roving around downstairs. Guiltily I inched the dressing gown open and had another look at myself, one breast at a time. The nose of the right one came round the edge of the flannel material like a puppy sniffing around a corner. The breast was full enough to make the material slip away down its outside slope. I looked at it with a certain amount of pride. The nipple was closed like a sleeping eye, but the skin was pure and creamy with not a blemish or mark upon it. I made the other one appear in the same way, the flannel going up one slope, over the soft point and falling away down the other. The valley between the two was curved at the bottom, but there was no girlish sagging with my breasts. They stood of their own accord bright and full. I was very pleased with them. In a way I felt sure they would help me in my life. I was going to need them.

At my middle there was still a bit of roly-poly flesh, but I breathed in, expanding my bosom and making my stomach flatten. As it backed away the newly-grown bush of hairs around the crease at the tops of my legs rose. I had begun to notice it some months before, and, because I knew nothing of how a girl grew, and since at St Bernard's there was no one I dared ask, not even our Mary, I worried in case I was turning into some sort of monkey. I had watched my face anxiously for any sign of hairiness there. Then I had found a couple of little bushes under my armpits and I went mad with anxiety, imagining I would be swinging through the trees in no time.

I was saved from thoughts of suicide by discovering a picture postcard of a naked lady concealed between the pages of a pious book, in the room at St Bernard's which we used as a chapel and a library. There were a few dozen broken books in there for the children to read and this picture had fallen out of one when I picked it up. This person was standing with a few flowers dangled around her but her pubic hairs and her bosom clearly on display. After noting with relief that she was far hairier in that place than I was, and making up my mind to ask my sister about it, I stood wondering where I could put the picture to get the most fun. At the end of the room was a thick reading stand with a Bible on it. Mr Fagence used to read from it every evening after tea. I put the nude lady in the middle of the Bible. I remember watching his expression when he turned right away to it that evening at prayers. He gave a start, made a quick guilty glance around and then put it slyly into the inside pocket of his jacket. Then he read the lesson.

My little collection of hairs was quite pretty, I thought, gazing at them in the mirror. Fair and springy, like the hair on a doll. I was enjoying looking at myself now. I let the dressing gown fall right off and had a view of my arms and shoulders : then, turning around, at my bottom, and finally at the front of me again. Just as I had been glad at the way my bosom was forming, I felt glad that my whole body was not fat any longer, that my legs were becoming slender and my skin was clear and fair.

The feel of the soft bed under my bottom again reminded me that I had intended to sleep for a while. I heard Davie coming up the stairs again and, because for some reason I did not want to disobey him, I put the dressing gown on and climbed between the covers.

My weariness caused by being without a proper bed for three nights sent me to sleep almost right away. I tumbled straight into it, but I had only been dozing for a few minutes when the sound of something falling and breaking woke me. At first I was frightened, not realizing where I was. Then I knew it must be Davie up to something. It was.

Climbing swiftly from the bed I went out on to the short landing. The noise had come from the other bedroom. I went in and was shocked to see a girl, about my age, standing there. She was facing away, wearing a grey pleated skirt and a short coat with what we used to call a pixie hood over her head. She had white ankle socks and white buttoned shoes. On the floor was a broken china money-box, which had been a pig. I could tell because the head was still in one piece. The coins from the box, mostly pennies with a few silver coins, were spread around the floor. The girl stooped to pick them up.

This I took in while I stood mesmerized at the door. I could not move but my sudden breathing made her turn round. I cried out aloud. It was Davie!

I don't believe I have ever been so stunned since. 'Davie,' I managed to get out. 'Davie what you up to?'

'Disguise,' he said calmly. 'Good innit? Nobody will be lookin' for two *girls*, Nell.'

'But . . .' I stared at him. I didn't know why but it seemed so creepy. There was something bad about it that I did not understand. Somehow it was not funny, like dressing up.

'I'll keep the pixie hood up,' he said. 'So's it covers my hair. Then I look as good a maid as you.'

I nodded, still dumb with surprise. But he did truthfully make a good girl. He had blue eyes and small features and even dimples.

Then, I don't know why, something in me I suppose, made me ask him: 'You got everything on? Of 'ers? Like underneath?'

Boldly he lifted the hem of the pleated skirt.

'Fancy putting them on!' I almost shouted. I was aghast. 'Her drawers.'

'Why not?' he replied. 'My pants are soaking anyway. And if you're going to do something, I reckon it should be done all proper.'

They were white flannel. He lifted his skirt higher and I could see him bulging through the material.

'They're all right,' he shrugged. 'Just the same as mine, 'cept I'll have to pull 'em down to be havin' a pee.'

I couldn't find anything else to say about it. 'Fancy breaking the money pig,' I said. 'That's somebody's. It belongs to her.'

Davie stared at me with those biting blue eyes. They seemed even sharper coming from beneath that hood. 'What you expect then?' he asked. 'You expect me to get it out with a knife? There b'aint be time for that. I reckon we ought to be going. On our way see?'

'All right.' Now I know that somehow I felt insanely jealous of his wearing that unknown girl's clothes, especially underneath.

'Well don't be so durn flighty about it,' he said. 'You'd think they was your things.'

That, I realized, I would not have minded. 'We'd better go,' I said. 'They might come back early.' He looked at me in the overloaded dressing gown. 'You'd better get some of her clothes for yourself,' he said. 'There be plenty in that wardrobe thing. Her drawers is in the drawers.'

He sniggered because he had made a joke. I just sniffed. 'It's a pity she's got no brother,' I said haughtily. 'I could be wearin' his trucks and things. I reckon I'd look all right in boys' trucks.'

I thrust my leg out of the dressing gown, right up to the top as I had done before the mirror. His eyes went right up to it and I say he coloured under the pixie hood. 'Naw,' he said. 'That wouldn't be any use, now, would it? We'd still be a boy and a maid, and that be what they be lookin' for.'

Still hardly able to believe what he had done I said, 'What we goin' to call you now then? Be no use callin' you Davie. Not with you dolled up like that. Somebody might be listenin' in.'

He took the idea seriously. 'You're right Nell,' he said. He gave it a bit of thought. 'Daphne, I reckon,' he said.

I started to laugh. I could not help it. But he cut me short bad-temperedly. 'Well, what's wrong with that?' he demanded. ' 'Tis a proper maid's name innit? And it sounds a bit like Davie, anyway.'

His face was odd, really nasty under the pixie hood. 'All right then,' I said, '... Daphne.'

five

During my strange and busy life, I've had a good many odd days and a great number of odd nights, but never so odd as when Davie (or Daphne) and I made our way through the countryside in the early May of 1945. At first I found it difficult to say anything to him at all. It was like travelling with a new person, someone I did not know. When I called him Davie he would look around to see if anyone might be listening and give me a warning look. When I called him Daphne he was just as difficult, saying that I did not need to call him that all the time. In the end I found myself just clearing my throat and saying 'Hmm' before I spoke.

We made our way by bus and often on foot, keeping to the map we had managed to dry out. I would never have found my way but Davie – and under the pleated skirt and the blouse he was still Davie to me – was very clever with things like maps and directions, even using the sun to calculate our way. He should have been an explorer. Dressed in a different way.

On the second day after we had changed our clothes we came

to places that I knew were near my home because, although I had never been to them, I had heard people talk about them in everyday conversation. Newton Abbot, Buckfast, Totnes market. In the afternoon Davie decided he wanted to go to the picture house. It meant using up a lot of our money but he wanted to see the film which was a war film about the Japanese bombers. He suggested that to conserve our funds he should pay to go in and then help me through the lavatory window. It's difficult to know why now, but this struck me as a reasonable enough plan, and I made no suggestion that *I* should go in and he should get through the window. He could persuade you to do things.

'Be careful of your voice then,' I told him before he went into the cinema foyer. 'Don't you forget you're a girl.'

'One sixpenny, please,' he mimicked from under his hood. He had worn that hood so long now it was like travelling with a small monk. If it had not been, that is, for the ankle socks and the pleated skirt.

I was not surprised that his girl's voice was so good. He seemed to be able to do anything. 'Put a hankie to your nose, just in case,' I advised. But I knew it would not be necessary. Looking from under the rim of that hood he looked just as much a girl as I did. 'How will I know the window?' I asked him.

'It's bound to let out on to the alley down the side there,' he said pointing. 'Wait down there and I'll go into the lav and throw something out of the little window. If there's a big window and I can get it open, I'll do it. If not you'll have to get through the small top one. Now you understand, Nell, don't you?'

I said I understood and he went into the foyer of the cinema. I hung about outside and I heard him make his Daphne voice. It sounded convincing enough to me and the girl at the cash desk did not even look up. I counted up to a hundred and then I went around to the side alley. Nothing happened for five minutes and I worried that I had made a mistake or something had gone wrong. Then, mercifully, a piece of newspaper floated out of a small window three parts of the way down the alley. I hurried to it.

'Davie,' I whispered. Then '. . . Daphne.'

'Nell. Come on.' His hand was waving at the small fanlight

window at the top. 'You've got to get through 'ere, Nell,' he said hoarsely. 'I can't get the other bugger open. It's all rusty.'

In all my life I had only been to the films two or three times and then never through the toilet window. But climbing was nothing to me. I got a foothold on a water pipe and then a knee on the sill before pulling myself up to the window. It was a squeeze, and I hoped that no one would come along the alley and see my bottom bent over as it was, but I was soon dropping head first inside and there was Davie, standing on a toilet pan to help me down.

'It's a good thing you remembered to come to the ladies' place,' I said when I was on my feet. 'I meant to tell you.'

'You should have,' he grunted. 'That's why I was such a long time Nell. I didn't think about being dressed up. I went straight into the men's lav and stood there while some old man finished pissing. I forgot I was supposed to be a maid. It was ever so strange. When e'd done 'ee turned hisself around, with his old thing still hanging out and 'ee just stared and stared at me. 'Ee must have thought that t'was 'ee was in the wrong lav. Then he looked at the troughs what they only 'ave for men and 'ee knew 'ee 'adn't made no mistake.'

I had begun to giggle, but Davie said sharply, 'Don't mock, Nell Luscombe, t'was dead serious, I tell 'ee. There 'un was with the old pig danglin' out from 'is trucks and there was I dressed like this. And the dirty old gaffer just stood and a big smile came all over him. All bad teeth 'ee 'ad too. 'Ee took 'old of that thing and began swingin' it around like a rope. And just smilin' straight. T'were nasty, I tell 'ee, Nell.'

'T'was terrible, Davie,' I said trying to keep my face straight. 'What went on then?'

'I give 'un a shove,' said Davie. 'Pushed him right back into the pee troughs. I pushed 'un a bit hard because 'ee sat down in all the wet. Then I buggered off fast and came in 'ere, in the maid's lav.'

'Is he gone, I wonder Davie?'

'I hope so. Let's go in quiet. It be dark anyway.'

We went from the toilet into the main part of the cinema. Even in the dark you could see it was almost empty. We crept sideways down a row in the middle and sank down in the seats. The main film was just starting and I could see Davie's eyes, bright points of anticipation. I watched for a few minutes, but the weariness of being without a bed came over me and in the dusty warmth of the picture palace I sank lower and easily to sleep.

I don't know how long I slept but I was roused by a dig from Davie's elbow. When my eyes had focused I saw that sitting by him was an old man with a bald head and a nasty overgrown moustache.

Davie saw I was looking. ' 'Ee be back,' he said flatly. 'The old sod from the lav.'

'What be 'ee up to?' I asked, still drowsy.

' 'Ee be feeling of my leg,' said Davie in a matter-of-fact way. 'Rubbin' like.'

'What you goin' to do then?'

'Got a pin or anythin' like that?' His voice went down to a whisper.

'I got a safety pin,' I said. I found it in my pocket and handed it to him in the dark. He nodded his thanks.

Nothing happened for a while and I began to think that the old man had gone back to sitting quietly watching the film Then Davie leaned towards me. ' 'Ee be gettin' un out now,' he confided. ' 'Ee's fumblin' for it.'

The elderly molester, I could see, was having some sort of struggle. Then he leaned over closer to Davie and I could see his randy old eyes twinkling.

Well, then they stopped twinkling because Davie stuck the pin in his dick and he let out the biggest screech you ever did hear from any man on this earth. He jumped up like he was on springs and as he did Davie stuck the pin up his backside and he howled like fury again.

'Oh! Oh! Oh!' he blubbered and went hopping down the empty row of seats like a castrated kangaroo. We held on to each other for laughing but we knew that it was time to get out. Soon the manager and maybe the police would arrive and we did not want to be there then. We marched steadily to the far exit and let ourselves out into the street. Still laughing we went through the market place and beyond the town to where the open road leads to the south and Upcoombe.

It was in the evening when I first saw something I recognized, the spire of the church at Hopewell poking, as it always did, through the easy mist that came at that time from the creek. We were coming from a strange direction for me but I felt the thrill of thankfulness that it was still there, as I remembered it, and that I was nearly home.

From the high ground where we looked out we could see the South Hams, fields green and red and curved beyond the town, coloured by the evening light and after the fields, in one triangle, the sun setting on the sea, sailing away like a ship. I held Davie's hand.

'We be nearly there now,' I said. 'This is where I went to school.'

'Will they have built that house of yourn that quick?' he asked. ' 'Tis not a year yet.'

'They will,' I answered confidently. 'They work hard down here and it was only a little house.' I glanced unsurely at him, not wanting to give the impression that we had lived in poverty. 'But it were a very *good* house,' I said. ' 'Tis always possible my dad is back there now. Back from the army.'

'I thought your dad was on secret missions,' he said. ' 'Ow could he be on secret missions and sittin' in your house at the same time? 'Ee couldn't. Stands to reason, don't it?'

This made me a bit sulky. 'The war's near over so they say. Maybe he got out first because of us to look after. Mary and me.'

He sniffed unbelievingly. ' 'Ow far is it?' he said. 'Much further? My feet are barkin'.'

'Oh it's only a couple of miles,' I told him. 'No way at all. Come on. Let's get there afore it's dark.'

We left by the familiar road at Hopewell and went through the snaking lanes hanging with scents, and we came to the head of the little hill at Upcoombe. I felt full and strangely frightened now. Frightened by what we might find. Or what we might not find. We walked down towards the Chapel Cottages past the houses where lived the people I knew. I did not want to show myself right away, so we kept low and ducked out of the way if we heard voices. Then I heard something else, the sound of my stream. My stream where I had spent so many hours paddling and playing. It made me smile to hear it and I stopped Davie and told him to listen too. But he was impatient. I suppose there's nothing more boring than other people's nostalgia.

It seemed to me, though, that the stream sounded very clear. I thought at first, that this might be because I had not heard it for so long, it was coming new to me. Then I wondered if there had been a lot of rain and it was in flood. But then, the real answer came like a chill. The reason I could hear it so plain was that the houses, our little row of houses, which had shielded the sound in the days before, were no longer there. They had not built them again. We had come all this way for nothing.

We reached the brow of the village and looked down to where Chapel Cottages had been. It was just black debris. They had not even bothered to clear away our burned-out kitchen dresser and the coconut mat from our passageway was lying rotten among the bricks and broken wood. I walked towards it all, in the light that was just going for the evening. I don't know what I felt, disappointment, despair or the deepest loneliness, but the tears were dripping down my face and on to my chin. Davie hung behind and shuffled down after me. We stood in the old damp-smelling rubble. I went and stood in the place where the kitchen had been, just where my mother used to do the ironing and we used to sit by her. I looked around me and then across the unbroken space to where dear Granny Lidstone's house had been. Now she and mum were both in the gravy-yard. Davie kicked his shoes into the thick mess. 'Not much here,' he said hollowly. 'Better be goin' Nell. Somewhere else.'

'Yes.' I tried to sniff back the tears so he wouldn't see them. 'Let's go somewhere else.' We trod over the rest of the mess and back on to the lane. It was almost dark and the stream was gurgling loud at the bottom of the lane. Where would we go? I did not know. I left it to Davie.

On the day that the war was ended, the German war that is, we arrived in Plymouth. We had some idea that we might be able to get a ship from there to some place where we could be happy and no one could ever find us.

For a girl of nearly twelve whose only experience of the war was one bomb, even though that bomb killed her mother, it was astounding to walk into a city where hardly one stone seemed to be left standing upon another. From the flattened buildings the odd wall stood up like a ghostly tree. But people went about as if nothing had happened. Even a child could see for miles through the open spaces. The smell of the sea came right off Plymouth Hoe and went inland with nothing to stop it. 'This is where *I* used to live,' said Davie with a funny bit of one-upmanship. 'There weren't just one bomb here. Look at it.'

I did not argue with him because you did not when he said things strongly like that. Some things I had already learned. People were gathering in the ruined centre of the town to celebrate the last day of the war. They started singing and as they got towards later evening there was music booming from a van with a loudspeaker and everybody seemed to be drinking from bottles and dancing, and then they all began an orgy of kissing and hugging.

Davie and I had bought some chips and eaten them. We must have been looking scruffy and rough by now because more people were looking at us with curiosity. I had tried to get Davie to put his own clothes back on, but he insisted that we had to keep up the disguise. 'When we're free,' he said in that important way he managed to put on. 'And only when we're free, Nell. Then I'll be Davie . . . again.'

The jolly crowd in the centre of the city drew us towards them. By the time it was dark there must have been thousands singing, dancing and cheering. A message from Mr Churchill was broadcast over the loudspeaker and they all went mad. People were crying and laughing at the same time but Davie said that was because they were drunk, which was probably true. There were lots of men and women in the mob in uniform, especially sailors of course, with some soldiers and some airmen. I had a quick look at one or two of the soldiers in the hope – or rather in the *idea*, not the *hope* – that it might be my father. But wherever he was going berserk that night it did not seem to be in Plymouth.

We found ourselves gradually dragged into the celebrations and we began to enjoy it. After all, we had been a week on the run, keeping away from people and living rough, and now here we were in the middle of a great big party and feeling as though we were welcome. A lady gave me her bottle of stout which I tried to drink but could not swallow, although she kept telling me it was black champagne. Davie was smoking a cigarette – a Camel – which an American had given him from a packet. I was worried in case we got separated by the mob and I called out 'Davie' towards him. His scowl shot at me from yards away. Then I realized what I had said. 'Sorry,' I cried. 'Sorry, Daphne!'

I moved towards him through the jostle and then, at the moment I reached him, we were grabbed by two big and jolly land army girls. They were wearing fat farm breeches and their green knitted sweaters bulged like the udders on a couple of prize milking cows. They had great mouths and red faces that glistened, all ruddy in many lights. They caught hold of us and shouted roughly, 'Come on girls – let's all dance!'

Well, I did not know about a lot of things then and it seemed all right, even if it was a bit embarrassing to be dancing like that with another female. She caught hold of me and smashed me into her voluminous chest with arms like gateposts around me. My eyes wobbled and my body bounced and I could see Davie caught by the same agricultural grip. He was trying to keep his pixie hood on so that she would not see his hair.

We did some wild prancing dance with the two landgirls chortling like fiends and us two little ones crushed and suffocating in their sweaters. 'Hoik! Hoik! Hoik!' mine was shouting just as though she was trying to turn some old pig on its back. She rubbed me violently right across her bulging front from one tit to the other and back again. I could feel them rolling against my face like bags of hot water. It was terrifying.

Then, just when I thought I would pass out through lack of air, they let us go having seen some of their friends swigging cider in the distance. I staggered to the edge of the crowd and Davie followed me dizzily.

Our faces were thick with sweat, my hair was sticking to my forehead and Davie's pixie hood had almost been torn from his head. We were still panting when two equally rumbustious sailors came towards us. They waved bottles of brown ale, and, gasping as we were, we accepted a swig each. Used to drinking rough cider, I drank my mouthful, but I noticed, with some sort of smugness, that Davie spat his out.

We handed the bottles back to the sailors, but they did not move off. It was obvious by their faces that they wanted some repayment. They stood beaming expectantly at us while the creeping feeling that further trouble was on the way grew in my breast – the appropriate place for it, because the sailor in front of me was staring down at my girlish swellings just like he was looking into the deepest waves of the sea.

'Righto, girls!' he boomed suddenly. 'I'm Jack and he's John. Let's 'ave some dancing.'

There was only chance for one wild glance between Davie and me before we were again carted off into the crowd, our trembling legs only just scraping the ground. Jack crushed me close to his barrel chest almost as fiercely as the landgirl had. Then he started sloshing great big kisses all over my head and face. Horrified, I screwed my eyes around to see if the same thing was happening to Davie. It was. I began to bleat with worry.

'Come on my darlin',' encouraged my sailor. 'Give us a kiss.' I thought if I did he might be satisfied so I held my lips up, only to find the lower half of my face and then my neck engulfed with great wet smacks. It was like being hit with a jelly.

He loved every sloshing minute of it. He had me tight, bouncing to the music, alternating with gurgles from his bottle of beer.

'You can call me Handsome Jack,' he shouted above the din of the celebrations. It was impossible for me to call him *anything* because I had no breath for two words. I wagged my head at him while he banged me up and down like a rag doll. 'I bet you'm enjoying this,' he bellowed beerily into my face.

Handsome Jack hauled me through the great jumping crowd. It was like being dragged through the waves of an ocean. His big chest heaved against me, his bristling chin scratched my forehead and his great booted feet pounded the ground all around my thin shoes. From head to toe he was a constant threat. Desperately I tried to see what had happened to Davie, but he had been washed away by some other human current. I wondered if I would ever see him again. Jack's enormous round knees were now pummelling my middle like pistons.

'Jack! Jack!' I managed to cry. 'Stop. It's killing me.'

Immediately he stopped and became all concerned. 'M' dearie,' he said, his trunkish arms about me. 'What be the complaint?'

I began to cry and he led me with overdone gentleness to the edge of the crowd. There he found a shipmate waving a bottle of whisky. He grabbed at this like it was a passing gull, held it and poured some down my gasping throat. I felt like I was on fire. It hit the bottom of my belly and seemed to rise up through me in hot streams. While I was still gasping he poured another mouthful into me.

What happened after that I was not very clear about. Somehow Handsome Jack got me into the backyard of what must have been a brewery and there he tried to rape me across a beer barrel. Rape, I suppose, is too strong a word. I had no resistance. Exhaustion and the whisky had seen to that. In any witness box I would have had to confess that my protests were feeble. Jack, presumably to cover himself in case of prosecution, kept bellowing at me: 'Say you be sixteen, Nelly! Say you be sixteen!'

'I be sixteen!' I cried out in panic. I thought it was the only way to stop him shouting and battering me with his giant caresses. We were against the barrel which was on its side, with some sort of wedge beneath it to stop it rolling. His horny hand went up my skirt and he began hauling at my knickers.

'No, Jack, no!' I pleaded. 'What you be about?'

'You know what I be about darling,' he leered. The booze on his breath was so overpowering that, even in those straits, I wondered whether it was worth arguing if he was going to rant as well as rape.

'Handsome Jack. Now you stop it!' I tried again. I used his full name to try and please him.

'Not now, I b'aint stoppin',' he bellowed. ''Tis for the war, Nelly, for the war!'

Christ, I thought bitterly, not that one again. ''Tis finished, Jack,' I protested. ''Tis done. The war's over.'

'Against Japan,' he bawled with leering triumph ''Tis for that war.'

By now I hardly cared which fucking war it was for. He had me naked to the waist. I was wriggling like a fish but I could feel my strength sapping. 'Now there's a pretty thing,' I heard him say as if to himself. Then he produced what was anything but a pretty thing.

God it was like a white gun! From my position pushed back on the beer cask I could see it coming towards me in the gloom. His hands felt me out. They were like blocks of wood and about as gentle. He opened my legs and I felt the night air rush up them. His beer burped horribly and I could see his big broken teeth gnashing with enjoyment and naval lust.

Then that great, girt thing was pressed up between my thighs. It seemed to fill the whole space from one leg to the other. The rounded wood of the barrel was splintering against my buttocks and the backs of my legs. But I had no fight left. Handsome Jack would have his way.

He was having some drunken trouble in finding the proper place. 'Where be it maid?' he kept demanding. 'Where you gorn and hid it?' He pushed my legs further astride. I thought he must split me in two. Then, with a grin you could have seen a mile away on a dark night, he connected and began to push his jumbo into me. I closed my eyes.

Then, like the heroines in all the girls' stories I should have read but haven't, I was saved from this fate by fate itself. He was rocking the barrel now with his shuttling movements, trying to get himself home. I felt it move beneath me and on the downward stroke my feet touched the cobbles of the yard. I waited for the next time and once I felt them touch I pushed with every atom of strength I had left, pushed and then threw my head and my weight backwards over the barrel.

It worked brilliantly. The barrel rolled back a complete turn, taking us with it. With a horrible cry Handsome Jack was pitched over the top of me. I had a memory of seeing his shape flying through the air above me, his jumbo standing up as though in shock. A short but amazing sight.

I landed on the back of my neck on the cobbles, my legs still over the barrel and pointing up at the Plymouth stars. Jack had flown yards further and had pitched on his head somewhere behind. I pulled myself together, kicked the barrel away and turning around kneeled up, pulling my drawers up with one hand as I supported my trembling self with the other. Looking back I saw what had happened to Jack.

Now he looked far from handsome. His head must have struck the ground first for he was cradling it in his hands, crouched down with his white rump stuck in the air like a big boiled egg.

Staggering to my feet I still had enough conscience to whisper 'Jack … Jack … are you all right Jack?' His reply was to slide slowly sideways and lie curled on the cobbles. I completed pulling my clothes into shape and ran quickly out. I heard his groans echoing from the yard. Poor Handsome Jack. He was the first man I had left groaning. But far from the last.

It took me a tearful hour to find Davie again. I went through and then around the fringe of the crowd which was pounding about in the street, even bigger in numbers than before. It was amazing how many servicemen came to offer their services or to ask if I'd like to celebrate the end of the war with them.

Eventually I found Davie sitting in a large cardboard box in a shop doorway. Only his head was showing and he eyed me with dull suspicion. I had to speak first.

'What you be doin' in that box, Davie?' I said. 'You cold or what?'

'Hiding,' he said sulkily. 'Hiding these girl's clothes. Men keep trying to get me.'

'Get you?'

'Well, you know, *get* me. You're a girl, you ought to know.'

'I know,' I sighed. I sat on the step beside him. The sounds of the celebrations floated over the roofs around us. 'I know all right. Oh Davie ... that sailor tried to be filthy ...'

He looked at me without his expression changing. 'What d'you think mine did, then?' he sulked. 'Black and blue I am Nelly.'

'At least he couldn't *do* anything to you,' I said innocently. 'I mean you're a boy. You're different to a girl.'

'That's what I told 'im,' said Davie.

'And what did he say?'

' 'Ee reckoned it was better.'

I did not understand this but I was so hurt and confused now, and I was getting cold, that I did not ask him any further, except to find out how he had escaped. 'Well 'ee went and give me his bottle to have a drink, like. So I banged him over the head with it. They took him off in an ambulance.'

'We'd better get away from here,' I said. 'We'd better find somewhere safe.'

He stared at me, his head sticking very strangely out of the box. 'Where's safe?' he said hopelessly. He began to stand up. His girl's clothes were muddy and torn now and he had lost his pixie hood. I felt overcome with pity for him – he always had that effect on me when he was downcast – and I put out my hands and helped him from the box. 'Where we goin' to go Nell?' he asked, all assurance gone now. 'Where'll be safe?'

We found the answer amazingly quickly. Only a few yards along the street a small door was swinging open. Someone must have left it to hurry to the dancing in the streets. We looked in carefully. It was a sort of storehouse with boxes and crates standing in piles like dark walls. No sound came from the shadows. We walked carefully through the corridors of goods. Then I put my hand to one side and touched something soft. 'Davie,' I whispered. 'There's some mattresses piled up here. Let's climb up.'

He seemed uncertain. 'We got to get right *away* from 'ere, Nell,' he said. 'Abroad. We've got to stow away or something. We can't go on like this.'

I patted him in the dark. His shoulder felt hard and thin. 'Let's lie up 'ere for a while, Davie,' I said. 'Then we'll work out what to do.'

I sensed his nod. We climbed up the pile of mattresses and fell into them. Then we rolled protectively towards each other. His body felt damp and warm but small next to mine. I put my arms about his neck and put my face next to his cheek.

We felt each other trembling but, lying like that, we seemed to calm and before long we went to sleep. It was some drunks shouting and singing in the alley behind the building that woke us up. We did not speak but lay there listening to them and, when they had gone, to the wind rustling in the darkness of the store.

'Davie,' I whispered. 'Do you think they'll be back to shut the door?'

'Don't know, Nell.' He stirred. We were warm and luxurious in there, away from the noise and the dangers of the world outside. It seemed nothing but natural that we should turn to each other and embrace. I could see his eyes looking at me in the dark.

'Do you know how they do it?' he asked quietly.

'What, Davie?'

'You know what Nell. Like the sailors tried to do.'

'No Davie,' I said. 'But I expect 'tis easy. I don't reckon it's anything you have to be clever for. Anybody can, even simple-minded people.'

'You want to have a try, Nell?'

'Aye, Davie, if you like,' I whispered.

He stirred against me and pushed his face against my chest. It was very strange because we were still both in the clothes of girls. We made no attempt to kiss each other but we began to touch, explore and rub each other with our hands. He rubbed my breasts, gently and around and around, as though he had a polishing rag. I felt the blood hurry through me and I put both my hands down to his bare legs under his skirt. First I rubbed his knees and then worked my way up until I felt his sturdy little jumbo inside the girl's drawers. I stroked it with my fingers and felt it give a throb. A great feeling of suffocation came over me. I rolled on to my back, my legs open for a second time that night. But this was different. We were that rare thing, instinctive lovers. His right hand went around to my bottom and his left slid along the cleft of my legs. He stroked it back and forward. It was though we had planned it and rehearsed it many times.

Davie withdrew his face from me and said as though in ordinary conversation: 'Nell, I reckon we ought to stop playing about now and do it proper. Do you still want to?'

He saw me nod in the dark. He brought himself to his knees and lifted both our skirts up. Then he pulled my knickers down and he did the same with his. I could almost see his penis glowing in the dark. I reached out and touched it. It was like a warm velvet pencil. I was trembling again, with anticipation, not fear now, and I released him so that he could guide it to me. He was careful, so accurate you would think he had done it all his life.

I moved my bottom and opened my thighs wider. He found the place with no trouble, first time. Thousands would have missed. I was still sore from Handsome Jack's efforts, but I ignored that. I felt it enter, its head poking into my darkness, then the body followed. I don't remember any pain. All I remember is that delicious young rod travelling up inside me. It was all I could do not to cry out with the unusual pleasure. I wriggled beneath him and he began to withdraw.

'No, Davie, no. Don't do that.'

He was collected as ever. 'I be taken 'un out to see if us both is all right,' he said mysteriously. 'T'will go back in you soon, Nell, you see.'

He withdrew it and shifted up to his knees and looked down at it in the dark. 'Is 'un all right, Davie?' I asked him anxiously.

'Dunno. 'Un seems all right. But I can't see 'un proper.' He looked at me beneath him in the gloom. 'I reckon us'll 'ave to be wed, Nell, if we go on like this now.'

I laughed and I heard him chuckle. Then he began feeling

around in the pocket of his skirt. 'I got that there weddin' ring we found in the house by the river,' he whispered, still fumbling. ' 'Ere 'un is. I'll put it on your finger.'

He did too. It was miles too big of course (I am certain it was a curtain ring). I moved it around on my finger. Then I did a truly amazing thing.

I took the ring in one hand and his small jumbo in the other, and I slipped the ring over the head of it just as easily as if it had been a finger. We both went into gusts of laughter, rolling about on the mattresses like a couple of pups.

'Nell Luscombe,' he threatened, 'now I'll show you.' And he threw me back, mounted me again, and thrust himself home, still wearing the ring. We started laughing again at the thought of the ring inside me. He bent over and for the first time we kissed lip to lip.

Then from behind us, and slightly below, a torch shone at our backsides. A policeman and two other men were standing staring at the amazing sight of two half-naked schoolgirls in bodily embrace.

'God 'elp me, Fred,' said the policeman. 'Now I seed everything.'

six

Davie and I were never taken back to St Bernard's. But we were separated the day we were caught and we did not see each other again for many years. They took Davie off to some place in another part of the country and I went to a big downtrodden house in Cornwall, a sort of hostel for difficult girls. I liked it there. It was an exciting place to be, high on some cliffs where it was always misty, or windy, a shaggy old house that looked haunted. Inside it was exciting too, because some of the inmates were very delinquent and kept setting fire to the place or having intercourse with soldiers, or chasing each other with carving knives or kettles of boiling water. There was a riot once and some of the bigger girls made the matron take off all her clothes, pick up a shovel, and stoke the boiler with coke.

I was younger than most and much quieter. I was constantly interested in what was going on but I was always in the background. Some of the girls were very strange, I thought at the time. One came into the bathroom once, when I was in the bath, and asked if she could wash me. I refused, and then she begged me to allow her to kiss me on the breasts. Very shocked, I would not allow this either and she went out weeping and tugging her hair. Not much trouble came my way though, and I was regarded as an inoffensive child, which indeed I was. I only got into trouble once and that was due to a mistake. The girls had to go and have their hair cut short at a scruffy old woman's place in the nearest village. Each was given a ticket with a special rubber stamp on it and when the old woman had cut her hair, she would hand in the ticket and the woman would be paid at the end of the month.

After I'd been in the hostel a week or so one of the staff gave me a ticket and said brusquely: 'Get your hair done.' And, unknowing, I took her at her word and went to a proper salon in the neighbouring town; I sat there, feeling like a duchess, had a shampoo and set and a special styling and then (never being one who knew when to stop) I had a manicure as well. When I handed them the ticket from the hostel and explained that it was instead of payment they went crazy, telephoned the matron and caused me all sorts of bother. My pocket money was stopped for two months, but I was able to walk about, among the basin-headed girls, with my hair looking beautiful.

It was at the hostel, however, that they discovered I could sing. It was a discovery for me too. When I was with my mother at home, I used to sing around the house and to myself when I was paddling in the stream. Absent-mindedly I suppose, for I used to hate singing in school because it meant tedious warbling up and down scales. Since then I hardly sung at all because I had not had much to sing about.

But I was glad to join the choir because this meant that you went to people's houses and to church halls and the like, to give performances, and people gave you gifts or cakes or sometimes money. We went into some quite grand places and the audiences used to sit with damp expressions on their faces while we harmonized songs and things like 'Abide with me'. It was while they were held in this sort of charitable trance that some of the choir used to lift bits and pieces from tables and sideboards and pocket them. There was a pawnbroker in the town who had no scruples about buying anything they brought.

It was through this singing that I first met the Commander, one of the few men I have honestly loved. It was approaching Christmas and we were told we were going to sing carols at a special hospital for wounded officers. The delinquent girls liked the sound of this because they thought they might do themselves some good from the social point of view.

But when we went to the place and we were taken into the ward, we all came to a stop inside the door just as if we were afraid of moving another step. It was terrible to see them, the poor men, lying broken and wounded by the war. In one moment I saw how horrible it had been and would now always be for these officers. They would not be able to live again. Some were blinded and others could not speak; others had ghastly burns and scars, no arms or no legs. One man was in a bath of oil because he had been burned so much.

I almost choked with tears while we were doing the carols. The poor souls were trying to sit up and listen to us and some tried to sing with us. One officer, all covered with bandages so that you could hardly see he was a human being, sang like someone calling out for help when they have been gagged. His bed was quite near to where I was standing. The hem of my dress was caught on the bedside chair, showing the backs of my legs, and I was going to pull it away, but for some reason I did not. It was my instinct, I suppose, and I think he knew I had left it hitched up there on purpose.

It was terrible when they tried to applaud, bandaged hands going together all muffled and strange, and distorted noises coming from their mouths. Some of the girls were frightened and when we had finished, they hung around in a group like ewes, waiting for someone to take us out. But I looked at the man in the nearby bed and I could see by his half-buried eyes and the way the dressings were shaped around his mouth that he was smiling. I smiled back. He patted the side of his bed and without a tremor I went and sat by him.

'What's it like inside there?' I said.

'Dark,' he replied. His voice was faint, not because of the

bandages but because apart from everything else he had a throat wound. It came out in a faint croak. 'Dark and hot.'

'How did you do it?' At the time it did not seem like a silly question, even allowing for the fact that *he* didn't do it, the Germans did. It seemed a natural way to carry on a conversation. After all you can't start by asking somebody trussed up like that if they've had an interesting day.

'Fell downstairs,' he joked from his hollow. 'Drunk.'

I must have laughed because his hand, which was outside the bandages, in fact was one of the few parts of him that seemed to be uncovered, patted mine. It seemed to be quite a young hand.

'How long?' I asked him. 'How long until you're better?'

'Don't know,' he answered simply. 'Have me fixed up in time for the next war, I expect.'

He suddenly leaned back on his pillows as if the conversation was too much effort. I asked him if he was all right. He nodded but did not speak. It was time for us to go. One of our staff came in and started making a fuss because I was sitting on the officer's bed, but a nurse from the place told her not to worry and then smiled nicely at me. Encouraged, I said to the officer: 'Would you like me to come and see you again?'

He nodded but did not seem able to speak. The nurse was on the other side of the bed. She looked at me quickly. 'Would you like to?' she said. 'Really?'

'Yes,' I answered. 'That's why I said.'

'We could get someone to fetch you from the hostel,' she said. 'And get you back.'

'There's a bus,' I answered. 'I'll get on that. It's not far.' The other girls were all standing like ravaged virgins, open-mouthed at this conversation. All this time the officer in the bandages kept nodding encouragement to the nurse and to me.

'You could come on Saturdays, if the hostel people will let you,' said the nurse. 'We play housey-housey then. The Commander needs somebody to shout for him when he wins. He keeps missing out. You could do that.'

I nodded. 'Right, I will,' I told her. 'I'm allowed out on Saturdays.'

None of the other girls said anything to me until we were outside the hospital. Then one young slut said: 'Jesus Christ, fancy doing that.'

'Doing what?' I replied. The others were crowding around very ominously.

'Well, what you just done. Gettin' yourself in with the officers.'

'Bleedin' cheek she's got,' said another.

Then the first one again. She was a low, conniving sort of girl. Her face came right up to mine. ''Ow d'you know what he looks like?' she rasped. ''Ow can you tell under all those bandages?'

My heart went cold. I was tempted to hit her in the face. Instead I said simply: 'Go and get fucked.' I bet she was too, thousands of times. It was the first occasion I had ever used that word to anybody.

From that day I would get the Saturday afternoon bus to the hospital and sit by him while we played housey-housey. Because of his wounds he could not hear the numbers very well and for the same reason he could not shout if he won. But I sat on his chair or the edge of the bed and we played it like that. Quite often – for there were only twenty or so players – we would win sixpence or sometimes a full house of half-a-crown. I would take a penny from the sixpence or sixpence from the half-crown as my commission and to help with my bus fares. They were very unusual and peaceful, those afternoons, and I used to look forward to them. He was still inside all those bandages, like a man inside a hollow tree looking out, and I could see by his eyes that he was always pleased to see me.

When I think of it now, how odd it was that I had no idea what he looked like, how old he was, or even his name. I never asked. I simply called him the Commander. That was good enough for both of us.

When he had enough strength in his voice he would ask me about my life and I would tell him about my mother and the bomb and some of the other things that had happened to me. I was now twelve.

I went to the hospital throughout the winter and into the spring. One day, I remember, I saw some daffodils blooming in somebody's garden and quietly stole half a dozen to take to cheer him. Then they told me at the hostel that I was to go back to Hopewell. My sister Mary, having been retrieved from St Bernard's at Bristol, had been taken into full-time service at

Hopewell Manor, and it was decided that I should go too, returning to the village school until I could leave at fourteen, and living with the other staff in the manor house.

Even bearing in mind that it meant I would have Sir Waldo Beechcroft breathing down his long nose at me like some pale dragon, I would have been glad to go. I missed my sister sometimes and it would be fine going back to my old school after all my travels and adventures. But my first thought, when they told me, was that I would have to leave the Commander.

'It's a pity you have to go away now, Nelly,' said the nurse who used to look after him. 'In a couple of weeks he will have his bandages off and you'll be able to meet him properly.' Then she said thoughtfully, to herself rather than to me: 'But maybe it's just as well.'

'I'll come back and see him,' I promised. 'It's not all that far, and I'll be earning some money when I start at the manor. I could still come.' The tears were forming in my eyes. I managed to stem them.

'You don't even know his name do you?' she asked.

'No,' I shrugged. 'I've never thought to ask. But I'll have to know now. I reckoned on writing to him to tell him how I am getting on.'

She smiled. 'Good. I hope you will, Nelly. After you've finished housey-housey today come and see me and I'll write down his name for you to take with you.' Then she did a surprising thing. She said: 'You're a lovely girl.' And she kissed me on the cheek.

It was terrible the last day. I could hardly speak for sadness and inside that great cocoon of bandages, I knew the Commander was upset too. We won sixpence and I took my usual commission. And then it was time to go. I stood up. Once more I was going to be alone.

'I'll write you a letter as soon as I get there,' I said, trying to choke back the crying. 'Nurse is giving me your name and address.'

He seemed surprised at this because the bandages gave a little jerk. It's interesting how you can see people's reactions even when they're covered up like that. I remember that very day I was leaving, when I got to the door of the ward and looked back, he was sort of sagging in his sitting-up position in the bed, just like a bandaged thumb bent over.

'Write then, Nelly,' he said in his firmest and best croak. 'I hope we'll meet again.' I walked back to him. He patted his hand against mine. I leaned over and kissed the dressings in the general area of his forehead and he kissed me with the charred lips that lived in the hole in the bandages. I hurried out with only that brief look back at him. I had to go into the toilet and have a cry before I was able to come out and get the name and address from the nurse. She had written it on a card. It said: 'Lieutenant Commander Sir Frederick Harrie-Young, RN, GC.' and the address of the hospital, which I knew anyway.

Nothing in the world would have made me ask about the 'Sir'. Instead I said: 'What are the letters? I know the RN, but what are the others?'

'The GC is the George Cross,' she said.

'And he's got that?' I said. 'A medal like that?'

'That's right,' she said bitterly. 'He's got that Nelly. Instead of a face.'

It was more than a year later when I saw him properly for the first time. I had kept my promise and written careful letters to him, writing on the flap of the envelope S.W.A.L.K., sealed with a loving kiss, and when he wrote to me he put the same letters on the flap of the envelope too. Mrs Chandley, the house-keeper at the Manor, used to ask me who would write such rubbish on the back of an envelope. She thought it was 'some silly boy' because his handwriting was ugly and difficult since he could not hold a pen properly, something I had not realized before.

But the letters were wonderful. It must have been so painful and difficult for him to write at all because of the damaged tendons in his wrist, and each letter took him a week or more to complete, so that he had just finished one and my next one would arrive and he would have to start all over again.

He would write about the most amazing and beautiful things. Even though he was trapped in those bandages and imprisoned in that ward behind the gates of the hospital, he sounded so free. Everything that happened in the ward he found worth some comment, including the results of the housey-housey session. He had not replaced me as an assistant but had made an arrangement where he was allowed to bang an enamel cup on the metal part of the bed to show that he had a full house or a complete line. Although there was only the one window near him, and he had difficulty in working his way around to look out of it, the *things he saw*! The birds and the aeroplanes and the shapes in the piles of clouds were truly astonishing. And he noted them all and wrote to me about them. These letters always arrived on a Monday and, while I was still in school, I would sit in lessons, the unopened letter warm in my pocket, waiting for playtime so I could go to the lavatory and read it in peace. I was always astonished at the amount of things he could write about. Although I was much freer, I did not seem to have half as much to say.

All these letters he simply signed. 'The Commander' and, after thinking about it, I never used his title or full name or his decorations on my letters to the hospital. But they reached him anyway.

In between all the other things he would write about, he would sometimes mention that he had begun what he called his 'jig-saw-puzzle' operations, skin grafts and the like, and that they were 'getting the pieces to fit quite nicely'. They had taken his bandages away, or most of them, and I was especially glad about this. I had been lying in bed thinking about how dark and lonely it was inside all that wrapping.

But I was never able to visit him. My sureness that it was only a bus-ride away was demolished when it turned out to be fifty miles and many buses and more money than I had. I thought I might see if I could get permission to take two days to go and see him, but nobody would listen and I began to think I would have to run away again to do it. But he wrote, promising to come and visit me as soon as he was 'all ship-shape', as he joked, and when the time came he kept his promise.

I guessed the time was drawing near because his letters had more news about his operations and how he had gone outside for the first time and sat in the autumn sun in the hospital garden. Because his skin was all new – like a baby's, he said – he had gone back into the ward with quite a brown face. In my kiddish way I began to imagine him as a bronzed, handsome man, in naval uniform, dripping with medals. A thousand times I must have romantically imagined our reunion, me an almost grown girl now, not all that far off being a woman, and he a hero of ... how old? I did not know how old he was. Nobody had ever told me. I had never asked and parcelled up like he was in the hospital there was no way I could judge. I thought he could be twenty-five or he could be forty. In fact he was forty.

He came to see me one day towards the end of that year. It was raining and I was doing my afternoon job of cleaning the cutlery with silver polish. Mrs Chandley came in all of a flap and said: 'Nelly there's a gentleman come to see *you*. None of the family is home except Master Parsifal so he couldn't have told *them* he was coming. But he's left his card for the master and he's Sir something-or-other.'

I thought my heart would jump from my body. My face had gone scarlet. I could feel it burning. But I tried to treat it in a matter-of-fact way. 'It's Sir Frederick Harrie-Young, Lieutenant Commander, RN, GC.' I recited. I had never forgotten that. 'He's my friend.'

'Your friend?' she said unbelievingly. 'Your friend?'

'That's right, Mrs Chandley,' I said, getting up and putting the knives back in their box. 'I know lots of Sirs, you know; hundreds of them.'

As I went from the room I heard her loud cowish sniff behind me. She said: 'He's got a very odd face. Very odd.'

I trembled but I walked on through the passage until I came to the room near the front door. Callers were always shown into there. I hesitated and then knocked on the door. His familiar croak answered and I went in.

I had never seen him standing before. That was something I had forgotten. He was quite tall, close to six feet, and he must have been well built at one time. Now he looked as though there were wires holding his body together. He was in naval uniform and it hung about his frame. He was standing, but leaning against a table, and he had positioned himself, purposely now I realize, in the darkest part of the room because of his face. It was badly damaged but it was not ugly. His jaw and the lower parts of his cheeks were stretched with new tight skin, discoloured at the edge of each patch and square where they had done the grafting. His neck was a general mess and on the right side he had no ear.

But his eyes were clear and blue, his forehead very strong and handsome and his hair dark and thick. I smiled at him, standing as I was near the door.

'Hello Nell,' he said. 'How do I look?'

'Taller,' I said, trying to prevent myself shaking. 'Much taller than I thought.' I couldn't help myself then. I rushed towards him, the tears spouting down my face. I threw my arms around his waist and held him tighter than I have ever held anybody in my life. His arms went around my head and he held it against his chest. I could feel him trembling too. After a full minute he was trying to say something.

'Let's go out and have some tea shall we, Nell? Then we can have a talk. Can you come out now?'

Drawing myself away from him, and turning my head swiftly so he could not see my stained cheeks, I went towards the door. 'I'll get my coat,' I said. 'Mrs Chandley will let me come. Just wait here for me, Commander.'

I got my coat and announced to Mrs Chandley that I was going out. She knew better than to argue when someone important was involved. She gave one of her sniffs and said: 'Don't forget your manners then.'

Now I felt excited and glad. I hurried back to the front room and I remember how he walked forward quite naturally and helped me to put my coat on.

He had a taxi waiting outside and it took us into the main street of Hopewell where we went to the Queen Anne Cake Shoppe, which was somewhere I had gazed at with ambition ever since I was old enough to want the better things of life. It was quaint and chintzy and even during the war had served teas and home-made cakes and sandwiches. We went in there and I sat down dumbly and looked around at the comfortable people. We had a proper tea with sandwiches and pastries. I told him what I had been doing, which did not take long, and he told me what had happened at the hospital, which did not take much longer. But we were not uncomfortable or embarrassed in each other's presence and he told me some good jokes and made me laugh with my mouth full of bread and butter. Afterwards we went to the picture house where we sat together in the dark and watched *Strike Up the Band* with Mickey Rooney and Judy Garland. It was shown on television not long ago and I kept a cabinet minister waiting while I watched it and had a cry.

When he took me home in another taxi we were both feeling sad. He said he was waiting to hear if he would be going back to the Navy, which he wanted, or whether they were going to throw him off the deck, as he put it. He told me he would keep writing to me and he asked me to write to him also. Sir Waldo was still not home, so he left his card and his compliments with Mrs Chandley, and drove away. We kissed each other on the cheek before he went and I waved until the taxi was gone into the gloom at the end of the drive. With him that was how it would always be.

It was true what they said about Parsifal, the mad son of Sir Waldo. He was a poor simple wretch, a boy of about fourteen, who spent most of his time crouched in the barn launching beans into the air from the end of his stiff penis. He never seemed to get bored with this and, naturally, it was a great matter of interest with the young housemaids around the place. It was my sister Mary, who was now eighteen, who promised to take me to see the unusual performance and with two of the other girls we hid in the bales and watched him at his lonely pastime.

He had a great strong member and very springy too, probably because of the way it was constantly put to use. He would crouch and bend it like a catapult placing a flat bean on the end of it and then letting it go so that the bean flew up in the air. The poor lad would make little whoops of happiness if the bean flew a long way. The other three girls were all laughing in their hands, but although I giggled with the rest of them at the first sight of the oddity, I felt very downhearted about poor Parsifal and the thing that he was doing. His parents never seemed to speak to him or care what he was about. His father simply ignored him and his mother grieved over the loss in the war of her other, normal son. You could see she wished it could have been Parsifal, but of course he had been too young to go to the war, and in any case, they did not take mad people. I used to see her watching him while they sat at breakfast (all his other meals he took in the kitchen with us), sloshing his food about, but otherwise eating in a sort of crazy silence, with everything going on around him completely unnoticed. His mother's eyes would go across the table, full of agony, towards him while he spooned his porridge everywhere but his mouth. His father hardly ever looked beyond his newspaper.

After the first time watching him in the barn, I would not go and spy on him again, although Mary, who always appeared so right and proper, was always prepared to go and have a giggle provided some of the other maids would go with her. Then one morning, when I was taking some kitchen waste to the chickens, I had to walk past the barn door and I heard him doing his bean flipping, making little grunts of satisfaction or disappointment depending on how far the bean was flipped.

Foolishly, and only because I felt so sorry for him, I went in through a low side door. There he crouched, his member stretched out like a springboard at a swimming pool. He had a pot of beans at his side and he fumbled inside it and took a bean – after throwing away a couple he must have thought unsuitable and placed it carefully on the flat head of the thing. He pressed it back an amazing distance (I've since known men who could do quite extraordinary tricks with erections, but I've never known one who could do what Parsifal could do) and then, leaning back so as to be out of the way in case the bean sprang back and hit him, he released it and it flew in a high curve, several yards across the barn floor. My heart swelled with pity for him. I could not help it. Coming from my hiding place I walked across the floor towards him and stood a few yards off so he could see me. He looked up but he showed no shame, no embarrassment, not even caring that I was there. He just selected another bean and did it again and then glanced up at me to see if I thought it was clever.

'Parsifal,' I whispered. 'Why be you doin' that all the time?'

'Ah,' he said as if he had a secret he was willing to share. 'It's my bean flipper.'

' 'Tis not a bean flipper,' I said soft, approaching him. ' 'Tis not for that, Parsifal.'

'It's my bean flipper,' he said sternly.

Now I was just in front of him. He was sitting on a wooden box. I bent at the knees in front of him and looked into his barmy eyes. He was just like a little cow to look at in the eyes. He looked at me puzzled and nervous because I was so close. But I smiled at him and a softer look came over his boy's face. 'You want to touch my bean flipper?' he said. 'Look, this is it.'

I just nodded and I put out my hand and touched it on its soft nose. His expression altered to one of excitement and surprise. He took my hand, uncertainly at first, but then firmly, and ran it along the skin. I remember doing that, when I was a little girl in the stream, for the poor lonely American soldier, and now I was doing it for a mad boy. First I let him guide my fingers up and down, but then I put my other hand to it and began to work them all over. He had gone puffy in the face and his eyes were nearly jumping out of his head. He was making purring noises way back in his throat. His hands went out and touched my face. I did for him what I had done for the American soldier. I caressed and rubbed him until the last seconds and then I cradled him.

I went outside and dipped my hands in the rainbutt. Inside the barn there was a great silence. And then, to my shock and horror, there came the most horrible cry. I looked through the door and saw him running about in crazy circles, his hands on his little thing, and crying: 'Oh my bean flipper! Oh God! Oh God! That girl's broke my bean flipper!'

The incident that sent me away from Hopewell Manor for ever happened at breakfast time; after being there two years I was considered old enough to wait at table. It was well-known among the maids that Sir Waldo was apt to behave very wickedly in the early part of the day and more than one had returned to the kitchen in fear and tears because of some gross but casual indecency performed on her person while she was serving or waiting at the breakfast table. A complaint to Mrs Chandley only brought scornful disbelief or the opinion that 'Sir Waldo is a bit absent-minded in the mornings.'

It was true he performed these things in what seemed to be an absent-minded way, usually when he was reading *The Times*, but the general opinion among the kitchen staff was that he knew what he was doing all right. The maids, and there were five of us including my sister Mary (who, typically, was inclined to put down the assaults as 'accidents'), used to draw lots and the unlucky one had to serve breakfast. This lottery used to take the form of closing our eyes and putting our hands in the silver drawer and selecting a knife, fork or spoon. We would then look at the silver marks and whichever had the lowest letter of the alphabet as it's date-letter had to do the chore. I managed to avoid this by concealing a piece of cutlery with a high letter up the sleeve of my dress and dropping it into my hand when I was making my selection.

Unfortunately I overplayed my hand and it was quickly noticed by the other girls. One morning they made a combined rush at me and pinning me to the table found a teaspoon in my sleeve. After that I had to run the gauntlet for a week.

On the first morning, Sir Waldo's mile-long nose came out of his newspaper like a trunk as I busied myself around the table. I imagined that I saw a nasty bright light come into his eye but I looked away quickly and went around the other side of the large table where Madam was cracking dry toast in her teeth while staring blankly at the wall. Parsifal was moonily slopping porridge over the table cloth.

But nothing happened until my third day, when Sir Waldo took me firmly by the wrist and instructed me to stand at the side of his chair. I did so trembling, frightened at what might occur, but unable to prevent it. My whole body vibrated and my feet were hot in my shoes. Hopefully I looked at Madam but if her husband had thrown me to the carpet and raped me repeatedly, it is doubtful if she would have noticed it over her machinations with the toast. And as for Parsifal, all you could have counted on from him was a mad faraway smile.

And so I stood, like some little sentry, at the side of Sir Waldo's chair, waiting. He was in no hurry. In fact perhaps that was part of the pervert's pleasure, his delaying and my suspense. Eventually he made a move. He leaned around the outside of his paper and whispered: 'How old are you, gel?'

'Fifteen, Sir,' I mumbled. I kept staring at the paper. I remember it said: 'Attlee Anxious About Next Move.' So was I. I concentrated on reading the words underneath the headline, anything to keep my mind off what I knew was about to take place. There was nothing I really understood because, until then, I had taken no great interest in politics. Then he began putting his hand up my dress.

God I can feel it now. Just like a spider climbing up the spout. Oh you *low* man, I thought. You dirty, *low man*. Strangely enough my shaking ceased. It was probably the uncertainty that caused it. Now I stood rigid, letting him do it, suffering it.

The maids all wore black lisle stockings, held up with garters. His hand went up the rough material and touched the naked flesh at the top of my leg. Not for a moment did he look up from his newspaper, which he managed to balance expertly in the other hand. The thin fingers went inside my garter and hung there for a moment or so. Then they continued the journey to my private places wrapped inside my drawers. A scream was trapped in my mouth. Silently and closing my eyes tightly I began to pray. 'Oh Almighty God, our heavenly father, who sees all things, please in Thy mercy stop this dirty man doing what 'ee be doing right now. For our Lord Jesus Christ's sake. Amen.'

Nothing happened, which was much as I expected. I've learned not to put too much faith in praying, especially in emergencies, since prayers seem to take longer than they ought to reach their destination. And by that time it's usually happened.

While I was still muttering privately to God, the hand went further with its explorations. First it massaged the outside of my drawers right below the arch of my legs, then it wheedled its way up the leg, breaking the elastic as it went. Wartime elastic was never very strong. It was amazing that this was going on and yet nothing in the room was moving. He continued with his newspaper, I stood stiff and terrified, Parsifal was scooping some of the blobs of porridge off the cloth, and the only sounds were the explosions of Madam gnashing her toast.

Thinking of it now I am amazed that I did nothing. My memory is that I braved it out, hopelessly, in the way that you fight your way through a nightmare, knowing that there is nothing that you can do to change it. Eventually he removed his hand and folded his newspaper. Madame looked up as though she had seen me for the first time. She had finished all her toast and I suppose that is what made her look across to me. Perhaps he had timed the end of the assault on me to coincide with the last crust. He knew exactly what he was doing. 'Go and get some more toast girl,' she said sharply. 'Don't just stand there as if you'd been struck by lightning.'

I stumbled out of the room thinking I would have preferred lightning. At least it never struck in the same place twice. Returning with the toast I set it on the table and then looked up just in time to see his randy eye lifted above the edge of the paper. Then, at that moment, I thought: 'Right, you filthy bastard, I'll get you tomorrow.'

From the moment I had the thought I knew I would see it

through. In fact, once I had formed my plan, I could hardly wait until the next day to carry it out. It would be necessary for me to make a quick escape and to have everything ready for that. Fortunately it was the day after we received our monthly pittance from the hands of Mrs Chandley, so with a pound or so I had saved, I knew I would be able to travel and exist for at least a week until, with luck, I found some refuge. I was very cool about it. I packed everything I had in a cardboard box and tied it with string before putting it under my bed in readiness for my flight. I put my street coat with it. It was a good plan.

The other maids, including Mary, stood grinning stupidly, as I carried in the trays to the breakfast room.

The scene was as before, indeed it never seemed to alter. It was like a working model in a wax exhibition. He was reading *The Times*, the idiot boy was distributing porridge and his mother was munching the toast. I did what I was supposed to do and, sure enough (and to my relief, because I had a feeling that perhaps that day, of all days, he would not be feeling filthy enough to make his indecent assault) he caught me by the hand and held me at the side of his chair. He continued with the newspaper and I found myself reading a speech by a man called Ernest Bevin which had upset Conservative members of the House of Commons. A few more days like that, trying to take my mind off what was about to happen, and I might have become a political expert. But, right on time, the wandering hand left Sir Waldo's side, as though going off of its own accord, and found its way to the hem of my skirt. Up it crawled, up the servant's black stockings, a slight twang of the garter and then a busy fingering of the flesh of my thighs. That was the moment.

I closed my legs, quietly but firmly, trapping the hand between them. A little start came over him, but he was conceited enough to think I was enjoying it and joining in. A wicked smile sniggered beneath the long nose and he looked at me questioningly, taking care to stay under cover of the newspaper. Now I had him. From beneath an extra tureen on the serving table on my other side, I produced a primed mousetrap. He did not see it, so taken was he with my cooperation. I did it beautifully. I thrust up my skirt and held it against my thigh. As his fingers crept up my leg the trap was sprung and caught his hand.

Christ, you ought to have heard him! He screeched out and shot a foot up in his chair. The howl actually froze on his face as he pulled his hand away and the mousetrap was still clamped on his fingers. He bounced up and down in agony, tugging at the contraption to get it off. He collapsed on his chair. I leaned over, calmly picked up Parsifal's bowl of porridge and emptied it over his father's head. What pandemonium!

Madam went berserk, firing toast crumbs all over the place in her frenzy, letting loose a terrible high howl. Parsifal banged his gruel spoon on the table and screamed: 'She broke my bean flipper! She broke my bean flipper!'

It was time to go. I did not rush or even run. I turned briskly and walked out, passing an avalanche of servants heading in the opposite direction to see what had happened. Upstairs I took my cardboard box from beneath my bed, kissed Mary's pillow (as a substitute for taking farewell of Mary herself) and went out of the back door. It was a fresh early winter's day. I could smell freedom. Through the garden and out into the lane I went and ran down the airy hill towards the town. All the way I was laughing and crying at the same time. People turned and must have thought I was very odd. I suppose I was really.

This time I was on my own. There was no Davie to help and guide me. From the moment he had been hauled away, I had heard not another thing from him. Three times I had written and I sent him a Christmas card and a two shilling postal order as a present, but he had not replied. It would be a long wait before I saw him again. The Commander had gone back to sea, he had written to tell me so. ('Dearest Nell, I am now sailing to Gibraltar, en route for the Suez Canal and the Orient. It is very lonely being the captain of a ship.') So I could not turn to him, and in any case I would not have gone to him in any trouble. There only remained my father and, even if I could discover where he was, I knew that after the first emotional play acting, the kisses and the rubber tears, he would have sent me straight back to Sir Waldo or handed me over to the police and asked for a reward.

So I went, alone and blindly at first, just wanting as many fields between myself and Hopewell as possible, and quickly. My happy childhood had turned sour. Instinctively my first flight was in the direction of the bus station, thinking that this was where Davie would have headed. Just as I reached there a bus was pulling out and on the destination board it said 'Exeter'. That seemed far enough away for a start. I ran and jumped aboard. I sat on the top deck and watched the Devon lanes and pastures go by, just as though they were running away from me, not me from them, and the red winter furrows, and cattle, and smoke fingering up from chimneys and blowing slowly through the cold air. People in the villages and small towns that we passed all seemed to belong to the places and to each other; they had a set sure life, somewhere to live and somewhere to work, family and friendship of other human beings. It did not seem a lot to want. My cardboard box of belongings lay very light on my lap. But I got to thinking about what I had done in the breakfast room in Hopewell Manor. I began to giggle, and I was still giggling when the conductor, a spherical, red-faced man with a little tuft of white hair, came up the stairs.

'Ah,' he said. ' 'Tis nice to see people laughing. Even if 'tis by theirselves. Where be you going m'dear?'

'Exeter,' I said firmly. 'Just Exeter.'

'Now, which part?' he asked. 'I b'aint want to be charging you too much for the ticket, do I?'

That caught me. 'The middle part,' I filled in hurriedly. 'As far as the bus goes.'

He looked at me strangely. Then he said: 'Going to see somebody be 'ee?'

'N ... no, I b'aint. I be ... going for a job.'

He gave me the ticket slowly, then said, 'Well, m'dear, I 'ope you get it.'

Then he went downstairs. I cursed a country that was trained to look out for spies. The normal Devon man's curiosity was enough without adding anything. I felt sure he was suspicious of me. Perhaps a cordon had been thrown around the district to capture me for the police. I took a pair of sewing scissors from my box. I had reckoned that I ought to be entitled to a going away present from the Manor, so I had helped myself to these, intending them as a defensive weapon. The rough memory of Handsome Jack the sailor still lingered.

But nothing worrying happened. The bus went through what was already a foreign land to me, even though it was only a few miles from the place where I was born. Rivers broadened and the hills became flatter and eventually we drove through the streets of Exeter, again all crumbled from the bombing of the war. It astonished me. To think that all around there had been such destruction and that we in our village had seen nothing of it except the bomb that put paid to my mother and my childhood.

At the terminus at the centre of the old town the conductor said goodbye to me and, in an odd, knowing way, wished me good luck. It encouraged me for a while but that feeling and the enjoyment of my freedom soon went as the day drew on and the afternoon closed in, dim and damp. Everyone around me seemed to have plenty to do and places to be going, while I wandered aimlessly through their busy day. I went to a steamed up café and had sausage and chips and a cup of tea. It cost me more than I thought and I knew that if I were to survive I would need to conserve my money better than that. On the other hand it was not, this time, all in pennies and half pennies, so there was no question of it weighing me down as it had when I escaped with Davie.

Probably because it was the only place I felt any connection with, I wandered back to the bus station. I had some vague idea of looking at the route map in there, and the waiting room, bleak though it was, seemed more comfortable than the chill of the bare street.

I bought a tacky bun from the refreshment counter and sat in a corner of the waiting room, wondering what to do next. Then I saw the conductor of the bus I had been on, coming across the floor towards me. I tried to hide behind the paper bag and the bun.

'You still here then?' he said, standing a couple of yards away and looking at me kindly.

'Yes.'

' 'Tis because you be lost.'

'I b'aint lost. I just don't know where I be going.'

' 'Tis cold.'

'Aye, 'tis gettin' that way.'

He leaned forward and took me by the hand. He was not someone you could fear or be suspicious about, so I went with him. I did not think he would take me to the police or hand me over to anybody else. And he did not. We walked instead through the chilly old streets, me silent, holding my cardboard box against me as though it kept me warm, and him whistling cheerfully through his teeth. After reaching a small street we turned into an alley and went to the front door of a house, almost a cottage even though it was in a city. Dark though it was I could see that the outside was carefully kept and there were things growing neatly in the patch of garden at the front.

His wife, who looked so much like him she could have been his twin sister, made a cup of tea. Somehow I did not feel nervous telling them my story, even to the embarrassing parts. They sat one each side of me, with the fire on all our faces, while I related what had happened that day. When I got to the part about Sir Waldo's indecency towards me they kept shaking their heads to and fro just like clockwork. I looked from one to the other but I could never get a full face at one time. Then when I told them about the mousetrap they pealed with laughter and hung on to each other's shoulders, reaching across me and holding each other. 'Oh that's a good one!' the bus conductor chuckled. ' 'Tis indeed a good one.' When I had finished the lady began to cry a bit and her husband patted her. Then she got up and cooked us all sausage and chips.

I could see they did not know what to do with me. After the meal they allowed me to sit in an old deep chair with another cup of tea and listen to Tommy Handley on the radio. I sat and laughed. They went into the kitchen and did the washing up, refusing my offers of help, and I could hear them discussing my plight – and theirs now – in their fruity voices. They had no idea what they should do with me and, at that moment, I thought I would have to save them the trouble by leaving the house in the early morning and going on my way.

It was not difficult. I awoke automatically at six-thirty because that was the time all the servants got up at the Manor. The cottage was cosy and quiet. I could hear the clock clucking downstairs. They had put me in a little room, almost filled by the bed, and there in the dark, I got dressed and, taking my cardboard box, inched my way down the creaky stairs. There were still embers in the fire from the night before and their big white cat was rolled up like a cushion on the mat. It was a really homely place and I was sorry I would have to go. But there was nothing for it.

First I wrote them a note which just said *Thank you. God bless*, and with two kisses after it. Then I quietly let myself out into the small garden and crept to the gate. It was still dark and everywhere was cold as iron. I reached the gate and, turning around, I saw an oil lamp lit in the upper window. He was looking right down at me. For a moment neither of us did anything. He must have been thinking, weighing things up. Then he just waved goodbye to me, a small wave as if he thought a bigger one might wake his wife. And I thought I saw the shadow of a smile. I waved back, gratefully, and went on my journey.

seven

Why I went to Weymouth I do not know. It was just that the roads seemed to lead that way and in some unconscious manner I felt happier and safer if I kept to the seacoast. By the time I reached there I had only two shillings of my money left. I would have to do something definite before long or surrender.

My hand was on that two shilling piece, just as though I was keeping it warm and it was doing the same for me, as I walked aimlessly along the chill seafront of Weymouth. The beach was empty and so was the sea, except for gulls and other December birds. A couple of minutes of sun occurred, pale as lemon, and a few old people, stiff and freezing, came out walking, trying as they do to keep healthy and have a longer life.

All that was in my mind was to find somewhere to *be*, somewhere where there would be no trouble, no cruelty, no fear. Somewhere certain.

There was a nudging hunger inside me and I stopped outside a café by the side of the small port, all comfortably steamed up and full of men who worked on the ships in the docks. It was my last two shillings, but as I stood there the door opened and the smell of the frying wafted out. Two grinning, satisfied-looking men came out and before they had time to close the door I was inside.

It was too early for the main midday meal and in that sort of place anyway breakfast just ran on to supper time with hardly a break. In one corner, away from the rest, there was a table, yellow marble cracked like a spider's web, and I sat there alone. An easy-looking man in an apron all splodged with tomato sauce, fat and tea-stains came and asked me what I wanted and I ordered fried egg, chips, bread and butter and tea, which I calculated from the chalk menu on the wall came to exactly two shillings. Some of the men around me looked at me curiously and I expect some made a few guesses at what I was doing there, but they left me to myself and I ate hungrily what I knew could be my last decent meal for a long time. The appearance of a solitary sausage on the plate worried me because I had not ordered it, nor did I have the money to pay for it, but it looked glistening and hot and, although I had half an idea to take it back when I had finished the rest, I could not resist the aroma and I sliced it up and ate it. Having now gone over the top of what I could afford to pay for, I might have then decided to be hung for a sheep as a lamb and ordered a second helping of everything with treacle pudding to follow. But my nerve failed. Even then, as I stood up to go to the counter, I felt my legs tremble.

'Two and tuppence lady,' said the woman behind the till. Her hair was sticking to her forehead in the way my mother's used to do when she was steam-ironing. She had fat forearms and heavy elbows as ladies in that sort of café seem always to have. Her apron was stained in the same kind of pattern as the man's, like an artist's palette.

'I've only got two shillings,' I said. 'I thought it would come to two shillings.'

'Two and tuppence,' she repeated. Then she called: 'Harold!'

Harold was the man who had served me. 'It's two and tuppence, dear,' he nodded.

There was nothing for it but to stand my ground. 'I didn't ask for that sausage,' I pointed out. 'You put it there without me asking.'

'You scoffed it,' Harold pointed out amiably. 'How much have you got?'

'Two shillings,' I replied. 'And that's the lot.' I knew that all the men had stopped eating now and were looking around behind me.

'Aw, Christ,' said Harold with a sigh. 'I'm not going to be arguing about tuppence. Two bob it is. The sausage is freeman's.'

'Thanks. Very kind of you I'm sure,' I said. I put the coin on the counter and turned to walk out in as dignified a way as I could. When I had reached the door the lady called after me. 'Want to do the washing up dear? There's plenty of washing up.'

I heard some of the men laugh and I thought she was making fun of me because I had no money. That was very nearly the last straw because on top of the embarrassment of the whole thing, the memory of the meal was already fading and there was a space in my pocket where the two shillings had once been. Turning quickly I was just about to give them some choice thoughts when I saw that they were looking at me in a friendly way through the steam. I stopped myself.

'Yes,' I said instead, the relief filling me. 'I'll do it. Anything you've got.'

All the men clapped and laughed at this. One of them shouted: 'You pay 'er union rates, Flossie!' and another smacked my bottom in a friendly way as I went back to the counter. Not thinking, I put my cardboard box down on the counter and they stared at it, realizing then that is was my luggage. 'There's a lot of it,' said the woman in a low sort of voice. 'Mountains.'

'But we'll feed you and pay a bob an hour,' said Harold. 'Is that all right?'

I grinned at them. Their grins came back at me through the vapour. Gladness filled me like their tea. 'That's all right,' I whispered. 'I'll start on it now.'

The months that followed were, in many ways, amongst the most settled in my young life. Everything was so simple. I worked in the café, washing up at first, then they got an old woman to help with that and I became a waitress. I slept in a room above the café and they paid me a shilling an hour and all my food. For me it was contentment, almost luxury.

The winter of that year was arctic. The harbour froze and even the edge of the beaches had what looked like thick finger nails of ice. Everything became very still, nothing seemed to move from one day to another, as though the air and the whole of Weymouth and the world was frozen solid. The café was steamy and warm, a good place to be, and the heat drifted up through the ceiling into my little room above making it as warm as a nest. I began to be very happy.

Every afternoon I was allowed an hour off and I always went down to the frozen beach. My feet, warm inside a pair of sailor's socks and wellington boots which had been given to me, would crunch on the sharp sand. The sea broke the ice at its edges as it came in with the tide but the coating soon formed again as soon as it came to the ebb. There were no winds and no storms. The cold air and the cold sea seemed to be joined together. Gulls still flew, their wings creaking.

Harold and Flossie Crouch, the couple with the sauce-splashed aprons who ran Hal's Café ('always something hot') were as kind as parents to me. At first they made no inquiries about where I had come from, or why, at just fifteen, I should be wandering about with no roots and apparently no family. Then, one afternoon when it was snowing freshly and it was too cold for me to go out, I sat in the little kitchen behind the café and told Flossie my story. I can see her now, wet-browed, cigarette bent and broken in her nicotined hands, leaning forward to hear every word of what I had to say. She was quite overcome by the things that had happened to me and twice she had to call me to stop because she had begun to cry uncontrollably and had to blot up the tears with her stained apron. When I told her about Sir Waldo and his deadly wandering hand her eyes burned with amazement and anger and she kept muttering: 'The bastard, the foul bastard,' and jabbing the point of a huge breadknife into the top of the table. It was as well for Sir Waldo that he never dropped into Hal's Café for a cup of tea and two slices of bread and dripping.

Because I was afraid my new life might be discovered and I would be dragged away to somewhere, I did not write to Mary. By this time I knew that I could not rely on her as a sister, or her on me, and that we would now grow into life by our separate ways, me, as it turned out, to be an international whore and her as a pastrycook in a baker's shop.

I did, however, write to the Commander, at the hospital, hoping that they would forward it to him as he had returned to sea, but no reply came back which made me sad, although somehow I knew that we had not seen the last of each other. I would wait for him.

The winter had really bitten deeply into everything that year. There was snow and ice until the end of March and then the frozen weather was broken up by the spring tides and storms. The café was almost on the harbour front and it was thrilling for me at night to lie in the enclosed warmth of the loft and hear the wind and the waves throwing themselves across the shore. And then, one morning, most unexpectedly the spring arrived. The storms and the cold went almost at once and I awoke to the huge sun, a long sky and the blue channel. It was to grow into one of the most beautiful of all summers.

Naturally a great many of the men who came into the café from their work on the docks or the boats became familiar and friendly. I was the sort who could laugh off their bantering remarks and their well-intended pinching. I could give as good as I got from any of them. Waltzing around the tables with my arms loaded with hot plates, brushing off the rude jokes and reaching hands, I was completely happy. I knew that some of the young fishermen who came in smelling of haddock and mackerel looked at me with a more serious interest. I often caught them glancing at the line of my bosom as I went about my work or heard the banter stop abruptly when I bent my bottom over. I was pleased and flattered and indeed several of them I felt were very appetizing themselves, young and strong with bright eyes and always with a laugh. If it had not been for the overpowering smell of fish they would have attracted any woman.

One of these easy lads was called Rainbow by all the others. He worked a small fishing boat with his father who was small and creased and quiet. His father was also deaf and, as far as I can remember, was known as Hooter. They would come in after a night in the Channel, niffing to heaven, and sit and eat a huge hot breakfast. They lived together in a house at the back of the town with no woman there because old Hooter's wife had died.

Rainbow was very lively and popular, always raising a shout or a laugh from the other men when he arrived in the morning from his boat. The old man used to slouch in after his son, looking very miserable and blank-eyed, not seeming to take any notice of anyone there. Sometimes the customers would shout: 'Where did you catch him then, Rainbow?' and everybody would roll about laughing, although the joke was well worn.

Rainbow would reply, and always the same reply: ''Un got caught in the net. I thought 'un was one o' they mermaids.' And that would get a rousing laugh too. They were simple men and they never asked a lot of life.

I guessed that Rainbow liked the look of me, particularly as he always spoke softly to me without any of the loudness I got from the other lads. He seemed almost shy. Of course it did not take the others long to catch on to this and they would always banter us. Flossie said to me one day: 'You want to beware of young Rainbow, Nelly. He's got that look in his eye. And he ain't spotted a shoal of mackerel neither.'

Nor had he. He began to come into the café in the evenings, sometimes, before he and old Hooter took their boat out for the night and, in truth, I used to look forward to seeing him, because he was a handsome boy and I liked him too.

Then one night in the spring, just as the evenings were lighter and you could see far across the sea even at nine o'clock, Rainbow asked me if I would go out fishing with Hooter and him. I guessed he meant nothing innocent because he did not look at me when he said it but kept his head half turned away and asked me from the corner of his mouth.

'All right, Rainbow,' I agreed. 'I never been on one o' they boats. I'll come with you.'

It was true. Although I had always lived within a whiff of the sea and I was familiar with tides and storms and gulls, I had never actually been on a boat. My only experience of a vessel of any kind was the little skiff that sank beneath Davie and me in the river, and since we were only aboard it for about two minutes it was scarcely worth counting.

I told Harold and Flossie I was going and Flossie frowned with doubt and repeated that I ought to watch young Rainbow carefully. But Harold said he was all for it, provided I arrived back in time to do my work in the morning and I did not fall asleep over the breakfasts. So at ten o'clock, when the last bar of silver had gone from the channel, I waited for Rainbow's boat at the harbour. He came whistling through the darkness with a little lantern swinging in front of him and old Hooter grumbling along behind. It was Hooter who was carrying the nets. Rainbow was delighted and seemed surprised to see me, as if he thought that I might change my mind. The old man, although he had come into the café dozens of times, stood and looked at me in the light of the lantern asking: 'Be this the one? Be she? Be she?' He took the lantern from his son and ran the lantern up and down to get a good look from head to foot. Apparently he liked what he saw because he muttered: ' 'Tis all right,' and turned and climbed down to the deck.

Rainbow's boat was called *Dainty Girl* and she reeked of fish. She was short and stubby, and the winter's new paint had already been knocked off in great patches by the clumsy sea. But the narrow wheelhouse at the back, like a watchman's hut, looked very jaunty and Rainbow said that although we might run into a 'bit o' a sea' that night the trip should be a good one. He helped me very courteously on to the deck and I could feel how powerful his hands and forearms were as he held me. His almost Spanish face looked very romantic in the lanternlight, gentle but with some sort of threat in it. I felt wonderful.

Rainbow sat me in the wheelhouse right beside him and the old man went below and started the engine. Rainbow kept calling short instructions to him down a small brass tube, giving a whistle before every order. Since Hooter was supposed to be stone deaf I did not know how this worked. Later I got the suspicion that it was all done to impress me and that Hooter never even answered the other end of the tube but got on with starting the engine on his own. But impressed I was. The sky was ragged with clouds and the sea came at us with a steady slap as we left the harbour. Sitting there, next to handsome Rainbow at the wheel, watching the land and the sky move on, made me feel like some glamorous star of a film about the Spanish Main.

As we left the stone harbour and the channel spread all around us, Hooter came up to the deck with three mugs of tea. He took his and began busying himself with the nets on the deck. It felt grand being out there in the night, drinking tea, warm in a large woollen jersey. There was a pane of glass missing in the window of the wheelhouse and the wind ran through it and blew at my hair. How wonderful it all was. Then the sea began to get heavier. I laughed when it pitched over us the first time, but the laugh was thinner when it threw us the opposite way the next moment. I had finished the tea and I could feel it swilling around like bilge in my stomach. Then the wooden nose of the boat went straight up in the air, just like it had suddenly scented something far off in the oceans. I tipped backwards. The tight wheelhouse was suddenly rattling and shuddering and the stench of the fish assailed me in gusts.

'Oh Rainbow, oh God,' I remember saying, although my voice seemed miles away from my body. 'I b'aint feelin' all that healthy.'

Rainbow was all surprise and consideration. He tied the wheel with a piece of string and shouted something to his father who was stumping about on the deck as easily as he would walk about a Weymouth street. Then, supporting me firmly about the waist, he took me down the few steps to the deck and told me to breathe the wind. But the more wind I breathed the more fish I breathed as well. Then the boat pitched again and despite his support I tipped over and slithered away across the scaly deck. A cowardly wave gushed over the side and hit me when I was down. I began to cry.

It took both Rainbow and old Hooter to get me up this time. They held me to the side so that I could be sick. One of them, and I suspected it was the old chap, had his hand on my arse, the horny fingers flattened out like a seat. Not that I cared. The whole world was spinning and dipping and the air full of noisy gusts.

'Down,' I managed to get out. 'Down, down.'

'Down? Down?' They started to repeat it to themselves like a pair of comedians. 'Down? Down?'

'Under,' I belched. 'Below. Down below.'

That was their language. They got me across the deck, shaking with sickness, wetness and cold, and helped me through the tight hatch to the place under the deck. God, there it was worse!

The reek of the engine oil and the increased smell of fish had me reeling again. And it was so low and confined. Like a coffin. But there was no going back. With Hooter's hand still three parts of the way up my bottom and with Rainbow holding me conscientiously under the breasts, I was almost frog marched to the middle of the boat and there heaved up on to a bunk.

'You 'ang on there, m'beauty,' said old Hooter in the dark. It was the first time he had ever spoken a sentence that long in my hearing. Rainbow heaved my bosom on to the bunk as if it were a kit bag. Then he hung a foul fish bucket from a hook on the side of the bunk and said if I felt sick that was the place to put it. Then they slumped off back on to the deck.

I hung there spread out like some stricken flatfish, unable to see anything but only knowing the terrible black movement all around. It was like being in your grave in an earthquake. But a sort of coma came over me, I became drowsy and dozy and eventually the movement itself seemed to rock me to sleep. When I awoke there was a lantern burning in the cabin, the sea had calmed and the boat was moving sedately. And there was Rainbow sitting stark naked on the stool beside the bunk.

My eyes took him in. His body was powerful and the lamp-light made it smooth and olive. He looked at me as though ashamed and said: 'Durn it! I went and got wet.'

'It gets wet at sea,' I said logically. 'Did you come down to change, Rainbow?'

'Aye, that's it,' he agreed. 'The wind 'as dropped off now. The old man's got the nets over the side. I got a bit o' spare time.'

On his body he had several strange tattoos and these he showed me, holding up the lantern to illuminate the various places. He had some daggers and hearts on his forearm and the words 'love or death' and these I had seen before. But over his heart he had a heart in red ink and below his belly-button a sort of scroll with the words: 'For good girls only' and some little arrows pointing down to his fine, dark jumbo. Then he turned about and I sat up in the bunk and held the lantern to see what he had to show me there. It made me laugh. Sailing across his bottom was a fleet of tattooed fishing boats, the leading vessel just disappearing into his backside crack.

'You're just like a picture show,' I said. I knew my voice sounded croaky, but I was not sure whether this was because of my recent sickness or because I knew what was going to happen. He was very gentlemanly, his jumbo was hanging quietly during all the conversation just as if he wanted me to see that he did not expect too much.

But he was a handsome lad and I was primed for someone like him. 'I'll show you what *I* got, Rainbow,' I said throatily. 'But 'tis not tattoos.'

While he squatted there dumbly I wriggled out of the tight trousers I was wearing, pulling away my drawers at the same time. I could just about sit up in the bunk, with my head bent forward a little. In this way I pulled the jersey away from my body and took off all my other things.

Rainbow sat staring as if he could not believe what he saw. Then when I was naked he stood up and held the lantern so that he could see me properly. I could almost feel it making shadows across my body. 'Be I all right then, Rainbow dear?' I asked.

'Aw, Nell,' he said in a respectful whisper. 'Aw Nell, you certainly be a real pleasant sight.'

This was my first really grown-up sex and, in some ways I now see, it began a new life for me. All the things that have followed have stemmed from that one night in a little boat on an abruptly windless sea.

It was amazing how calm it had become. The vessel now moved about as easily as a cow strolling across its meadow. All my sickness had gone with the waves, although it made me feel weak. But not all that weak. I looked at the comely Rainbow with his now upstanding jumbo and his fine smile and waited for him to climb upon me.

'Be it all right then, Nelly?' he asked with his fisherman's politeness.

' 'Tis all right,' I whispered. 'I'm true fond of you, Rainbow.'

He climbed up with hardly an effort, just easing himself from the floor and lying half on top and half alongside me, keeping most of his weight off my body, a politeness I have always appreciated in a gentleman. I could feel his member burning eagerly against the top of my leg. My fingers went to it and encouraged it. Considerately, with my other hand I put my nipple between his lips. He sucked for a while like a child and became very excited in a powerful but contained way.

There was not much room for romance. Every movement needed some guidance and encouragement. I was pleasantly surprised to find how good I was at it. Although my experience had until then only covered an American soldier and poor Parsifal (neither of which could be counted as the real thing), the drunken efforts of Handsome Jack the Plymouth sailor and the juvenile love of Davie – although that was all, I seemed to be moved by instinct.

I moved below him, gently pushing his stomach up until his

body was arched above me, his chest wide and with a pretty tuft of hair flowering at its centre, and his tattoos animated. A quick dance with my bottom and I was directly below his anxious eyes, his arched stomach and his eager pointed lance. It seemed to glow with anticipation. I could feel myself glowing too, a flush on my skin, my breasts warm, and between my legs like an oven. I opened them wider and guided him to me. It was amazing. He seemed to fill my belly with himself. He slid home with never a moment's hesitation and all in one deep breath. There was no doubt he was a splendid and healthy lad, even if he did smell fishy.

Having run in for his entire length he did nothing else but just lay there like some landed fish himself. I turned and looked at his comely face just at my shoulder. His eyes clouded and then closed and I had a short silly fright that the experience might have killed him. I did not want that to happen on my first real time. But his face was moving and he seemed to be trying to say something.

'What is it Rainbow dear?' I whispered. 'What be you on about?'

'I be prayin' Nell,' he said simply. 'I be prayin' to thank the Lord God for this thing we be up to.'

I let him pray, although I would have preferred to have got on with it. But, perhaps, I thought, it was like grace said before a meal. It was the only prayer he knew but worded approximately for us he prayed: 'Oh God, bless us who go down to the sea in ships and occupy our business in great waters ...' Now, after all this time, I can appreciate how charming it was, but then I must confess, I thought it was a bit strange and only caused an avoidable delay. When he had done he opened his seaman's eyes and began moving like a piston engine. What a thing he possessed. I truly thought he would burst me at the seams. He began to sweat busily and his grunts of young pleasure were in rhythm with the beat of the boat's little engine. His fish-cutting hands had my buttocks held so fiercely that it was all I could do not to cry out, and I feared he might damage me for he had a strange liking for banging those buttocks together like cymbals in a band. His thighs rolled on mine and his gasping open mouth on my neck.

He blew out as quickly as the storm and lay there wallowing lazily like the boat in the easing sea. To my surprise he wasted

110

no time before slipping fast asleep and began to snore unmusically. At that time of course, I knew nothing of the strange disinterest of men once they have had what a few moments previously they wanted before anything else in the world. I did not like to wake him although I was getting cold and stiff in the bunk. I pulled a blanket around us and dozed myself, letting the moving of the sea and the rasping snores of my young lover become a lullaby. When I awoke again he had gone from my side and was bumping about the deck with his father.

I searched about for my clothes, washed my face in a bucket of reasonably clean water and, straightening my hair and my expression, I climbed the ladder up through the companionway.

As I reached the open deck the knifey air caught me and the new morning's sun fell on my face. It was a great salty sunlit sight, the sea reclining bright blue towards the green land only a short distance away. Seabirds were whirling and squawking around the mast and the funny little wheelhouse and there were baskets of silver fish on the deck.

'Did you catch much last night then, Rainbow?' I called as he was sorting the nets at the stern.

He returned the look gravely and steadily. 'Aye,' he said.

Old Hooter did not glance from the land ahead. He was at the wheel and he stared straight over the bow as though he had never entered Weymouth harbour before. Being a useful sort of girl I turned and went below and found the kettle and the teapot and made three mugs of tea. I took them above and father and son accepted them without a word. We stood together on deck and watched the land closing on us, like Columbus coming to a strange world.

Before long we slipped around the stone breakwater and into the early-morning harbour. Other fishing boats were heading in and we waved to several crews. One man shouted, 'Did you do all right then, young Rainbow?' and I heard him and the others laughing across the summery water. I glanced at Rainbow and saw that he was flushed and angry for that moment and he turned away and went and did something with the ropes at the stern. The old man took the boat alongside the jetty and they tied up.

'I've got to go now,' I said to both of them at once. They

were standing awkwardly on the deck, wearing high boots and dim expressions. A seagull came down and grabbed a fish from one of the baskets. Rainbow shouted something at him in fisherman's gibberish. 'I got to,' I said. 'I promised I'd be back to help with the breakfasts.'

It seemed there was something else. Something they wanted to do. I smiled at them and went to climb up the ladder to the jetty.

Rainbow said something sharp, quickly to old Hooter and then turned and went in a hurry down below. The old man simply stood on the deck, caught in some indecision.

'Bye, bye,' I said as cheerfully as I could. I climbed the scaly ladder to the jetty and turned to wave again. Then, as I turned to walk towards the town, old Hooter shouted: 'Girl!' I turned to see something bounce on the stones. It rolled and then stopped and shone in the sun. I took two paces towards it, hesitated, stooped and picked it up. It was half-a-crown.

Quickly I put it in my pocket, turned and walked away. Not for the first time in my life, I did not know whether to laugh or cry. Still I took it. I clutched it in my hand as I began to run along the cobbles.

That was the start of it all. I had done it for money. I was a whore.

After that I began going out on the boats of Weymouth with various fisherboys and sailors. Often I could be seen making my way, in a quietly brazen manner, down to the harbour as the night came on and the same watcher would have seen me return on the peaceful morning tide with a deck full of mackerel and satisfaction on the face of some wholesome seafaring lad.

Never again did I go with Rainbow and Hooter on their boat. It turned out that I had been an eighteenth birthday present for the boy from the old man because despite his brave tattoos, until that night he had experienced even less than I had. But after that he stuck to fishing and even when he came into Hal's gave no sign of those rocky hours we had spent in each others arms. But the word had gone round, of course, and various lads asked me to go out to the Channel with them and I often went. Naturally my charges went up with the increasing demand. One sunset I sailed with three jolly brothers and during a force nine gale blowing nor' nor' west I obliged each in turn. I stepped ashore with over a pound.

Needless to say this new career was not helping my work at the café. Sometimes I was so dog tired I would drop off to sleep over the till while waiting for someone to take the money from their pocket to pay for a meal. Once I fell into a big pan of potatoes and another time let the washing up sink overflow and flood the kitchen floor.

Harold and Flossie were patient with me. They realized from the beginning what was going on. One night, when I was in bed, I heard them arguing about me. I was very surprised because they seldom had a cross word and it upset me that I should be the cause of any disagreement.

Their room was next to mine and the walls were only plywood. It was rarely they said much after they had gone to bed because they worked such long and heavy hours and they were exhausted by that time.

Occasionally they would murmur some reminder to order more potatoes or grumble about the late delivery of the eggs (it was strange, but they never served fish, on the principle, I suppose, that fishermen don't enjoy eating what they've caught). On this night, however, I heard my name mentioned and I lay, suddenly wide awake in the moonlight spreading from my window, listening to them.

' 'Tis a thorough bad life for a girl, Flossie,' he said. 'A carnal life like that for somebody so young. It might be money, but it's trouble and in the end it's shame as well.'

Flossie used to wear a heavy cloth nightdress, so heavy that I swear I could hear her putting it on even though there was a wall between us. 'Shame? Rubbish!' she replied. 'After what's been done to 'er, who can blame the girl.'

I felt glad that she should come to my defence in that way. 'She's never 'ad a morsel,' she continued. 'And she never will 'ave, 'tis certain, washing up in a place like this. But she's got *one* thing. She's 'andsome, Harold, she's real 'andsome. It's the girl's gift. I don't see why she can't be using it to make a bit o' money.'

' 'Tis immoral,' he argued. 'There's nothing good about it. She'll find no good in her life if she goes about at prostitution.'

The word came through the wall like a bullet. Somehow I had never used it when I thought about what I was doing. It's a foul word anyway. *Prostitute*. Even in those early days, and little as I knew, I tried to think of myself as a courtesan (a term I had found in a romantic novel), which sounds so much more elegant. It has a palatial air about it; it sounds like fine dresses, string music, and ladies curtsying.

But that is what Harold said: 'Prostitution.' I buried my face in the pillow, a lifetime of furtive street corners and stained beds suddenly confronting me. Then I heard Flossie again. 'She'll be the best, that one, you mark my words, Hal. She's got carriage and beauty and she'll learn because she's clever. Take it from me it's her only chance to make good.' The bedspring harped as they got beneath the blankets. 'Look at us,' she said. 'Work till midnight and what are we? Poor as a couple of shithouse spiders.'

They must have been facing away from each other because I heard the bed twang again as one of them turned. 'You sound as though you'd have liked to do that yourself Floss . . .' Harold said accusingly, but softly enough.

I heard her laugh coakily. 'Me? Oh, Hal! I don't deckon I'd have done much good as a prossie. I would have had to have been a bargain.'

'Oh I don't know,' he said good-humouredly now. 'I reckon I'd have spent a bob or two on you.'

'Go on,' she giggled. I smiled now in my moonlit bed. 'I'd never have charged you for it, love.'

The next day in the shadows at the back of the café Flossie came to me diffidently and said: 'I'd like to be giving you some advice Nelly dear. Now you're growing.'

I felt myself blush but she was as practical as she was kind. She placed in my surprised hand a small square packet.

'Give one of these to the lad,' she said secretly. 'And make sure he uses it. You don't want no babies.'

It was the most touching and the most useful present of my life. All through the years that followed I had no child. More's the pity I think now. My good sister Mary had five. I like to think that she had mine too.

eight

My time at Hal's came to an end, as it happened, in an unexpected way, although abrupt conclusions and quick beginnings have been part of my life since then. From time to time
a larger vessel than the everyday fishing boat would come into
the harbour, perhaps a coaster of several hundred tons, and
it was aboard one of these, the *Charlie Harry II*, that I sailed
unintentionally from England.

I was by everyone's account a fine-looking girl with a ready
smile and a generous heart. My early apprenticeship aboard
the boats was over and I had a greater control of what I was
about. My charges went up to ten shillings (I now had nearly
fifty pounds in the Post Office Savings Bank, the reward of
loose living in the trawling grounds and a sum which delighted
the old dearie in the Weymouth Post Office who thought I was
earning such good money at the café) and, in addition, I had
become accepted in that small, salty world. I went out at the
start of the season (the fishing season I mean. My work was
continuous) with the little fleet to hear the Bishop pray from the
bow of a boat, for God's blessing on the catches and the men
who caught them. I prayed with my eyes as tightly shut as the
next person.

A hot summer had settled on the southern coast, days of
huge skies and easy seas, when the people started going back
to the beaches now the war was over. They came to Weymouth
in their thousands although the barbed wire and the buried
mines were still in some places, and watching the busy children
on the sands with their mothers and fathers made me, for a
moment only, sad because of what I had missed.

But I was making up for it now. I am afraid I was to be
found in some of the lower public houses of the town, laughing and drinking and not thinking of either yesterday or tomorrow. I had, at last, written to my sister Mary and she replied
and told me how well she was getting on at the bakery in
Hopewell, where she had gone after the disaster at Hopewell
Manor (well reported in the newspapers, of course, and hardly
needing detailed repetition here) when poor Parsifal poisoned
both his parents at the breakfast table and had to be taken

away to a refuge for the simple-minded. Neither Mary nor I ever heard a word from our father, although Mary was told that he had been seen in Plymouth with a one-legged woman. It was of no great interest to me. Then, however, before the affair of the *Charlie Harry II,* I received a letter from the Commander. He had gone to Hopewell and inquiring after Mary had traced her to the bakery and had obtained my address. He wrote and asked me to go and see him in London, enclosing three pounds for my first class railway fare.

I was full of excitement and a sort of compressed terror. What if he should find out about the life I was now leading? I trembled in my bed to think of it and I refused to go out in the boats for a whole week before I went to London in case there should be signs of debauchery in my face; also I did not want to smell of fish because there was no doubt that a whore takes on the aroma of her customers very quickly when she works in a certain area or among men of a certain profession. Charlotte the Harlot, who I knew in later years in London, had worked in the region of a tannery for years and always had that niff of hide about her, something which put off quite a number of potential customers. In fact it ruined her for general practice in the end and she had to go to the chemical works area in the Midlands where it did not notice so much.

Anyway, I was bubbling over by the time the day arrived for me to go to London. I had never been there in my life, of course, and it was like setting out for a different and distant country. There must have been a dozen of my friends at Weymouth Station to see me off, with much anxious advice about keeping hold of my money and watching for pickpockets and pimps who preyed on innocent girls from the country and the sea.

All the journey I sat rigid as a virgin in the corner seat, not speaking to anyone and even refusing haughtily the offer of a young man sitting opposite who wanted to give me a cucumber sandwich. I hoped he thought I was some fine lady, even though I was travelling third class. (I couldn't bring myself, when it came to it, to buy a first class ticket.) England looked lovely though, from the carriage window. I had not travelled by train very much (not, in fact, since Mary and I were taken from Hopewell to Bristol in our early forlorn days). It was May and everywhere seemed breathing happily and freely now there was no war. There was blossom on the trees and cows in the fields, houses and rivers and people and bicycles. Some people, not just children but grown-ups also, stood at the side of the line and waved at our train. It was just as though they had never seen a train before and they had come out specially to see us. I waved back, a bit haughtily, just the merest turn of the glove at my wrist. In a way I felt like a queen.

Mind you, I did this partly to show the young man with the cucumber sandwiches that I was aloof and aristocratic and when I opened my corned beef sandwiches from their grease-proof paper I took only dainty bites at them, munching the mouthful like a lady, the lips tightly together, and wiping the crumbs off my mouth with a flick of my imitation lace gloves.

I thought that the young man was duly impressed by all this high-class behaviour, but I was mistaken because we reached Winchester and he got out, raising his cap (which pleased me, of course), as he opened the door. But then he stood on the platform, just outside the open window and, leaning in, kissed me fully on my surprised lips and said: 'I reckon you'd make a fine shag, my love.'

He strode away jauntily, leaving me trying to be aghast for the benefit of the other passenger, an elderly, nodding man. 'I don't know what manners are coming to!' I sniffed with all the high disdain I could find.

'Aye,' said the elderly, nodding man looking me in the eye. 'But he's right though.' In those days I never knew how men could tell.

He was there to meet me at the station, not the tall, gallant naval officer I had imagined in my girlish fantasies, but an ever-wounded man, his face aged with pain and scars, a man supported on two sticks and with legs as stiff as the sticks themselves.

But his voice was strong and gentle as ever. I walked, then unable to help it, ran along the platform towards him, my happiness at seeing him again almost flooding away the sadness of his condition. I scrambled all my first words together in my confusion and we stood, a pace apart, him smiling, me choked with emotion. Then, very carefully, for I was afraid I might topple him over, I put out my arms and folded them round him. It was the first time we had touched each other as adults. His body was as meagre as a pole. He could not return the embrace because he could not let go of the walking sticks. He stood rigid, as though helpless with shock, while I pressed myself to him and put my face against his damaged face. There was nothing I would not have done for him. He was someone I loved.

'I have a taxi,' he said hoarsely in my ear. 'It's waiting.'

It was the first time I had seen a London cab, a black box on wheels, but I understood how useful it was for him because he was unable to bend his legs at the knee and in the back of the taxi there was room for him to stretch out in front of him. We sat while the cab set off through the wonderful strange streets to an address he had given. But now it seemed that we did not know what to say. It was as though everything that we had in common had been said in that embrace at the station.

'I've got some change for you,' I said eventually, awkwardly.

'Change from what, Nell?' he asked.

'From the train,' I explained. 'I couldn't bring myself to come first class. It seems such a waste. So there's twenty-five shillings change.'

He laughed in his throat-crackling way. I often wondered what his laugh was like before he was hurt.

'With that, Nell,' he decided, 'you must buy yourself a hat. I think you would look beautiful in a hat.'

'Where are we going?'

'To the home of a friend,' he said. 'Diana Seagram. We will stay there.'

A sudden coldness came upon me at the mention of another woman, an immediate jealousy such as I had never experienced in my life. And she sounded rather grand too, this Diana Seagram, with a house in London. I looked at him, half afraid, half accusing, as if I had any claim on him. He still thought of me as a child. He smiled into my face.

'You'll like her,' he said, not understanding my look. 'She has a very pleasant house too.'

'Commander,' I said, deciding to blurt it out. 'Is she . . . is she . . . your . . . lady?'

He laughed joyously, and I felt myself flush to my neck.

'My lady?' he repeated, enjoying it. 'No, she's not Nell. She's just a friend. She's the widow of a man I knew in the war.

He was killed on my ship. She's wonderful but she's not my ...
er ... lady.' He laughed again and put his arm about my
embarrassed shoulder. 'You're my only lady, Nelly Luscombe,'
he said.

The house was near Westminster. It had been damaged in
the bombing but despite the patching up it was pleasing and
comfortable. The lady was the same; sweet faced, middle-
aged, slim and assured in a gentle way. I stood in the hall when
we first arrived, staring up as she came down the fine staircase,
feeling once more like a country house maid. But her eyes
were kind and soft, and she took me to my room talking all the
time to make me feel at ease. It was amazing the things she
knew about me.

'He told you all these things?' I said.

'Yes all of them,' she answered. We had gone into the room,
the best room I had ever slept in, until then. Diana drew back
the curtains and the sun fell in. Outside was a walled, small
garden. There were bees walking on the window sill.

'You were very important to him,' she said simply. 'When
he needed some help. Did you know that Nell?'

'No,' I answered truthfully. 'I didn't do anything. I just
played housey-housey with him, that's all.'

'It was very important,' she said. 'Almost everything.' She
touched me on the shoulder. I felt I liked her very much.
'You helped him survive all that.'

That afternoon they both took me to Bond Street and I
bought the hat he had promised. I can remember it exactly now
and it makes me smile. It had a little lacy veil, like a small
fishing net, that dangled over my forehead and my eyes and
made me feel very beautiful and cool. We went into other
marvellous shops, the Commander sitting down, his legs stuck
out in front of him ('like a damned wheelbarrow,' he said), and
Diana and I looking at and trying on the clothes. She bought
herself an expensive, tasteful blouse and she wanted to buy me
a skirt, but I would not allow her to do so. I had some of my
immoral earnings from Weymouth, which I had drawn from
the Post Office Savings Bank the day before, and in one shop I
bought myself a pair of gloves which I paid for with my own
money. I had never paid so much for anything in my whole
life. But I did not show it. My face, I know, was composed, I
gave the assistant the money and thanked her with what I hoped

sounded like a rich voice. Diana and the Commander were watching me closely and they both smiled and nodded.

In the street once more I was caught up with the fresh thrill of that exciting and expensive place. The shop windows were draped and displayed with things the like of which I had never seen, the road was full of cars and buses and those taxis like squat hearses. The pavements flowing with people.

There were also strangely loitering ladies in the street, wearing smart suits and shoes, but who seemed to be on some kind of patrol, walking and waiting and then walking again, and conversing with random men. I watched them and their expensive clothes and faces and I saw that here there must be better pickings than among the fishing boats of Weymouth. Trying to hide my interest from the Commander and Diana, I nevertheless was able to see what these ladies were about and how busy they became even in the middle of the afternoon. Nobody seemed to notice them or mind.

They filled me with an irrepressible and illegal thrill. I wanted to see them again and find out more about them. I was shy and unsure but not afraid. The following day Diana had to go out and the Commander said he would take a rest because his legs were painful after the previous afternoon's excursion. Did I mind amusing myself? I said truthfully that I would be glad to do so and I went out saying I was going to visit the zoo. But, as soon as I was clear of the house, I brazenly got into a taxi (it is amazing how quickly even a country girl slips into such easy city habits) and told the driver to take me to Bond Street.

On edge with anticipation, I walked along the crowded pavements and saw again the elegant prowling ladies. Then I took to some of the side streets, being careful not to lose my soundings (as they say among seafarers), and I was amazed to find even more expensively dressed loiterers down where there were fewer shops and more privacy. Eventually I found myself in Curzon Street and then in the narrow courtways of Shepherd Market. Wandering women were on the loose everywhere, waiting outside smart shops, taking afternoon tea in the small cafés, and making secret signs and signals to each other as they cruised around.

Amazed and fascinated, I tried to overhear what conversation went on between them. It was basic, trade talk, like signals one to another.

'Done it yet Emmy?'

'Three times love, one double time.'

'You're so lucky, darling. Had to go to bloody Marlborough Street to pay my licence. Haven't had a thing since.'

Breathlessly I listened. Licence? Was a licence needed in London for this sort of occupation? Did it permit the business? I hung about, watching and walking up and down the pavement. Eventually a buxom and handsome lady, in a red costume and with a fascinating blackened eye, took to watching me and after a while approached me.

'Why don't you fuck off?' she suggested.

I was dumbfounded. I felt a flush fall over my face like a curtain.

'Why?' I managed to say. 'I'm not doing anything.'

'Listen dearie,' she said, leaning close so that I could smell her powerful perfume and see the lines protruding around the black eye. 'We've got enough girls on this stretch as it is. There's no more room. Where you from?'

'Paris,' I decided brilliantly and followed it by a string of gibberish which I hoped might be taken for French.

'Well just fuck off back there,' she advised. 'There's too many working this pitch. And, anyway, this is the pricey pavement. Two quid a time here. If you want to work in London go and try Soho, all right?'

I replied with a further stream of gibberish and minced off with a pounding heart within me and what I hoped was a show of utter disdain without. Soho? Ah, I had heard of Soho. The Weymouth fishermen talked of it as something in their dreams, in the same way as they might talk of a huge catch of mackerel, or a chance of a salvage prize money. It was something beyond them.

I stopped another taxi. 'Take me to Soho,' I said with polite highness, and sat back in the seat feeling stifled with the thrill. Driving through the London Streets I knew that my future was there.

Soho did not frighten me at all. Considering that I had been born and brought up among the good clean fields of Devon (where, certainly, there was sin, but in a secret and silent country way), I found the tight streets, the brassy lights and the strange foreign people only fascinating.

Leaving the taxi, I wandered entranced by the aromatic alleys and delighted by the doors from which strange sounds and dark movements came. It was a warm afternoon, and the Soho ladies were lolling from open windows or walking the narrow pavements. They were not so well tailored as the Curzon Street women, they wore common red shoes and chewed gum. But furtive men stalked them along those streets. I wondered how much money they made on an afternoon in a heatwave.

The way I was meandering about, taking my time and looking at everything with such intense curiosity, made me a target for several men mooching through the courts and alleyways. I had the fresh, fruity look of the country girl, bright eyes and my hair at its finest, with my bosom bursting beneath my blouse. I soon had a little contingent of prospective and eager customers following obediently. Three times men coming in the opposite direction fell conveniently over their own feet as they neared and lurched into me full of apologies and pleasure.

A squat, swarthy fellow I took to be Italian kept popping up out of doorways and turnings all over the place. He would slide from one opening and walk towards me, eyes almost revolving, go past and then a minute later emerge from yet another exit twenty yards ahead. He had a magician's moustache and was wearing an overcoat despite the warmth of the day. I began to laugh because of his antics and this encouraged him to approach me.

'How much you want – only to talk?' he whispered.

I may have been from the country but I was not slow. 'How much you pay?' I asked sweetly.

His face beamed at my willingness. 'Only to talk for ten minutes,' he repeated reassuringly. 'I give you two pounds.'

This seemed like a very reasonable proposition. 'Where do we talk?' I asked, suspecting there had to be more to it. 'Where do we have to go?'

'Here-a in da street,' he nodded encouragingly. 'Just-a walk and just-a talk. I give you two pounds.'

'What do you want to talk about?' I said. 'Anything special?'

'Oh-yes, verra special,' he nodded. He was taking two pound notes out of his crocodile wallet and pushing them towards me insistently. I took them and put them in my bag. 'Now we talk,' he said. 'Me – I talk.'

So we walked along the street, my arm casually through his like old acquaintances. There were people everywhere. We walked through the vegetable market and then along Old Compton Street. He began to speak in a steady confiding tone. 'I would like-a to peess all down your beautiful back,' he began.

Now this surprised me. There was no chance of my allowing such a thing – in those early days I only knew the plain and simple ways – but the very idea amazed me. I turned quickly to him. He hardly glanced at me but said: 'I pay two pounds. I talk 'ow I like. Okay?'

There was nothing I could do but nod and we walked for ten minutes through the byways of Soho with this amazing one-way conversation going on in my left ear. He spoke in the same low voice and with the same low thoughts. What he said he wanted to do with me was enough to make my young rural eyebrows go up and down as if they were on strings.

My face, I knew, was scarlet with embarrassment, but I walked solidly on with him until he had apparently attained the satisfaction he acquired in this most curious way. At that point he bowed politely and shook my hand, inquiring whether I would care to meet him for further conversation the following day. I hesitated but he forestalled any refusal by putting the fee up fifty per cent. Three pounds was three pounds in anybody's life, so I agreed to meet him in the same place at the same time.

The following day I made an excuse to be by myself in the afternoon and the Commander and Diana smiled knowingly. 'I think you have met some nice young man,' the Commander said, sitting stiffly in his chair. 'You must bring him here, mustn't she Diana?'

Diana smiled agreement and I had a brief picture of the Italian whispering that he would like to peess all down her beautiful back. So I denied meeting anyone but said I wanted to buy some presents for the people in Weymouth. Half an hour later, my ears now plugged with cotton wool, I walked round and round the little garden in Soho Square while the small Italian talked earnestly of his strange ambitions and interests. I heard hardly any of it, and at the end of the stroll I was three pounds better off, more than some people earned for a week's work in those days. It seemed an easy way of making a living.

He wanted me to return on the following afternoon but it was to be my last day and I was looking forward to spending it with the Commander. The Italian took great umbrage at my refusal and there in the street began to get awkward and angry. In the end the only way to get rid of him was to give him a mouthful of West Country curses. He looked shocked and answered primly: 'Don' you talk-a to me like-a that.' I thought it was a trifle odd coming from him. He went away still muttering.

On the afternoon following I took the Commander boating on the Serpentine. It was my treat. He had taken me to several restaurants and to see *Annie Get Your Gun* and now I insisted that I would take him to tea by the lake and for a row along its summery green water.

I can see him now, as though in a happy dream, stretched almost full out in the boat, his unbending legs sticking out, while I rowed between the ducks. I had become quite good at handling small boats, for the Weymouth fishermen sometimes asked me to assist them in more than my usual way. The London sun shone on us and he joked and pretended that his stiffened legs were the barrels of twin naval guns. He fired them in all directions giving orders and instructions to a make-believe gun crew. It is strange how men are such great pretenders.

That hour or so is pictured in my memory in soft colours like an old miniature painting. To be in his company was always a pleasure. To laugh and float about like that under the sky and the overhung leaves was pure joy. I felt I loved him so much.

'Commander,' I called from my rower's seat. 'Have you ever had a wife?'

His legs stopped firing. He seemed to wait an eternity before answering and I was fearful that I had said the wrong thing to him. But his voice returned eventually, as careful and calm as ever.

'Yes Nell,' he said. 'I had a wife. But we separated. She's married to someone else now.'

There was another silence, only the simple splashing of the oars and the talking of the ducks making any sound. I was

124

afraid to say more. Eventually he said: 'She did not want a husband like this.'

nine

From London I returned to Weymouth feeling empty, sad and suddenly lost, but my adventure aboard the *Charlie Harry II* soon put all other things out of my mind and my life was once again changed.

Until that time I had only occupied my business in small waters, among the crews of the little fishing boats that had their homes in Weymouth bay. Larger vessels, of course, came into the port and I had occasionally stood on the quay and watched them and wondered about their possibilities as far as business was concerned. About this time also the ferry service from Weymouth to the Channel Islands was resumed after being stopped by the war, and it crossed my mind that, if it could be arranged with the more or less permanent booking of a cabin and that sort of thing, I could make a steady living from likely men going on that passage. The crossing, in those days, took about ten hours.

I did, in fact, make one experimental trip (my journey to London having made me keen to travel and to find new opportunities) and booked a cabin on the overnight boat. On board was a Welsh rugby team and their supporters going to play in Jersey. I caught the eye of a square, randy-looking fellow first and eyed him to my cabin where, at the door, I asked him if he wanted to spend some money. Either he had taken too many drinks or they did not practise prostitution in Wales, or he was plain stupid, but whatever it was he did not seem able to understand the proposition. Eventually, fearing our doorway discussion might be spotted by someone in authority, I pulled him into the room and demonstrated what charms I was making available. A bright light dawned on his dumb face and he said: 'Oh, it's a shag you're wanting, lovely! Oh fine, all right. Always ready for a shag. You look like you're panting for it.' Then he piled on me as though he was going into one of

125

those scrum things they have in rugby, gave me a terrible seeing-to, pulled up his trousers and marched out with a triumphant grin all over his Welsh face. I couldn't seem to make him understand that I wanted paying for my services. He seemed to think that it was *he* who was doing the favour.

The news, needless to say, was passed around quicker than the ball they play with. While I was still lying back panting and cursing my luck and lack of business sense, there came a knock on the door and outside I found the rest of the team and a number of supporters. I found one man who was not so drunk as the others and who seemed to understand English and explained that I was doing this as a living and not as charity. Appropriately enough (although I did not appreciate this at the time because the word was unknown to me), this man was the hooker of the team. He shut the others out, passed over a pound – which he was careful to explain was payment also for the original fellow who turned out to be his brother – and pushed me back on the narrow bunk. I felt a lot better about this and he seemed to enjoy it, the only drawback being I was almost smothered by the thick rugby scarf which he insisted on leaving wound around his neck. To take it off he indicated between lurches and grunts would be bad luck for the team.

Afterwards he went outside and explained to those that remained (some had gone back to singing at the bar, for Welshmen have strange priorities) that it was on a commercial basis and that he would collect money. I stepped very quickly outside and said I would prefer to collect it myself and the collection would take place immediately before giving my services.

'Oh, all right then, lovely,' he said amiably. 'I was only seeing you wasn't going to be cheated, that's all.'

During the course of that crossing I think I must have seen to the whole team, the reserves, the secretary and the treasurer, who cried all through his fuck because he was something to do with the chapel and he didn't think he ought to enjoy it. I was exhausted but richer by some nineteen pounds seven and sixpence. The shillings and pence came from one of the reserves, a cherub of a lad, only sixteen, who pleaded with me to accept the reduced fare saying it was all he had, his father was on the dole and his mother had left home with the coalman. It was a heart-rending story, accompanied by a smattering of Welsh tears, and he looked so comely that I accepted the seven and six. He had wiped his eyes with the hand that held the coins and they were wet with his sobbing when he handed them over. I was very touched. But then he came at me like a young pig and gave me the most frightful going over before strolling out whistling some song they sang in their bloody valleys.

I was tired by the time the ferry reached Jersey. I stayed ashore for two days, recuperating, and then returned to England with the same team. If I thought I was going to get richer I was mistaken. The team had lost heavily (and some of them had the effrontery to put the blame on me) and the entire return trip was accompanied by maudlin songs and dismal drinking. Indeed, I ended up crying and singing with them, as plastered as any, and finished the night with the club captain and the secretary sharing my little bunk, at the conclusion of which I was given a life-long honorary membership of Abercowan Rugby Club, which entitled me to go and see any of their home matches free.

It was now obvious and inevitable that there was for me no escape from a wicked life. If, in the solitary nights I had, I experienced any pangs of worry and remorse I soon dismissed them and went soundly to sleep. I liked the physical demands and the interesting and varied men and I hoped right from the start it would lead to more rarified things. If I was not born to it then I adopted it and it adopted me with equal willingness.. As Flossie had said that night, it was using the one talent and advantage I had – an enticing and willing body and a giving nature. And through this horizontal life I have risen from being a homeless waif to become a famous lady. My bed has been shared by a Prime Minister, three international footballers, a circus strong man, several millionaires and powerful industrialists, the editor of a Sunday newspaper, sundry actors *and* actresses, and a sly rural dean. All on different nights of course.

Within a week of my return to Weymouth – where my work at Hal's Café had, of necessity, become part-time – I was standing on the quay when the *Charlie Harry II* chugged into port. There were few things very handsome about her – and that went for the captain and the crew as well – but she looked quite jaunty as she pushed through the harbour mouth on an August evening's tide. As she passed she gave me a little toot-toot on her siren and I waved and laughed because I was sure it was intended for me.

As it happened I was right. The crew of the vessel, which had been plying in and out of Weymouth for a year or more, had seen me serving in Hal's and had heard from the local fisherboys of the other activities. This had interested them a good deal, especially the mate who missed his wife a lot, and they had decided to entice me aboard their ship.

That evening they came into Hal's and sat eating their chips and eyeing me. I was not worried for I had been surveyed many times before and when the mate (Jock they all called him – it was that sort of informal ship) invited me to accompany him and two others for a drink in the town I went along easily as I always did. I was still particular, but not as particular as when I started. Most men look alike if you close your eyes and count your money.

They seemed a very friendly bunch, laughing and joking a lot, and buying rum and whisky and port for me. Port, appropriately now I think of it, was my favourite drink. It never failed to lull me into a receptive mood.

They were sailing around the coasts of Europe, going wherever there was a cargo to be hawked, taking their old leaky ship in and out of harbours along the English Channel, down through Biscay and into the Mediterranean ports. She was an old vessel, damaged several times during the war, and apparently quite unsuited for the cargoes she carried. Bits fell off and sank or floated away regularly but the crew sailed on.

'One day,' forecast Jock the mate confidently, 'the wee old tub will sigh and slide below the waves and we'll all be left to swim. I'll give her twelve months and no more.'

He was eleven months short in his estimation.

There is little I can remember of the next few hours. Lifting the glass of port became difficult and I began to laugh a lot. The next sensation was an aching head and the familiar roll of a vessel under my bottom. I wondered which of the fishing lads I was voyaging with that night.

But there was an unfamiliar atmosphere and a strange hot smell about the darkness into which I woke. The place felt to have more room, I could sense it all about me, and there was no smell of fish. I stirred and realized I was lying naked in the warm darkness.

I felt around with my foot first, touching the wall by the wide bunk in which I lay. My toe touched a switch and I pushed it down. A dim, electric light bulb, as naked as I was, glowed in the bulkhead. I looked over the hills of my breasts, between them and around them, still lying flat on my back, surveying the place with caution. There was a man lying in another bunk across the cabin. I could see he was watching me. It was Jock the mate.

'Och, so you're awake, lassie,' he said.

'Where's my clothes?' I said quietly.

'Dryin' out he replied simply. 'Ye fell out of the wee dinghy when you were coming aboard.'

'I don't want to be here,' I said. Like Venus I put my hand modestly over my pubis. 'I want to go back.'

'Lassie,' he said. 'Ye wanted to be here last night. You wouldna' be any place else, and that's a fact.'

'Somebody gave me something,' I said adamantly. 'Put something in my drink. Where are we going anyway?'

'South by south west,' he said. 'Unless the captain's drunk again. Heading for Finisterre. Then down the Bay to Bilbao, then who knows where lass? Who knows where?'

The news staggered me. 'I can't,' I said, sitting bolt upright. He stared at my breasts. I lay down and covered them with my spare forearm. 'I can't go to Bilbao, wherever that is. I haven't even got a passport.'

'Stowaways don't as a rule,' he replied simply. 'Would you have a liking for some coffee?'

'Stowaway!' I howled. 'You Scotch bastard! You shanghaied me! I've been kidnapped!'

'Keep your voice low lass,' he said urgently. 'The skipper doesn't know. Yet.'

'Then he's got to know,' I said sitting up again. This time I drew a blanket up between my legs and held it around the back of my neck. I sat in the dim light like a prehistoric woman in a cave.

' 'Tis better he doesna' know,' warned Jock. 'He's a hard man. Especially with girl stowaways.'

'I'm not a bloody stowaway,' I said, prudently keeping the protest below a shout. I don't like the sound of the captain. 'You drugged me and brought me aboard this fucking hulk.'

'Hulk is correct,' he nodded wisely. 'Fucking? Well, we shall see. Meself I'm wondering if she'll last the trip. There's more water inside her than outside. The pumps are going all the time. And as for whether you're a stowaway or not, the matter is of no matter. All stowaways say they've been shanghaied. That's the story they all tell. But maritime courts, if it ever got that far, are inclined to believe the officers. I'm thinking that the furthest this will go will be the captain. And that would be bad for you Nelly, lass. I told the truth. He's a bad one with girl stowaways.'

I felt myself collapse hopelessly within, and I sagged in the blanket. He handed me a mug of coffee which I took without thinking and drank. It made me feel better. 'You make it seem as if you had a lot of girl stowaways,' I said dully. 'That's how it sounds.'

'Aye,' he agreed, having thought about it. 'We seem to have a wee few. They seem to be attracted by us.'

'What do I have to do?' I asked, knowing full well.

He advanced heavily on me. 'For a beginning,' he said with throaty romance, 'you can comfort a man who's far distant from his lovin' wife. That's me.' He was bare chested and wearing an old pair of dungaree trousers.

'I charge you know,' I said, thinking I might just as well make the most of the situation. 'I do it for money.' I wondered how far Bilbao was.

'And you'll be paid lass,' he said. 'Paid right well, I promise.' He waited, his face quickly sad. ' 'Tis my pretty Jeanie McAllister from Glen Donal that I miss. That I'm yearning for. Be pretty Jeanie McAllister for me, will ye?'

'Aye,' I replied, getting right into the game (this is a talent you need to have in the business).

'Hoots,' I murmured as he slipped his trousers down. 'There's a grand sight. Hoots again.'

To be honest he was a fine looking chap with that sort of hungry look about his body. He closed his eyes and he closed with me and came into me muttering, 'In the glen, sweet Jeanie. In the heather in the glen.' I had not the heart to ask him about money then, but I thought it would be all right.

I lay back and closed my Devon arms about his Highland back and brought him to my breasts. There were only a few occasions when I truly relished it, I had already got over that, but I must say his fatless body and his Scottish mutterings were not without enjoyment.

'Dear Jeanie,' he kept saying and I dutifully muttered back, 'Aye, aye, I'm right here in the glen with ye', and all sorts of pantomime like that. At one point he paused to correct my pronunciation of a word, which made me understand how important it all was to him. Then the pipes started, at least that's what he said, because he could hear them through the mountains and the mists.

'The pipes, aye, the pipes. The Campbells are coming,' he cried.

The Campbells weren't the only ones. He was a fraction before them and we lay exhausted as the hills and glens vanished and were replaced by the dark bunk in the pitching sea.

'Ah, that was grand, Nell,' he said kissing my face. He levered himself up and, watching him, I wondered why Jeanie McAllister allowed him to roam so far from home.

'Now,' he said stepping towards the other side of the cabin. 'Ye have to be paid.' He returned and pressed into my hand what looked like a small brown coin with a hole in its centre.

'What's this?' I asked staring at it. 'I want some money!'

'Hush woman,' he said. 'The captain will hear ye – and then there's trouble. He does terrible things to girl stowaways.'

'What *is* it?' I demanded, but whispering.

'A token,' he smiled. 'Everything on board is paid for by tokens ye see, you'll be able to buy things with it. Tobacco, sweeties, all sorts of merchandise. It's worth all of five shillings.'

'Five shillings! I charge more than that.'

'That just from *me*,' he pointed out. 'I'm the mate on this ship and if I tell the others it's ten shillings a time, at the end you'll have a wee fortune in those tokens.'

'Others?' I said. 'You expect me to do it for the others? For tokens?'

'Aye,' he said. 'There's six others. Fine gentle lads, all o' them. All missing their dear wives and sweethearts. They'll be glad to have you aboard, Nelly.'

It would not have been so bad and at least it would have helped my pride a bit if perhaps just *one* of the crew had called me Nell and not pretended that he was with someone he loved, or said he loved. Sailors are terrible romancers and hypocrites. The loneliness of the sea gets into them and they cry as easily as they drink and pray and then are often remorseful.

During the next few days in that leaky and lumpy little ship, I was called so many names in the welter of passion that I began to wonder who I really was. True, Jock the mate came back three times and I was Jeanie McAllister each time, so at least he was faithful in his fashion. But the charade I played with the others sometimes verged on the edge of treachery.

First the bosun's mate, a horny type of bandy man with a bright eye, came into the cabin and, having deposited his token, stood looking at me like a ferret staring from a rabbit hole. 'I'll call you Dorothea,' he said, a suprisingly high voice coming from such a low slung body. 'Or Rose.'

'Make up your mind,' I sighed, leaning back. 'It's all the same to me.'

'Torn between them, I am,' he sniffed, 'Dorothea in Tilbury and Rose in Gibraltar.' He thought about it. 'No, I think I'll call you Maggie,' he decided.

I surrendered then and became Maggie for the next ten minutes. When he had finished he was in penitent tears and trembled, 'Oh Audrey, how could I do these things to you?'

In those few days I took on the names of twenty far-flung women and had a few real surprises. One deckhand kept murmuring, 'Granny, oh granny', in my ear and the cabin boy, a sweet lad, howled for his mother and his Uncle George.

After almost a week I was weary, bored, robbed of identity and worrying about where I could change the pile of brass tokens I had accumulated. Then there came a private knock on the cabin door and in came the mate and the rest of them, like a deputation, and stood bashfully around the door. Seen together they made a pathetically downtrodden bunch for words and moving his hands like paddles.

'Jeanie,' began the mate pleadingly. The others followed all together.

'Dorothea,'
'Rose,'
'Beryl,'
'Zara,'
'Audrey,'
'Kate,'
'Pussy,'
'Granny,'

'Mum and Uncle George,'

'Nelly!' I bawled at them. 'Won't you learn. I'm Nelly Luscombe from Weymouth!'

'Ah yes,' nodded Jock. 'And who else could you be, lass?' He waited while they all muttered 'Nelly, Nelly, Nelly,' like some prayer of the seven dwarfs. They were still all cluttered together looking embarrassed by the cabin door. 'Nelly,' went on the mate. 'We've come to ask a favour of you, just one wee favour.'

'I should think I've done enough favours,' I said glancing at the pile of brass tokens by the bed. 'I've got enough of those things to keep me in sweeties to the rest of my days.'

'It's just one thing,' he insisted. 'One favour.'

'What is it?' I asked impatiently. I was getting fed up with all of them.

'Do you think you could do a bit of darning for us? Darning and mending. We're none of us any good at it.'

Nothing surprised me any longer. I leaned back and sighed. At least it would mean working with my hands, which would be a welcome change. I nodded.

'And the cook on this ship is a madman,' went on Jock plaintively. 'He'll kill us all yet. He leaves the giblets in the chicken, doesn't he boys?'

'He leaves the giblets in the chicken,' they echoed like slaves.

'So you want me to cook as well.'

'Just now and then. So we can have a decent meal. We'll get him drunk, which will be no trouble, and give you the run of the galley.'

'All right. All right,' I sighed. 'But if I cook and sew I want a rest from working on this bed. Is that agreed?'

They agreed with unflattering eagerness. My body was being willingly swopped for mended socks and edible food. Inwardly I shrugged.

'And we'll keep the donkeyman away – promise,' piped up the dim cabin boy. The others nudged him furiously. He looked shamefaced.

'Who?' I demanded. 'Who did you say?'

'Er ... the donkeyman,' he blushed.

I looked at Jock. 'Who's the donkeyman?' I demanded.

'Och, 'tis only the laddie that works the donkey engine,' he said. 'He's a wee bit crazy. He keeps wanting to come in here, ye see, like to ... well, to join in the fun. But we won't let him in. We took all his tokens away. And we won't let him get at the drink. Just so he wouldna' bother you.'

'Thanks,' I whispered. The thought of a crazy donkeyman coming in was unnerving. 'Just keep him out of the way then.'

'We will, we will,' they recited and then they shuffled out. The first consignment of socks was in my cabin in ten minutes.

I locked the door carefully, for now I was fearful that the hideous donkeyman would come wandering down. In my cabin I darned socks and mended shirts for two days. It was getting stuffy but I dare not show myself in case I should be seen by the donkeyman or the captain.

In the event the weather on deck, according to the crew, was spiteful for the season. The vessel pitched about a good deal but this no longer worried me. Whatever else I had lost I had found my sealegs. What did concern me was the awful creaking and straining of the vessel. At night she groaned like someone dying.

Half the crew's time seemed to be spent trying to keep the pumps working and there were bets struck that we would reach the bed of the sea before Bilbao.

They did, however, manage to pour enough drink down the unresisting gullet of the cook and I was smuggled into the galley to prepare a meal for them. I had never been much of a cook, but what I gave them seemed to them like a feast and for a while made everyone forget their loved ones far away and the fact that the ship was falling to pieces by the hour.

The cabin boy was told to help me with the washing of the dishes but we had only just started clearing the galley table when there came a terrible roar from the companionway and Jock the mate came tumbling down backwards followed by an enormous and wild man, oil all over his face and dungarees. His eyes were blazing and oaths tumbled from his monstrous mouth. When he saw me he howled like a gorilla.

'The donkeyman!' cried poor Jock, trying to get up from the floor.

'The donkeyman!' howled the cabin boy.

I stood transfixed. The crew came tumbling pathetically downstairs after the wild man, trying to catch him and hold him, but he was brushing them aside like King Kong.

I backed away stiffly. He was clear of the crew, who were left sprawling in all directions, and now there was only the cabin boy between his desires and the object of them – Nell Luscombe. Soon there was no cabin boy either for he went gallantly under the galley table. I turned searching frantically for an escape, for a weapon. It was my fortune that I picked on the best weapon I could have wanted – a bowl of washing up powder standing by the sink. I threw the lot in the donkeyman's face and followed it with a bowl of water, a combination which resulted in the amazing sight of the frenzied creature blowing coloured bubbles all over the galley.

It was enough. I went over the top of the table like a deer and ran along the lower gangway. I dashed up a flight of stairs and found myself on the open deck. It was dark and the ship was pitching about, apparently without hope, in a strong sea. There was a light on the bridge. There was nothing for it but to go there.

Up the ladder I went, the furious sounds of battle coming from an open hatch as I passed it. Flinging open the bridge door I discovered the captain standing there, peaked cap, black beard and woollen combinations tucked into sea boots.

'I'm a girl stowaway,' I said.

We met the donkeyman on the companionway as we set off for the captain's cabin, leaving the bridge in charge of a myopic crew member who, logically, had been given the charge of the wheel. This old fellow had actually been introduced into my cabin by Jock – it was his idea of an act of charity, although not towards me – and was so short-sighted that he failed to see me in the dimness. I kept very still and he struggled out again complaining about people making jokes with old men who were nearly blind.

The donkeyman came charging up the stairs and there was a confrontation between him, the captain in his 'combs', and me trembling behind that powerful, flannelled posterior.

'I want 'er,' growled the donkeyman. 'She was promised.'

'Out of the way,' the captain bellowed in his face. 'Get back to your duty or I'll have you in chains!'

The donkeyman hesitated. The captain's big hairy leg took a step towards him. 'While I wear the uniform of the captain of this ship,' he said strangely, 'I am in command. Back to your duty or it's mutiny.'

The huge oily man retreated, growling and cursing, and we went once more towards the captain's cabin. By now I was glad to be with him.

We went into his pitching cabin. A photograph of an old lady on the wall was going to and fro like a pendulum. He sat on a stool and held me at arm's length before him.

'Now, let us have a look at you,' he growled amiably. I felt reassured. He held out his hands and took mine, keeping me at a distance like a large uncle. The opening at the front of his flannel combinations gaped like a mouse-crack in a wall. His beard was like a huge bunch of seaweed.

He reached back and took a half full bottle of whisky from the table behind him. The level had been swaying from side to side with the ship. Still holding me by one hand he took a gigantic swig of the scotch.

'Can you sing, girl?' he roared to my astonishment. 'Can you dance?' Then: 'What's your name anyway?'

'Nell,' I said carefully, 'Nell Luscombe.'

'Well what about singing and dancing?'

'I can a bit.'

'Do you know "The Good Ship Lollipop"?'

'No, I don't.'

'Shirley Temple sang that. What a pretty little girl.' He seemed to make a decision.

'Come on, sit here on my lap and *I'll* sing it to *you*.'

'Now?' I said incredulously.

'Yes, come on girl, now.'

Hardly able to believe it I sat on his lap, my face close to his reeking beard, his arms around me, and he began to sing 'The Good Ship Lollipop' in the most appalling voice I've ever heard. What a sight it must have been in that wild cabin on that doomed ship.

Where it might have led to I don't know, although I have some ideas, but whatever was intended to follow never did because suddenly there was a tremendous blow on the hull and a great square piece fell out of the side of the ship. The cabin woodwork splintered and a section of that dropped out also. The captain stopped singing and we both looked out of the shattered bulkhead into the night and the rolling ocean.

'I think I ought to be on the bridge,' said the captain, with what seemed to me to be something of an understatement. He got up from the stool, placed a peaked cap on his head and, in his boots and combinations, strode out to the storm.

By this time I was naturally frightened but I knew enough about ships to realize that there must be a life-jacket around somewhere. I found one that looked as though it had been a feast for mice and then discovered another in reasonable condition.

The revealing hole in the bulkhead was allowing large slops of sea into the cabin as the ship heeled to starboard. But it was not, at least, pouring through, although the place was awash around my ankles.

There was a wardrobe on one wall and I staggered to it and took out another pair of combinations and a short thick reefer jacket. I clambered into these garments and then pulled the lifejacket over me. All the time I kept telling myself to keep calm and think clearly. It was good advice.

I got outside the door and as I did so the *Charlie Harry II* gave the most pathetic dying groan and lurched to one side, never righting herself. I heard the sea roaring into the captain's cabin and it suddenly broke through the door behind me and rushed savagely around my legs. I cried out in horror and stumbled for the companionway.

It took all my strength to get to the open deck. Once there I saw instantly it was hopeless. Not only was the vessel sinking by the bow, but some incompetent sailor had triggered off a distress rocket which had shot straight through the bridge window and set the whole structure merrily on fire. We were both sinking and burning.

There was no sign of any of the crew, which even in my confused state I realized was only to be expected. They would logically have abandoned ship at the first opportunity, certainly before any order was given, always provided they could find a lifeboat or life-raft that had not rusted to its fittings.

Turning, I saw that the wheelhouse and the bridge were well ablaze and the sea was coming over the starboard side in great bites. I began to feel as alone as the boy on the burning deck. It must have been a violent pitch and shove that sent me into the sea, but suddenly there I was in the chilly water, hanging on to what at first seemed to be a large ornamental trunk. It had a convenient brass handle but, such were the distractions all around me, it was some time before I realized that my raft was a coffin. The ship was now several hundred yards away across the pitching waves, the fire and the water racing to devour her. All at once she gave up the struggle and let the ocean have her, descending with what seemed like an outrageous breaking of wind. The fire was gobbled by the sea, leaving only sudden blackness, and I was left floating with my life-saving coffin.

The sea was cold and dark all around me, but at least it was not as rough as I had imagined. Indeed, although the waves were large they seemed to roll in fairly orderly fashion and I floated well enough on them.

In the rolling and sliding of the sea I was tiring and the coat I had taken from the captain's cabin was weighing me down. I knew I would have to climb on to the coffin. I had gathered enough muscle to make an attempt to get on to the lid when a new advance of water conveniently lifted me and I made it first time. I doubt if there would have been a second chance. Now I wondered who might be inside.

Flat on the pine lid, in this outlandish situation, I hung on to the handles and oddly, tried to read the inscription on the brass plate. My eyes had become used to the darkness and indeed I now realized that it was quite a bright night wide with stars and a trace of moon. Almost as soon as I had begun travelling in this odd way, I saw a light only a few waves away and shouted with all the power in my salty throat. No one appeared to hear me, at least they did not answer, but a couple of minutes later my coffin had drifted quite close to what I now saw was the ship's dinghy. It was the one they used for ferrying to and from the shore.

I paddled my coffin eagerly towards it and hung on to the stern. Exhausted now I heaved myself up and saw two prone figures in the bottom boards. One was Jock the mate, and the other the daft cabin boy. At first I thought they were dead, but true to form they were merely drunk.

It was no use expecting any help from them so I heaved myself over the stern, falling right on top of the cabin boy who only grunted. I even had the presence of mind to hitch the coffin on to the rope at the end of the dinghy so that we were towing it. Then, utterly spent, I crawled on my hands and knees and fell alongside the sprawled body of Jock.

He turned and nuzzled a whiskery, whisky-sodden face into

mine. His eyes cracked into small crevices and he smiled dreamily.

'Och, 'tis ma bonnie lass, Jeannie McAllister,' he crooned. ' 'Tis fine to ha'ye with me, lass. Fine. Fine. Fine.'

We were only two hours in the small boat, which was just as well because, I learned later, within minutes of scrambling into the thing, Jock and the cabin boy had, typically, disposed of *all* the emergency rations and the bottle of medicinal brandy. They had opened the locker right away and tucked in as if it were a picnic, while the ship was burning and going down, while their shipmates were floating about in the sea and while I was travelling the waves on a coffin.

My uneasy feeling even in these dire circumstances, that I might be travelling with someone on the lower deck, as it were, was unfounded. It transpired that the coffin was kept on board for the personal use of the captain himself. His name was on the brass lid. He had a fear of dying at sea and he didn't like the thought of being tipped overboard sewn up in a canvas shroud with the ship's carpenter putting the final stitch through his nose in the traditional seafaring manner. He knew the incompetence of the carpenter.

It was a pity, in a way, that, having voyaged the coffin aboard the *Charlie Harry II* for ten years, he could not make use of it when the occasion arose. As it was, he apparently floated away in his combinations and was never seen again.

Of the rest of the crew, at the final count ashore, only the donkeyman was missing and he turned up in a bar in Bordeaux about a month later, sitting there waiting, he told the police, for his ship to come in.

Two hours after the *Charlie Harry II* sank, we were picked up by a French fishing boat and taken into a small port about a hundred miles up the coast from Bordeaux. The fishermen did not like the look of the coffin we were towing and cast it adrift with the dinghy. Perhaps it still sails the oceans of the earth, shunned by suspicious sailors, to become for ever one of the mysteries of the deep.

When they discovered that underneath the combinations and the life jacket I was wearing there was a female body, the French sailors became agitated and I thought at first they might think it unlucky to have a female on board, for some ships think it spells disaster – and judging by the experience of *Charlie Harry II* they might well be right. I was exhausted when they got me aboard and lay me first on the deck alongside Jock and the cabin boy, both of whom they were sure were dead. It was just dawn and they all gathered round to have a good look at me. The French captain himself took off my life jacket and felt my heart. He was amazed and pleased with what he did feel under those soaked combinations and he carried me bodily down to his cabin for a reviving cognac. Fortunately he could see I was in no state for socializing and he gallantly allowed me to sleep alone in his bunk until we put into port in the morning.

We were taken to a small local hospital, where we found the rest of the crew, the donkeyman apart, sitting comfortably in bed smiling above their breakfasts. There were emotional reunions until I was taken away to a small private room where a nice worried young doctor examined me thoroughly and, for me, quite enjoyably in my drowsy state and pronounced that after a rest I would be fully recovered.

I must have slept for twenty-four hours, and, awaking in a room full of calm sunshine, I luxuriated in unaccustomed comfort. I asked for a brush and did my hair and they gave me some coffee and a neat boiled egg. In the afternoon a representative from the British Consul in Bordeaux came to see me, a solemn and considerate man, who said he understood all my papers and belongings had gone down with the ship and he was sure I would want to contact someone at home to tell them I was safe. This caught me by surprise and at once saddened me. For at the moment I realized there were few people indeed who would have missed me had I drowned that night. Not many tears would have been shed, even if anyone had realized I was aboard that ship. For all my gay and busy life, and the many men I had known, no one would have noticed I had gone. I did not have anyone. The last thing a whore can expect is to be remembered.

In the end I sent a telegram to Hal and Flossie who must have thought I had walked off for good. The representative from the Consul said that I came under the heading of 'Shipwrecked Mariners' and gave me what seemed like a large amount of French money before shaking my hand, smiling and leaving. It was the only time a man has ever left me in bed with money in my hand and never wanted anything in return.

Later that day I borrowed a robe and crept along the corridor of the small hospital to visit Jock and the rest of the crew. They were in a jovial mood, trying to make French nurses understand their quips and requirements, but as soon as he saw me Jock lapsed into melancholy.

'Ah, Nelly, dear,' he said guiltily. 'Since the crisis I've been thinking I should be telling you of Jeanie McAllister.'

'Not again,' I sighed. 'Soon you'll be able to tell *her*. As soon as you get home.'

'Na,' he mumbled. 'She doesna' exist, lassie. She's a mere figment of a poor man's distracted imagination.'

I was amazed. 'You mean all that moaning and groaning about Jeanie in the glen and the bagpipes, and all that stuff, was not true?'

'A figment,' he nodded. 'A sailor's got to have something, Nell. He needs to have something to remember, y'see, even if its no' the truth.'

That was another thing I learned. A man would rather have anyone but a harlot. Even when he is in the arms of one.

That evening my life turned yet another of its famous odd corners and I moved into a time of luxury and strangeness which opened my surprisingly innocent eyes to many things.

I was in my room, now bored in my bed, when a visitor was announced and in came one of the most beautiful women I have ever seen. She was tall and smiling, slender and with that grace of movement you either have throughout your life or you never have at all. She was about thirty-five, her clothes were of a style and quality beyond anything I had ever seen and there was about her an assurance, you might almost call it modest vanity, which I have since envied in some women and tried to copy myself. Indeed this lady, Madame Amantine Bougain, taught me all the manners and airs, the conversational tricks and charms, the very tactics of society that eventually enabled me to move and live among the most particular company, and have intercourse with many of its members. I had a lot to thank her for.

'I have read in the paper of your ordeal, you poor child,' she said after introducing herself. Her English was better than mine. There was just a flicker of an accent about it, but even that, I suspected, she could have eliminated if it had not been so effective and so charming.

'It is said that you clung to a coffin in the sea!' she exclaimed. 'Ooooh, that must have been so horrible for you!'

'It was empty,' I shrugged. 'There was nobody in it.'

She seemed delighted with the answer. 'Ah,' she smiled. 'You have a sense of humour also. And you are just as pretty as your picture in the newspaper shows.'

'My picture in the paper?' I asked, hardly able to believe that an unknown English girl, shanghaied by the randy crew of a doomed ship, and saved by a floating coffin, could have been of any value for a newspaper. From her bag she produced the cutting from the evening's paper. I must say I looked very grand, a heroine of the sea (which is what the paper called me), for the photograph had been taken just after we were landed from the French fishing boat.

Carefully I took the cutting from her. Her gentle perfume reached me. Apart from Diana Seagram in London I had never met anyone like her before. Her hands were faultless, long fingers, the nails shaped and painted with minute care. She wore a glorious diamond ring and a wedding ring. I had a passing wonder what her husband might be like. Would he like me?

'Are you recovered?' she asked. I noticed that although her English was so good, she hesitated before each thing she said, as though making sure in her mind that it was quite correct. This was very charming too, of course, and when I knew her better I saw her using the trick to keep some dumbfounded man on tenterhooks while they conversed.

'I'm all right,' I said confidently. 'I could walk out of here now. But I don't know what they are going to do with us.'

'How did it happen that you, a young girl ... How did you happen to be on that terrible ship?'

I must have blushed because she smiled to encourage me and in a moment my hesitation had vanished. 'I was kidnapped,' I confided. 'Well sort of. I'm afraid I had too much to drink and so did the crew and I ended up on their ship.'

Her eyes went wide. They were extraordinary; amber, like the eyes of a prize cat. Then she laughed, a fire-bubbling laugh that ran all over her body. 'Oooo-là-là!' she exclaimed. 'It is like a romance story!'

I laughed with her. 'Oh they were all right,' I said. 'The crew, when they realized what they had done, they were very kind and considerate. I had a cabin to myself and every attention.' I thought that was a truthful enough summary of what happened.

'In England,' she pursued. 'Your mama and papa know about this? They have been told of course?'

It seemed a good opportunity to tell her the story of my life, which I did, cutting out certain adventures and incidents, but giving a general summary of the things that had befallen me over the past few years. She listened, obviously fascinated, with tears when I told her about my mother and the bomb, and with laughter when I told some of the other things. In the end she sat with her face hidden behind her fingers, looking at me through the little space between them. 'What a singular young lady you are, Nellee,' she said. 'Would you like to come and stay in my house? Until you are ready to go back to England?'

As she said it I could picture it, rising like a backcloth in a Christmas pantomime, the fairy castle, accompanied by fanfares and rainbows. It was not quite like that. For a start it was not a house but a very large apartment, but it had every touch of luxury and a great deal of excitement.

It was not difficult for her to arrange my discharge from the hospital the following day, since she appeared to have enormous influence in the area and a word from her was sufficient to make sure that everything was done with speed. At nine o'clock the next morning a complete new set of clothes arrived, all fitting to the inch, and an hour later a silent French motor car, with a silent chauffeur, arrived to take me from the hospital. I dashed in to say a quick farewell to the crew. Jock was heartbroken. 'I'd such plans for ye, lassie,' he moaned. 'Ye and me, roaming along the lochside in the dim of the day ...'

'What about Jeanie McAllister?' I laughed and went out. I left quickly, hearing all the pleadings coming from the ward behind me. I ran down the corridor towards the glass doors that led to the new world, away from the hands and the fantasies of sailors, to where that marvellous motor car waited to take me to my new life. Madame Bougain had said it was for a few days, but I have always known, some instinct has never failed to tell me, when my life was about to become something different. And this was one of those moments.

ten

Madame Amantine Bougain and her daughter Aurore lived in a white and wealthy apartment on a hillside that over-looked the tight streets of the town and the enormous sea that spread beyond. One room, very large, had french windows opening on to a roof garden and terrace, hung with bougain-villaea and other sweet flowers. The first morning I arrived we sat out there in the warm autumn air and talked and drank dry, colourless wine.

Aurore was as slender, as beautiful and as gentle in her manner as her mother. She had long hair and a fawn face and the same amber eyes. She was seventeen and still at school.

There was a Monsieur Bougain, but he was dismissed very quickly as 'living in Paris' and, apart from an early instance when we discussed his portrait, was hardly mentioned again during my stay, which in the end, all things being considered, did not surprise me.

It might have been expected for me, a raw English country girl, even with my outgoing nature, to have felt clumsy and embarrassed in the company of these two fine French ladies. But they were so kind and so natural that not for a moment did they let me feel out of place. They admired my skin and my facial bones and even the texture of my hair, which was hardly looking in its glory after its submersion in the sea. We had lunch, served by a pretty maid on the terrace, and drank some more wine and Madame Bougain insisted that I repeat my life's adventures for the benefit of her young daughter. I can see them now, sitting with the casual sunshine on their elegant features, sighing contentedly and making small ex-clamations while I recounted the long story. At its conclusion they both sat there, as if waiting for some more, and when they realized I had come to the end, they both rose and kissed me, one on each cheek.

The next three days were like an expensive dream. I wandered about the beautiful apartment with its pictures and porcelain and stylish furniture, hardly daring to touch anything. I slept in a large downy bed with a latticed door on to a little balcony from which I could see the movements of the ships in the harbour. I waved sentimentally to them and their crews. Madame Bougain had insisted on taking me shopping several times and I was now attired like some princess in what seemed to me the most delicate of French fashions. I could hardly believe my good fortune. Then, standing on my balcony, looking out towards the port and remembering how all my life I had been *used*, I came to a conclusion that for all this there had to be a reason.

One strange thing about the apartment was the portrait of a florid and ugly man that dominated the entrance hall. If it is true that portrait painters always flatter their sitters then this man must have been a terrible sight in true life. On my third afternoon I was standing looking at it, the only unsightly thing in that tasteful place, when Amantine came, almost silently, to my elbow, and looking at the painting said: 'It is a rossignol. Our nightingale.'

'What does it mean?' I asked. 'Your nightingale.'

'It means something that is always with us, something that is hanging about and we cannot rid ourselves of it. Our rossignol is Monsieur Bougain.'

'He's very ... impressive,' I said, not knowing what to say.

'His bank balance is but he is not,' she said. 'Will you come and listen to me play the harp?'

By this time nothing surprised me and I said that I would like to hear her play. She took me by the hand, as if I were a small girl, and led me to another room which had a piano and a large golden harp standing like some sort of footman near the sunlit window.

'Sit down, Nellee,' she said softly, 'and I will play.' She sat against the harp and touched it with real tenderness. 'This,' she said when she was ready, 'is Debussy.'

I would have known no difference, my experience of music being the lusty West Country songs we had to sing in school and the rowdy ballads with which the sailors at Weymouth accompanied their beer and spirits. But as she played, there came upon me a feeling like a dream: the room, the woman and the playing, each muted and fragile. It made me feel sweetly drowsy, as though we were in a garden, not a room.

'Did you enjoy that, Nellee?' she asked, rousing me from my trance. I saw that she was standing very close to where I was sitting. 'Embrace me, Nellee,' she asked. It was half an order. 'Put your arms about me.'

I put my arms about her waist, still sitting, and, my heart suddenly hurrying, looked up at her. The composed face was smiling down. Something unknown but compelling drew me up and I found myself in an embrace with her. Frantically I tried to organize my spinning mind. I tried to tell myself that this was just French friendship. Then she kissed me on the lips. I could feel her breasts pushing against mine and her thighs flush against the front of my dress. The kiss and the feel of her went right through my body.

Nothing further happened then. She was a very cool lady. She released me in a way that indicated that, after all, it was just a motherly kiss, and with a light laugh she took me by the hand and we went out on to the terrace where the pretty maid was laying out a fine tea service. I was still enthralled by what had taken place in the music room. I could not believe it. If I had been held by some handsome prince I would not have been more pleased. After all the rough and terrible things I had known, to realize that someone so clean and so beautiful really *wanted* me was blissful. 'Oh Amantine,' I laughed as I went with her to the terrace and we came to the set table. 'I could just do with a nice cup of tea.'

In the mornings the light seemed to float in through the window. I would wake to find the sun golden all about the room and from the outside the softened sounds of the streets and the noises of the ships in the harbour and the outgoing sea.

For the first three mornings I lay in that soft and expensive bed, feeling my skin flush against the flimsy nightdress and wondering what amazing luck it was that had brought me into all this luxury. Rising from the bed on each of those days, I went to the window and then out on to the terrace, feeling so airy I swear I could have floated to the top edge of the hills above or to the town below. My shoulders felt the touch of the morning on them and the bougainvillaea would crowd my head with its scent. The walls of the town appeared as a pale yellow, with the narrow streets sunk in shadow. Down the hill beyond a closed garden, with a wall low enough to see over the top, was the courtyard of a monastery of some kind, with a single silent bell and a few monks moving about like prisoners taking exercise. Standing high above it all on that balcony I felt truly rich and free, and I knew then that was how I would always want to be, and one day I would be in my own right.

On the fourth morning Aurore came through my door with a briefest knock, while I was still drowsy in the bed. The fresh light rippled all down her as she stood, paused inside the door. She was wearing a long pale garment that was gathered at the neck and prevented from opening by the inward slopes of her breasts. She had come in quickly, with no hesitation, but now she stood inside the door, her face fresh and composed, but not seeming to know what she wanted to do next.

'Aurore,' I said sleepily. 'Good morning.'

'Nellee,' she answered quietly and saying nothing more she walked across the space between the door and the bed. At the side of the bed there was another hesitation while I stared at her, my heart suddenly awake and banging like a bird at its bars.

At the edge of my bed she made another brief delay, but this was replaced by a small smile from her and an uncertain one from me. Did I understand what was about to happen? She carefully opened the side of the sheets and coverlet, and then leaned sideways and on to the bed so that the pale gown dropped open, still caught at the neck, like the entrance to a cool tent. Inside, in the shadows of the garment, I could see her body, the stomach curving inwards and then moulded into her thighs, warm and fawn, her legs bent beneath her bottom on the bed. The gown still sloped across the tops of her breasts but the under globes stood out, full and curved with no change in the colour of the skin. She leaned right across to me, kissed me first on my doubting forehead and then, with a sudden consuming appetite, on the lips. I lay back gasping, my mouth agape. She was so wholesome and lovely. I could not help myself. It was as though my hands and arms had suddenly begun to float from the rest of my body. They went out to her slowly then, each hand almost leaping to the swollen skin of her bosom.

'You mustn't be late for school,' I said.

Her answer was to open the sheets wider and to climb right into the middle of the bed, her face intent on mine, searching it, mesmerizing me, her hands now delicately feeling my body. 'Mama sent me,' she said, as though that explained everything. Now her entire slender form merged into mine. She was much slimmer to hold than she was even to see, my one arm being plenty to encircle her waist and draw her closer to me. We kissed again, fully now, hanging on to it, a clean lovely kiss after all those rough, fish-and-drink soaked kisses I had known in the recent past. As she drew away she made to release the fastening at the throat of her gown, but I stopped her with my hand. Puzzled, then amused, she waited, but then seemed to realize how much I liked to see her in that sweet garment, flowing from her body like the wings of a butterfly.

We kissed again, our four breasts rubbing against each other like friendly cats. Mine were still within the bodice of my night dress, although they were bursting to be released and caressed. Her cool hands went to them and, carefully, she brought them out from the silk like someone taking kittens from a basket. The sight and the feel of them excited her instantly and she pushed her head against them and ran her young tongue up their lobes and curled it around the nipples until I could feel my stomach boiling like a kettle. How long this went on I do not know. It seemed she would never tire of it and I lay back wallowing in the engulfing, loving feeling, something I had honestly never experienced before.

I could feel my whole body blushing, a warmth that spread from my knees to my ears, and my breasts swollen and almost bursting with the intense pleasantness. My hand fell to stroking her back and then her small buttocks, polishing them with the most gentle enjoyment for both of us. My fingers slid down between her damp legs and she lay back her head and groaned when I touched her. 'You like me a little, Nellee?' she inquired breathlessly, as if there still might be some doubt.

'I love you Aurore,' I choked. 'Honestly. More than anyone.'

Then to my astonishment, as though she had just remembered something urgent, she came from the trance into which she had so readily tumbled, and in a matter-of-fact voice, like someone recalling a lunch appointment, she said: 'We must go. Mama is expecting us.'

Without saying more, she slid like a python from the bed and came around to my side, taking my hand and leading me from the room. As I walked towards the door, entranced still, my nightdress finally dropped from me, as if it were exhausted, and lay around my feet on the floor.

'Leave it,' Aurore said, quietly but with authority. She looked at me closely, all up my body as if to make sure I was all there. Then she smiled that marvellously innocent smile again and whispered: 'Come. Mama waits for us.'

We went along the corridor like two children wandering around their house after rising too early from bed. I was naked and Aurore in her trailing gown. We held hands and walked without speaking along the padded corridor, with portraits of French poets staring down on us, lost for words. The pretty maid came up the stairs ahead and I gave a start but Aurore held more firmly to my fingers and the maid walked by without a second glance.

At the door to Amantine's bedroom Aurore knocked with great care, almost selecting the spot on the panel, and we heard her mother's musical voice call for us to enter. It was so strange. I felt as I had done years before with my sister, going to kiss our mother before going to school. My heart began to echo within my chest again. Aurore opened the door.

Her mother, the stately Amantine, was lying like a queen in the huge bed, a fragile teacup in her hand, her hair and her face composed. I tried not to think of what might happen next.

'Mama,' said Aurore politely, 'I have brought Nellee.'

'Nellee,' she breathed happily from the bed and I felt the warmth run all through me, the lovely wonderful feeling of truly being wanted; welcome to someone so fine and extraordinary. I walked forward trembling but happy all over.

'Nellee darling,' Amantine said, her eyes soft but still fixing me. 'Please Nellee you will kneel by my bed.' It was an order.

'Kneel?' I asked, not in protest but surprise.

'As you do when you say your prayers,' she encouraged. 'By the bed.'

Dumbly I did as I was instructed. I slowed my movements

as if I were performing a ritual, but within me my heart was racing. The sun was coming through the gauze curtain and I felt it run all over my back and my bottom as I dropped beside the bed. Aurore stood back and watched, her slender hands held before her like a choir girl, a sweet expression on her peaceful face.

As I knelt I let my head go forward to touch the bedcover and the body of Amantine. My hair had fallen wildly over my forehead and the bed. Nothing happened for what seemed a long time and then I felt her hand reach towards me and begin to stroke my hair and my neck. I had hardly cooled down from Aurore's caresses and now this firm willowy movement sent my blood quickening again. I reached up helplessly and groped for a touch of her, *any* touch. My fingers found her toes, as she swivelled so that she was sitting upright with her feet curled under her. I held on to her while she continued to stroke my hair and my neck, my ears and then my back.

'My dear Nellee,' she said firmly. 'Come to Amantine.'

She turned quickly on the bed now and her legs swung like a gymnast until she was sitting directly before my face, imprisoning my cheeks with her warm smooth thighs. I felt Aurore move behind me and then her hands holding my long hair. She gently brought my face up until I was looking into the eyes of Amantine sitting above me. Nell Luscombe's mistress.

Amantine's hands came down to my breasts, now staring up at her, still quick and full from the stroking of Aurore. Her fingers played as easily on my nipples as they had on that harp the previous day, until I was in such a state that, frankly, I would not have been surprised if my bosom had exploded with a loud bang. I was speechless and indeed what was there to say?

She moved forward a fraction on the bed so that her thighs and the deep soft channel between her legs were open to me. She encouraged my head to it and, to my amazement, for I had never done anything like this before, I began to kiss it.

It was sweet and her body began to vibrate with the pleasure I gave. I was hardly conscious of Aurore moving in what seemed like the shadows behind, so enclosed was I in my lovely world, but I felt her flowing hair tickle my buttocks and the tops of my legs as I knelt against her mother. Instinctively I parted my legs to give her the passage she required and she lay against me and kissed me and lapped at me in the same way as I was doing to her mother.

It was unendurable. We wriggled, each just joined, the force of the pleasure running through us, one woman's body to another. I was experiencing both of them and it felt as though electricity was flying through my blood vessels. I began to shudder from my very foundations and I could not stop. I felt the same shaking going on in front of me and behind me and in a moment we were all clutching each other desperately as the travelling orgasm surged through us. It was the first time I had ever experienced a climax.

We tumbled then on to the floor, lying like beached fish, naked on the carpet, gasping, holding on to what ever parts of the others we could locate. The maid came in while we were like that, and after inquiring if Madame had finished with her tea tray, removed it from the side of Amantine's bed, stepping across our prostrate bodies to do so.

I loved it. I truly did. I might as well confess. After all the crude times and the uncomfortable and stinking places, after all the foul advantages which had been taken of me, to find a loving and giving experience like this with two people so beautiful was something honestly wonderful.

Looking back on it now, and knowing what I now know, I still smile with pleasure. And to think I might have enjoyed it even more if I had been a lesbian. But you can't have everything.

Despite my busy sexual life among the fisherfolk of Weymouth and the adventures that had gone before it, I was still quite ignorant and innocent about many things. Homosexuality, for example, was something I had heard about, a subject of jokes and banter among the men I had come to know by the English Channel, but I had no idea how people of the same sex made love, what methods were used to achieve their ends.

So, to me, my amazing experience with Amantine and Aurore was like falling into a rushing river and finding it full of warm and slow water. I knew nothing of their world and their enjoyable diversions until that time because in Dorset and Devon sex was simple. My loving with that beautiful mother and daughter was the most novel and luxurious thing that had happened in a life that was, admittedly, plain and often sordid. But for all my enjoyment of them and for all my enthusiasm for almost all the sexual things they did and they taught me, and all the kindness and the cleanness that I appreciated so much, it was not possible for them to turn me into one of their sort. You are what you are, even as a professional sex-vendor, and nothing can change that. There have been times when the comfort and consideration of a female lover have been like a breath of gentle air after some of the depradations of the male sex, and I have welcomed them more than a few times. But although my body has been eased and sometimes entertained, my heart is not in it. It is always a mere diversion.

Amantine and Aurore, of course, sensed this very quickly with me and, for them, it was a matter of great regret, not only from their point of view but particularly for me. It was like going to a house of singers and having no real ear for a song. As Amantine put it: 'Men are all right in their place, but Nellee there is nothing like the real thing.'

But we continued to be comfortable and gay in that exquisite home on the hill while the summer waned all around us, the sun a little more shy each day, the wind from the sea a trifle sharper. We lived a life of great leisure, and the days slipped easily and idly on. Aurore would go to school each morning in a plain grey dress with her hair tied tight behind her neck and come home each evening to tear off her garments and rush to embrace me on the terrace.

It must have seemed strange to outsiders that a girl so desirable should not give more than a dull glance to any man or boy. As she went to school each day, I would stand on the terrace with my morning glass of orange juice, and watch her walk down the steep hill into the town. Her carriage was that of a model, her sway timed to perfection, her head level and her arms and hands held delicately. There was undoubtedly a look of innocence on her face. Men and lads in houses, apartments, shops and gardens on her route used to hide in hedges, trees, on balconies and in windows just to glimpse her as she passed. I watched them clearly from the terrace, looking from above them. It was like seeing an army waiting in ambush, crouching, creeping, straining, just for a moment of her walk, and then to utter a wish or even a prayer of which she was the object.

Once a middle-aged man, a fellow fat as a ball, actually fell out of the tree in his garden while he was hanging like a globular monkey in an effort to get just one more look at her backside as it undulated down the hill.

When I told Aurore of this casualty and of all the attention she received as she walked to school, she exploded with genuinely surprised laughter, loving to hear the details of the gauntlet she ran each day. She called Amantine to hear and we all rolled about with mirth at the poor stupidity of men. The following day Aurore, who had a lot of jokes in her, placed a pretty red garter above her right knee, just below the hem of her schooldress, so that it was exposed at every other step. My God, the effect that had! Amantine and I stood on the terrace and laughed until we cried at the antics of those poor, denied males.

When she had finally gone out of sight and beyond the view of those frustrated men and they had slunk back into their normal shadows, we sat down in the pale sunshine and Amantine, after thinking about it for a while, said very quietly, 'I must tell you, Nellee, that Aurore is not my true daughter.'

This surprised me considerably. I had thought how much alike they looked, but it was probably the young girl's style, her walk, her carriage, her clothes, her hair and the way she laughed and talked which made them seem related; things she had learned from Amantine.

'She came to me as you did, from nowhere,' she sighed. 'And as *you* will Nellee, one day she will leave and go back, or go to some other place. She was thirteen when I found her, her father had been killed in the war and her mother had vanished, as so many people did. She was living in a poor house in St Nazaire, with a devilish family. The husband was only waiting for her to grow for another year. He could hardly control his desires. Through some influence I have in that city I was able to bring here away to live here.'

I could not help it. 'She learned everything from you?' I said. 'Everything?'

She did not seem offended, nor did she seem to consider that any offence was intended. 'She learned very well and easily,' Amantine smiled. 'But she was born with it. She is natural. Not like you Nellee, you will never be.'

'I know,' I said. I found myself saying it in a dull way, as if it were something in which I had failed. Something that gave me a sense of shame and regret. 'I can never be.'

'But,' she replied, half a sigh, half a laugh, 'it has been wonderful. You have enjoyed your stay here, Nellee?'

'Oh I have,' I said truthfully. 'I have so much, Amantine.' I was suddenly afraid that I had offended her after all and that I would be sent away. My fingers went out anxiously to touch her sunlit hands and she smiled her gratefulness.

'You have been beautiful to me,' she said. 'And also to Aurore.'

She laughed again and rose gracefully. 'Tomorrow,' she announced, 'there is to be a party. It is at a house about thirty kilometres away, a most elegant house. There it is possible that you may meet a boy you would like. It will be a change for you.'

The house – I believe it was called Val de Plaisir or something like that, it was many years ago now – was more like a small château sited on one lump of a valley that was terraced with vines. We arrived in the late afternoon while there was still some sun lying in the floor of the valley and all along one side. As we approached between the slopes the house, which was on the sunny side, looked golden, as an apple does. It had some small turrets and a pennant was ruffling from the top of one of these, very bravely, giving it the look of a knight's fortress. I was thrilled to see it and so was Aurore who had never visited there before. She squeezed my hand as we sat in the back of the car, just girlish excitement, making some remark about how fairy-like the house looked in the sun. Amantine, who was in the front with the driver, turned to make some comment of her own, and her eyes went straight to our clasped hands. The look was so definite that both Aurore and I released fingers at once. It was over in a moment but in that instant I knew that we three would not be together for long. Where love is so is jealousy.

The owner of Val de Plaisir was a minor nobleman of some sort, as befits somebody with a small castle, and he greeted us as we left the car. He was florid and unappetizing, paying a lot of attention to us in turn, with many kisses and embraces. When he kissed me, a great slobbering smack full in the face, his hands went without hesitation to the underneath of my breasts, as if he thought it necessary to hold me up. Had it been anywhere else I would have hit him (or charged him anyway), but here I could only blush. Blushing is something I could still, surprisingly, do. And I can now.

There were other cars, very expensive cars too, parked outside and there seemed to be relays of servants to fetch and carry our luggage into the house. Each of these servants, I noticed at once, whether male or female, was young and good-looking. I began to wonder what the party was to be like.

'She is so beautiful,' the minor nobleman said for my benefit in English.

'Yes she is,' said Amantine. 'Very beautiful.'

Her voice troubled me. There was the jealousy again. I glanced at Aurore and saw that she had sensed it too. I felt a quick shot of sadness and a returning of my old loneliness. Before long, I thought, I will be going. It was to be sooner than I imagined.

Although small by comparison with some castles I have known, the house was hundreds of years old. I always have this strange idea that buildings grow with age as people do, or trees, and that something centuries old must naturally be spread everywhere. But it was very fine inside, with halls and paintings and a staircase down into the main room like the entrance of a stage.

A young manservant and a petite, pretty maid took me to my room although I only had one suitcase and a small valise. They fussed about with the curtains and the bed and the lights before finally leaving me and making exits each with a bow and a *wink*.

The room was airy and rich, and I was getting a taste for these things now. I undressed and, wrapped in my robe, lay on a large enveloping bed and considered the carved ceiling, imagining, not for the first time, that one day I would own something like this in England where I could be a lady and invite my friends. By then I would have some friends. Somewhere I would have to find some.

All at once I felt unsure and frightened. What was I going to do after this? After all this comfort and luxury, how would I again be able to face a tight bare room and grunting fishermen. I wanted to be rich and, as Flossie told Hal that night I had listened through the wall, I had only one talent, one advantage.

There was only one thing for me. One way to travel – on my back. But for the future, I thought, I must rise in the world, learn more things, make new contacts and a new richer life; become a better class of whore. It was the only way I would get my castle and my friends.

Soon all this would end, all this fine fantasy, I felt sure of that. I could feel it approaching in the very looks that Amantine sent my way that day. Soon I would be on my own again. I had to know where I was going. Downstairs I heard a large clock chime. It was time to get ready. For what?

There are orgies and orgies and I have attended a few in my time, but never one quite like the affair that took place at Val de Plaisir that night. I have been present when such functions have developed into something not unlike a game of football, and others where people just sat around nibbling sedately at each other as if it were a Mothers' Union tea party. I have also been presiding ringmaster at an orgy for perverted elderly people, which was very worrying because the participants kept getting cramp and attacks of asthma and had to be banged on the back. Once I also found myself in charge of a teenage orgy in Paris, where one boy cried bitterly because he was under the impression that he was going to play table tennis, and in London there was an orgy for shy people where the nearest they got to doing anything was shaking hands.

But at Val de Plaisir they were apparently experienced orgiasts, myself apart at that early time in my career, and everyone knew what to expect and what was expected of them. It began with about forty people at dinner, a jolly but conventional affair, with the estate's output of claret being notably diminished, and then followed what seemed like a rowdy but decent party in the large room with the staircase, and here the dinner guests were joined by another group and, significantly, by all the men and maid servants of the house, the handsome young people I had noticed when we first arrived.

These youngsters seemed to be the organizers of the sexual activities, offering themselves, encouraging others to take off their clothes and stretch and roll on the many large cushions that were brought and rolled out and placed on the carpet for the purpose. The lights were dimmed and the whole affair was accompanied surrealistically by an elderly woman playing a mournful saxophone and a languid youth on the drums. They were the only people who remained clothed throughout the proceedings, even the police spies who were amongst us taking off their garments and taking part in the pursuit of both their work and sexual enjoyment.

It was very warm in the large room and the dimness of the lights seemed to make it warmer. I sat on the fringe of the activity, not really knowing what to do, having no experience of this wide-spread form of sex, watching and wondering how I should take part. It was like being a child at school, hesitating on the edge of the playground game, wanting to join in but not sure how to go about it.

I had seen Amantine and Aurore only briefly since we had arrived at the small castle. Before dinner I had stood with them during cocktails. Not speaking French I feared that I would be adrift in the conversation without them. But at dinner they had been at distant places at the huge table and now I could not see them at all in the gloom. I began to suspect that before long I would not be wanted. Not by Amantine anyway.

Then Amantine herself appeared through the warm shadows. She was wearing a loose robe and I could see by the way it fell and the places where it touched her body as she walked that she was naked beneath it. She had with her a young girl, pretty but looking surly.

'This is Francie,' said Amantine. 'If you like her she is yours.'

She sounded like a cool, experienced saleswoman in a store. As though to add to the picture she tugged at a bow around the girl's neck and the long rose-pink garment Francie was wearing dropped swiftly away from her. I thought she shivered.

The girl was dark-skinned and slim with tight conical breasts like coat pegs in a Devon chapel. Her eyes dropped sulkily and she reached and pulled her hair cloak-like around her shoulders.

Amantine was regarding me, smiling to see if I approved. 'Nellee,' she said as though reminding me what was happening. 'Do you like her?' I felt uneasy. Stretching up towards her, I whispered close to her perfumed cheek: 'You said I might have a boy, for a change.'

Her smile then, I thought, was one of relief. Perhaps she was thinking that Aurore was safe after all. 'Ah, you are right,' she nodded. 'I promised. Come, Francie.'

The girl let off a brief smile as if she too were relieved that nothing had come of our meeting, and took herself to some other place in the room more to her liking. I waited and in a few minutes Amantine came back accompanied by a white-skinned young man, his short, fair, curly hair looking like little flames in the beam of light above my head. He was wearing a short loin-cloth and an expression of happy insolence. He was not tall, but very broad across the chest and slim at the waist. His legs were thick and his skin like white paper. 'He'll do fine,' I said confidently to Amantine. 'He'll make a nice change.'

This young fellow's name was Etienne. That much he understood. I was Nellee and he was Etienne. After that word of mouth ceased. But he was a really unusual young fellow because he began to perform a series of acrobatics in front of me like a fairground tumbler in olden times. I sat there fascinated, but unable to make up my mind whether he was displaying himself peacock fashion or just limbering up for what was to follow.

No one, apart from me, took the slightest notice of these gymnastics, revealing though they were. He did a remarkable cartwheel and then stood on his head, stationary, like an upside-down statue. Since he wore nothing under his loin-cloth these antics resulted in a display of sexual attachments such as I had never seen.

As a fisherman's harlot, what with the confined spaces, the poor lighting, the pitching of the ship and the hurry, I never had much time for viewing. Now I sat astonished and admiring. He had a true sense of the theatre because he contrived to have the single lightbeam in that part of the room shine on the centre-piece of the exhibition in the most ingenious and alluring way.

It was a performance (although one he had certainly given on other occasions) just for me. The droning crone on the saxophone and the dim boy on the drums played on, long drawn-out, muted, tuneless, appropriate to the scene. All around were little heaps of people, playing, slithering and sliding like one of those Dutch paintings where everyone plays in the snow. There was quite a lot of subdued beating going on, and biting, and a fair deal of tying with ropes and cords, not to mention one couple with a chain that could have pulled up a draw-bridge. It was all a far cry from Hal's Café in Weymouth.

Etienne had now completed his circus performance and with a smug smile squatted in front of me and inserted his hands into the loose folds at the top of my gown. I made no move towards the boy because I felt, as a beginner, I ought to sit quietly and see what developed. What did develop was the sturdiest and palest jumbo I have ever seen. A true white elephant. (Years later I witnessed the feats of Swan-neck Swanson, the vile man of Cockfosters, who for sheer length could have left young Etienne standing.) Fascinated, I watched this pallid trunk creep beneath the hem of his loin-cloth as he fondled my breasts. An enjoyable bubble was growing inside me, like a pot coming to the boil. I realized that in the past I had been far too busy with sex to enjoy it. That required leisure.

My hands went out to this creeping creature which, amazingly, continued to wriggle away from its master. My horny sensation hardened my stomach and for the first time in my life I was suddenly desperate. I made a move to throw myself back on the cushions but with a serious and experienced smile he restrained me. His fingers were magical, now stroking my hips and then cleaving into the pocket between my thighs. He moved his hands easily and delicately, like a bored man washing dishes, and through my half-closed eyes I wondered how one so young could be so refined in this sort of activity.

His wrists pushed aside the last edge of my garments and I lay exposed to him. But, strangely, he seemed to get more enjoyment out of himself than out of me. It was as though *his* hands, not *my* breasts or what was between my legs, were the objects of his pleasure. By now I was in one hell of a state, sorely tempted to grab him and rape him. But there came an interruption, and it was obviously something they had all been awaiting, for there was a muted buzz of anticipation.

I found myself panting although I had not moved from the cushions. Etienne coolly eased himself up as if he had been engaged in a bit of carpentery, and watched with everyone else while Amantine, naked and very beautiful, walked with grace up to the landing of the central staircase. A gong sounded in the shadows. Breathing seemed to stop. All eyes were there. Two young men, wearing only coloured scarves around their throats, brought a harp on to the landing and a little stool with a satin cushion. On this Amantine placed her bare bottom and then leaned forward and took the harp between her legs like a tall golden lover. She began to play eerily, filling the place with the most overpowering sound. Everyone seemed to have forgotten what they had been doing previously and sat and watched and listened intently.

Then on to the stage, a collar and chain around her neck, her wrists secured, walked Marianne, the pretty maid from Amantine's apartment. She stepped straight and upright, her eyes closed. On the other end of the leather lead was a large, black-haired handsome woman. She carried a riding cane.

I felt my breast touched from one side and turning saw Aurore crouching like a naked hunter on one knee, looking at what was happening on the stairs. I responded to her touch, contacting her fingers in mine, although, truthfully, I felt a disappointment, a fear that she might have come to replace Etienne. But I need not have worried, in that place there was plenty for all.

The ritual on the landing, or the stage as it was, unfolded to gasps and sighs from the audience in the shadows, and to utter astonishment from me. Marianne was led to a stool, like a long piano stool, and bent across it by the big dark woman. This woman's expression was such that she might have been putting a cloth on a table. It was important to preserve the seriousness of the event, something I myself realized in later years when I was ringmaster at several orgies. Once a Conservative Member of Parliament was blackballed (in his case not an inappropriate term either) from the Westminster Strangeways Society because he could not stop laughing at moments like this. It spoils it for the others.

Poor Marianne, having been stretched across the stool, and with Amantine's fingers still brushing the harpstrings in the dimness behind, was tied by her wrists and legs to the stool. Her thighs were clamped by leather straps to the wooden legs, so she was bent over and could not move. Her hair trailed forward on to the ground before her. Her garment was opened behind.

'It will hurt,' I muttered to Aurore. 'It won't half.'

She smiled, still not taking her eyes from the stage. 'The girl likes it,' she said. 'Which in its way is a pity. Also she is well paid.'

At that moment the riding whip came down. People shrieked

160

all over the room. I hid my eyes. Then I felt Etienne stir and put his white hands out to me, guiding me on to the cushions, still not taking his gaze from the stage. And Aurore, as casually as if she were joining in a dance, came to my side and began to caress my stomach while lifting her dilated eyes to see how the exhibition was progressing. As for Etienne – well he was enormous and energetic, that boy, moving like something driven by an engine.

I was now only aware of what we three were doing. My hands had grasped part of him and part of her. I was aware of the harp music and the howls of Marianne the maid, but then everything happened in a dazzling instant. Etienne came, I came, and Aurore came, and an inspector of the French police arrived too.

He stood above us, while we lay gasping, and tapping us each politely on the shoulders, asked us to rise and provide him with names and addresses. All around similar policemen were making similar inquiries. It was a sad end to an unusual evening.

Never again was I to see Amantine and Aurore. After that moment of interruption in that exotic place they went from my life forever. When I was free and back in England again, I wrote to them, not wanting them to think I was ungrateful for their great friendship and kindness, but no reply came. Many years later, when I was able once more to visit that area of France, I went to the apartment and found that it was owned by a German diplomat who used it as a summer house. He was a wealthy, lonely man and he invited me in and walked around the rooms with me. The result was that I spent several days there in his company, a strange reliving of the past (although not quite!), but that is another story.

After the police raid on the Val de Plaisir (they had inserted spies into many of these orgies, drawing lots for who should be the lucky ones. In fact the raid was not made until every senior officer in the local division had claimed his turn as a spy), I was taken away by one police inspector, a mournful-looking man in uniform, one of those, I thought, given entrance to the castle by the spies inside. Presumably he was mournful because he missed the show. It was during the confusion within the orgy room that this officer approached me and, by a tap on the shoulder, motioned me to follow him. I had climbed back into my gown but was wearing nothing else, although compared to some around me I was decidedly overdressed. Policemen with smirks of enjoyment on their faces were taking off naked and semi-naked people to the vans parked outside. Three gendarmes were quarrelling over who should be permitted to release Marianne from her bondage across the piano stool. The big dark woman had struck an inspector with her riding crop and Amantine was gamely fighting them off from behind the strings of her harp. I saw Aurore in the distance passionately kissing a policewoman. She would always survive.

In all this confusion the morose inspector took me away, alone, and putting me into the back of a small Renault, he drove me silently away from the castle and towards Bordeaux.

I shivered with cold and worry in the back of the car. After a few miles I asked for a coat and, although he apparently spoke little or no English, my dumb-show of becoming frozen had its effect and he threw back a police greatcoat to me. It felt damp and musty, as though it had not been used for a long time, but after the first couple of minutes I was glad to have it around me. The seat of the car was made of some plastic material and kept sticking to the backs of my legs and my bare bottom. I felt very miserable.

After a drive of about half an hour we arrived at a dark building which contained one room and a small cell into which I was put. No other policeman appeared and I wondered why I had been singled out for this solitary confinement. It was warmer in there, but not much, and I crouched down on a bed in the corner of the cell throughout the whole night, feeling lost and cold.

At eight o'clock the following morning the inspector visited me and instructed me to stand up while he walked around me peering closely at my form. I had some bruises – made by Etienne or possibly Aurore – on my hip and he insisted that I life the hem of my gown, so that he could study these minutely. Every now and then he would sanctimoniously write something in a black notebook.

I was given a breakfast of coffee and rolls and jam, served by a pop-eyed lad, who became so agitated by my presence that he slopped the coffee out of the jug all over my knee. He insisted, rather gallantly for one who looked incredibly stupid, in kneeling down and mopping it up with a handkerchief.

An hour later a stout, studious man with a gladstone bag entered the room and stood outside my cell eyeing me through the bars.

The inspector brought the keys and opened the door. 'Police doctor,' he informed me, pointing at the studious man. Then he left. The police doctor appeared very flustered, dropping things, and going red as a sunset in the face. Eventually he indicated that I should let my gown drop to the waist. With a shrug I let it fall. His eyes trembled. With shaking hand he produced a stethoscope and listened over almost every inch of my chest.

He asked to see my tongue and looked down my throat, getting so close I thought I could have easily bitten off his head. Then he ran his fingers all over me, prodding and feeling me in places where no doctor had ever explored before. I sniffed: 'Doctor Livingstone, I presume,' but it was lost on him. He now had me standing with my gown around my ankles, shivering with chill and embarrassment. Then he stood in front of me and took one of my breasts in each hand and weighed them, comparing one with the other like somebody judging turnips at a suburban garden show.

Only fear and uncertainty, reinforced by the appearance at regular intervals of the inspector's head around the door, prevented me from attacking the nasty little man. He grew in confidence as the examination went on and I continued to endure it, standing nude and flushed with shame. He even began to hum to himself, so happy was he in his work.

He eventually left with a polite, 'Good morning, mister,' which I thought in the circumstances was an error of some size. I sat on the cell stool and pulled my gown around me. I cried.

Later that day another police officer arrived with a tape-measure and a notebook and proceeded to measure my body from every angle and every end. Once more it was insisted that I strip and stand for the examination while he ran the tape measure all over me, even noting the distance between the point of one breast and the other. He muttered 'Twenty-three centimetres' and wrote it down.

On the following day yet another police inspector arrived with a camera and a tripod which he proceeded to erect in the cell. This inspector then proceeded to photograph me, nude naturally, from every view and angle, taking hours, it seemed, to get the lighting the pose and the focus right.

Now by this time most people would have suspected something was amiss. But I was an ignorant country girl, suddenly thrown by a French policeman into a solitary cell. How was I to know what the procedures were? I had read about Devil's Island and about some of the terrible things that were done there.

It was while yet another inspector who was introduced as the police masseur was rolling up his sleeves that I realized that each of these men wore a uniform with a button missing from the right hand pocket. Each man was wearing *the same uniform*! They were changing into it before coming into my cell.

Suddenly I screamed and picking up the so-called masseur's bucket of mud I emptied it over his head. Then I laid into him with my stool, knocking him around the cell before finally he managed to crawl out of the barred door. He ran from the outer room cursing. He wanted his money back!

I was left alone for about an hour. Then the original inspector appeared and I told him what I thought about him and his perverted friends with every swear word I could summon. Without saying a word he manhandled poor me from the cell and hung me with shackles from the wall in the outer room. There I was suspended like some poor bastard from the middle ages, naked, and with the man in the uniform sitting drinking glass after glass of wine and gloating over me. Hanging there helpless in those cruel chains I shouted: 'I want to see the British Ambassador!'

The British Ambassador did not arrive, but the real police did. A few minutes later the outer door burst open and they burst in. They had a good time getting me down from the wall. They said my tormenter was a former policeman who had gone mad but was quite harmless. He had, however, been sane and crafty enough to insinuate himself into the police raid on the castle and, having got me in his private dungeon (under his house), he then hired out his uniform and my degradation to any of his friends who desired to practise their strange satisfactions on me.

In the police station they all rolled about laughing at the ingenuity of the bastard who had so debased me. I sat in the corner and cried and wished for the civilized fisherboys of Weymouth.

eleven

My first marriage, to George Turnbull, champion of the two-foot paint roller, took place (solemnized, as they say) in the spring of my eighteenth year, 1951, in Dover.

Dover was the first place in England I reached when my adventure in the Bordeaux region of France was concluded. Glad as I was to see those cliffs protruding like large grinning teeth and to hear the English seagulls, I was again penniless. I left the ferry from France and walked into the town. It was the furthest I could afford to go and I was there for more than the next year and a half of my life.

People said that George Turnbull was as thick as paint itself, and paint, and the art of applying it to walls and other surfaces, was the great absorbing interest of his life. He was broad and young, with a kind, thoughtless face and an island of baldness in his thick hair where he obsessively scratched in a puzzled manner, because beyond his own glossy world he was a man of extreme indecision. Only when challenged by an unpaintable job or suspended in the sky with a giant roller and a bucket of white emulsion was he sure and in his element.

I arrived in Dover, feeling at once a stranger in my own country, in clothes and on a rail-boat ticket provided by the British Consul in Bordeaux from the store of such things he keeps for the stranded and destitute. The clothes would have looked better on Granny Lidstone of long ago, the ticket was third class (which meant hours across France on seats made of the hardest wood any bottom ever suffered) and they gave me only enough money judged to be sufficient for my needs until my first step on my native soil.

Indeed as I stepped ashore from the ferry into the edgy autumn day I possessed only the garments I wore, plus my gown from the orgy at Val de Plaisir, and one brass token which I had somehow retained from the useless payments received aboard the doomed *Charlie Harry II*. Here was I, Nell Luscombe, once more starting life again.

I had spoken to hardly a soul on the long journey, although one or two Frenchmen on the train had looked at me with a prospective eye. But I was too tired in body and broken in spirit to respond. And so at Dover, in the blowy air, I was more solitary than I had ever been since leaving my village in Devon. Instead of coming home, as I had dreamed, I was just like a stranger arriving in an unknown land. It was getting towards evening and the comfortable lights of the town seemed to mock me. There was a cold smeary rain in the air and the gulls were searching unnervingly in the dusk.

There seemed to be nothing I could do, nowhere I could go. Like some old lady, in my strange elderly clothes, I stood and began to cry. Looking back on that moment, I feel sure they were genuine tears but, with me, there was always a slightly theatrical touch about such emotion. I looked cagily through my wet fingers to see if I was arousing anyone's sympathy.

It was a policeman who came gallantly to my sobbing side. He decently put his cape around my shoulders and took me to the police canteen before accompanying me to the immigration authorities where I showed the temporary documents given to me by the Bordeaux Consul and told a little, but naturally only a little, of my story. There was a surge of rough British sympathy throughout the little warm office and a Salvation Army man and his wife were summoned from the town.

With the real kindness of their sort, they took me into their hostel in Dover and gave me a bed and some food. There were three other drifting girls in the room, two on their way out of the country and one not knowing where she was going next.

During the night the two outward-bound girls got up and went off to burgle a wine and spirits shop, which they had spied down the road. They returned in an hour, scattering banknotes and with the Dover police two minutes behind them. They shot into the small dormitory and leapt into bed fully clothed, while the police banged on the hostel door downstairs. Peeping fearfully from over the edge of my bedclothes at all this, I looked down and saw three white five-pound notes lying in the moonlight on the floor. Like a lizard I slid from the sheets, collected them, rolled them up like a cigar and hid them where only the most personal of searches would have discovered them.

Then the police came with the poor, distressed Salvation Army lady. We had to get from our beds, two of us in our innocent night dresses and the other two in incriminating trousers and sweaters. There was a dashing chase around the dormitory with the girls, the police in pursuit, going over the beds like some sort of steeplechase, and one-pound and five-pound notes flying all about, until eventually they were cornered and taken away. The hostel lady was weeping by this time and I went over to comfort her. I minced across to her, my legs hardly parting. I walked like a Japanese geisha girl, with the tiniest steps, but with a glad heart, for I knew that once more good providence had nudged my shoulder.

During my long wooden journey on the French trains, I had plenty of time to think about what I should do when I reached England again. The number of people I knew as friends were accounted for on the fingers of one hand. There was Hal and Flossie in the café in Weymouth and the Commander and Diana Seagram in London. The only other person who would recognize me was my sister. I doubted whether my father would know me, or want to know now. It was not a very comforting list.

My sister and my father could be eliminated in the same brisk stroke. I was reluctant, too, to journey halfway across southern England merely to return to the scullery of Hal and Flossie, kind hearts though they had. In any case I had no wish to carry on business once more with the Weymouth fishing fleet. London beckoned temptingly, but I would not allow myself to contact Diana Seagram and certainly not the Commander in my destitute state.

I had it in mind to find my way to London – which with the lucky money that had floated my way I could now do – and to throw myself into the fortunes of that crowded and chancey city. I remembered the Italian who only wanted to whisper ruderies in my ear, and I thought there must be simpler ways of earning a good living if they were only sought out. But strangely perhaps, after all I had experienced, I was still nervous of the big town and more nervous of getting into a life of common vice, from which there might never be any escape. In my naïve way I had assured myself that all the amoral things I had done until then were merely temporary, a means to an end, and that once I had attained some stable form of living I would be able to cease and begin a normal life; sex would be a pastime, not a necessity.

For this reason I hesitated about going immediately to London. I also thought it prudent to wait for a few days because if I were seen boarding the train, questions might be asked as to how I came by the fare. When I went to the city I wanted to go firmly on my feet with no worries about making a living and finding a home. So I decided to stay, temporarily, right there in Dover, on the doorstep of England, until I had gathered enough substance to make a sure and steady change.

There was no thought in me, either, to open up business as a harlot in Dover, although the town being the busy port it is, I expect I would have prospered. Apart from the seafaring men (and I was sick of sailors anyway) there was, at that time, the first traffic of the great holiday activity to the Continent and back that came in later years. I could have in all probability set up a thriving business among travellers. I could have been the first and last whore in Britain.

That day I decided to remain in Dover I went out from the hostel, like the stout-hearted young girl nobody could deny I was, to find myself a job and a place where I could live. The job I found in a yellowing milk bar in the town, working shifts, and I found a room above an undertaker's shop, spacious and warm and cheap since nobody else would take it because of what lay underneath. I had some uncertainty myself, but I decided it was a bargain and I took it. Walking down the street I saw coming towards me the other lost girl who had shared the dormitory at the hostel. She was glad to see me for she had no friends, and impulsively I asked her if she wanted to share a room. She embraced me in the street. Her name was Gwenny. She had walked from Wales. Round, talkative and irresponsible, she had lived half her life in fantasies, and she became my first real friend.

Suddenly I began to feel confident and assured again. It was very cosy there above the coffins with a view across the Channel, thrilling on screaming winter days and restful in the calm weather. We had a small gas cooker, a kettle and some pots and pans, two armchairs, a wardrobe and our beds. We used a bathroom down the corridor, which was shared with the business and which smelled of embalming fluid, and we had a key to let ourselves in through the shop when we came home late at night.

The first evening we moved in we bought a bottle of sweet,

cheap sherry and drank to our health and our future. For the first time in my life I felt that I surely might have one. It was my home.

Gwenny, however, had a weakness. She was incapable of keeping a job for more than a week. Occasionally she had several posts in the same week, sometimes the employment only lasted a single day, and once she had two jobs in one day.

Born clumsy, she set fire to the Honeypot Tea Shop on her first afternoon, sending swarms of retired ladies tumbling into the street. She allowed a mass escape from the pet shop where they tolerated her for three days, permitting a monkey, a herd of white mice and three *tortoises* to run away.

Gwenny was then hired to push an elderly gentleman in his invalid chair and each afternoon she would trundle him along the seafront, dreaming her dreams, with the old fellow nodding off to sleep. One afternoon, Gwenny let go of the wheelchair to admire somebody's baby and the vehicle went bumping off by itself down the slipway and into the cold sea. The poor old man was up to his waist in waves when he woke up. Gwenny said she was sorry.

In these circumstances her money was uncertain and for much of the time we shared the room above the undertaker's it was my earnings from the milk bar which paid the rent and whatever food we could afford.

I was able to nibble at bits and pieces at the milk bar, although it was hardly filling or nourishing, and during Gwenny's brief career at the Home and Colonial we had plenty to eat every night because she always came home with half a dozen tins under her coat. They caught her after three days.

One of her real talents, however, was the ability to throw the most realistic epileptic fit I have ever seen. She did it one night in the room, scaring the wits from me, and we adapted this imitation to our needs by having her throw a fit in the grocery department of a store and while everyone's attention was diverted, I would put as much as I could into the shopping bag and make a run for it.

Two jolly humpers – young men who carried the loaded coffins for the undertakers – took us out to a public house sometimes or to the cinema. At funerals they would sit in the hearse with the coffin they had humped and would sing ribald songs under their breath while the procession made for the cemetery.

One night when we let ourselves into the shop below our room (something we now did as a matter of course, it seeming no different than, say, a sweet shop) I gave Gwenny a playful push. She was a solid round girl, and she stumbled back and collided with a coffin on its trestles, tipping it and depositing the body of·a poor old dead man on to the floor.

We jumped about horrified, squealing. There he was in his best suit, sprawled out on the floor as though he'd gone to sleep there.

'Oh God, Nelly, what are we going to do?' gasped Gwenny.

'Put him back,' I trembled. 'There's nothing else we can do. If they find him there they'll know it was us, and they'll throw us out.'

'I don't like it,' quivered Gwenny. 'Oh Nell, I don't at all.'

'Neither do I,' I admitted. 'But we got to do it. Come on, let's lift him back. Just pretend he's asleep. Kid ourselves.'

It was the most awful experience. In the light from the street coming in over the shop blinds, we crouched, one each end, and replaced the coffin and then bent to lift up the old dead man. God, we were petrified. We both trembled so much it was a wonder we did not shake the poor corpse to pieces. Then his false teeth fell out.

'Oh Christ, Nell!' Gwenny shrieked. 'His teeth. They've come out.'

They were sitting on the floor grinning invitingly at us like death itself. In some ghastly way they seemed worse than the actual corpse.

'Put him in,' I gasped. 'Get him back in the box.'

We lifted him up and dropped him into his coffin. The exit of his teeth had caused his mouth to relax into a gummy smile, as though he might be enjoying it. Once he was back we stood staring down at the teeth, luminous in the half-light.

'I can't,' whispered Gwenny. 'I can't pick them up Nell. Honest I can't.'

'Nor me,' I trembled. 'And we'd have to put them back in his mouth too.'

'Oh no!' she shuddered. 'Oh God, I couldn't. I just couldn't.'

'Let's throw them in the dustbin,' I suggested.

'No we can't,' she whispered superstitiously. 'It's tampering with the dead. And he'll need them. You know, weeping and gnashing of teeth and that, like they say in chapel.'

I had an idea. 'There's a coal scuttle in the back room,' I said. 'And there's a pair of fire tongs in it. Let's pick them up with them.'

She crept into the rear room and came back with the tongs. They were cumbersome for the job but between them we managed to pick up the teeth. Getting back into the mouth with them was a different matter. We kept dropping them on the corpse and in the coffin and having to fish them out again, until eventually, shaking every inch of the way, we manoeuvred them towards his gums and slotted them in. They did not go in straight and indeed they sat there grinning back at us in a most gruesome way. We could not stand it a minute longer. We shut the lid down and went upstairs. We spent the rest of the night clutching each other to fight off our nightmares.

Those months in Dover with Gwenny were, I suppose, now I come to think of it, the most sexually innocent of my adult life. I told her nothing of my immoral past, only describing the general things, and she was strangely incurious for a Welsh girl. She told me of her growing up in Wales and the things she had done since. But we exchanged little information about our private past. And in all the time we lived together, no man slept in our room. I was making up for the innocence and carefulness I had missed in earlier years. I was enjoying this life. I began to think that, after all, I might not be on a headlong course for an existence of casual sin. And it was while I was in this mood that I met George Turnbull and he asked me to marry him. He thought I was a virgin.

It was at a two shilling dance at a village hall a few miles outside Dover that we met. He was a big, dull man, his feet being especially large as I discovered during our first quickstep. He moved like a tractor, those enormous feet plonking down one after the other like caterpillar tracks; on his face there was ever an expression of good intention and earnestness. He was, I suppose, handsome in a stony sort of way but he was steady to the point of hardly appearing to move at all. The only time when George was seen to be truly alive was with the two-foot paint roller in his fists, and for that he was famous.

'I painted a ballroom last weekend,' he told me on that first night, after wrestling inwardly to find some form of conversation which might interest me. 'By myself.'

'By yourself?' I asked. 'A ballroom?'

'Three hundred feet long by seventy-five wide, by thirty high,' he quoted modestly, lowering his under-face into a pint beer mug. 'Wore out four rollers.' His decent frank eyes turned to me. 'If you want to come and see me working, I'm doing the front of the Red Lion next week,' he said. 'There'll be a lot of people watching.'

Walking through the town the following Wednesday, I saw a crowd filling one pavement and staring up at a building on the other side, their mouths open in the manner of upward gazing crowds. A policeman, presumably sent to disperse the obstruction, was fixed in the gutter also looking up as though some famous comet had appeared.

There was a ladder and at the top was the amazing George Turnbull, the Leonardo da Vinci of the Kent coast. He was performing at a tremendous rate, running his roller, as though it were part of him, over the flaky face of the Red Lion Hotel.

I felt a certain proprietorial pride as I watched him perform and saw how he continued to entrance the people, just like a tightrope man or acrobat, their heads moving hypnotically with the mighty strokes of his roller. Hurrying to the edge of the watchers, I waved and shouted and for a moment the famous man paused in his work, waving the roller in salute, an action which sent white paint sploshing over the crowd like seagull shit. 'Nell Luscombe!' he called down. 'Will you marry me?'

The watchers, all delighted, turned for my answer. There was nothing for it. 'Yes,' I shouted back. 'Yes I will.' People gazed at me with a sort of awe. I was to wed the great George Turnbull.

The only person who did not approve of the match was Gwenny, who knew she was incapable of leading a proper life alone, and I worried about her until, with unexpected fortune, somebody she knew in Wales offered her a job as a tea girl.

'Where is it Gwenny?' I asked happily, but wondering if she would be able to cope.

She dropped her eyes because she knew that I was thinking of her clumsiness. 'In a steel smelting plant,' she mumbled.

But she was able to be my bridesmaid. It was something, she later wrote, which gave her happy memories after her accident, while she was confined with eighteen steelworkers in the hospital at Ebbw Vale. That day she looked fascinating in the gown of turquoise through which she had, however, accidentally pushed her foot.

I was, naturally, in white. George Turnbull believed that he was taking an untouched maid to the altar, and who was I to spoil his day? In any event the previous years of my life were now fading behind me like a dream and here was I walking up the aisle as happy as any true and intact virgin.

During the service George seemed to be lost in a gaze that took in the entire east wall of the parish church, longing to measure it by rule of thumb and a squinting eye.

There was a lot of Kentish beer drunk at the reception, held in the same village hall where George and I had first danced. The groom, because of the paint that lodged in his throat, could roll away a dozen pints, one quickly on the heels of the pint before. The best man, a ruffian I can only now remember as Wild Mickey, was also an indiscriminate beer swigger and he and George, keeping pace with each other, fell to arguing drunkenly as to how long it would take to paint the interior of the hall where we were celebrating.

'Four days,' said Wild Mickey, pushing George on.

'Two days,' argued George, at once becoming belligerent. Nothing stirred him like paint. They drank more and the dispute became louder while I sat beside my new husband and tried to prevent an outburst of fists.

Eventually George, with a streak of beery gallantry, threw down a challenge. It was like some grand gentleman of the olden days. If he had not been standing there bulging out of his best blue suit, his neck hung over the edge of his collar, I would have imagined him in some silk ruffle with a sword ready in his hands. 'I'll paint this place I will,' he challenged. 'Before I takes my bride to bed tonight.'

There were howls and pleas all around, not the least from me, but there was nothing that could stop him then. Somebody was sent for his overalls and his rollers and paints and scaffold boards. While they were gone and I surrendered myself to gloom and Babycham, he drank another five pints of beer, took off his coat and strode up and down measuring the place out first with his giant feet and then with his thumb. Eventually when all his equipment had been brought by an obliging man with a milkcart, he clasped me to him and rubbed a rough kiss into my face. 'Wait for me Nell,' he breathed. 'Wait for me.'

Numb, dumb, I looked around the walls and the ceiling of the place. It had not seemed very big but now it seemed acres. I sat and began to cry, comforted by various women guests including Gwenny who had cut herself badly while opening a tin of peaches and had fresh blood all down the front of her dress, just above the hole in her skirt. All at once I felt I had to do something to stop him. Like a woman trying to stop her man going to a pointless duel I howled: 'No! No! George Turnbull! Stop this madness now!'

Madness it may have been but it was too late. His overalls over his wedding suit, the confetti in his hair soon to be mingling with gobs of cream emulsion, George Turnbull set to, like an obsessed giant, to paint the walls. Everyone gasped at his speed and, sitting unattended at the table, I could not help but feel a certain pride as his roller covered the yards of wall so swiftly.

After four hours most of the guests had gone home and after another two I went also, leaving George solitary and still painting. Even Wild Mickey had gone. I walked alone (Gwenny became ill and had to be taken away) through the cold streets of Dover, a ghostly figure in a wedding dress, sobbing a little, but having a slight laugh between sobs.

We had booked a room for our honeymoon night at the same Red Lion Hotel from whose ramparts he had first proposed, and I wandered in, desolate, and went upstairs. The reception clerk instinctively realized what had happened. 'Gone off painting has he, Mrs Turnbull?' he said. The sound of my new name made the situation even more poignant. I nodded tearfully. 'There's nothing on earth is ever going to keep him from it,' he said solemnly. 'It's in his blood.'

I went to the room, bathed, put on my sad wedding nightdress and lay in bed waiting while the hours tolled by on the town clock. He came to bed an hour before dawn, stinking of topcoat and turpentine, but triumphant. He had done it! In two moments he was asleep. I smiled at his white face, so full of emulsion, and kissed his cheek. Poor fellow, I think now, he had few triumphs in his short life. I could hardly have denied him one on his wedding day.

He snored brilliantly all through what remained of that first night of our marriage. Perhaps it was overworked imagination but, lying there in the Dover dark, I convinced myself that a fine spray of paint was being fanned out with each snore. He lay on his back, his feet like tombstones. His large square rib cage would rise like a platform and then deflate, a pungent snore forcing into the room. It went on for hour upon hour. It was like lying with a machine. In the morning I would not have been surprised if he had done the ceiling in the night.

He had to go off to work in the morning, for he had left a coat of lime green drying somewhere and he could not leave it alone. Used as I was to all sorts of adversity and thoughtlessness on the part of men (why do they always call it 'mankind' I wonder?), I had a little, private cry, when he had gone, the whimper of a woman left for a wall.

I went around to see Gwenny who was under notice to leave the dry cleaning shop where she had been working since the beginning of that week. While I was there, sipping tea with her, a procession of customers came into the shop with wrong garments, burned clothes and one man bringing a pair of trousers with five creases in one leg. Gwenny dealt with them with the off-hand attitude of one who would be in another place at the end of the week. While we were there she chattily put a steam iron right through a shirt front. All sympathy for my problems, she comforted me with the thought that at least I had a husband who enjoyed his work. He could have painted all day long as far as I was concerned. It was the voluntary overtime he was so eager to work, what, in his trade, you might call extra-mural activity.

But on the evening of our first full day as wife and man he returned to the Red Lion Hotel (where they had given us a room for three nights, the cost to be set against future contract – a melancholy coincidence, as it happened), triumphant after yet another battle with paint and plasterwork. He spent the first hour of our evening describing every cornice, parapet and sash he had daubed that day and I realized then this would forever be the pattern of our lives together. Eventually, like an afterthought, he asked me how I had fared that day and I told him bluntly that I had been crying.

Genuinely astonished, he was further amazed to discover that I was not proud of the fact that he had painted the interior of a hall on our wedding night.

Sorry and concerned, he insisted that we went to our bed very early and I changed into my bridal nightdress feeling happier and softer. He modestly donned a pair of stiff pyjamas, apparently made from some sort of compressed wood shavings. I swear they creaked when he moved. Then, from under the bed he produced, with a kind of coy triumph, a parcel and an illustrated book on sex.

I sat in bed, my beautiful unattended breasts lying half outside my nightdress, gazing in astonishment while this fucking novice opened the book at page one and began to read aloud. Worse was to follow, for the parcel contained the most horrifying collection of intercourse equipment I have ever seen. There were dozens of washable sheaths, jars of jelly and pots of French chalk (to dry out the sheaths after laundering them). There were pills and tablets enough to arouse a physical wreck. It was only a wonder that they had not included a puncture outfit. George smiled solidly as he looked up from the bundle.

'I didn't know rightly what to get, Nell,' he admitted. 'So I went and ordered the lot.'

It was one of the most humiliating nights I have ever spent with a man, not excluding my awful adventures aboard the Charlie Harry II. He even (Oh God, when I think of it!) produced a war surplus gas cape and spread it below my buttocks so that in the course of losing my virginity I would not damage the Red Lion sheets. When he had finally read the instructions (leaving the book open so he could refer to it) and had donned all his rubber, paste and jelly, and had taken two tablets (one meant for me) he hung poised above me. I couldn't help it. 'Why don't you give it a coat of paint as well, George?' I sighed.

The poor nincompoop eventually got himself pointed in the right direction and advanced on me like one of King Arthur's Knights, hanging with armour and with a blasted great lance sticking out in front.

What really worried him was that the instructions about what he kept calling 'piercing' could not be carried out. He

176

kept pushing and probing with that look of intense puzzlement on his face, not understanding why he had not reached the expected resistance. Every now and then he would refer to the book and then have another poke. Eventually he lay against me panting and gave the matter thought. Then, tragedy smashed all over his face, he lifted himself up, and on his great elbows said: 'You *are* one Nell, ain't you?'

'One *what* George?' I asked, staring at the ceiling.

'One of them virgins?' he said. 'You ain't been with another man, have you?'

Still looking up I shook my head. 'I've never been with another man, George,' I recited.

'But something's supposed to happen,' he said miserably. 'Something's missing, Nell.'

The born dolt actually began looking around the bed for something that had vanished years before.

Fortunately he had another read and discovered that a girl could lose her physical virginity in a number of innocent ways, for example, on a horse or on a wall. Not knowing anything about horses I said it probably happened to me as a child and I spent hours astride our garden wall, sometimes hopping along it from end to end.

He buried his big, simple face in my breasts, which he seemed to have been saving for some emergency, and muttered: 'Damn that garden wall, Nelly. Damn it.'

'Oh dear,' I thought. 'Oh dear, Nelly Luscombe. What have you gone and done?'

But if George Turnbull as a lover left a girl breathless with boredom, he was a good and generous husband, giving me the settled silent life I had wanted after all the storms of my youth.

And he had a sense for the dramatic too, for he had prepared for me a great surprise – a little house of our own. Nothing had been said about where we were to live after our marriage and during our three days at the Red Lion, surprising as it seems now, I had not worried very much about it, believing that we would get some rooms in the town and make them our home. Perhaps I was secretly afraid of anything too permanent.

But on the third day we were wife and man, he arrived at the Red Lion in his rattling paint-splashed van and, smiling with stony mystery, he drove us from the town and inland to where a group of new houses sat on a hill like a sort of camp or fortress.

I thought that he was merely taking me to view some new professional triumph. We drew up in front of a small house shining like a painted box in the Dover sun. Still with that large fixed smile he led me to the door and with one of the few romantic gestures of his life he lifted me across the threshold. It was ours!

I am sure that I was never so overjoyed about anything, and even since then, even in my grand days to follow, never has that simple and sudden happiness been surpassed.

The realization that this was *my* house, my very own, took my breath away and I began to laugh crazily, jumping from his arms and running like a child from little room to little room, banging on the walls (recently painted of course) and trying to embrace the windows that looked out on sloping green fields, the roofs of Dover and the English Channel, grey in the distance like a broad street. He came and clumsily joined me at the window. I put my arms, my poor wandering homeless arms, about his hefty waist and we gazed out together.

'Look at the sea, Nell,' he said. 'It looks like it could do with a few undercoats and a nice gloss, don't it?'

It was difficult to answer that. I swear he would have liked to have given the rainbow a new top coat if the chance had been offered. And it was his work that had brought us our house. The builder was so keen to have George that he had given it to us rent free providing George would paint the houses all around him. He was to be allowed three days a week to do other work, so that he could earn the housekeeping, and the rest of the time paint the windows and doors of our neighbours. I realized I was married to a champion!

At first there were no neighbours. We were gladly marooned on that hill overlooking the sea, and I began to sense the happiness I had always felt might come if I could only find somewhere to settle, where every day would not bring a new trial or adventure. You could not be further from adventure than marriage to George Turnbull.

Three days a week his little van would trundle down the hill, all colours, like a large moving flower, and I would be left to the comfortable work of a young wife. Occasionally I would think of the old hairy days but, at that time, with no great longing. Then some people moved into the little estate and I was invited to coffee and tea and would stand gossiping on the muddy paths like any other woman. I began to dream about carpets and cocktail cabinets and perhaps even babies. Each day I lived in my house, doing the easy chores, while Frankie Laine and Johnny Ray sang to me from the radio.

George built a small shed in the garden where he kept his paints and where he spent much of his evening time pottering and making small things for the home. At one time I thought he was getting notions of parenthood himself because I went into his shed and saw that he was building something that looked very much like a cradle.

'What's that you're making in the shed George?' I asked him.

'Oh that,' he said. 'That's for the builder's yard. It's just a rat trap.'

Now of course, I realize that it was never in my nature to live that life, even if I had convinced myself that it was safe and happy. The change came with the seasons. Autumn was with us again and the wind blowing down the Channel made me lonely. In the town I met a man, Theo Baldwin, another painter, but a painter of canvases, not walls. He looked like that sort of painter ought to look, in his fifties, his hair long, grey-gold, his face lined with artistic worries. It was his voice that was so handsome.

'Mrs Turnbull,' he said on the day we first fell into conversation and introduced ourselves in the public bar of the Red Lion (so much of my life at that period was connected with that place). I was there waiting for George. We went out once a week to the films and I would meet him there. People in the cinema used to move away from us because of the smell of turps that hung about my husband, something to which I had now become accustomed. 'Mrs Turnbull,' said Theo Baldwin. 'You are a lady of great beauty you know. Would you permit me to paint you?'

Now I've seen enough films and suchlike about portrait painters to know that they want to have you pose in the nude and then, eventually, to persuade you to make love to them. Theo was not like that at all. He had me across the bed before he had ever touched a brush to the canvas.

I was shocked at myself more than at him. To think that I slipped into it so easily again after all my telling myself that I was cured and free of such things. But it happened as if it had all been arranged the moment I agreed to visit him at his studio in the town. And I went, eyes open, into it as if nothing had ever happened to make me change my ways. Once a whore always a whore. Throughout the previous day I had felt guilty excitement simmering inside me. George rolled off in the morning with his brushes and rollers and his customary satisfied grin. I waited and made myself a cup of coffee. Then I sat on my plastic-topped stool in my fitted kitchen and tried to think clearly, to deliberately put this temptation behind me. It was as though I were praying. The radio played and the house felt safe like a cloak around my body. Was I to leave it and start a life of adventuring once more? Surely not. I was.

I left it until the last possible moment, in case something might happen, like George returning with lead-poisoning or a neighbour calling for a chat, which would play my hand for me and prevent me risking all this good, steady life I had managed to form. But at eleven o'clock no interruptions had occurred. It would not even rain to give me an excuse. Head bent, hell-bent, I walked down the grassy slope of our hillside, with sea-wind in my face, feeling again the ghostly nudging presence of Nell Luscombe, travelling trollop from Weymouth. It's not surprising, I suppose, that I cannot, even now, visit a seaside place without hearing in its wind the whisper of a proposition.

Guiltily, I went into the town and, after walking along the main street, window-shopping, I snaked down a small alley where his home and studio lay. I trembled as I rang the bell and stood dumbly when he opened the door.

'Good girl, Nell,' he said like a secret agent meeting an accomplice. 'You got here.'

I walked into the gloomy house. There were paintings and canvases everywhere (he was not a particularly successful painter as far as actually selling his pictures was concerned) and I walked, still nervously, between them, trying to see what they portrayed.

'Come in here, my darling,' he said unhesitatingly. He was

180

wearing a sort of loose smock with signs of the zodiac on it.

I felt out of practice and he took my uncertainty as some sort of innocence. I was loitering about and he was making circles around me like some artistic shark, putting out his hands and then withdrawing them without touching me.

'Proportions, proportions,' he muttered. It was like George measuring up a wall, with his thumb. Theo used his hands, holding them at angles like frames and advancing and backing away as if he were on elastic, until he came right in close and framed my right breast with his outspread fingers. 'Exquisite,' he murmured. 'Rotunda exquisite.'

'Thank you very much, Theo,' I said uncertainly. 'I can't stay long. I've got to go to Liptons.'

'Of course, of course,' he agreed. He was one of those people who keep saying things twice. 'Would you ... would you just take your clothes off dear. At the top.'

I sighed. After all, I was there snared by my own irresistible attraction for grimy adventure so there was no point in being coy. I said nothing but began to undo the buttons on the front of my dress. Theo stepped back as if he expected an avalanche. I pulled the sleeves and shoulders of the dress down over my arms and let it hang there from the waist. I was wearing a slip and a bra. Theo started making more framing movements with his hands. 'Beautiful, beautiful,' he recited. 'Rotunda, rotunda.'

He kept up a commentary as I continued to strip. 'Skin, smooth, pink, curves, sublime, neck, sexually arousing, waist dainty, shoulders creamy, arms slender ...' Then: 'Oh what a lovely pair of titties.' Flinging me back on the four poster spread behind me like a soft trap, he at once fastened on to my left nipple as though making sure of a connection, so to speak, and then rolled passionately across to my other breast and hung on there. He went to and fro several times, spoiled for choice it seemed, in a long curve like a windscreen wiper.

'My darling, my darling,' he gabbled. 'My dear darling, my dear darling.'

His artistic beard was as stiff as one of George's abandoned paint brushes and he jabbed it all over my anatomy. He was wearing something or other under his zodiac robe and he tore this garment away and released a long thin appliance that sprang around like a ship's bowsprit in a gale. He was taking a long time on his approach, so I wriggled out of the bottom half of my clothes and kicked them away down the bed. This gave him another excuse to explore and exclaim. He tracked over my lower landscape, nose down, beard tickling down between my legs, puffing, burrowing so deeply that I almost lost sight of his head altogether. He came out red-faced and breathless, like an inspector of drains, gave a pathetic moan and climbed close to me.

In a lifetime of beds and men I have known some strange performers, but Theo the artist was the most unusual I had met up to that time. He began using that long starved thing of his like a paintbrush, dipping it into my personal palette and painting my legs, my stomach and my bosom in the most odd fashion. I lay there astonished, wondering where he would start work next. As he brushed me with his penis he muttered, eyes closed: 'Crimson ... ochre ... aquamarine ... violet ...' as if he were painting by numbers.

By the time he had finished this performance I was nicely on the boil, and ready for the real thing. Unfortunately what he had been about *was* the real thing as far as he was concerned and I left the studio puzzled and dissatisfied and clutching a small etching he had given me as a parting gift.

Several times more I visited Theo, each time emerging with a frown and a worthless drawing or painting which I dropped in somebody's dustbin. I would wait guiltily at home for my own painter, George, to return and satisfy me. But George was a man whose passions were less than occasional and after his tea he would go out to work in his little wooden shed, leaving me to wonder where I was going to dispose of my pent-up energy and love.

The answer was provided by Garth, a stringy young husband who lived three houses away. He had the haunted look of a man who hopes for and needs a lot more than he gets. His wife was a jug-faced, fussy girl who went to evening classes for rug-making and it was during one of these absences and while George was working late over some expansive wall that Garth asked me if I would like to come into his house to see his cat's kittens. I would have had to have been as blind as a kitten not to see that he intended to show me more than that, because you can only take a certain amount of kittens and once you've seen one you've seen the litter; and anyway he had that dry, desperate look about him. When we had inspected the kittens he asked me if I would like a drink and I could see his hand shaking as he poured it. He missed the glass with the first two lumps of ice.

'Nell,' he said through clenched teeth. 'The telephone's out there. Please, please ring nine-nine-nine for the police.'

'What's the emergency?' I said.

'There will be one shortly, Nell,' he muttered. 'I think I'm going to rape you.'

'Why tell the police?' I said. 'And what do you mean you *think*?' An explosion of amazed pleasure transformed his face.

'You mean ... you mean ... you'll let me?'

'Then it isn't rape,' I said. 'Not technically. If I let you.'

'Well call it what you like,' he gasped. 'We've got half an hour. Beryl will be knee deep in rug wool now.'

The use of his wife's name seemed to strengthen his resolve. He caught me by the wrists and kissed me agonizingly and we charged up the stairs. He had the curtains drawn and his trousers down in one swift sweep of his arm. I slipped out of my clothes while he stood transfixed on the far side of their bed which was covered by a hideous gold quilt.

'Oh God,' he whispered across the bed. 'I've watched you and watched you Nell, every day I've spied on you. I know every curve of your body by heart. It's been driving me mad and now you're here.'

'I'm here,' I smiled and nakedly leaned back across the quilt.

'Er ... Nell ... not that side ... please. That's Beryl's side.' I sighed at his hypocrisy and moved over so I would not defile Beryl's bit of the bed. He was really hungry, poor soul, starved; holding me and caressing me with the enthusiasm of a man trying to rub away a stain.

We were both lying panting gratefully after it was over, when there came a ring on the front door chimes. Poor Garth went rigid with fear. His eyes seemed to revolve in his slim, pallid face.

'Lay low,' I whispered. 'They'll think there's nobody in.'

'But I'm *supposed* to be in,' he trembled. 'I'm baby-sitting. And it's bound to be someone from around here.'

'Better go down,' I said. 'Shall I stay?'

'No. Oh God, no.' He shook.

'I'll creep out the back door,' I decided for him. 'Trust to luck nobody sees me. Bye.'

He did not even answer, but tucked his tell-tale shirt into his trousers and stammered down the stairs. Long practice had made me able to dress quickly and I was only just behind him. I had intended to turn off and creep through the kitchen to the back door, but just as we reached the front door the letter box popped up and a pair of eyes pinned us.

'Open up Garth,' called the voice. 'I can see you, old boy. And that lovely Mrs Turnbull.'

The game was up before it was properly started. Garth shuddered forward and, ashen-faced (the back of his neck was ashen too), slowly opened the door. It was Bernard Winters, the motor car salesman who lived on the opposite side of the road. His face was all grinning triumph.

'Ho! Ho!' he exclaimed. 'Caught in the act, old boy. Nabbed you rotten.'

'Mrs Turnbull came in to see our kittens,' said Garth huffily. 'You're a bit much Bernard, a bit too much.'

Bernard laughed and patted us both on the shoulders and made man-of-the-world noises. He was a dark, handsome fellow, but a bit sure of himself.

Just how sure he was it did not take long to discover. I had hardly returned to my own sitting room when our newly-installed telephone rang and it was Bernard. 'Nelly,' he said. '*I* think you're desirable too. Why don't you visit me sometime? Margaret goes to pottery on Thursdays.'

I paused. Then, right, I thought. This is the true crossroads. 'All right,' I answered calmly. 'It will cost you five pounds.'

'A fiver!' he exclaimed. 'Jesus, you're a girl, aren't you!'

'That's why I'm charging a fiver,' I said. I heard him guffaw over the line. 'I bet you didn't charge old Garth that. He hasn't got a fiver to his name.'

'That's none of your business!' I said. 'It was a trial run. I was just seeing if I could still do it.'

'Christ you *are* something,' he said. 'All right, Nelly. On Thursday then, when Margaret's gone to pot.'

'Start saving your pennies,' I told him.

*

That's how it began. A one-girl vice ring in the middle of a little estate of boxy houses, stuck on a hilltop meadow in Kent. You don't have to explore far to find a market for flesh. I was passed from husband to husband like a secret game of rugby, gathering fivers as I went.

That first Thursday with Bernard Winters was worth a fiver of anybody's money, even mine. Here, at last, was an out-and-out bastard who enjoyed sex and especially illicit sex. He was genial, unhurried, unworried, getting me a couple of gins beforehand and a well-brewed cup of tea afterwards. Fortunately it was now the darkest side of winter so that moving about the district was not so difficult as it would have been on light evenings, although it occasionally meant climbing a garden fence or two. Bernard was not the type to merely pay up as a customer. It was his nature to get involved in business, and soon he was acting as my agent, with husbands all over the estate and even organized visits from Dover and the surrounding villages.

At first it was merely a quiet phone call from Bernard about Harry Venables, a draughtsman from the far end of the estate, whose wife was another Thursday potter. I paid Harry a half-hour visit and came away with my fiver. Then there was somebody else whose wife was doing French, flower arrangement and metal work for beginners. This man worked overtime on these evenings and then rushed home to spend his overtime on me. God only knows how it went on so long undetected.

The only real embarrassment was the money. I honestly did not know what to do with it. I thought of opening a bank account, but there was a risk of George discovering that. And it was not as though I could even go out and spend it. George would have soon noticed anything new – although I would have dearly liked a refrigerator. Bernard offered to 'invest' my takings for me, but I prudently declined. What was I to do with this fortune that grew so readily as my contacts and customers increased?

Our house was so small and modern that there were no crannies or niches where such an amount in notes could be concealed. The garden was bare of possibilities – except for George's little hut down by the fence. One afternoon, when I was getting desperate with a hundred and fifty pounds in five and one pound notes under our mattress, I decided to look at the shed.

It was confined and crowded, full of tidy paint pots and brushes and his bench where he did his odd bits of carpentry and other work in the evenings. Suddenly I felt very sad for him and very guilty for what I was doing behind his back. Shamefully, I could imagine him in there at his lonely vice while I was sharing mine on some neighbouring bed.

Shame, however, would never find a hiding place for the money. I searched around with no success until, just as I was leaving and I was outside the workshed, I chanced to look down and I saw that the floor was raised from the ground a few inches leaving a hollow beneath. On his shelves were a line of jam-jars, some containing screws and nails and other oddments, but several standing empty. I took down one of the jars which had a screw-on lid and took it inside the house. My ill-gotten money curled in there very cosily and I returned to the garden and pushed it into the space under the floor. Within a few weeks it was joined by another, also full of notes. I had more than three hundred pounds.

The disgusting business was booming. I found myself mornings, afternoons and often evenings making my way to some randy husband, with my bag containing one of the new electric vibrators which I had heard about and purchased as a professional aid.

There was a touch of pantomime about some of the visits I made. On one occasion the husband had been left to watch several simmering pans on the cooker. He explained smugly that his wife made her own jam and marmalade. Unfortunately he became engrossed during the next half hour and forgotten pans flowed over and hung, black and burning, down the side of the cooker like lava from a volcano.

Another client had wailing two-year-old twins in his charge and we had to perform on the nursery bedroom carpet because they would not let daddy out of their sight until they were asleep. They were a couple of intensely ugly, chocolate-mouthed boys, and they stood at the side of their cot and leaned over and watched us on the floor, murmuring and muttering, like two yokels at a gate.

One man brought his father and we all three got into bed, me rolling log-like from one generation to the other. On another night I was the whore-in-residence at a blue film performance attended by eight eager husbands.

Before long another jam-jar was stuffed with notes and I began to wonder where it would lead. George continued on his plodding life, apparently not noticing anything, not even my signs of fatigue. Then in the middle of one night, a terrible thing happened. I woke up and saw George standing against the window with a red glow reflected around the room.

'Nell,' he said ponderously, turning as he saw I was awake. 'My shed's on fire.'

With a screech much louder than justified the loss of a garden shed I rushed to the window beside him. It was burning furiously, just the bones of the framework visible through the flames. His pots of paint were bursting like bombs. I almost choked just watching it. He went at his usual slow gait to telephone the fire brigade but by the time they arrived the little building was just hot ashes and the jam-jars had cracked and melted and my precious money had burned away. All that for nothing.

Two days later George Turnbull painted his last wall. It was at the side of the Red Lion, a blanked-out elevation with no windows or doors. He was painting it a jaunty blue and when I last saw him and waved to him he was on the top rung of the ladder using his two foot roller with his everyday cheerfulness and vigour.

I waved back and continued down the street to a grocery shop. While I was at the counter a commotion began outside and I saw people hurrying. Somehow I knew it was George. I put down my shopping basket and went to the door.

Down the street a crowd had gathered at the foot of the blank wall of the Red Lion. There was no doubt about it being my poor husband. From the new blue area at the top of the wall a great rounded streak of paint, a perfect quarter circle, curved down the wall like a layer of the rainbow. And at the foot of that rainbow there was no crock of gold but George Turnbull. He had reached too far, the ladder had toppled sideways, but faithful unto death, he had kept his roller against the surface all the way down, a trail like a doomed aeroplane.

When I got to the crowd I could see it was terrible. To start with, dear, dying George was covered head to foot with blue paint. A policeman who had his head in his lap had it all over his trousers and tunic and it was rolling away, oddly like a bloodstain, from beneath the form of George. I took the blue head from the policeman and laid it properly in my lap. He died there a few minutes later, only opening his emulsion-covered mouth once and that was to say: 'I'm sorry Nell, but I always counted the jam-jars.'

The funeral was at the church where we had been married only a few months previously and all the neighbouring husbands came and stood around the grave but none of them would look up and look me in the eye. I went up the hill to our house, alone, adrift again, not knowing then whether the coroner's pronounced 'accidental death' was the truth and never to know.

That I had to be away from that place was obvious. I could not stay there now; there was no point. I packed the things I had and set off towards the town again, going somewhere I did not know. I sent a note to our best man, Wild Mickey, asking him to sell the contents of the house and always put fresh flowers on poor George's grave. I don't know whether he did.

Now was the time, I told myself, when at last I should go to London, where someone loose like me would be at home among my kind. But I still wavered, still afraid. I got on the London train but at Canterbury I got off again and wandered aimlessly down through the creaky old city until I saw the cheerful front of a fish and chip shop. I bought two shillings worth wrapped in paper and went into a small, cold park to eat them on a bench. I felt miserable and sorry for myself and sorry for poor dead George who had trusted me and asked for nothing, which was as much as he got.

The paper the fish and chips were wrapped in was *The Times* – Canterbury being that sort of town where fish and chips can be wrapped in *The Times*. I never read it in my life, except over Sir Waldo's shoulder, but sitting there, in that wintry garden, with nowhere to turn my steps, I began to read the grease-smeared small advertisements on the front page. The third in the column I screwed up my eyes to read: 'Young nanny/companion required. Widower with three grown children. Resident France. Interviews London.'

There was a telephone number. I gaped at it and then slowly turned the newspaper up until I could see the date at the top of the page. It was only three days old. Almost mesmerized I got up from the bench and walked to the post office where I telephoned the number. Yes, I was experienced. Three years with Lord Sutton, two with the Duke of Dorset. References? Of course. Yes, I could be in London that evening. Seven o'clock. Thank you so much. Goodbye.

Still glazed I came out of the telephone box. Liar that I was I *knew* I was going to get the job. I was going to France once more. Nelly Luscombe had done it again.

twelve

Walking along the Promenade des Anglais, Nice, in the very spring of my life, the fine sun on the fine sea and France rising all around me, I could not help but think of the strange turns of fortune in my life and the chance that had brought me, a near penniless widow of Dover, to this rich and marvellous place.

There had been no trouble with Mr Sheridan who had advertised in *The Times*. I went to the house in Eaton Square and let my eyes shine. Poor Mr Sheridan's French wife had died a few months before (the poor lady had drowned in a revolving vat of flour while visiting a mill owned by her husband; a fate oddly similar to that suffered by my George). He had been interviewing a parade of starched women of the professional, housekeeper class and when I walked into his room you would have thought I was a summer's day. We discussed our twin tragedies and I dimmed my eyes accordingly and then he began telling me of his children, Sirie fifteen, Anton sixteen and Paul twenty-one, who was in military school in Paris. Slowly I turned up the lids of my country eyes and directed them on to his face. I could see he was not going to ask for references.

I was engaged immediately and I even received an advance of salary and was invited to make myself at home in that lovely house in Eaton Square. I was given a room overlooking the gardens and I stood in the window that very evening and watched the lights of London moving in the night. In three days

I would be travelling to Nice, to a house, so he described, like a gem in the hills above the sea. A house called L'Horizon. I stood in the window and practised saying the name to myself. I felt rich and comfortable. Goodbye George Turnbull, goodbye Dover, I whispered.

I bought a new coat with some money given to me by a gentleman in Hyde Park, in payment for a ten minute trick in the back seat of his Rolls as the chauffeur cruised around the park. This was the first time I had performed in London and I was really pleased with it. For a start I had only been walking in the park – not even provocatively walking because I was not aware that Hyde Park was a place where this type of thing happened. It was a mild winter's day and I had found myself strolling by the water, looking at myself in the lake and giggling at the ducks, when the car drew up, silent as a ghost, and the driver startled me with his shout: 'Miss, are you working?'

It seemed a very curious question, but I answered honestly: 'Yes I am. I've just started.'

The next thing I knew was that I was in the back of the car with a lusty, lunchy sort of young businessman, ten pounds better off, and leaning back over the softest seats while he gave me the benefit of his better nature. It was really most luxurious and pleasing, all the more so because it was so unexpected. He even had a nice little cocktail bar in the back of the car and he poured me a drink of champagne before depositing me within walking distance of Marble Arch. 'Goodbye, Nelly,' he called cheerfully, pulling up his trousers. 'And thank you so much.' A gentleman.

That afternoon I found Diana Seagram's house near Westminster and timidly rang the bell. She was, as always, the most kind lady and we sat and had tea while she gave me the news of the Commander and I told her at least some of my adventures. I wondered how she would have reacted if she knew that an hour before I had been rolling in a Rolls-Royce with someone from the City.

She told me that the Commander had gone to live in a house in Shropshire. She wanted to tell me something else, I could sense it, and eventually she decided she would.

'He has asked me to marry him,' she said quietly. She stared into her teacup as though she had just seen the answer there. A quick, unreasonable pang of jealousy touched me. 'What will you say?' I asked her. All at once we were not girl and woman but woman and woman. She looked up as though wanting help. It was the first time anyone like that had looked at me as though they needed advice.

'I truly don't know what to do, Nell,' she said shaking her head. 'We've known each other a long time. He and my husband were great friends, and now it seems almost like a merger of lost souls. He suffers a great deal, as you well know, but the worst thing is his frustration with his handicaps. He gets so violently angry with himself, you know.'

'I didn't know that. I've never seen him angry.'

'No you wouldn't. He wouldn't let you see that. He wouldn't show you. But a man like that is bound to kick over at times. God, he can't walk, he just stumbles, and his voice sounds as if he's trying to speak through a tube. It hurts his pride.'

'Diana,' I said feeling oddly wise. 'Do you love him?'

'No,' she said simply. 'No, Nell. Nor does he love me. As I said it would be a sort of merger of souls. But he needs me and I possibly need him, I don't know.'

We both knew that I could not tell her what to do. She had merely wanted to tell me the matter. We finished our tea in an aimless sort of way and I left her. We kissed each other at the doorstep and I felt the loneliness of her come through to me. How strange, I thought, that this woman with her poise and her house should really have nobody and here was I, now in fortune, going to a new life in a new rich place.

The day after I drove with Mr Sheridan in his large French car, retracing my journey to Dover which I had left in such despair shortly before. It seemed so odd going through those streets, seeing several people I knew, and going right by the wall of the Red Lion where George had died. Nothing had been done about continuing the painting of the big blank wall and looking out from my deep seat I saw again that terrible arc of blue that marked the crash dive of my late husband. The wall of death. His memorial.

Mr Sheridan had been silent most of the journey and now sat dozing beside me. I had only my thoughts. We returned to the ferry terminal from which I had emerged nearly two years before, without hope or money, after my adventures in France. Now I held out my passport with a certain smugness, a waif now a traveller.

We reached Paris by early evening and Mr Sheridan said he would have dinner in his room at the hotel, leaving me in the company of the chauffeur, a wooden-faced religious man called Perrington. He took me on a tour of all the dreadful and sinful places of that city, to show me, as he said, to what depths some poor creatures can fall. We went to a cabaret where a man with a dog-whip pretended to lay it across a naked girl who crawled across the stage.

'It makes me want to weep for her, Miss,' said Perrington, straining forward at every stroke. 'Imagine the degradation of that wretched young lady's soul.'

We remained dutifully for further equally disgraceful acts and went along some streets, dozens of them, where the Paris prostitutes waited for customers, and Perrington again was almost in tears at their plight. He studied several very closely, even staring into their faces, as if he was wondering if it might be worth saving them. Apparently he had already made some attempt at this because several smiled as if they really knew him. After two hours of dragging around what seemed, even to me, to be the most sordid places, I was ready to return to the hotel. Mr Perrington, a bulky man who sweated, was almost breathless as we mounted some steps at Montmartre to visit a cabaret which he described as the most terrible in all of Paris.

He was a good judge. Even I sat there blinking at the depravity on the stage. My own sexual adventures, not excluding the exotic business near Bordeaux, were all light and purity compared with the performance displayed there that night. In any event, I do not approve of animals being involved in such matters, especially dumb sheep. As Mr Perrington became more annoyed so he seemed to swell with sweat. It oozed from every pore and he became more enraged as the acts went on. Then, not being able to stand it a moment longer, and despite my attempts to restrain him, he suddenly leapt to his feet and charged like a wet hippo down the aisle towards the stage shouting God's vengeance. He scattered the entire show, men, girls, sheep and everything else. One of the monkeys ran up the curtains. It was an amazing thing to see and I sat shaking but transfixed. Mr Perrington then flung himself on his knees and began to pray loudly for God's forgiveness for these people. The curious thing was that nobody did anything about him. Not immediately anyway. He was allowed to kneel there praying like fury, much to the obvious enjoyment of the cast of the orgy, who now stood back and watched (one naked girl cuddling the monkey and the other sitting astride the puzzled sheep) while the audience shouted and cat-called with huge gusto.

I stood up. 'Mr Perrington!' I called. Then, hardly knowing what to say, 'Mr Perrington. I think it's time we left!'

The people understood and there was tremendous applause from both the stage and the audience. I felt like Sarah Bernhardt. 'Mr Perrington,' I shouted again. 'Please.'

That was it. The whole show began a slow handclap and chanted Mr Perrington ... pleeeeese ... Mr Perrington, pleeese.' I felt myself go scarlet in the dark. There was nothing for it. Shakily I stood and went, like some schoolteacher trying to instil discipline, down the aisle through the middle of the audience, jumped on to the stage and grasped hold of Mr Perrington who was still on his knees praying like fury. My appearance brought howls and wolf whistles from the people, mostly, but by no means all, men. The naked cast began to applaud and I looked about me embarrassed, but then began to feel rather thrilled by it all.

A beautiful bare black man came across the stage and put his arms around me, and a girl, the one with the sheep, came and kissed me on the cheek. The sheep put its nose up my skirt. Then there was a great hollow howl, Mr Perrington, who had seen the attention drift away from him, looked up with reddened eyes. The cast, after further embracing me, unceremoniously picked him up, took him to the side entrance and dumped him in the alley. When I hurried to him after several more naked hugs and kisses from the performers, he was sitting on the cobbles with his knee showing through a split in his trousers, very much like a large defeated boy. Without a word he got up and walked into the main street, where we took a taxi back to the hotel. All the way he was hushed, his eyes fixed straight ahead, but when we reached the hotel he took me by the elbow and said plaintively: 'I would be greatful, Miss, if no mention of this reached Mr Sheridan.' He paused and said secretly: 'I don't want word of my crusade to get around.'

The death of Mr Sheridan's young wife (his second) in the flour hopper (she had tumbled in and been whirled around and around in hundreds of tons of flour – she drowned in it before they could rescue her) had, it seemed, ruined the poor man's life. He sold the mill right away, retreated into his own thoughts, and would never again have any bread, biscuits, cakes or anything made with flour in his house.

He had apparently adored her. But she had been less popular with the other members of the household. Once at L'Horizon, in the kitchen, I asked Mr Perrington about the tragedy and he recounted it with smug enjoyment.

Fascinated I asked: 'How did she look when they got her out of the flour hopper?'

'White,' he replied with brief relish. 'Very white.'

The house was well named for it was set in the pines and hills above Nice, on the road to Grasse, looking over the random distant roofs of the city and on to the long blue sea. It had cool balconies and bougainvillaea lolling from the walls. It reminded me in that way of the terrace of Amantine and Aurore on the other coast of France. Mr Sheridan was, of course, very rich, and there were many beautiful things in the house. But he took little pleasure in any of them now that his wife was gone.

If I had thought at the outset that I had been engaged as a possible bed companion (and I *had* thought that) then I was in error. Never once did Mr Sheridan touch me or say anything untoward to me. He was kind but in an almost absent way. Sometimes however, I saw him glancing in my direction as if he felt guilty and, catching my eye one day when this happened, he looked quite crestfallen and felt he had to explain. 'When you move about the house, Nell, I sometimes catch a glimpse of my Giselle.' I felt very sorry for him.

But his children, the children of his first wife whom he had divorced, had apparently got over any effect of their stepmother's death. I thought perhaps she had been one of those people who can be intimately concerned with only one other person. For the children, once she had gone she had gone.

Sirie was slight and pretty in a wan way (strangely pale for a girl who lived much of her life within reach of the sun). Her black eyes never looked immediately to you, they wandered, almost floated upwards. They were full and lovely but they told you nothing. She was quiet, inward, given to reading filmstar magazines and listening idly to Chinese music. She was still at school and went silently every day dressed in a plain blue dress, driven by Perrington in the Citroen, her expression the same when she left in the morning as it was when she returned in the afternoon.

Anton, the younger son, was a year older and in many ways like his sister although he spent more time away from the house, driving a huge and dangerous motor cycle around the mountain roads. Before the death of his stepmother, his father had forbidden these journeys, but once she was dead he never bothered again.

My duties at L'Horizon could almost be defined as simply 'being there'. It appeared that I had been engaged not to perform tasks, or even take responsibilities, but simply to take the place left by the floury departure of Giselle. It was as if I were required to walk about, to occupy a chair, to complete the landscape of that house.

And yet I could have been in no way a replacement for the late Mrs Sheridan as far as her mourning husband was concerned. He made no demands on me except an occasional smile. I had seen pictures of Giselle and she had been an undoubtedly lovely woman, but with a sharp look in the very corners of the eyes, the sort of sharpness many French women have, as though they are keeping some clever secret. It was the look I had seen in the eyes of Amantine.

The children required me even less than their father. They were like a small secret society, spending much silent time in each other's company, sitting in the fine room or out under the trees on the sloping grass of the cool garden. Then, without a word, almost as if some signal had passed between them, they would rise and go their separate ways, she to her room to play her Chinese music and he to his great big red motor bike. When I saw them in the green garden, sometimes they reminded me of a pair of birds, like flamingoes.

I would do what I could around the house. There was a complete staff of servants and there was little left for me but to straighten a cushion or tend the potted plants on the terrace. After a few weeks in such a sunny, luxurious place I began to wonder what on earth I was doing there. I began to lounge about like the others, like some sun-tanned ghost, padding about the marble floors, cool and half-naked, while the silences of the place piled one on top of the other. I would sleep for an hour in the afternoon and then perhaps walk down to the town or the beach. I loved the shops, the Promenade des Anglais, the flowered squares and arcades of the town. The beach was always strewn with people like the dead after a battle. After a while, however, like the sea it became boring, eternally unaltered, lolling in the sun. It was a different kettle of fish to the cold but lively Channel I had always known. One night there was a storm that had been waiting in the mountains. It flew along the Riviera coast, flooding the streets and stirring up the sea. Early in the morning I ran down to see the waves banging on the shingle.

But the storm rode off and the coast was left as before, golden, hot and the same day after day. I sat in the shade of the terrace balcony, giant geraniums planted in pots on the verandah above, trailing down to give me shade. I drank a glass of dry, cold wine and wondered why I was so vacant and unhappy.

The gate of L'Horizon was at the foot of the garden with a long climbing drive up to the house. It had two stone columns, flaking and covered with creeper, topped by a pair of ornamental pineapples. One morning, the sound of a show-off sports car came down the curling road from the hills, barking and braking, and then it choked back as it ran along the road at the other side of the garden wall before swirling into the drive. It was a handsome green Alfa Romeo. It snorted and paused like a horse and then the driver turned it up the drive towards the house. I was sitting idly in the shadows, wearing a light wrap over my swimsuit.

I knew it was Paul, the elder son who was expected that day on leave from the Ecole Militaire in Paris. 'You will hear him making a lot of noise as he comes through the mountains,' Perrington forecast with a sniff. And so it proved.

From my idle shadows I carefully watched him bring the car more sedately up the drive. He was in uniform, round-faced, leaning out like some pilot of the First World War taxi-ing his plane home after a dog fight. Paul was another romancer.

He was a pale, overfed young man – strange for a soldier – who walked about the house for the next few days in white slacks and a white shirt. He looked like a French cricketer. His attitude when he arrived was to be seen in his swagger but the lethargy of that house soon put its hand on him, as it did everyone else, and he became bored and restless. Once or twice I could see him looking at me but he kept his distance until the third day when I was sunbathing beneath my window. Then, as though finally making up his mind, he walked beneath the trees and the trailers and sat in an attitude on a canvas chair next to me. His leg hung across the arm. He was in his whites and he remained immaculate and military in a stagey way. He would have jumped to attention at the least shout.

'Ennui,' he sighed. 'This house should have been named Ennui. It's a place of boredom. Don't you feel bored?'

'Yes,' I said honestly. 'But I'm paid to be here.'

'I could go and sit in a café in the town,' he shrugged. 'I know many people there, you know. I am very popular.'

This raised my eyebrows, but I did not know whether it was boasting or the way he framed his English. 'Why not go and sit at the café then?' I suggested.

'I can't be troubled,' he sighed. 'It's hot and I feel just nothing. It's this house. I don't come here on leave, I die.' His forearms had become brown in the sun and so had his face. In the Military School he worked as an instructor in some kind of army office.

'What about Sirie and Anton?' I said and this brought a thoughtful smile.

'Ah, the secret pair,' he said. 'They are just for themselves. I do not come into their thoughts very much as you can see. And as for my father, well, he is busy with his sorrows.'

'Yes, I know. It is very sad.'

'Yes. She was very white when they pulled her out you know. Giselle, I mean, from the vat.' He sniffed as though smelling the flour again.

'So I believe.'

'It was terrible. Like a dream. In fact I have a dream about her. There is a gigantic cake and Giselle is in the middle of it. It is not very nice.'

'No, it can't be.'

'Is there a chance that you might like to come to my room?' he said quite suddenly but without changing his tone. 'I could show you my birds.'

He did not have the nerve to look at me when he made this proposition but just stared ahead as though he had seen something fascinating at the far end of the lawns. But a small

197

encampment of perspiration had gathered on his forehead, and his lips had become hard and dry.

'You have some birds?' I said. 'I did not know. No one mentioned them.'

'They wouldn't,' he shrugged. 'To my family they are a joke. Will you come and see?'

I could see it was taking every fibre of courage he had, which for a trainee officer was not a lot, to get me to that room. The plump Napoleon-like attitude he struck, where he would stare out like a Field Marshal over-seeing a battle, and his roaring sports car were both fronts for a shy and fearful youth.

'All right Paul,' I said, standing up and putting a beach wrap around my swimsuit. He stared at my bosom as I stood and his eyes went quickly down the length of my body to my thighs. He saw I had caught this and he blushed. 'The birds are very interesting,' he mumbled. 'My grandfather left them to me.'

I was pondering this while we walked into the house and the coolness fell over us. We walked without speaking up the stairs and along the top corridor to his room.

'Who feeds your birds?' I asked. 'When you are away? Nobody has mentioned them to me.'

He smiled strangely. 'There is no need,' he said. 'You will see.'

At that he opened his bedroom door and I stopped in astonishment. From the ceiling was supended a full-sized stuffed swan, wings out-stretched, beak fixed nastily ajar. And all around on shelves and stands were owls and gulls and various birds of prey. A stuffed pelican squatted beside the bed and there were two penguins on each side of the adjoining bathroom door.

'Christ!' I said.

'They used to frighten me,' he shrugged, closing the door behind us. 'But not now of course. When I was a little boy.'

'How amazing,' was all I could say.

'My grandfather,' he sighed. He sat on the bed right alongside the pelican. 'He collected them. He went mad.'

'I don't wonder,' I said staring around. The eyes looking through the feathers stared back from every corner.

Paul looked around morosely. 'He loved birds. He went all over the world to shoot them. But he was rich,' he added. 'Very rich, and when he died he made it a part of his will that I should have these creatures in my room. I was only five. He thought they might amuse me.'

I reached up and gave a touch at the swan's backside feathers. It rocked to and fro above the bed, it's great neck casting a long shadow. 'Nice hobby for a lad,' I said.

'It was terrible,' he said, rolling his eyes at the eyes around the room. 'These monsters. I would lie, just a little boy, in my bed in terror unable to take my eyes away from these bastards. They flapped through my nightmares and when I woke they were still there. Especially this fucker.' He jabbed his finger at the swan's undercarriage, but pulled it away again as if he were afraid to do it some hurt. He smiled wanly at me. 'Can you think what that was like? The fear. Every night?'

He looked at me hollowly, the grown youth once more a little boy surrounded by feathered fear. I felt a surge of pity for him, and my own needs, both sexual and maternal, began welling up within me. I began to unfasten the bra of my swimsuit.

His haunted stare became one of disbelief, his eyes wider than owls'. His boyish mouth fell open and his hands began to make ineffectual movements towards me, away from me, and aimlessly in the air about him. I stood very still, by the bed, while he was rooted six feet away. I took the bra away slowly and smiled while I was doing it. My heavy breasts fell an inch when I took away the support. He was staring at my nipples and I knew they were returning the stare.

He made no movement at all now, but remained solidified, as if he were fearful that anything he did would shatter the moment. I wriggled out of the bottom half of the swimsuit and sat sedately on the bed. 'Come over here,' I invited. 'To me.'

He stumbled forward and fell on his knees in front of me, dropping his head into the cleft of my bosom and making a wet sort of moaning. I pushed him back firmly and unbuttoned his shirt. He scrambled out of the rest of his garments himself as if afraid I might vanish or change my mind. He had a body like a baby white elephant. He was pale and flabby but with an endearing innocence and eagerness. I lay back easily on the bed and invited him to me. He came clumsily to me and lay on top of me with the sigh of a boy who had reached the end of a long sorrowful journey.

I had to restrain him all the time we were making love. He

would have run off like a stampede if I had not held him and coaxed him and whispered that everything was all right, that he had nothing to fear. Afterwards he lay against me weeping quietly.

'I thought that soldiers never cried,' I said tenderly. I was grateful to him too.

'Soldier,' he sniffed sarcastically, 'I'm no soldier. Just a fat clerk instructor in an army office. Until today I wondered if I was even a man. The only women I have known have not been for love. They have been the loose women of Paris. That sort, Nelly. Loose women.'

I was tempted to tell him that his luck had not changed. I patted him sympathetically. 'We cannot always choose our lovers, darling,' I said.

He lay completely still for some time. We cooled together. Then he did the most extraordinary thing. Slowly he levered himself away from me, a look of dawning wonder on his podgy face. When he was upright he threw his arms above him and emited a whoop like a Red Indian.

Jumping from the bed he cried: 'I'm a man! I'm a real man!' and rushing about the room began throwing the owls everywhere.

I lay transfixed as he picked up the stupefied stuffed birds and hurled them across the room. They collided with walls and with each other, heads fell off, eyes rolled out, and there were feathers and frowsty stuffing flying all around.

'I'm free! I'm free!' he howled, capering about. 'Fucking oiseau!' He picked up the pelican from the bedside and hurled it across the room, then he banged the pair of penguins together and threw them likewise. Then the swan. He loved that moment. His swinging arms sent the poor elongated thing see-sawing wildly above the bed. I lay there naked, backing away, hardly able to credit my eyes. The swan swung and then swung again. Then it began to break up like an aeroplane disintegrating in flight. I could almost imagine it squawk a final squawk.

Now the room was raining feathers and foul old stuffing. I removed a few bits of swan from my torso and, replacing my swimsuit, stood up and moved towards the door. Paul was standing, a nightmare figure, pale and naked in the middle of all this mayhem. He stopped and turned as I went. His light of triumph dimmed. Anxiety crammed his face. 'Nell,' he said. 'You leave – do you think I'm crazy?'

'No,' I replied. 'Just getting your own back. I'll go and get a dustpan and brush.'

In the evening, dinner being the only time when the entire family met together, Paul, a new smiling Paul, relaxed and assured, carried the conversation through what was generally an uncomfortable, quiet hour. The father was usually enclosed in his own thoughts and would only emerge to make an apologetic smile around the table and ask some slight question and then return to his own deep world. Sirie and Anton rarely spoke either, although it was never hostile, just enveloping. It seemed impossible for them to find a way out of the silence. We ate like monks.

Paul's transformation livened up the whole table. Everyone talked and smiled. Sirie and Anton exchanged glances and then smiled knowingly at each other, at their brother and at me. It was the best evening I had spent at the house and after a while I began to tell them something of my early life. As I told some of the things that had happened to me, a deep attention fell over the family. I only repeated the adventures that were repeatable but they kept their faces to me and even seemed to hold their breath as I told them about the village and my mother and the German bomb and all the things that followed, as though I was telling them of life in a country of which they had never heard.

No one laughed, even when I told them how we had ambushed Mr Fagence, the terrible man at the Bristol orphanage, before Davie and I ran away, or even when I described how the little boat had sunk below us in the river. I must have gone on with the story for a long time because the night wind began to come in through the french windows and stir about the room. Never before had I told the whole length of my adventure (when I described the shipwreck and the floating coffin, the girl's eyes widened like lamps in the dimming room) and I became very interested with it myself, as though seeing it from a distance for the first time.

When I had done, it had become dim in the room and both Sirie and Anton had tears running down their young cheeks. I began to feel quite pleased with myself.

When the evening was finished Mr Sheridan kissed me on the cheek and so did the two children (I think of them or did then, as children because of their simplicity and sombreness). Paul and I sat in the subdued evening on the terrace and drank pastis, the drink from Marseilles. I had never tasted it before and even now I can sense vividly the peppermint feel of it and the taste of the night air. Paul was attentive and hardly able to take his eyes from me. When we had finished our drinks we walked out to the front of the house to look over the dropping land to the brilliant lights of Nice and the glowing sea, to the moving headlights of the cars on the Corniche, and an aeroplane coming into land at the airport by the shore.

The romantic sights and sensations of the night were all around us, engulfing us and stretching far out to the horizon. We closed against each other and kissed with deep passion.

I took my arms from around him, rested my thick hair against his cheekbone, and reaching down undid his fly. It was a zip, only then coming into fashion, but so much easier than the fumbling buttons of old. They played havoc with a girl's fingernails. I felt his whole frame come to attention as I fumbled into the cave at the front of his trousers.

We went a few paces from the terrace, away from the diffuse lights of the house. The hard dry grass led in a slope down to an arbour where there was a large hammock, lying like a docked boat. We sat on that, romantically, like some couple from a chocolate box or a birthday card. Then we eased ourselves back on the hammock and it creaked as if we had woken it up. It was amazing but within hours he had become a different man. He even looked different, firmer, stronger, the face more masculine, the eyes definite. He kissed me with passion and I returned the kiss. It was time for confessions.

'There is something I must tell you, Nell,' he said thoughtfully. 'It has been with me for what seems like a long time. I must tell someone of it. It is about Giselle.'

Giselle again. Self-raising from the flour. 'Yes, Paul,' I said. 'What about her?'

'She did not fall into the flour hopper. I pushed her.'

I must have become very good at surprises, having had a lot of practice, for I did not stiffen or make a sound. Instead I made myself relax even more against him. 'Did you hear me, Nelly? I pushed her.'

'That's what I thought you said,' I replied. 'Why did you do it?'

He held on to me. 'She was a monster,' he whispered. 'An evil spirit. She made us all cry in our different ways. The children hated her. My father she treated like an animal. And then she came to me one night, in the room with the birds, and she seduced me and tormented me, my own stepmother. Then she humiliated me so long and in so many evil ways that I could stand it no longer. We were all standing together looking at the mill and the flour swirled around and I gave her a little push. There was only a short rail and over she went. She was drowned in the flour. I am a murderer, Nelly.'

Thinking of it now I am astonished at my own calmness. My youth had taught me much. I turned his face to me. He was crying. I kissed the wet cheeks and then the mouth and felt for him below. 'It does not matter, Paul,' I murmured. 'I won't tell.'

thirteen

When Paul had returned to Paris I was left with his guilty secret and my own loneliness. I did not love him but we had helped each other and I missed our hours together. Now around the house and in the town I felt as tight as a bomb. The weather became hotter, a haze shimmering through the mountains and the sun glaring along the coast. One afternoon, sitting in the shade of the garden, I saw Anton come in on his big, red motor cycle, and I began to study him carefully.

In all my life I had never set out to seduce any man or boy. It was always they that came towards me. Lying there with a lime juice in the shade of the hanging geraniums and the bougainvillaea, I thought about the possibilities of Anton, but curiously, at a loss as to how to go about it.

He walked up the lawn towards me, such a handsome boy, his red shirt open almost to the waist, his crash hat held below his arm like the helmet of a knight. He smiled from about fifteen yards away and said: 'Beautiful.' But I could not tell whether he meant me, Nell Luscombe, the day, the scenery or his roaring ride in the hills.

'I could hear you, Anton,' I smiled. 'I could hear you riding around in the mountains.'

'From this place?' he said. He seemed genuinely surprised and pleased. 'I was so far away for most of the time.'

'I know,' I nodded, sipping the lime. 'But the echoes came through the valleys and I could hear the roaring from here. I knew it was you Anton. Nobody rides a motor cycle like you.'

It was a bit of bare-faced flattery to a mere boy, but he smiled as though he was wise enough to detect it. He walked the two or three paces left towards me, and said: 'You will be missing my brother Paul, Nellee.' Then he leaned forward, very calmly, and kissed me on the cheek. His lips were dry and young. I felt a shock of real delight go through me. But before I could look into his eyes he had straightened up and sauntered off towards the house. The sound of Chinese music was coming from Sirie's window.

Now, Nell Luscombe, I said to myself. You are a young woman, and a woman who has felt a good many beds on her bottom. Anton is sixteen and although he is a grown lad (and how beautifully he has grown!) it would be very wrong of you to take advantage of his youth and inexperience, even though the weather is so hot and you are so tight and horny, and the boy walks about so enticingly and sleeps his boy's sleep only yards from your door. There is no excuse. It is taking advantage of the young and it must be resisted. If at all possible.

I lay in my bed that night, the dark hours seeming even hotter than those of the day. I was naked with the crumpled top sheet drawn up between my legs. There were sounds coming from across the garden, creatures, and the midnight noises of Nice mumbling up to the open windows. My breasts were hard as marble and faintly luminous. From my pillow, I only had to squint down to see their outlines like the roofs of some eastern temple with the nipples like oriental points. A bead of sweat wriggled down my stomach, my thighs and my private valley felt heated and damp, my very skin seemed to throb. All I could think of was that boy lying, doubtless cool and sleeping, along the corridor. Restlessly I rose from the bed and went naked to the window. Why was I like this? Why could some women be born and live as wives or farm maids or office workers or assistants in a shop, like my own satisfied sister. Why could they go so calmly through their lives, unashamed, untormented, content? Why was it that I, a simple West Country girl should want so many desirable, undesirable things? I looked up at the stars that night, my stomach throbbing, my face damp, and wondered why God allowed such emotions. But the sky (or God if that is his face) just looked blankly back at me. It was no help. After calling on conscience, logic, religion, morality and all the others, I could only come to the conclusion that I was born randy.

Even the garden seemed ill-at-ease. I stepped on to the confined balcony outside my window and, as though I had trodden on a secret switch, a light came on and glowed behind the lace curtains of the window opposite, across the narrow paved courtyard. Anton's window.

I stiffened with excitement, standing naked as a statue but in the shadow. My blood began to rumble in my veins. There was a movement behind the curtains. I had my hands against the back of a small cane chair on the balcony and they felt wet. Dark air pressed against me.

Then, oh God I still thrill as I remember it now all these years later, the pale curtains of his room moved and Anton, naked as I was stepped out on to the little balcony. Then the curtain moved again – and the lovely young Sirie, nude and slender, came out and stood beside him. What a moment! I remained and looked across at them and they looked at me. No words were said. I could have screamed. These things never happen in cold countries.

The two children, and it is impossible for me to think of them otherwise, stood like junior gods, slightly apart from each other. I could see the deep hair on his loins, and her little breasts like two dark eyes. Their hands moved across the space between them and joined. But neither their faces nor their bodies moved. The train of sweat trickled down my leg. 'Bit on the warm side tonight,' I called.

There was no reply (really I suppose it would be difficult to make one to an observation like that) and we continued to stand and gaze across at each other. A car went by beyond the garden wall on its way over the mountains. The top circle of its headlights curled over the wall. 'Please,' called Anton softly. 'You must visit us.'

'When?' I whispered nervously.

'This moment,' said Sirie. I thought I saw the shade of her smile.

'I will,' I said. 'I'll come now.'

I could hardly keep my fingers still as I pulled on my robe. I folded the silk around me, feeling it slide and roll against my skin. Quickly, and wondering why, I arranged my hair, opened the door and went like a ghost in a hurry along the shadows of the corridor. I tapped, merely touched Anton's door and pushed it open. All the doors in that house opened easily. I stepped in.

What can I say about the scene that met me when I entered that room? It was amazing, astounding. It was dim and sound-less, the only movement being the fidgeting of the lace curtain at the window. But at the far end, lit up like a religious scene, was a bed with an oval back and sitting up in that, meekly and beautifully, were the boy and the girl, Sirie and Anton.

They were both unclothed to the waist the sheet negligently lying over their thighs. The boy, manly and serious with a tuft of hair in the middle of his brown chest, his expression sober. The girl, slender as a deer, with the amber light lying sweetly over her slim torso and the dozy little breasts. She had that silent, puzzling smile as if she knew everything in the world but was not inclined to tell. Around each neck was a plain gold chain. They were side by side in bed, their shoulders touching. 'What an interesting bed,' I said throatily as I walked towards them.

They had been sleeping together ever since early childhood. When they were seven, they said, they were separated but on the first night Sirie got up from her bed and went immediately back to her brother. At ten they were told sternly that they must keep to their separate rooms, but they disobeyed and returned to the familiar reassurance of each other's bodies as soon as they could. When their father, who knew nothing of all this – or if he did he had taken no heed – married Giselle they had kept to their own rooms, but crept in to each other for an hour or two's company in the early hours. When she had died they had gone back to sleeping with each other again.

This was all explained in the most amusing and matter-of-fact way while I sat on their bed, like some aunt, and they sat upright projecting from the sheet, the damp light on their lovely bodies. My passion had, strangely, cooled, as if it were ashamed of its ambitions, and I was watching them and listening to them quite happily and with a new and pleasant innocence.

'Nellee,' pleaded Sirie. 'Tell us some more about your life's adventures.'

'Now?' I said.

'Ah, there is no better time. It is too hot to sleep,' said Sirie. 'And we love to hear people tell us stories, don't we Anton?'

'Yes we like that. You don't have to tell us the truth all the time. We do not mind if you make things from your imagination.'

'I'll tell you the truth,' I said. 'There is plenty of truth.'

Then, while those two naked beauties sat attentive as children, I told them of the days when I met the Commander and of the dirty lord who had put his hands up my dress when I was a servant at his breakfast table, and how I had taken revenge with the mousetrap. And the poor idiot son with his bean flicker.

At this they both broke into ripples of laughter and spontaneously leaned forward to kiss me. My hands went out to them and in leaning I touched his hard young chest and her small velvet breast.

When I had finished Anton said formally: 'We have something to tell you.'

'A secret,' confirmed Sirie.

'We have told no one but we must tell you,' he added. 'We have been waiting until Paul left us.' They glanced at each other as though uncertain who should speak. The girl nodded briefly at the boy and it was he who spoke.

'Nellee,' he said. 'You know that our stepmother Giselle is dead because she fell into the container of flour that goes round and around at the mill?'

I nodded dumbly. They knew about Paul then. 'She did not fall. She was pushed into the flour,' continued Anton.

'And *we* pushed her,' said Sirie smugly.

I felt my brain swim. 'You?' was all I could say. 'But Paul ...'

'Hah! Paul told you it was him,' nodded Anton. 'I thought he would. It was not. He lies to protect us. We pushed her, Anton and Sirie.'

'But . . .'

'Because,' put in Sirie, 'she came into this, our room one night and came upon us like this together. She was very angry and said she would tell our father and we begged her not to. So she said she would punish us herself and she returned here the next night and used her golden hairbrush on our derrières, how do you say it?'

'Our arses,' put in Anton.

'Yes arses,' said Sirie.

Anton said. 'She made us ashamed and angry. And it hurt also. So the next day when we visited the mill we gave her a touch of our hands and, *voilà*! Into the flour she went.'

There was not a lot I could say. 'Of course I will not tell,' I promised. 'But Paul . . .'

'What he told you is not true,' said Anton firmly. 'He says it to make-believe he is romantic and tragic and, he believes, I suppose, to protect us. But we are safe. Nobody knows.'

Sirie smiled. 'When you have pushed your stepmother into a million kilos of flour,' she said logically, 'then it is something truly different is it not? It is no pleasure if you do not tell someone!'

They sat smiling, almost laughing at my expression. I was still sitting on the bed, and with that same spontaneous movement they so often showed, they turned back the sheet, moved a foot or so further apart and invited me into the middle.

It was all so logical, so amazingly innocent. I did not know how to respond. I glanced at each face and they were smiling confidently. So I climbed in, like a visiting cousin in a crowded house, and all three of us slid down naked beneath the sheet and slept.

It was still warm and dark when I felt the boy move against me. With an easy fish-like roll, he turned on me and with never a touch of exploration pushed his slim penis into me. The girl was snuggled into my other side, her breasts against my ribs, her mouth against my breast, and deeply asleep. Anton whispered as I woke and realized what he was about, 'Tomorrow I will take you on my motor cycle in the hills.'

*

Since my arrival at L'Horizon, Mr Sheridan had spent all those hours closed off in that room of his and I could not help but wonder during my listless days what he did or what he thought about in there. Then one morning he told me.

He was standing waiting, it seemed, in the corridor as I came in from the hard sun outside. 'It's you, Nell Luscombe,' he said, holding my hands.

'What is, Mr Sheridan?' I asked. He was staring at me, shaking his head, and coming into the gloom from the bright light I could not see him properly. 'It was you all the time.'

'Me, Mr Sheridan?' I continued. Had he found out about Siric and Anton? Because of the light I was unsure whether it was a smile or a grimace coming towards me. It was a smile.

'Dante,' he said. 'Please call me Dante.'

'Yes of course, Dante.' That was encouraging anyway. 'What was me all the time, Dante?'

He took me by the arm and we walked into the cool house together. It seemed like a cave after the brassy sunshine outside. In the next few minutes he said more words to me than he had done in the whole time since our first interview in London. 'Come, Nell,' he smiled. 'I will show you my room.'

Another room! In this house there were always surprises in rooms. I walked with him, his hand still holding mine, wondering what I was to see this time. It turned out to be, for once, unremarkable. A solitary sort of room, a trifle stuffy, with a bedroom and bathroom adjoining it, with books and papers everywhere. The sort of room where a man spent a great deal of time alone.

The one remarkable piece of furniture was an enormous red velvet chair, high backed and wide-seated. 'That,' said Dante, seeing me looking at it, 'I call my thinking chair. I have been using it a great deal lately, Nell.'

He approached me familiarly, as though he had suddenly remembered why he had brought me to France in the first place. He was an attractive man, I suppose, with a good figure and the spreading of grey around the ears and temple which to so many young women brings unmentionable memories of their fathers. In my case, of course, it did not.

'For weeks, Nell,' he said, his hands on my elbows, 'I have been sitting here thinking of *someone*. Thinking, thinking. Making hopeless pictures of her. Never quite making them fit.

I thought it was Giselle I was day-dreaming about. I imagined her walking in English fields, along the beach in Rousillon, down a street in San Francisco. The backgrounds were all authentic. They fitted perfectly. But somehow the figure, the woman was wrong. And there was no face. I wondered where on earth the face had gone. Then, only last night I fitted another face to it. It was your face, Nell.'

I felt a flood of pity for him. Fitting faces to dreams here in this empty room. 'I'm glad you found me,' I said simply, as though I had been waiting for him all the time.

'May I kiss you?' he inquired seriously.

No one had ever asked me before. Quite often they expected a great deal more without asking. I was amazed and impressed at the politeness.

'Of course you can,' I laughed. 'I'm here.'

And he kissed me and as I returned that kiss, a whole nightmare began flashing in front of my imagination. I knew then the question he would ask. He would ask me to marry him. How could I marry a man when I had already been intimate with his sons? How?

'Nell, let's sit in my chair,' he suggested. 'Will you?' I smiled and he sat in the huge red 'thinking chair', patted his knees and I sat on his lap. I felt enjoyable. Like a girl with a good father. 'You are a lovely young woman, Nell,' he said eventually. 'I am much older, but I have wealth and I can make you very comfortable and I would try to make you happy. If you will marry me?'

I put my fears aside quickly and decisively. 'Oh yes, Mr Sheridan . . . Dante,' I said. 'Please.'

You can hardly hesitate about an offer of that type, not when you've spent years as a sexual gipsy. Racing through my mind was the thought that somehow I would have to come to some arrangement with Sirie and Anton and, of course, Paul, but I felt sure they would understand. And there was the matter of Giselle and what I knew of her fate in the flour hopper.

He kissed me again, very lightly and decently, and we walked the length of the long, manly room to the bright window over the garden. Sirie was sitting in her usual ghostly way under the shade. She ruffled through the pages of a magazine but never paused to read anything or even look at a picture.

'Sirie is very bored, I'm afraid,' said Dante, putting his arm about my waist. Despite the weather he was wearing a jacket of some light, rough material and I liked the comforting touch of it around my bare midriff. 'They are strange children but I hope one day you will have something in common with them.'

'I'm sure I will,' I mumbled.

'I will not ask you to be a mother to them,' he said. 'That is asking too much. And as for Paul . . .' He paused in a worried way as if he had suddenly thought about something concerning Paul. 'Well . . . he is not even younger than you,' he laughed quietly. 'He will not be able to call you "Mummy", will he!' I swallowed and joined the tail end of the laugh. Difficulties were already beginning to pile like hills on my horizon.

But immediately he reassured me. 'Sirie and Anton will be returning to Paris in a few weeks,' he said. 'I have arranged for them to start some new studies there. It is difficult to imagine what they will do for a living. Anton could be a motor bike mechanic I suppose, and Sirie would make a wonderful mistress for a rich man.' He made a noise of annoyance and I turned to see him blushing. 'What a thing for a father to say,' he tutted. 'What a thing.'

I was profoundly relieved to know that the two young people would not be in the house continuously. 'Dante,' I said. 'You are very sure aren't you? About marrying. It was *my* face you saw in your thoughts?'

He put his greying head against my cheek, very tiredly. 'It *was* you,' he said. 'You were very clear. And . . . Nell . . . I think there is something you should know about Giselle.'

'Oh no,' I thought. 'Not again.' I looked at him, trying to appear unknowing. 'What is that?' I asked.

'I pushed her into the hopper of flour at the mill,' he said simply. 'I loved her very much but she had hurt me so much that I took the opportunity to give her a nudge. The children were there, also Paul, but there were so many people on the gallery looking down that nobody saw me do it. She has been haunting me of course, but I can conquer her. I feel it is something I have to tell you. You are marrying a man who has done his wife in.' I pulled back, but not forcefully, from his arm and regarded him with amazement.

'You killed Giselle?' I whispered. '*You* did it?'

'Yes. Does it worry you?'

By this time it was not so much worrying as intriguing. Why

should they all want the credit for pushing her in the flour?

'I loved her overwhelmingly,' he said hopelessly. 'But she taunted me and tortured me, and the night before she even boasted that she had committed adultery with Paul, my own son. It was a lie, of course. A fabrication to injure me. I could not allow that sort of thing to be said. So I gave her a jog. When they managed to get her out she looked very unpleasant. All white.'

'So I believe,' I answered stupidly, adding: 'Perrington told me.'

'Ah, Perrington,' he nodded. 'Not always the silent chauffeur he appears to be.'

'Servants generally aren't,' I said, slipping very easily into the voice of the lady-of-the-house.

'A good chap,' he said, now apparently having completely disposed of his confession concerning Giselle. 'But sometimes strange. Do you know Nell, I discovered quite by chance that he goes on a sort of rampage in the dens of vice in Paris? He does it regularly, making out he's some kind of religious fanatic, trying to save everybody from sin.'

'No!' I managed to exclaim. 'Not our Perrington!'

'Our Perrington,' he said, accepting that I now owned Perrington too. 'It's apparently the way he gets his thrills. It's become so regular that half the erotic cabarets in Paris have come to know him, welcome him almost. People follow him from one cabaret to another, he is regarded as part of the entertainment.'

I sighed. 'Well as long as he doesn't start that sort of thing in Nice.'

'Indeed, you're right, darling,' he agreed like a husband. 'He's a good chauffeur, and it's quite fun really, I suppose, to have a *tiny* bit of secret scandal in the house. It stops life becoming dull!'

It would be difficult to imagine two weddings further apart in style than my first and my second. Once more, of course, I married in white, but this time I knew the groom would not spend our first night painting the walls of the reception hall. In the event he spent it searching for the bride.

The ceremony at the large church of St Phillipe in Monte Carlo and the reception at the Hôtel de Paris were very costly, lavish and lovely, with hundreds of guests. For a family that kept so much to themselves, the Sheridans seemed to know an enormous number of people, who came in their cars and their finery.

In the church the atmosphere was thick and holy with incense clouding everywhere. Not wishing to be disqualified on a technicality, I had assured Dante that I was a Roman Catholic. The priest towered over us like some archangel. When the organ sounded and the choir sang it was so beautiful I would not have been surprised if my groom and I had started to rise to the ceiling.

And for this girl, who had been pulled by fishermen and wrecked by sailors, walking down the aisle, radiant in the reflections of the stained glass windows, through a large, rich congregation, to the arm of my distinguished husband, it was a triumph.

My conversion to Roman Catholicism being so sudden it left some gaps in my knowledge as to what was going on in the church, but I joined in and chanted the tunes bravely with the rest, although the words I sang were 'Tom Peace, Tom Pearce, lend me your grey mare.'

Incense drifted up my nose and the rosy light shone upon me. In the front pew, with all the family guests, sat the angelic pair, Sirie and Anton, and the upright and uniformed Paul, singing soberly and all three kissing me with perfect propriety after the ceremony.

There were three hundred guests at the reception, and sitting proudly next to Dante, my husband, a champagne glass hinged on my lip, and surveying the array of bobbing heads and the servants carving through the crowds, it came to me that the cost of this extravagant day was probably more than the cost of my entire previous life all put together.

But I was in no mood to think nostalgically of poorer days, although when a group of singers took the stage in front of the orchestra and sang French part-songs in harmony, my mind did return for a moment to that first wedding reception of mine, when Wild Mickey and some poor George's painting pals sang 'Drink To Me Only'. It was a different world.

Then, as has been usual throughout this eventful existence of mine, something happened. Among the guests I had noticed, I could not help but notice, a funny little fellow with ill-fitting morning dress, moving in and out of the various tables. He looked like a street violinist, bald, small, saggy. Or a pick-pocket, for he had a furtive way about him. I found my eye attracted towards him every time he appeared in view. He seemed to be alone, to know no one, but to be cruising around on some errand, a glass of champagne moving just in front of his nose. There was something ominously familiar about that stoop, about that walk.

Then, when the chanson group – two ladies in long white dresses and two men in brown tailed suits – were singing in fine French style, the little soiled man suddenly mounted the dais at their side. Then, relieved, I thought that he must be a musician or a vocalist perhaps, or a comedian. But the singers were at once upset by his presence, like a clutch of hens joined by a fox. They fidgeted and moved over, trying to keep their harmony and distance. Some guests began to snigger and then some to laugh outright and a cold, cold hand from years ago crept across my heart. The clown in the baggy trousers suddenly darted to the front of the singers, scattering them, and, throwing his arms wide, burst like a hideous off-key bird into: 'There's an old Mill by the Stream, Nellie Dean.'

'Oh God,' I thought. 'My fucking father!'

At the awful moment of realization, three bystanders approached and carried him still upright but bodily away from the dais and out of the room, his baggy legs running protestingly in mid-air as he went.

Over the heads of the amused people I could hear the cackling Devon voice shouting: 'She be *my* girl! My lovely daughter. Nell ... ie!' I seemed to smell the cider reeking across the room, a memory that made me catch my breath, and for a strange moment saw my little home in Upcoombe and my childhood.

'Dante,' I whispered to my husband, 'I must just leave you for a moment dear. I'll be back very shortly.' He smiled his gentlemanly smile and I kissed his cheek. I got up for the moment, aware of my trembling, and the puzzled guests parted to let me through. I saw nothing but blurred faces. I ran the last three yards out of the door and saw my father still held by the three men who were discussing what to do with him. Only one was needed to restrain him. The man had pinned him against the wall with one hand held on his chest, like a specimen moth. My father's face was yellow, his eyes bulged, his mouth dribbled.

'Please, please,' I asked, going towards them. 'Let him free. I ... I know him.' The man who held him let go obediently and my father dropped from the wall to the floor. His terrible iodine face turned to me and smiled, not with those jagged teeth of old but with a frightening set of dentures that somehow seemed bigger than his mouth. 'Nelly my little maid,' he howled, staggering towards me.

For a moment I stood transfixed, helpless. Then (how could a daughter not?) I stumbled towards him and cried as I embraced his skeleton body.

'Oh Nelly,' he blubbed convincingly, 'I've been looking everywhere for you, my darling girl.'

'Dad,' I trembled. 'Dad ...' I was crying now, wiping my eyes with the lace sleeve of my bridal dress. 'I've been and got married today.'

'I can bloody see that,' he said, immediately sour. 'And you didn't ask your old dad to give you away or even to come and have a drink with you.'

Something got caught in my throat and I felt my face redden. 'How could I?' I sobbed angrily. 'When you buggered off all those years ago? I haven't set eyes on you since!'

'Don't you shout at me my girl,' he snarled. 'You'm still my daughter!'

People began to look out of the main room and those passing in the foyer stopped to stare. The three men who had removed my father from the dais hovered around, obviously eager to remove him still further. Something had to be done, the bride at a society wedding could hardly be seen brawling with a derelict man.

My father, on to my indecision like a ferret, caught my hand: 'Come on outside a minute Nell. Then I'll go away. God's honour.'

Knowing him, I should have learned. But, just to save the embarrassment of that moment, and with only a quick guilty look about me, I followed him out of the door. Blood is thicker than champagne.

Innocent, bewildered, I followed him out to the steps of the hotel. 'I've got a car,' he said urgently, pulling me. 'Come on Nelly.'

A car! My senses were so fuddled I allowed myself to be dragged down the steps and a moment later the door of a big car at the kerb opened and I was flung into the back between two Negroes. My father, squeaking with triumph, jumped in beside the driver and we shot off at such a rate that I was thrown back between the black men. Stiff with terror, my white wedding dress up around my waist, I was fixed there, trying to scream but making no sound.

Eventually that stoatish face turned from the front seat and the layers of teeth smiled in the gloom. 'I read in the papers at home about you, Nell. "Society Wedding of Orphan Girl!" it said. Read it with my own eyes. And bloody offended I was, as you can believe. After all you *do* have a father. So I decided to come here to see you on your happy day.'

'Where are we going?' I managed to demand. If the Negroes had not been holding hands across my front, I would have scratched his face. 'You'll be in prison for this! My husband . . .'

'Now stop it my girl,' he threatened. 'Just remember who it is you'm speaking to.' This piece of effrontery left me speechless. 'I came down here specially,' he said. 'Foreign parts. But I seem to have got into bad company, Nelly. I owe a lot of money for cards, and I told these gents that you'll be able to pay. You will won't you Nell? For your old dad?'

I don't suppose another woman in the entire world has ever spent another night like that. Not only was my distracted husband without me – and had the Riviera police and even the small Monte Carlo Army searching the towns and villages of the coast – but I danced on a table, clad only in my white bridal stockings and a suspender belt and I slept with a large hairy Corsican. Some women, I suppose, are simply born bad.

Certainly they had to give me some wild, doped, drink to make me do all the things I did, but I cannot help feeling that a *decent* woman would never have performed like that whatever she had been forced to take.

Inside some of us seems to be a casket of wickedness and it only needs to be unlocked for our lowest natures to take over. Looking back over the years of sin and regret I can only console myself with the thought that I am what I am. A trollop. My father and the other men took me to a sort of thieves' kitchen, a room behind a bar in the narrow hill streets of Nice. It was crowded with louts and whores and they were obviously waiting for me because as I staggered through the door, encouraged by a sharp push from my father, and stood there in my wedding gown in the thick smoke, a huge approving roar went up from the bottle-crammed tables. What a sight I must have looked, crumpled white lace, and my flowered head-dress hung over my ear. I stood looking down on the riff-raff, furious but fearful. 'I'd like you to meet my friends,' my father said with his terrible smile.

What they gave me to drink I can only guess. At first I would not touch it, but a whole gang of them, not roughly, quite goodnaturedly in fact, poured some down my throat and it was easy for them after that.

I don't know how much the sneaky bastard had lost at cards (the suggestion that he should repay his debt with me had been made by him and planned after the people who ran this den had studied my picture in *Nice Matin*), but whatever it was I more than repaid the score that night.

There is not much of it I can remember, which is as well, but according to appreciative eye-witnesses, I was completely at home and entered into the spirit of the foul den and its low customers. The second and third drinks of whatever potion they were giving me did not seem so difficult to accept as the first and then I vaguely recall Spanish music twanging from somewhere and me mounting the large central table in my long lovely wedding dress. It was the most spectacular strip-tease ever seen even in those parts, if only for the fact that everyone knew the costume was authentic. Off came my head flowers, off came the lace dress, off came the silk underclothes I had chosen so carefully for the delight of my husband, and eventually I danced brazenly in my satin shoes, my white stockings and my suspender belt, and – God damn me – the veil I had worn so religiously in the church only hours before.

Like a nightmare I can still see the beaming criminal faces all about the edge of the table, the boards of the table itself, stretching out like a stage before me, the bouncing of my own bosom right under my nose, and I can still hear the rhythmic clapping, the randy shouts and my father's piping Devon voice over it all. 'That's my Nelly! You show them Nell! You show them!'

If I did nothing else I certainly *showed* them. To such an effect, apparently, that hot men were offering my father a fortune for the pleasure of the night with me. He was conducting this degrading auction while I was still banging the table with my heels (one of which I broke I recall, delicate shoes not being meant for Flamenco dancing). The owners of the place apparently moved in, however, and took the matter out of my father's hand and paid him a percentage from the highest bidder, the large and hairy Corsican. All this I heard next day from one of the whores who came by to see if I had survived – the Corsican apparently being a hard man to satisfy. She was weary but very pleased and said that my efforts had substantially increased her own earnings and those of her friends. My father, apparently, had gone off with his percentage, leaving his love for me and the promise that we would meet again some day. If he were in a condemned cell, I vowed to myself, then I would go. Gladly.

I was in a cubicle bedroom. I had a vague memory that the Corsican had kept colliding with the confined walls. I sat on the edge of the bed sore, sad, helpless, bedraggled, on what should have been the first wonderful morning of my life with Dante Sheridan, whom I had promised to cherish and love and be faithful to only the previous morning. I was naked. My poor stockings and the pretty belt were hanging over a light bracket just outside the door. I saw them as soon as I looked into the desolate room. Tables and chairs were thrown and scattered all over the place and an old woman was beginning to mop the floor. As I watched she picked up something from beneath a table, examined it disdainfully and threw it away. It landed on a pile of bottles in the corner. It was my expensive and beautiful wedding gown. There was a towel in my cubicle – it was the sort of place that short-time prostitutes use – and I wrapped it as best I could about my body, and, weeping now, I stumbled across the room to where she had thrown my dress. I picked it up. It had more holes in it than any lace dress ever had. It was splashed with wine and smeared with dirt. But it was all I had. With the mopping-up lady watching intently, I put it on, feeling the sad shame of what I had done, wishing my father dead and me dead also, but less painfully.

Head down, I walked out of the wretched place, not knowing where I was going. I could never go back to L'Horizon now, I would not let Dante suffer for what I was like. For what my family was like. I would have to go out again on my poor travels. I could never go home.

As it happened I did not have to travel far. I walked through the blank, sunless alleys, until I reached a small square. There was a café and I sat, huddled at a table, my dress hanging down like a soiled rag. The waiter arrived and with that blankness cultivated by all waiters in that part of the world, he took my order for coffee without a lift of the eyebrow at my wretched condition. I had no money. But it did not matter. Just as I was about to drink it I felt a hand on my shoulder and an English voice said: 'Make it another coffee, will you?'

Slowly I looked up and there, smooth and suave and handsome in the Riviera morning sun, was my Davie. My Davie from long, long ago.

fourteen

Davie had lived in Marseilles and at other places along the coast while he pursued his career of burglar, bank robber and general thief. Those years before, when we were on our childish journey through the West Country after running from the institution at Bristol, I had often watched him and thought to myself that he was bound to be an exceptional person when he grew up. I remember, on those nights when we were little fugitives, when we were resting in some place, how I would ask him what he wanted to be when he was a man and he would sit and seriously consider it with his confident attitude, giving the impression that he would be offered all the most wonderful positions in the world and would merely have to thumb through them and take his pick.

'Nell,' he used to say then, ''tis a difficult thing to make up my mind. I reckon all the places in the world have been discovered now so I don't see any use in me being a navigator. There's acting I suppose, on the films. Or I could be a famous sportsman.'

'I didn't know you could play sport, Davie,' I had said.

'Oh I could learn,' he replied. 'Any sport.'

'Or I could be a boss,' he went on. 'Like of factories, and have cars and cigars. I'd be a doctor, one of those surgeons with the masks on, but I can't abide blood, Nell. Can't abide it.'

As it turned out he did wear a mask in his work, even if it were in a bank rather than an operating theatre. He had made his first bank raid before I met him again in Monte Carlo. It was in Antibes, and according to his own account had been executed with great audacity and cleverness, but with no luck. The haul only amounted to about two hundred francs, due to some incompetence by the cashier who handed it across. But as an artistic operation, he said, it was perfection.

'I realized Nell,' he said gravely when we were driving high above the sea on that first day we met again, 'it came to me like a flash from heaven, that there's no room for people like me in the world, the ordinary, legal world. It's all fixed against you. It doesn't matter how clever you are, there's your place – down there at the bottom – and that's where you have to be, so that's it. So I reckoned I would put my talents where they would make the most for me.'

I nodded. The breakneck rocky road soared above the patterns of the sea and rose up towards the silk blue sky. I was still in my torn and defaced wedding dress, but now the sun warmed me. I wondered how my husband Dante was getting on without me. I felt sad for him, but I looked at the grown-up profile of Davie, my childhood hero, sitting beside me and squeezed his arm because I knew now that it was him I had loved all these years. Even though I had almost forgotten him.

'I think you're right, Davie,' I agreed. 'You could have done anything, you could.'

'Anything,' he agreed grimly. 'Anything.'

His voice now was a strange muddle of Devon, London and Marseilles French. He had been on the Mediterranean for two years, working for various small gangs to gain experience, he said, before branching out on his own. He told me he had been very successful and had stolen a lot of money, art treasures and other good things.

'Somebody in my position can't trust *anybody*, Nell,' he said, making the car screech. It was a rugged Renault, not very new but chosen for it's anonymity, he explained. 'When I've got to know you better again, then I'll tell you some of my secrets.'

His apartment just off the port quarter in Marseilles was suitably impressive, good light rooms and a view over the docked shipping and the quays, but far enough away not to have the hot, dusty noises that blew from there every day of the summer. The only thing amiss with it was that it seemed a shade feminine, the décor and the oddments and especially the main bedroom which had lace and chintz and smelled of perfume. In one closet I found a whole rack of women's clothes.

'Well,' explained Davie carefully. 'I don't really *own* it, see, I'm renting it from a lady.'

'But she's left all her clothes and things,' I laughed uncertainly.

'Yes, well, as a matter of fact, she's away where she doesn't need all these things at the moment and she asked me if I'd mind keeping them.'

I went to the wardrobe and ran my fingers along the materials. They slid over my fingertips like water ripples. 'These are very nice,' I said. 'Very expensive. She must be rich.'

'Yes,' he nodded. 'Very rich.'

'Listen Davie,' I laughed. 'Don't be embarrassed, darling. I haven't seen you for years, why feel embarrassed about living with a woman here? I could hardly expect you to wait for me. I didn't wait for you. My God, I got married only yesterday.' Then I added anxiously, 'Perhaps you shouldn't have brought me here. Will she be back soon?'

'Not for five years,' he said, sitting on the bed and doggedly lighting a cigarette. 'She's in prison.'

'Oh dear, what happened?'

'She got herself caught,' he answered.

'Oh. So she let you have the flat while she's in there.'

I could see the old, small slice of shiftiness in his face. It was amazing to recognize it again after all these years.

'Well, if you really want to know, Nell,' he said. 'She doesn't actually *know* I'm living here. I just sort of moved in when she got put away. I had a key. But I reckoned she owed me a few favours. I mean, I set her up in the area. She had to clear out of Paris. So I'm keeping the place aired now, see?'

I could not help but laugh at him. Here was the half-apologetic half-defiant Davie I had just glimpsed in childhood. I moved towards him because he looked so juvenile in his sulk and touched him intimately for the first time in years. We had

221

kissed outside the café, where he had found me, but apart from my hand resting on his knee during the drive, there had been no contact between us.

'Are you alone now, Davie?' I asked slightly mocking. 'Don't nobody want you?'

For a moment I was afraid he was going to reincarnate one of his sudden childish outbursts of temper. It was still there, rotten within him. But he stemmed it and smiled cagily. 'I'm never alone Nell,' he said. 'Never. I've got thousands who know me down here, contacts, friends. That's how I knew where to find you. Eyes and ears everywhere. It's in the newspapers you know.' He sounded a trifle jealous then. 'Pictures, everything. Beautiful bride abducted and all that stuff. A photo of your husband crying into his hands. Very sad and touching I must say. He's got a lot of money hasn't he?'

'He's a good, nice man,' I said, looking straight at him.

'Why are you here then?' he asked craftily.

'Because I'm not sure I'm a good nice woman,' I replied still stiffly. 'I can't go back now. I don't belong with him.'

'And you think you belong with me?'

'I might. I started off with you. Where's the newspapers with my picture?'

'There's none here,' he said. 'You can see some later.' Then, after a wait: 'Do you want to do it again?' In a way I thought it was more like an inquiry.

'Again?' I laughed. 'Remember the last time Davie? Us two? In that warehouse, the night the war was over.'

'Oh ... oh yes, I remember,' he said as if he had only just been able to. 'Only kids we were then.'

'Oh Davie.' I was smiling when I moved towards him but by the time I had reached his chest with my cheek I felt desolate.

I thought it was strange but he seemed uncertain, almost as if he were out of practice, or shy. I opened his shirt for him and rubbed his chest. He seemed a little surprised that I should know what to do.

I undid his trousers but he got out of the rest of his clothes himself, in the way of a small boy who does not like his mother to help him when he imagines he can manage alone. He grinned a little embarrassed at me. I could see he was not excited. 'Why don't you have a bath then, Nelly,' he said surprisingly, 'and get that old wedding dress off.'

I was naturally surprised at his fastidiousness. He had come a long way from the warehouse in Plymouth. 'Yes,' I said. 'I suppose I'd better, I feel scruffy.'

'It's there,' he said, pointing at the bathroom. 'While you're in there, I'll do my press-ups.'

Now I was blinking at every sentence. 'Press-ups,' I said wanly. He nodded encouragingly, so I said: 'Yes, you'd better, Davie'. I went into the bathroom, full of perfumes and talc and enormous sponges, with a replica of the little boy statue from Brussels who provided the bathwater by peeing at an enormous rate and volume into the bath. I regarded myself in the full-length mirror. I looked like some Spanish countess ravaged by bandits. My face was grubby, my hair screwed into knots and bundles, and that poor, lovely white dress like some crumpled tablecloth in a tea shop.

But when I had taken the gown away from my body and I was naked, I stood reassured before the glass. My legs curved and slender, my waist tight, my breasts full and ripe and my arms slim and fawn from the sun. I had grown well since I last saw Davie.

The bath was swirling with warm, green-blue water, embroidered with bubbles. I turned off the manikin and stood in the drifting steam. I could hear Davie grunting in the other room. Although I had hardly put my foot into the comfortable water, I paused, then got out again and pushed the door. He was really doing his exercises, not press-ups, but standing on his head, nude, legs straight as flagpoles in the air, as slender as mine, his penis hanging long and limply over, pointing at his chin like a small pistol.

I applauded jokingly through the crack of the door. Then I called: 'Come in and wash my back, Davie.'

Moving towards the bath I stepped in and at the same time heard him drop his feet back to the ground. He padded towards the door and, quaintly, knocked.

'Come in,' I called from the suds. 'I'm only bare.'

He opened the door and, pausing, took in the sight of me in the luxurious bath. I was sitting up, the upper mounds of my bosom floating on the water line, skin slippery and shining. I could see he was staring, as though amazed that one person could have grown so much. I grinned at his expression and eased myself back into the water, so that my bosom became fully in sight, two hulls, keel up. The water ran in tides over the flats of my belly and gurgled down the gully between my legs as I eased myself further so that he could see more.

'How old are you, Nell?' he asked to my amusement.

'Four months older than you, remember,' I replied.

'You're a beautiful big girl,' he said inadequately. A sudden dream, a trance had come upon him as if he could not bring himself to make any action. He seemed to be searching for another compliment. 'You've got lovely hair,' he said eventually. 'Masses of it.'

He stepped forward then in the steam, his member remaining limp, and rubbed his fingers against my stomach. He kneeled at the side of the bath and reached for the scented soap. I handed it to him, and thoughtfully added one of the sponges. I watched him intently but he did not look deeply or even directly into my eyes. He moved like some monk doing a religious chore, slowly and with only a kind of languid interest.

His face was still Davie, narrow and different, but an anxiety pinned across it. He looked intent and worried. I eased myself on my elbows from the soft suds. Like a mildly romantic laundryman he slowly soaped and washed me, and to my further amazement began to whistle in a tuneless languid way. He seemed to spend hours on my stomach and breasts driving me crazy with his rubbing, then he mentioned that he would like me to kneel, motioning me over with his hands. I did so. He slowly lathered the tops of my legs and then went through between them, first with the soap, then the sponge, then his fingers, absent-mindedly, lazily. I was aching more than I would have thought possible by then. My eyes were down to slits. I felt as though my own breath was stifling me and any words I tried to say became moans before they came from my lips. God I felt so soapy, so randy.

'Nell, turn,' he muttered dismally, and I swirled slowly around until my back was towards him. He paid as much attention to my shoulder blades as he had to the front of my body, his one hand around to the front and holding my bursting bosom, just as if he were keeping me steady, while he soaped and sponged my back. Then he began to tamper around with my bottom. He slowed, and went slower and slower. Once I thought he must have dropped off to sleep because he stopped whistling and even moving for several moments, leaving me so tight I wanted to screech. But then he was back again, his fingers and that sponge reaching, touching every inch. Never can I recall feeling so clean and so dirty at the same moment. This boundless torment went on for half an hour or more. I kept seeing him, behind my closed eyes, as a lad, sitting opposite me in the bath that first night in Bristol. The night when he had shyly asked me if he could touch my breast and I had let him.

'If Mr Fagence could only see us now,' I managed to say.

He replied in his astonishingly matter-of-fact voice. 'No chance of that. He died four years ago. I went to his funeral.'

I could not handle all this at the same time so I said nothing. Davie took my hand and led me from the bath. He gave me some towels and a nod as if to indicate it was time I did something for myself. But he was soon back with a phial of oil which he proceeded to massage into my skin. I stood naked, helpless, hands hung by my side, blushing with desire. He used it on the palms of his hands around my legs and buttocks and his fingers in every place, drawing little haloes of oil around my nipples. For some reason I remembered from childhood the man who had swollen and swollen and finally blown up in the coffin in the front room. I felt sure that soon I would be sharing a similar violent fate. Then to my relief Davie led me back to the bedroom. I went carefully.

He gave me a feathery push back on to the bed and I tumbled there in luxury and anticipation, while he climbed towards me, still, astonishingly, with that lazy jumbo of his long and limp. It seemed to be the last thing he worried about. He hung above me and then with a tired sigh, relaxed and fell on to my body. We rolled together, locked, and made love, but without great passion. More an end than a means. It seemed it had all gone before and this was merely the way of releasing the enclosed tensions. It was brief and almost formal. Then we lay uneasily together in the silent hot afternoon room with the sounds snorting up from the streets of Marseilles and a ship somewhere grunting in the sun. The aroma of the bath and the oils hung around us like a cloud on a mountain. We lay flesh to flesh. I thought he was dozing.

'Davie?' I whispered, never being one to let well alone.

'What you want, Nell?'

'I thought you were asleep.'

'No, I'm thinking, Nell.'

'What about?'

'I was thinking it was a nice change to have a woman again – after all this time.'

That left me wide awake and staring at the ceiling for a long time.

Davie had a boyfriend, a Catalan queen called René, sometimes known as the Perpignan Pompadour. I should have known all those years before, I suppose, when he walked through Devon wearing girl's clothes so casually, although he undoubtedly did not know himself. Now it was a matter for a shrug. I decided immediately that I did not love him although I still felt responsible to him and for him in an odd way. To me he remained the lost boy despite all the change and the bravado. I could still see him hanging out of the window, while Mr Fagence swung him by the wrists.

'How did you mean you went to Mr Fagence's funeral?' I asked him.

The sly grin settled on his face. We were sitting on the small balcony with the smell of the streets rising to us.

'Wouldn't you have done?' he said. 'I got my own back on that bastard. I went to work in Bristol after I left school, in a lousy locksmiths – although I learned a few things *there* I can tell you. Anyway one day I saw in the paper that old Fagence had kicked off, so I went to the funeral, keeping quiet and well to the back. She was there, Mrs Fagence of course, all bowed and black, the old cow. Glad to see the back of him, I suppose. I just kept out of the way until the cemetery. The family were all around the grave as they lowered him in all sniffing and sobbing and the like. I sort of pushed my way in a bit between them and then I started to giggle.'

'Giggle? God what happened?' I stared at him knowing he was quite capable of doing it.

'Nothing for a bit. The vicar bloke kept on muttering the prayers and everybody started sneaking glances around and I just giggled a bit more and more until I was laughing out loud. Then I turned away and went laughing and skipping down the graveyard path. I got my own back in the end, didn't I Nell?'

To tell the truth I was shocked. 'But it was a funeral, Davie. He couldn't hear you.'

'I just wish he could,' said Davie, not realizing I was reproving him. 'That would have been even better.'

That was the first afternoon after our reunion. René the Perpignan Pompadour turned up about four, lisping for a drink and prancing about the place in a yellow sharkskin suit. He was swarthy and mean-looking, which made his piping voice and mannerisms all the more strange. He was one of a group, a gang would be an exaggeration, of associates of Davie that had gathered about him both as friends and occasional partners.

They were the biggest collection of quaints and misfits I have ever seen. They drifted in and out of the apartment, had a look (mostly disapproving) at me, and drifted out again. Their lives consisted of moving up and down the Côte d'Azur living on their wits and fingers.

There was Lennie, the Lizard of the Lounge, who hung about hotels poncing and trying to see what he could pick up both human and material. An hour after he first saw me he told me that he loved me eternally. He was not bad-looking but with a fatal furtiveness about him. One night when I was drunk at a party I let him roam all over me and eventually, mostly because I was too far gone to move, I permitted him to achieve what he proclaimed as the ambition of his life. It was so unimpressive (most of his endearments seemed to be directed at himself, which is no way to make friends with a lover) that I could have easily missed it altogether. When he asked again I said I did not have a spare minute and he went through my life from that moment with a perpetual sulk. He was, however, quite talented as far as drawing off wealth from old ladies staying in rich hotels along the coast, and in compromising careless men with photographs taken of them interlocked with girls that he had obtained. He was not, in general, an attractive person.

There was Sir Robart McAndrew, a flushed and flabby man who claimed to be a noble Scotsman and wore a dirty and disreputable kilt, the sporran as bare as a pig's ear. He relied on the kilt as an object of curiosity to make the acquaintance of the people he later cheated or robbed. He and his ways were exposed by a genuine Scots nobleman who perceived that Sir Robart's kilt was assembled from three different tartans (clans who had been enemies for centuries) and chased him along the beach at St Raphael with the knife he wore in his sock held for the kill. Sir Robart only escaped by running into the sea and swimming ponderously to a rock, from which he had to be rescued late at night, when the real Scotsman had gone grumbling back to his hotel.

Then there was Antibes Annie, a sloven who was a good safecracker. She had fingers like screwdrivers. She had opened one or two difficult boxes at various places along the Riviera over the years but what she did with the proceeds was a mystery. She certainly never spent them on herself. It was rumoured that she had a kept man who was a police department official and this may have been true because her information was excellent. She drank blackcurrant juice which had given her a permanently purple tongue.

These people were not settled members of Davie's gang, which was just as well since they would now all be in Marseilles prison instead of only going there in relays. He frequently worked by himself, or so he said, and when he needed help he brought in contact men from the organization in Marseilles. He said they were impressed with his cool attitude. They must also have been impressed with his lies, and not aware of the feet of clay I could now see so obviously enclosed in those pigskin shoes.

When this collection of disreputables met, slouched in smoke and making nasty noises in their throats, the bottle on the stained table replaced every few minutes, I would sit in the background and wonder how Davie had come to gain (although this is hardly the word) such friends and confidants.

When they were not slurring or slurping, when one of them wasn't folded face down on the table racked by a fit of coughing, they would plan all sorts of improbable raids and crimes. If boasts had been deeds they would have cleared every casino between Bains du Boulon and San Remo. But only rarely was anything decided and when they did work together they usually bungled it to such an extent that the police were at the scene of the crime almost before they were.

Antibes Annie went to gaol and so did Lennie the Lizard. He wept in the court and begged for mercy, while Annie, to her credit, filed her iron-hard fingernails, setting the teeth of every one on edge. The judge gave her two years.

'I think they're a joke,' I said to Davie. 'All of them. All your so-called criminal friends. Weak-kneed, incompetent riff-raff.'

He tried to put on his deep look, as though there were machinations I could never hope to understand. We had little sex after the first time, just the occasional flurry after a bath, because the Perpignan Pompadour kept turning up to take him out somewhere. I did not mind. I had a roof over my head. My only worry was when I had to sit and wait for the gang to return after one of their occasional sorties, biting my nails and wondering who would get back and how close the police were on their tails. I had written to Dante, a letter full of the true shame I felt at leaving him on our wedding day, not telling him the details, not mentioning my father, but merely saying that suddenly I had fallen among low people, which was saying the same thing.

'I'm better when I work by myself,' muttered Davie, still full of himself. 'Then I only have to trust myself, but sometimes I need the others.'

I sniffed. 'You don't need *them*,' I said. 'Not that clutch of nincompoops. And even when you work by yourself it's not exactly spectacular, not from what I've seen.' Predictably he rose to that.

'What do you mean by that?' he demanded, the Devon coming through in his tone. 'What do you mean by that, Nell Luscombe?'

I looked loftily. 'Well when like last week you come in with a diamond bracelet worth millions, so you said, and they're selling them in St Tropez for ten francs a throw, I think you're working on the wrong lines.'

The sulk puffed on his face. 'Anyone can make a mistake,' he said. 'That woman usually wears good stuff.'

'Davie, hardly *anything* works. Twice you've tried that trick of robbing a bank by pretending you're going to make a deposit there – and twice you've run out with less than you took in. That's not crime, it's not even good business.'

His sulk rolled down to this throat. His sullen eyes turned up to me. 'It's just that I'm having a terrible run of luck, that's all. God, there's so much loot around here, hotels, apartments, yachts.'

The fact was, for all his bravado, he had neither the luck nor the technique that brings its own luck. The weak side of his character displayed itself in his work.

'Hotels, apartments and yachts,' I repeated remorselessly.

'You were caught red-handed in that flat at Bandol and the old sod who caught you made you go to bed with him.'

He shrugged. 'It was better than the police,' he said. Then, remembering: 'Not much better, but better.'

I sat him down patiently. We were moving about the apartment like two mooching cats. 'Listen,' I said. 'Either quit this place or do something else for a living. You'll end up inside a cell, and French prisons are like French restaurants, you're there for a long time.'

Davie looked hopeless. 'What can I do, Nell? I've not been trained have I? I can only do whatever comes along.' He walked to the window and looked over the sweaty port. 'And I'm not slaving away doing work like those stupid bastards down there.'

'In that case,' I said quietly, and because I had thought it all out, '*I'll* be your partner.'

He turned from the window in astonishment. 'You, Nell? You come in with me?'

'It would be better company than you've been keeping lately,' I said.

He walked back across the room. 'It might work,' he nodded. 'It just might. I could teach you everything.'

'Don't bother,' I smiled. 'We want to be successful, don't we?'

I thought he was going to make some retaliation but instead he dumped himself in a chair, the thought still imprinted on his face. 'It's not a bad idea,' he agreed. 'We split. Sixty–forty. No seventy–thirty.'

I poured two glasses of wine. 'Right,' I said. 'We're partners in crime. As long as you're happy with thirty per cent.'

Our first bank raid in partnership was on the Juan les Pins branch of the Banque des Alpes Maritimes. It was perfectly positioned for my plan, its rear door opening on to a close street, and a short covered alley leading from that street and on to the seafront and the fashionable beach. The beach was important.

I believed I had a real aptitude for this sort of crime. It would be short, sharp, simple, but with a spice of ingenuity. As I explained it Davie's wry face rearranged itself into a smile. 'I reckon it might easily work, Nell,' he nodded. 'You've got a lot of cunning.'

The plan was that we should go to the beach at Juan les Pins, hire one of the beach cabins and sunbathe for an hour. Then Davie would return to the cabin and dress, leaving me lying alongside his empty deckchair. In the cabin he would take our coloured beach bag, one of the duffle-bag variety with a draw string, and turn it inside out. The inside I would line with black material and there would be two eye holes cut out. There was another, larger beach bag for the money we would steal and this was also reversed so it had a black exterior.

At eleven in the morning, Davie would walk into the bank through the rear entrance after coming from the beach. We arranged for a litle crooked man from Marseilles to block the front entrance by capsizing a handcart loaded with apples right in the doorway. Davie, now wearing the beach bag hood, would produce a gun and get the money put in the second bag and leave by the back door. Taking off his mask he would reverse it so that it became a beach bag again. Then he would walk through the alley and on to the beach, go into the cabin and strip down to his swim-trunks. He would take the cash from the second bag, reverse it, replace the cash, and then walk back to his place on the beach beside me. We would lie there like any other couple taking in the sun, our coloured beach bags by our sides, one loaded with loot, and wait until the excitement had died down.

Whatever his weaknesses in other directions, Davie, given the guidance, was cool and daring enough to carry such a scheme through with ease. Was he lucky enough?

After an hour on the beach, during which time we had ensured that we had a conversation with the beach attendant, so that he would remember that we were on his stretch of territory, I touched Davie's wrist and he winked, rose quietly and went back to the changing cabin with the two beach bags, the duffle bag inside the large one. Three minutes later he walked out in shirt, slacks and sandals, carrying the large bag, and slipped into the alley without fuss.

I lay back with my eyes closed. It hardly semed fair to pray for the success of such a venture but I did anyway, hoping God might be in a liberal frame of mind. After two minutes I heard the commotion in the street as the apple cart was tipped on schedule. Nothing more happened and I remained unmoving until, four minutes later, Davie came quietly down the sand again in his trunks and sat down casually beside me. He winked. It was done. I felt so elated. I grinned up at the sun.

After a further three minutes there came the expected uproar from the street behind us. The police sirens and the noise of excitement. With the other people on the beach we turned idly as though we too were mildly wondering what had happened. The loot was sitting right between us, and our crooked little friend from Marseilles, who had slipped off immediately he had upset the apples, would be heading home by now.

We remained on the beach until the sun began to run down towards the rim of the sea and then casually packed our belongings and went hand in hand from the place, wishing the attendant 'Bonsoir' as we went. By that time Juan was peaceful with indolent men playing boule under the pines and the dreamy late-afternoon feeling and light over everything. Outside the bank a policeman was standing guard in that quaint way the police have of guarding something once the deed is already done. We wished him a pleasant evening as we strolled by.

As a precaution against being stopped by any road blocks the police might put up, we had delayed until the roads along the coast were crowded with early evening cars. They would not hold up the entire Côte d'Azur at that time of day. As we drove towards Marseilles we saw police cars and motor cyclists by the rocky edges of the road scanning traffic, but we sailed by them with identical smiles.

It was not until we reached the apartment that we dared to open the bag to see how much the escapade had netted. We ran laughing up the stairs, like mischievous children, and locked ourselves in before opening the bag.

It was like opening a large Christmas present. The money was all in beautiful thousand franc notes. I peeled one from the top and ran it luxuriously through my fingers. In the bag there were francs to the value of £10,000. We sat and gazed at each other in awe of what we had done.

'Davie,' I whispered. 'What are we going to do with it all?'

The answer came within five minutes, for six of the most

sinister men I have ever had the displeasure of seeing on a doorstep came into the apartment and asked politely for a joining subscription to the Brotherhood of Marseilles. The crooked little fellow who had spilled the apples for us had then spilled the beans about us. We were allowed to keep a thousand pounds each for our trouble.

After that, however, we were permitted to practise but not in a spectacular way. The Brotherhood made clear to us that if we intended to work along the coast of the Côte d'Azur we had first to serve an apprenticeship as petty thieves. The big brothers looked after the major crimes.

There was no alternative but to work on a less ambitious plane until we were ready to perform one final major coup – after which we would escape to some other part of the world where the Brotherhood could not levy their dues.

We cleared a suite at the Hôtel Victor Hugo in Menton of jewellery including a pearl necklace so heavy that it felt like a horse collar on me. Unfortunately this particular piece was so well known and had been photographed so many times that we could not find a fence who would touch it. Eventually we got rid of it to a shaky man at Lyon who paid half and promised half but who disappeared the next day leaving us with a loss on the operation.

There was better fortune at St Raphael, however, where Davie purloined a fine yacht owned by a French industrialist who had gone ashore with his guests for dinner. He watched the two crew members left behind creep ashore for an unofficial drink and then started her up and took her three miles out to sea. I met him out there in a small motor boat borrowed from a jetty up the coast. We loaded everything of value on board, including a projector and a whole collection of wicked films, money, jewellery, champagne and three cases of Scotch, into the motor boat and cruised away with it.

What we had gained so far meant that our living had become more comfortable. I took driving lessons and bought myself a red Alfa Romeo, which I drove like the richest girl in the world on the roads of the azure coast. I took myself a lover, a comparatively honest and handsome Frenchman who owned a restaurant in the fashionable part of Marseilles, one of the most charming men between sheets I can remember. He always kissed my hand before and after the event. Davie was pleased because it meant that he no longer had to provide for my needs and he himself had moved up sexually and socially. He became, as he described it, unofficially engaged to a bronzed but homely Niçois boxing champion. Davie spent hours at the gym and they sparred around happily together, both south-paws.

The summer was drifting with each day now and the coast became subdued and thoughtful. I was thinking too; wondering where we should make our big take. We discussed various plans and possibilities and then, one warm day in October, we were sitting, Davie and I, at a pavement café near the apartment when the alarm bell of a small branch bank on the opposite side of the avenue began ringing. It stopped after a few minutes and then began again and eventually a police car arrived and we watched a bank official explaining something to the officers. I touched Davie's hand and nodded that we should stroll that way. Several people had stopped and were watching the conversation between the man from the bank, now joined by two others and the police. We stood with them, a couple of idlers, moved only by curiosity.

The bank officials were gesticulating, explaining profusely that the bell had a fault and the police were complaining at being brought out on a false alarm and repeating that it was not the first time it had happened. People living in that district had been woken in the middle hours of the night. There was a lot of French puffing of cheeks and spreading of hands, and the officials promised that they would again have the bell checked and corrected. The police went sourly away and the small crowd dispersed. We went back to the apartment and stood out on the balcony studying the exterior of the bank building through a pair of binoculars we had purloined from the yacht we stole.

'What's the idea then, Nell?' asked Davie. 'How d'you think we're going to get in?'

I sat down and had a drink and thought about it. It did not take me long. I had a natural aptitude for the business.

The evening we carried out the raid we had dinner in a small fish restaurant directly opposite the bank. It was warm for the time of year and it was not uncomfortable to eat outside so we sat at one of the pavement tables and watched the bank. Its all-night lights showed drowsily over the tops of the windows and the glass panel at the top of the door. A cat sat on the doorstep for an hour and washed itself eight times. Eventually it strolled on its way and so did the people in the street. We stood up, paid our bill and walked back to the apartment.

Davie had been out a few afternoons previously and returned with a pocket radio transmitter which, he promised, was guaranteed to activate any burglar alarm. We now took this and walked, like any midnight strollers, back along the avenue. In the shadows of the bank we concealed ourselves and Davie directed the radio waves towards the top of a barred window a fraction higher than our heads. In ten seconds the alarm began obediently ringing. My heart leapt like a rabbit but Davie calmed me and we walked from the shadows and went across the avenue to a small park, open to the street and popular with late lovers. There we sat on a bench, Davie's familiar arm around me. I smiled at him and he at me. We watched.

The alarm continued shrilling along the street and squares of irate light began appearing in the darkened upper stories of the apartments and buildings. Someone complained from his window: 'Stop that machine! Where's the police?' Other people responded from across the street. Nobody gave a thought that it might be a genuine alarm, it had rung wolf too many times. 'That thing has been going mad for two weeks,' shouted someone else.

The bored night police arrived without haste. They also had been called to too many false alarms. A few minutes later a Renault drove up with the flustered cashier who had the keys. Davie touched me lightly on the arm in the shadows of the park. 'Our man,' he whispered.

As soon as the door was opened the alarm was switched off and the neighbours in the avenue noisily pulled down their windows and the lights went off. A couple remained hanging out of the window to shout insults at the bank official and he, being in just as ruffled a mood as they, bawled insults back up the street. He went into the bank with the police, and finding nothing amiss returned to the pavement. The door was locked again and the men wished each other a sullen *'Bon nuit'*. Whereupon a man from a window shouted: *'Bon nuit! Merde! Bon matin!'* The bank man blew the Marseilles equivalent of a raspberry and everyone went home. After ten minutes Davie and I rose from the bench and, while I kept watch, he returned to the dark side of the bank where he once more activated the alarm. He came grinning back to the dim overhung park.

Up went the windows, on went the lights. People began shouting to each other all up and down the street. It was as though some famous victory had been announced in the middle of the night. This time the police did not even bother to appear. After three minutes (he could have barely had time to get back into his bed) the bank man appeared in his Renault, and waving his pale fist at all the fists protruding from the surrounding windows, he unlocked the bank and went in. The alarm bell stopped. The windows banged, the lights went off. Davie, pulling a nylon stocking over his face, walked across to the bank, strolled in the door, and put a gun in the bank man's ribs.

Pulling my stocking mask over my nose and chin I walked casually from the park and into the bank. I closed the door easily behind me. Davie was taking the official's keys from his stiff fingers. The man's face looked as if it had suddenly been frozen. His eyes protruded and his mouth was fixed in a small amazed circle.

Everything until then had gone beautifully to our schedule. I could feel myself flushed with the thrill of it. Davie's eyes were like bright points, shining through the mesh of the mask. Then things began to go wrong. The bank man had a heart attack.

He simply toppled down to our feet and lay there turning blue. Davie and I looked at each other with horror. There was no doubt it was genuine, no one could put on an act like that. 'Davie,' I said, aghast. 'We'll have to call an ambulance.'

We tried no further crimes for a month, so demoralized were we with our latest thwarted attempt. It was not so much incompetence as fate.

The Côte d'Azur newspapers were full of the story of the 'Chevalier' bank thieves who had saved the cashier's life by calling for help and losing the loot. We were glad to hear he had not expired, but pictures of him sitting smirking like a hero in the hospital were not much compensation for us for all that risk and no reward.

Silence fell over us and some of Davie's former associates,

236

the pink, puffing Sir Robart and the Perpignan pouf, came around to drink and gloat. This made me angry and Davie more sullen, but from his sullenness came the idea of our last and most fearful operation. He had been brewing it all day and half the night. At three in the morning he rose from bed and went out on the balcony to smoke. Seeing the red dot out there and knowing he had been restless, I got up myself and went out to him. We were a good distance above the street. I stood by him and we looked out to the weary, early-morning lights of the ships in port. The avenue below had a yellow silence. Not even a cat or a dog walked there.

'What have you thought of?' I asked him. It felt very good standing together like this. It was a shame we could not have been lovers, that he had changed.

'I have a plan,' he nodded. 'A good plan.'

'Not a bank again. I don't think I could stand another bank.'

He shook his head seriously. 'Not a bank, Nell. A *house*, a *rich* house.'

'But they all have burglar alarms and dogs and suchlike,' I said. 'How many house gangs have been put out of business down here? Dozens. There's always hidden safes, and getting rid of the stuff afterwards, and having somebody to ...'

I stopped because he had broken into a sardonic smile and it was still on me. Then I realized what he meant. 'No ...' I said. 'No Davie. We can't ... I couldn't do it.'

'L'Horizon,' he said. 'The perfect place. You know every inch of it. You know what's there. And if we get caught, you could always say you'd come back for something you'd forgotten.'

I shook my head, still hardly able to believe what he was suggesting. 'No,' I said. 'Not poor Dante. Not L'Horizon.'

I stood beneath the trees in the garden, watching the light in Dante's bedroom, brimming with a mixture of guilt and nostalgia. The perfume of the late Riviera flowers that climbed the walls to the balcony of my bedroom came to touch me like a soft hand. It had been six months to the day since our wedding. I wondered how my husband was.

Davie came like a wraith through the shubbery and studied the house as if he were an expert viewing a painting. He knew now where everything was, each room and what it contained, or, at least, what it had contained when I was last there.

There were no dogs, for Dante did not care for animals around the place. There was an elaborate burglar system, but I knew that one cellar half-window was not wired or at least had not been wired when I had been at the house.

Davie nodded me on with his head and we eased our way through the shrubbery and a curtain of elephant grass at one flank of the lawn. Davie seemed to know the way better than I did. He was soon at the cellar window, a half circle set close to the ground and sunk deeply into the stonework. There were weeds and cobwebs there and a dust as solid as cement in the crack. This window had never been intended to be opened so there were no hinges or locks to bother us. But it was set into the wall just as formidably as one of the actual stones.

But glass is always removable and, lying out on his stomach, Davie worked with a diamond cutter until he had carefully removed all three panes of glass from the low window. Then, with a pocket hacksaw, he went easily through the uprights. We could get in.

At least Davie could. He was still as thin as a ballet dancer and with no bottom or other projecting parts to bar his progress his slide into the house was simple. My legs and hips and waist were inserted without difficulty into the cellar, but the ledge of my bosom became jammed against the ledge of the window and there were anxious minutes of tugging and levering before I was able to drop down breathlessly beside Davie in the dark underground room.

There never had been a key to the cellar door, and it opened dustily but without fuss and we crept upstairs into the house. How strange it was, going through those shadows again. Everything as far as I could see was as before, the air of warm boredom, the silence, the patterns of pallid light through the windows. I paused at the bottom of the main staircase and listened up the well of the stairs. Was Dante, I wondered, with a woman in his room? I doubted it. The light was on and it showed in tight strips around his door. He must have been in there as he ever was, reading or brooding. Poor Dante.

At that moment his door swung open soundlessly. I thought my heart had crashed from my body. I stood stiff against the wall, while my husband stood on the landing above me. I could see his legs. Davie moved like a snake, backing lithely away down the passage in the direction from which we had come. I could not follow for Dante would see me. I thought he might call or go to the telephone for the police, or at least rouse the servants. But he was quite casual. He began to step down the stairs. Sinking back into a recess I watched as he came down the stairs and walked right by me. He was wearing a robe over his pyjamas, and his hair was like dull silver in the dim light. He paced on steadily through the gloom. He stopped and I guessed he was at the light switch. He touched it and the whole passage was lit. Then he walked on and I heard him go around the corner to the front hall of the house. I might have reached a window or another door then, but I did the strangest thing in my life. I ran up the stairs and into his bedroom. It took me twenty seconds to strip myself and get naked into the large soft bed. I pulled the sheet down so that it only just touched the underside of my breasts. Then I waited.

His footsteps returned along the corridor, the light went out down there and he climbed the stairs. He was at the same pace.

As soon as he walked into the room he saw me, his lost wife, lying beautifully in more ways than one. Astonishment jumped into his eyes. He made a half step forward, then stopped. 'Nell,' he said. 'Nell.'

From the bed, the light lying on me. I smiled at him.

'Hello Dante,' I whispered. 'I've come back.'

fifteen

For the next ten years I was Mrs Dante Sheridan, a pleasant and affluent experience at first, but one which soured when suspicion and nostalgia, a potent and nasty mixture, entered into our life. My husband became at first casual, then distant and eventually hostile. For my part I was good to him while he was good to me but after that I betrayed him. In addition he became almost mad with the renewed haunting of Giselle, eventually it became oppressive to live with him. Frankly I was not all that sorry when he hanged himself from the cedar tree in our garden in England.

We had moved to England very soon after my returning to him that difficult night at L'Horizon when Davie and I broke into the house. Dante, who although quiet was far from stupid, realized what I was about but forgave me for it in bed and questioned me no more about it. I told him nearly all the truth about my disappearance from our wedding feast and he generously forgave me that too. In fact I awoke on that morning, after my prodigal's return, with the sun of a new life once more shining in my eyes. I was determined that never again would I be disuaded from this good and exceedingly comfortable life as the wife of a rich and attentive man.

Davie was caught by the Riviera police a week or so later when bungling a burglary at St Raphael. He was sent for five years to the prison at, appropriately, Nancy, where he apparently had quite a comfortable and privileged time, because after his release he set up house with one of the warders.

Our house in England was called Banham Court, comfortable Queen Anne, set among the trees, streams and purple moorland of southern Hampshire. Here I learned to ride, to be a firm member of the Conservative Party, to entertain a household of guests at the weekend.

At first I was novel enough for Dante to banish the self-raising ghost of the floury Giselle and the frowns fell away from my husband as I entered into the rural English life at his side. He seemed to fit so much more easily into the damper English society and his solitude of the hot summer in France was all forgotten. I bought a lovely mare called Charlotte Brontë and we could sometimes ride across the blowy open country as far as Winchester, ten miles away, and back in a morning, racing the clouds all the way.

But Dante always remained thoughtful and a trifle slow in company and there were cocksure young men in the country who gave me looks across dinner tables and rooms that were both puzzled by my faithfulness and full of invitations to end it. It gave me a strange delight to joke with them, encourage them and dance with them, but always to leave them at the end unasked. Dante observed me at these games and would nod an approving smile across the room in my direction. He even began to wink.

I thought perhaps we were both cured; he of his trying memories and me of my natural-born shamelessness, and so we might have been, but for his gradual lapse into quietness with the occasional bursts of downright ill-temper. This I later discovered (when it was too late, of course) was brought about by his financial difficulties in his many business interests and not because of anything I had done.

It was in this period of my life, with leisure and money but with little work for me to do, that I began to read. Until that time I had hardly ever picked up more than a magazine, but with the enthusiasm of a discoverer, I now began to read from the library at Banham Court and also to buy books as they were published and reviewed. Being of my disposition of course, and ever ambitious, I even began to write adventures, both real from my life and imaginary, although I never showed these to anyone but kept them locked in a bureau in my dressing room. At this time, too, I began to take elocution lessons, secretly again, for I wanted to surprise Dante. Each time we had a dinner party or other company I would insert some of my new sounds, getting away from my old anonymous voice (a voice which had, over the years, lost even the individuality of its West Country roots). But nobody ever noticed, not even Dante.

Dante used to hunt twice a week in the season but I did not enjoy this and after two or three attempts to keep up with horses and the conversation, both before and after the kill, I excused myself. Instead I took Brontë on silent and solitary rides through the forest and the open Hampshire land.

It was on these lonely expeditions that I began to meet, by chance at first, but later with too much regularity for it to be an accident, a young man called John Thornbury who lived in a village ten miles away, towards Winchester, and who, like me, chose to ride away from the crowd. His wife was a compulsive invalid and he was always alone.

I suppose it was almost inevitable that he should be my first lover since my return to Dante at L'Horizon. For six years I had kept my pact and been faithful to my husband, but now was coming the time when he began to drift away from me and I from him. Instinctively I knew that before long I would have to find another man, a temporary man, and by the same sense I knew that it would be John Thornbury.

He was a handsome and quiet man and our first meetings

were shy and indecisive, our rides taking us across open country, slowly at first and then breaking into a good gallop as soon as we could see the sun reflecting on the stones of Winchester Cathedral. We asked little of each other then, only an occasional word, and company.

Then, when I decided quite abruptly one day that the time had come to take him as a lover, I found that he had been waiting for just as long. It was May, with the first real warmth in the season's sun. We had ridden across the open moorland of the New Forest and found ourselves in one of the glades that has remained secret and hidden from most people since the place was a hunting ground of kings. There were thick trees in that part and they hung low, while the new ferns reached high from the banks and knolls making a roof of green tracery above us. There, in the very nub of that green wood, was a small clear stream and we stopped to let the horses drink.

'When I was a little girl,' I said, 'there was a stream like this right behind the little house where I lived.'

'Where was that, Nell?' he said. We had dismounted and were standing as close as we had ever stood with that sudden knowing feeling locking us together.

'In Devonshire,' I said. I knew I had to be the first one to do anything so I turned against him and put my arms about him, lifting my face and kissing him on his face. He responded at once, enfolding me and kissing me in return.

'What part of Devon?' he asked as our faces parted. 'I know it quite well down there.'

'Upcoombe, in the south.'

His mouth was against my neck and his hands went to feel and clutch my breasts. My blood began to warm for the first time in a year. 'The South Hams,' he said reflectively.

'That's right.' My voice was getting very tight, so was my chest.

'I was reading about it the other evening,' he said, unbuttoning my shirt. 'A man called John Lelland, in the seventeenth century, wrote a book about Devon.'

'Did he?' I had the swelling of his member against me now. I pressed my hands around it. 'A book?'

'Yes. He called it the fruitfullest part of all Devon.'

'The South Hams?'

'Yes. Down there. Can you get your jodhpurs off, Nell?'

'They're one hell of a job, John,' I said breathlessly. 'They're not meant for making love. Have you got a knife or something we could split the seams with?'

'No knife. Got a corkscrew, though, in my jacket here. Want to try it?'

'Christ yes, I'm so hungry for you. Let's lie down over there, beneath that hawthorn, it looks lovely with the bloom on it, doesn't it?'

'Yes beautiful,' he replied. 'It's really summer now. I'm very hungry for you too, Nelly. Here's the corkscrew.'

I took it from him and while we both lay back and giggled foolishly I used the point of it to unpick the seam of his breeches between his legs. 'I'll be careful,' I promised. 'For both our sakes.'

Like many things that look difficult, it worked with surprising ease. The thread pulled away and he was open at the front and underneath. I was tempted to put my hands in and bring it out to my mouth at once, but he firmly held me and took the cork-screw from me and in the same painstaking way unpicked the seams of my jodhpurs. God only knows what any forest wanderer would have thought if he had come across the scene, a man using a corkscrew between a lady's legs. Now I did feel for him and brought his dear, imprisoned thing out into the sunshine. I kissed it right away and he undid my shirt completely and began to suck hungrily at my breasts. Soon we were joined in a frenzied outdoor game. The horses dozed and the birds sang and we were relieved and our spirits happy again.

We rode back circumspectly until we reached the place where we went our separate ways. We did not kiss but merely let our hands touch.

Several times we made love in the forest after that, although it never became a habit. Somehow we both seemed to sense when it would be, for I would wear my jodhpurs parted at the middle seam - a pair which I normally kept well hidden - and so would he. We never needed a corkscrew again.

Dante had many business interests, although they never again included anything to do with milling flour, and he travelled to many parts of the world in pursuit of them, sometimes taking me with him. He would not, as he put it, let me tax my brain with these matters and he rarely discussed them, although at times I overheard things upon which, had he had any confidence in my judgement, I might have had some worthwhile thought. But he never considered me like that. I was just a face and a body who was at his side. It was a pity. I felt wasted.

During the middle part of our marriage, at the time when we began to drift, we made one long journey over several months throughout America and Canada. Dante was delivering a series of lectures on business techniques. He had become quite renowned for this particular subject and throngs of businessmen would pack the halls wherever we went. Sometimes I would go to the convention centres or the huge rooms in ornate hotels to see him deliver his conclusions on commercial methods and I was astonished how popular and how well received he was. They would applaud tremendously and shake his hand and slap him on the back (although he discouraged this in his studied English way by saying to the enthusiasts 'no slapping on the back please, it hurts'). It was as if he had won an election or something. He would come down the platform, a small but assured smile on his jaw, give me a quick nod and hold out his hand for me to join him. American women were always gushing around him, making noises like blowholes and telling me how lucky I was to be married to such a remarkable brain.

There were receptions and dinners and I had some beautiful clothes and jewellery and received many complimentary looks from the businessmen. But they were always good-mannered, contained and courtly, no matter what they were thinking inside. With them business, the making of money, always came first.

But when the day was over and we were being driven back to our hotel suite, a weary quiet would drop like a curtain between us; not a comfortable quiet of two people content in each other's company, but the sharp quiet of a husband and wife who have nothing to say. I knew he was thinking of another woman, and worse than that, she could never be attained, she could never disillusion him, so that he could have her and then return to me, his wife. Because she was dead.

Towards the end of that long and increasingly dispiriting journey, we arrived at Miami Beach where he was to take part in a convention.

I was not looking forward to it. It was May and the weather was hot and humid. But there was a novelty.

'Nell,' Dante said in that manner of his which suggested that he had forgotten to tell you something long before. 'We're having a boat here in Miami. It's a luxury thing of course, all modcons. You'll be able to sunbathe. You won't want to be at the convention centre, will you.'

It was not a question. The boat sounded attractive, but I knew it would be lonely. It was on the intra-coastal waterway which runs up the Florida shore, only a few hundred yards inland from the ocean and the beaches, moored in an inlet, a large, beautiful, white, boring boat. By the end of the day I had counted thirty-two pelicans creaking overhead, sunbathed for as long as I dared, had a secret swim in the canal, and drunk half a bottle of gin.

Dante returned about eight and we went to a restaurant only a few hundred yards away on the beach. One of his business associates met us there and throughout the meal they talked about their eternal methods and techniques, while I felt myself almost crying with unhappiness. God, how I wished his marriage methods had been more successful. We returned to the boat and he worked on his papers until the cool empty hours. I could hear him breathing in the main saloon of the boat. On impulse I rose from the bed and walked to him in my nightdress, hoping that the sight of me might remind him that I was his wife. He looked up from his papers, blinking, puzzled, as if he did not know me.

'Nell,' he said awkwardly. 'I thought you were sleeping.'

I moved two paces closer to him, entering the circle of his lamplight, near enough for him to touch me if he needed or wanted to. He did not move. A look of desolation passed across his face.

'Why don't you come to bed with me?' I said quietly.

'I know. I know,' he muttered. 'I've been busy, you know Nelly. Conventions.'

'Are you ever going to spend some time with me again Dante? What about *our* conventions?'

'Of course. Don't be silly. It's just now.' His arm moved across the spread papers. 'You can see how it is.'

'Yes,' I admitted, dullness filling me like chilly grey water. 'Yes, I can see how it is.'

In the morning he went off early to his convention. I lay in the sleeping cabin staring at the bulkhead of the boat. During the night the off-hand slapping of the water against the hull had made me dream that I was a girl in Weymouth again, out with the rude fisherboys. That was a long journey back.

I showered and put on a swimsuit and robe, then took a cup of coffee to the area at the stern of the boat where there were some canvas chairs and a table. There was another vessel, a large opulent-looking craft, moored stern to ours and almost as soon as I sat down a brown and grey man appeared, sat at the table opposite and began to drink whisky in the sun.

' 'Morning,' he began right away, lifting an old peaked cap. 'Real nice day. Hardly a spit of wind.' He gobbed heavily over the side and watched as it plopped straight into the water.

He had that Spencer Tracy sort of face, sunned and knotted, with splendid eyes and chopped grey hair. His arms, protruding from the short sleeves of a shirt faded to the point of being colourless, were like pieces of wood and his knees and legs were the same where they emerged from his canvas shorts.

'It's certainly fine,' I replied. It was oddly like talking to a neighbour over a garden wall. 'Is that your boat?'

'Ain't she pretty,' he replied without answering. He swirled the bourbon around his glass and swallowed it like medicine. He made a face then poured another. 'Worth over a million dollars,' he said. He was not boasting.

'Are you by yourself on board?'

'Sure. I got a couple of Cubans who crew for me. But they wanted to go and see their mommy, so I let them. They used to make men down in Cuba. Want to go fishing?'

It was one of those times. I knew it. The coffee cup was half way to my lip and I let it stay there. 'I'd love it,' I said. 'But won't we need more help?'

'Ever been on a boat fishing?' he sniffed, regarding me critically across the few feet that separated the sterns. He seemed to be wondering if my arms would be strong enough. 'Out at sea, I mean. Out there in the ocean.'

I nodded honestly. 'A long time ago,' I said. 'But I did. I went fishing in the English seas.'

'Guess you'll fish anywhere then. Come aboard then, lady, let's get her cast off.'

Feeling as though I was playing some well-rehearsed part, I got up as I was and taking nothing from the boat I clambered across the rails and stood beside him. He shook hands formally.

'Ben Castairs,' he said. 'Pleased to meet you, lady.'

'Nell Sheridan,' I said, then added. 'Er ... Mrs Nell Sheridan.'

His face gave a kind of humph at this. '*Mrs* Nell Sheridan is it?' he remarked. 'Well. I'm *Mister* Ben Castairs, but it ain't going to make any difference ... Not to us fishing. Have a slug of bourbon before we cast off.'

The spirit burned my throat and brought tears to my eyes. He went forward and fired the engine. For the first time in months I knew that I was going to be happy that day. Just to show I knew what I was about, I cast off fore and aft and the lovely big vessel, like a swan, turned in her own length and eased herself through the waterway, her nose bowing eagerly as if she smelled the sea.

Sunshine flew along the deck, green palm trees waved over the limp water, gulls and pelicans lay flat against the perfect sky. I went to the wheelhouse with him and stood by his side, just as I had stood by the boy Rainbow's side all those spent years ago. God, Dante would be gabbling from the platform by now. If only he could see me!

'Any good with a cooking stove, woman?' asked Ben. I could see the spreading sea at the mouth of the waterway.

'Want something?' I asked, quickly adopting his short speech.

'Course I want something. Otherwise I wouldn'a asked. Git down and see what you can git in a pan.'

I went below. There was a saloon, expensively furnished and with a rank of books along a shelf. As I went by I leaned towards them and raised my forehead. Sex manuals, every one. How to do it, why you do it, why you can't do it, why you shouldn't do it, all the American best sellers on a topic of unfailing fascination. I grinned and cast a glance back to where his thick bare legs were just visible astride the wheelhouse.

'Are these yours?' I shouted up to him. 'All these sex books?'

'They're the wife's,' he replied at once. 'She likes to read that stuff. And I'm glad, because while she's busy reading about it she don't come looking to me. Right?'

'Right,' I laughed back in the American way. I went to the galley. Everything was easy, an age away from the old spitting, spilling stoves of the Weymouth boats. I made breakfast of bacon and eggs, toast and coffee and we ate it together on the wheelhouse as the shining ocean grew wider and wider about us.

'You must be very wealthy,' I said, my mouth full. 'With this boat.'

'Millionaire.' He waved his toast in his matter-of-fact bragging. 'Got so much I don't know what to do with it all. Next season maybe I'll get a new boat or a new wife. Maybe both. A bigger boat and a smaller wife.' He laughed uproariously at his joke and the bow bucked as though it heard the joke too.

He wiped the egg off the corners of his mouth with the last piece of toast, then tucked that away in his mouth too. He had fine flat teeth and his eyes were pale like the sea. 'Can you take her?' he said. 'I'll get the tackle set up.'

With more show of confidence than I was feeling I stood and took the wheel. I could feel her moving, trying to get her own way like a strong horse. Firmly I brought her back on course.

'That-a-girl!' he said. 'Keep her head right.'

'Okay Popeye!' I shouted. I do not know why I called him that; it simply came out. I heard him laugh hugely as he went to walk towards the tackle. Then he turned and gave me a smack with his hand across my backside, before going off towards the stern.

I stood against the wheel, a sensation of warmth and expectation all over me. I had never made love to an older man than my husband, who was then fifty-eight. That, I had a feeling, was something which would be changed before the sun set that night on the far edge of Florida.

What a fisherman he was. He had the most beautiful back I had ever seen on any man, the muscles built tightly in ridges and yet full of ease and suppleness. In three hours we caught half a dozen marlin, some yellow tails and a small grinning shark. I could hear myself laughing with triumph, holding on to him, helping to draw them in.

Then I went to the galley and got together everything for a salad and I opened a bottle of cold white wine. We put the sea anchor down while we sat in the stern and ate and drank. It appeared that we were alone on the long ocean, the sun and the birds for company, the land low on the rim of the water. It began to feel like one of the best days of my life.

When we had finished we lolled there, lulled by the sea. I looked at his strong brown face with its close crop of grey hair thrusting from under his cap. 'Popeye,' I said quietly.

'Yep,' he said just as calmly.

'I was wondering if you would like to make some love.'

'Strange thing, Nell,' he replied, still without changing his tone. 'I was just wonderin' that myself.'

We spent the next half an hour on the open deck, the sun burning first one back, then the other. He was the strongest and most energetic lover I had ever experienced and we savoured every rolling moment. When we eventually lay back he caressed my nipples with his hard hands and said thoughtfully: 'Shit, but you're a fine healthy girl. I ain't seen quality like this, not in years.'

He had made me satisfied too, taken all the tension from me, filled me and quietened my appetite. I would have liked to stay with him forever.

But the sun was trailing and I knew that, by the nature of things, I would have to return to my husband, to entertain yet another clutch of dollar-grabbing men with labels on their lapels (as if they were likely to get lost), eyeing me only from that greatest of distances, the respect of business.

Popeye sensed my reduced mood. 'Guess we'd better turn this tub around,' he said squinting towards the sun and the horizon. 'Ain't going to be able to stay out here for the rest of our lives, Nell.'

I put my naked arms to his hard chest and pulled my breasts to his stomach again. It was as firm as a board. 'Once more Popeye,' I whispered. 'Once more before I have to go back to him.'

He smiled gently, a surprising smile from one so hardened, and moved against me again. He had a beautiful penis, so smooth it might have been carved. Not a knot-hole or a bump anywhere. He pressed it softly into me and we joined without a murmur. My cheek close to that hard scrubby hair by his ear,

I groaned with the rough pleasure of him. His lips, firm and dry, went against my neck.

'God,' I breathed when we had finished. 'What could you have been like when you were twenty?'

'Shy,' he answered flatly. 'Very shy.' We dropped over the side and swam naked against the vessel. Then we climbed aboard again and he went forward, sadly I like to feel for I was sad too that our day was nearly complete, to the wheelhouse, pulling his old shorts up around his backside. I did not put my clothes on immediately but went up there with him, naked, and stood alongside him. I felt that we had been familiars all our lives.

'I gotta tell you something, Nell,' he said after being quiet for some time.

'Don't tell me you can't marry me,' I laughed. 'They all say that.'

'Nope it ain't that. It's the matter of this boat. I don't own her. In fact I never been aboard her till last night.'

I was genuinely astonished.

'I ain't kidding,' he shrugged. 'I was in a bar and this guy gave me the keys and told me to go and help myself. I was drunk and he was drunk, so I don't rightly know who he was. But it was real nice of him.'

I put my naked arm around him. 'She's been yours today, anyway,' I said. 'Ours.'

'Sure has,' he nodded. 'But I ain't no millionaire, neither. I been bumming up and down the Eastern seaboard for years. From Maine to Cape Hateras, the Carolinas, Savannah too. That's a goddam place, Savannah. Building boats, sailing them, all that sort of stuff. But I never did make enough money to be a millionaire.'

'I know millionaires who would give a lot to have what you've got,' I said truthfully, holding him against me.

He ruminated and turned the wheel carefully. 'Sure, sure,' he replied eventually. 'All I got is my health and strength.'

That evening when the plastic men with their plastic name tags and their plastic talk were crowding the saloon of our boat and I was in my evening gown and Popeye was alone on the boat on the next berth, I heard a car draw up and voices and footsteps. I went to the stern and saw some policemen taking

Popeye ashore. My heart went cold. I called to him and he turned. I looked around, no one had followed me to the deck.

'That guy who gave me the keys to the boat – he didn't own it neither!' he called jovially. 'Goodbye Nell.'

'Goodbye Popeye,' I echoed sadly. I waved as they drove him away and I turned and went back to my rich famous husband and his nasal friends. The very best things in life sometimes come unexpectedly and then only for a little while.

Once Dante fell into his unhappy valley he never again returned to the contented ways he had managed briefly to achieve with me. At about three o'clock one April morning I woke and found he had gone from the room. I sensed that he had been absent for a long time, and feeling inside his bed I found it cold. Uneasily I got up and went to the mullioned window which overlooked the stepped lawns of the house. The cedar tree spread its enormous branches like fingers trying to hold the night. A weary moon was yawning on the skyline. Looking down I saw what at first I thought must be a ghost.

It stalked, white along the shadows and into the long streaks of low moonlight, a thoughtful, sorry sort of ghost. I realized it could only be Dante once more communing with his dead, but never gone, Giselle.

Secretly I eased the window open and peered out. He muttered as he wandered and our household cat sat on the sundial at the centre of the lawn and watched with astonishment. Well it might too, for Dante was clad in a long silk dress, elegant and white, if a little old-fashioned by then. Giselle's.

Somehow I was not really shocked. I had always known that it was still lying within him. I had hoped that it would dry and disappear with time. I retreated to my bed feeling solitary again; all the things I had gained, wealth, experience, even (so I thought and hoped) love, all ashes. Nelly Luscombe was once more on her own.

I sat in the bed cursing quietly to myself. Should I now, once more get up and go, take the road and see to what new life it would lead me. The thought did not attract me. In the old days I had fled from nothing, only expecting to find nothing at the end of the journey. Anything better was a bonus. But here I had a life, a staff, a house, money and recognition. Could I balance them against married unhappiness and live with it?

The thought came. It said that I could no longer run away. I was too old.

In fact I was now thirty. I rolled in the bed to see if I still felt luxurious. I thought I did. I had taken to wearing calico night-dresses – some of them eighty years old that I had bought from an antique shop in Winchester. The smooth ordinariness of the old cloth against my skin that night, now I was on my own again, made me remember the solitary nights in similar nightdresses all those years ago in childhood. Slowly, as if the bed were the sea, I eased myself lower and lower into its deep-ness and safety and waited for Dante to return from his haunting.

He padded guiltily back into the room, now in his pyjamas, and pausing, whispered 'Nelly ... Nelly.' I knew he did not want me for anything, even less for comfort, but was only testing to see if I had woken. I let out a dreamy snore from beneath the sheets and I heard him grunt and climb back into his bed, to join his own dreams.

We had spent the previous evening at Sir Bernard Buffling's house in the Vale of Pewsey and, although Dante had been his usual and quietly withdrawn self, I noticed that several times he had looked intently at one of Buffling's nieces, a pale, fair, empty girl in her twenties. And it was this, I later realized, which had provoked his transvestite walk.

There were no more nocturnal walkings for some time after, but towards the end of the month we went to a grim Con-servative Gala Ball and once again, as I was dancing, I saw Dante standing alone at the side of the floor and staring blatantly at a similar type of blonde girl. That night he again sidled from bed and this time I followed.

It was a big secret sort of house, riddled with corridors and tunnels and rooms folded away and easily overlooked. I trailed him to the north wing and, crouched and sad, watched him unlock a cupboard within a cupboard and produce not one but a whole selection of his dead wife's dresses. It was amazing. He held them against him, comparing one with another, eventually selecting a pale blue number with thin shoulder straps and a mouldy looking corsage. He took his pyjamas off and wriggled into the dress, making little whining noises to himself. Then he went wandering.

I waited until he was muttering and pacing the lawn beneath

the spreading hands of the cedar tree and then, creeping back, I opened the first cupboard and found the second, with the key left in the lock. I turned it and pulled the door. Inside was Giselle's complete wardrobe, dresses, coats, shoes and lots of expensive underwear. I felt my lip curl in disgust. I ran my hands through it, feeling that old unwanted, unneeded sensation seeping through my veins like a creeping damp. 'Fuck you,' I whispered to the clothes.

Three days later, on an afternoon of dizzy, springtime sunshine, with the county rivers shining and the Hampshire birds full of song, I returned from my forest ride to see him (at a distance of a mile too, which was most disconcerting) dangling by the neck from the lowest and largest branch of the cedar tree.

He swung gently in time with the April breeze, the long pale nightdress almost touching the ground beneath his useless feet. I rode carefully up the hill, not hurrying for I knew I was too late and there was no need for hurrying. Indeed it had been too late for two years. I took the mare to the stable block and called Jarman, the groom. He came from the tack-room, a spidery man, his face crammed with lines and creases. 'Jarman,' I said. 'Please come and help me with the master.'

A lifetime of dealing with the foibles and dramas of horses had, I suppose, toughened him for the minor turns of human histrionics and he turned the corner with me to come upon the dangling Dante with only the merest flicker shading his expression, only half a step of hesitation in his walk. 'I'll get a ladder, Madam,' he said politely. 'People in that way are very difficult to get at without a ladder.'

He ambled away calmly and returned with the ladder. Between us we managed to get the wobbly body of Dante down from its gibbet and on to the lawn. As we stretched him out there, the springtime sun streaking teasingly across his dulled face, Jarman sniffed and said: 'I ain't never seen the master wearing that nightdress before.'

Looking down at the deeply dead Dante, a small swelling of pity rose within me. 'Do you think we could make it look like natural causes?' I said hopefully to Jarman. 'It looks very bad like this.'

'I doubt it, Madam,' he said sizing up the corpse. 'It would take some believing that would.'

'Well at least let's get that ridiculous nightdress off him and put him to bed,' I said. 'It's all so undignified like this.'

'You're right, Madam,' he agreed. 'People will probably talk.' He gave the alternatives some thought, walking in a small horseman's circle around the body. The two housemaids and the cook were off duty at that time of the afternoon or the whole thing would have become too complicated. 'Maybe,' muttered Jarman, 'we could put him across the back of old Nightmare and send him off on a gallop across country. We could make out the master fell off and broke his neck. Or we could drop him in the river and say he drowned.'

The vision of the three of us riding across country, with Dante held upright between Jarman and me, had its touch of romance, but I doubted if we could carry it off. And Dante floating down the river would look just as suicidal as ever.

'I think the best thing we can do is put his pyjamas on and get him into bed,' I said. 'Maybe we'll get away with pretending it's a coronary. We'll get Doctor Finneston. He's bound to be drunk.'

It was difficult not to admire his aplomb. 'Come on Mr Dante, Sir,' he said, just as if he were helping him on to his horse. 'Up we come.' He attempted to carry the corpse by himself but he was a very short man and poor Dante kept slipping over the back and trailing his dead head close to the ground. So I took my husband's feet and Jarman took the shoulders and we carried him into the house and into the bedroom.

The worst part was getting that hideous nightdress from him. She had fearful taste that Giselle, whatever her other qualities, and it did not suit Dante any better. He had however caught part of the material in his hand, probably the last movement of his life, and we tried to prise his fingers free of the silk. They would not let go. In death he was still difficult. But we managed to pull the silk through until it was free. After that, Jarman, touching his groom's forelock tactfully, left the room and I was alone with Dante.

Seeing him stretched out there, the first time I had seen him naked for about a year, it occurred to me that my husband had been a strong figure of a man and I felt a proper pang of regret that things had not been different between us. But it was too late even for regret. It was no use standing and admiring him. I took his pyjamas from their drawer, a conservative striped design, and with much pulling and tugging eventually got him dressed in them. Then I put his hand on his chest in the manner of one who might have suffered a sudden pain from his heart. The rope had made a nasty mark around his neck but I optimistically turned up the collar of his jacket in the hope this might hide some of the evidence. Then, when all was set, I called Dr Finneston, an Irish bottleman who could always be relied upon to give a false diagnosis, certainly in life.

Dr Finneston was in an early afternoon stupor but agreed to come at once, although, as he put it, death is never that urgent. He came into the room, brought up by the marvellous Jarman, as expressionless as a sleeping donkey, the doctor breathing a fiery cloud of whisky before him. He gave Dante the most cursory of examinations, before nodding carefully and saying: 'This man is dead.'

'Was it a heart attack?' I prompted, managing to squeeze a tear out of my eye. 'A coronary?'

'Aye, I'd say that's what it was by the look of him. A very sad day for you both, I've no doubt.' He stumbled towards the window, seemingly suddenly conscious of the alcohol he exploded with every breath, and stood blowing the fumes out into the garden.

'There's a very strange piece of rope hanging from the cedar tree down there,' he observed. 'Chopped off. As if a man might have hanged himself from it. It matches, I've no doubt, the nasty contusion around Mr Sheridan's neck. It looks like he may have hanged himself and then come up here to his bedroom to die quietly.'

At the inquest evidence was given that Dante's financial affairs were in a stormy state, something of which I was quite unaware. It made me feel a little better, however, knowing his death was not only prompted by his longings for Giselle.

Everyone for miles around was there, of course, in the coroner's court, cramming every seat and bench and lined up six deep against the terrible treacle-coloured tiles at the back. Jarman assured me that it was a mark of respect for my late husband to have so many people at the inquest.

I was summoned to the witness box by an usher calling my name like an echo without a voice. All around they rustled with anticipation and I stepped forward, slowly, with dignity, feeling within me the guilty thrill of the tragic actress. Pace by pace I went towards the witness stand, recited clearly the binding oath, and then waited for the questions that I knew must come my way.

The coroner had a face like a fat parrot. He leaned over to get a better look at me in my fine black clothes. 'Mrs Sheridan,' he moaned. 'Tell us, in your own words, the events of this most sad afternoon.'

My voice retreated into my bosom and I described how I had found Dante swinging from the tree, but omitting the detail of the nightdress which had remained a secret known only to myself and Jarman.

'Why, Mrs Sheridan,' said the coroner, 'did you take your husband to the bedroom and dress him in his pyjamas?'

My chin went down to my chest again. 'I was trying to keep him warm,' I whispered. 'I was trying to get him into bed. I thought warmth might ...'

'Bring about a recovery,' he finished for me. 'Well I've heard stranger things in this court, I must say. But not many.'

They brought in a verdict of suicide while the balance of the mind was disturbed and then everyone emptied out into the young spring sun of the street. Several people came to me and patted my arm and made sympathetic noises, but I noticed how a great many women, most of whom I knew by name, backed away from me. In that stratum of life it was not permitted to let one's husband get away with much, particularly suicide.

Everyone seemed to drift away across the streets, into the pubs for the discussion of the case, into cars and on buses, leaving me oddly alone on the pavement. The house servants, those of whom had been permitted to attend, and of course Jarman, remained with me, but a pace behind. He said we were waiting for the car. The coroner and the clerk came out and both raised their hats. The coroner wished me a pleasant remainder of the day. I was wondering about the remainder of my life. I turned around and the handful of staff who had come with me were staring at the back of my neck.

Everyone else had gone. The striped sunshine of the street was undisturbed now. It was a small street and there was no traffic. It was not until then that I realized that everyone was blaming me for what had happened, because he had hanged himself. I suppose I, the wife, was the natural one to blame. The thought struck me with such force – and my basic innocence was such that it had never occurred to me before. I have frequently been wicked but never intentionally cruel. Cruelty is the pastime of respectable people.

'I think we had better go home,' I said to Jarman. Surely *he* did not think it was my fault. His expression, as normal, said nothing. 'Home,' I repeated. 'Everybody else seems to have gone.'

As though he had been awaiting some movement, Perrington the chauffeur eased my car around the corner. It was strange how we had been just left there like that, on the pavement. Even as the car drew up I wanted to begin running. Just to get away from it. I would have to wait for Dante's burial. Then I would go again. On my own.

One of the most difficult things in the world, I suppose, is to throw a successful funeral. The basic circumstances are set against it, of course, and yet people expect it to be handled properly like any other social occasion and if it does not go right they grumble just as they would about a mismanaged wedding.

Fortunately the arrangements were taken care of by Dante's London solicitor, Maurice Benning, a long, careful and considerate man who knew more about Dante's life and dealings than anyone. All I had to do was to supervise the catering arrangements and look mournful at the graveside. This, as it turned out, was quite difficult, since it was decided that Dante's hunter, Roulette, should be part of the funeral procession, trotting saddled but riderless through the streets, with Jarman, face composed with horsey sorrow, at the halter. Roulette enjoyed the affair tremendously, pawing and neighing and finally enlivening everything by letting go the most colourful and noisy fart as the last rites were recited.

It rattled magnificently in the churchyard air and stopped the clergyman in the middle of his ashes and dust. I felt myself begin to laugh inside and had to concentrate heavily on the lid of the coffin so as not to allow the laugh to burst out.

Dante's children, Paul, Anton and Sirie, came from France for the funeral, of course, although in the years since our marriage they had hardly seen their father at all. He had pulled away from them and they from him, and considering our intimacies in the early days at L'Horizon, they treated me with remarkable resentment and disdain. They had accepted me as an employee of their father's, as a confidante and a companion, even, briefly, as a lover. But never as a step-mother. Now they acted out the day of the funeral with sullen faces as if they felt not so much bereaved as cheated.

Sirie and Anton, who, predictably, had grown into two of the most strikingly beautiful people, still lived together in Paris. Her habitual paleness suited the funeral perfectly, her black lace mantilla edging that sulky face and those downcast eyes. She looked more disgusted than sorrowing. He looked remarkably handsome in black and white, his fair hair just stirring in the graveyard breeze. They stood sides touching, aloof, perfect, and yet somehow amazingly rotten. Their polite mutterings of comfort to me were only just off the edge of insults. But I smiled to let them know I understood.

Paul, on the other hand, was more obvious. His languid fat had scarcely been held in check through the years during which he had clawed his way to the rank of full Lieutenant in the kitchen corps of the French army. His sulks were less subtle than those of his brother and sister.

'There is *nothing*,' he said bending close over my glass of sherry at the reception in the house following the burial. 'Nothing at all. You know that?'

'Nothing what?' I asked genuinely. People everywhere thought only of what wealth or what lack of wealth a dead man left behind. No one has loved money more than I, but it has always been my own, earned by me, not acquired, not borrowed, not inherited. I always thought of Dante's wealth as his. And the same went for his debts.

'There is *no* money!' rasped Paul through his fluffy pink lips. 'He was broke, bankrupt, penniless. The lawyer will tell you.'

I shrugged. 'What did you expect?' I asked.

He pouted, the way I remember him pouting in his room that day, a boy's sulk, unsure, unmanly, standing there among his stuffed birds.

'I thought he was rich,' he said blatantly. 'But I find *this* – only debts, mortgages, stupid investments. Not even this house is left.'

'You've still got your owls, haven't you, Paul?' I said. 'Or have you punched them all to pieces now?'

He glared at me. 'Another thing I want to tell you, Mrs Sheridan,' he said bitterly. '*Nobody* killed Giselle. She jumped into the flour herself. Everybody lied, thinking they were covering for my father.'

'Well I'm glad that's cleared up,' I sighed. 'I was waiting to hear that the butler did it.' I turned from him, determined now to make sure it was the last word with him. 'Goodbye Paul,' I said. 'Give my love to the owls.'

Every sentence Mr Benning spoke was delivered with great deliberation as though he examined each word for libel before he uttered it. He had about him, however, a stuffy legal kindness and when he approached me after we had put Dante away he touched my arm and spoke softly.

'I'm afraid, Mrs Sheridan,' he intoned, 'that you will be able to touch nothing. Not the house or anything else. Dante was in a difficult situation. Deep trouble I'm afraid.'

'Not as deep as he's in now,' I suggested quietly. I thought the corner of a grin took root on the extreme side of his mouth but it thought better of it.

'Is there anything here that you could call your own?' he went on. 'Separate from anything which Dante provided?'

'There's my soul,' I said. 'Can I keep that?'

'No one can take that from you but God,' he said. 'And he would need a writ and a good reason. Anything else? Your clothes, of course, no one could argue about those.'

I thought about it. Once again I realized that I had nothing. Then I said: 'My horse. I paid for that myself, so it must be mine, mustn't it?'

'Your horse,' he ruminated. 'Well, I'd say it was borderline. What would you intend to do with it?'

'I may have to eat it if all you say it true, Mr Benning,' I smiled. 'But my thought at the moment is that I may just mount it and ride away from this arseholing place.'

Not a wrinkle disturbed his expression. I suppose you hear everything as a lawyer. 'That,' he smiled quietly after some thought, 'might be a very good idea. I am giving you this advice very unofficially, you understand, but if I were you I'd

259

ride like fury. Get right away from this . . . arseholing place, as you put it.'

It was sound judgement. Everybody went, my stepchildren with their hateful bird-like pecks on each of my cheeks (I have never seen them since), everybody else full of sherry, chablis, pâté and assorted cold meats. They went off over the lawns towards their motor cars, gossiping among themselves, never once caring to look back to see me standing at the window alone, watching them. If I found it difficult to cry for Dante, I suppose I might have had some reasonable excuse to cry for myself. Through the house I walked and wandered, not feeling any great love or gratefulness to it, but simply wondering what my next roof would be. Left in the world with nothing but a horse.

It became dark mercifully early, rain clouds coming low and swiftly across the land and the trees. I sat in the drawing room by the unlit fire, gradually drinking my way through a bottle of champagne. The creditors would never get that. At nine o'clock, only waiting for the chimes to fade, I stood up and walked through the darkening corridors. I had sent all the servants packing as soon as the funeral fun had finished, only Jarman remaining in his cottage next to the stables. Walking through the house I stamped my feet heavily, defiantly at each step, until I arrived at Dante's secret cupboard. I opened the outer door and then the one within that. 'Come out, Giselle dear,' I called. It would not have surprised me to find that somehow her collection of clothes had been spirited away, but they were still there in their smug rows. One by one at first, and then by the armful, I took out her fine tat, my eyes now filling with jealous tears. How could any man marry someone and keep this sort of thing hidden away?

I opened the window in the upper corridor and tossed out the stuff by the armful. It floated down through the darkness to the lawn like a flight of dumbstruck angels. Then another load, then another, dresses, nightclothes, underclothes and shoes. I threw them all, in a controlled rage, my face wet, my lips trembling with her name. When I had finished and the cupboard was bare, I stood panting at the window and saw it all scattered on the lawns. Two dresses were hung on the tree where Dante himself had dangled.

Calmed at last I walked carefully down to the casement door below and went into the night. Oppressive clouds hung almost to the ground. A nightbird screamed far away and I could hear the horses were uneasy. First I gathered all the garments I had thrown and made them into a pile on the grass, just below Dante's gibbet branch. I walked over to the garage where there was always a spare can of petrol and took this back and emptied it over Giselle's clothes.

I did not light the pyre immediately. I went inside, changed my clothes, and took my handbag, then I walked to the stables and quietly saddled Brontë, who seemed glad to see me. I led her out on to the drive and she stood and watched me go to the pile of soaked clothes and throw a final match to them. They flared spitefully at once and Brontë gave a concerned snort. But I went quickly to her, pulled myself on to her back, and turned her away. I rode briskly away from the house, across the open country, along the ridge of little hills and down to the shingle road. On the brow of the last small hill I allowed myself to turn and look back at the flames rolling up from the darkness in front of the house. I could see some of the windows throwing back the reflections of the fire. I let out what began as a laugh but emerged as a sob, and then wheeling the horse I set out to ride through the darkness of the English night. Once more I was on the road.

John Thornbury's house was about a mile short of the town in the bottom of a wooded hollow so deep that the house seemed to be crouching, the top windows looking nervously over the upper ground from under their roofs. At that hour of the night the wood had, it seemed, closed in even tighter. Brontë eyed it unhappily but I encouraged her through it and we came to the yard beneath the back windows of the house. There was a light showing in the panes below the eaves. I hoped his wife had taken her sleeping pills.

I sat on my horse and gave the hoot of an owl, so realistically that a real owl fell out of the eaves just above my head and flapped furiously away. The light grew stronger at the window and I saw it was John. Indistinct as it was I thought I saw him smile. He opened the window. 'A midnight rider,' he called down softly. 'What news?'

'No news,' I called back. 'Only I buried my husband today.'

'I know. I was there. One of the thousands. I heard his horse fart at the graveside.'

'It did too. Listen, I have to sell Brontë.'

'Come in,' he whispered. 'All the doors are bolted. Can you climb up here, Nell?'

'She's asleep?'

'Whistling through her teeth. Can you climb?'

It was no trouble, and it had a touch of romance which we both enjoyed much better than him simply coming down to open the door. There was a window sill and an easy haul to the flat roof over the door. Then another few steps along a ledge and finally to his window. He hauled me in.

'Beautiful,' he said holding me.

'It was easy. This house was built for burglars.'

He put his long rough arms around me, letting his hands rest comfortably against my backside. 'How are you Nell?' he said genuinely.

'Unwanted, cast out. Running like a fugitive – again,' I said. 'That's why I want to sell Brontë. I'm going to London and I need some cash. I can't touch anything in the house. Dante owed millions.'

'So I hear.' He kissed me now, the friendly kiss of a man I had known and could trust. He paused, then said: 'It's funny, I was feeling alone too. I was wondering only an hour ago how you were.'

'Is Cecily not better?'

'Not one bit. I'm trapped with her. That's the worst type of loneliness. At least you're free. She's going really bonkers, I think. She came in screaming last night, said there was a grey ghost in riding boots in the yard ... You really want to sell Brontë do you?'

'I have to. I have to start a life.'

'Would you take five hundred?'

'That's very fair.'

'Splendid. She's a lovely animal. I'll give you half cash, half cheque. Is that all right?'

I nodded. He squeezed my hands and then went away from the room. He came back with an envelope and handed it to me.

'Do you want a receipt?'

'No. We're friends.'

'She's down in the yard. I shall miss her. She's very kind and dependable.'

'Not many people are like that.'

'No. Thank you John.'

I kissed him for thanks.

'Will you stay for a while?' he asked.

'No. There's a train at midnight. I want to get on it.'

'I'm sorry. I'll just have to remember the last time.'

'I will too,' We both laughed softly as friends do. He knew I was going and he took me again towards the window. Brontë was staring up, waiting for me to emerge. I felt very sad about her. She knew me very well. I kissed John again and put my foot over the window sill.

'What will you do in London, Nell?' he asked finally.

'What I should have done years ago, dear,' I replied. 'I'm going to be a high-class harlot.'

sixteen

Even after all these years I had no real idea how to go about it. By now the ladies who had patrolled Curzon Street and Shepherd Market in the days of my youth and wonder were no more. Their descendants had been banned from the pavements on threat of prison, and they now plied their trade in the confines of rooms and drinking clubs, with no fresh air and no walking; not nearly such a healthy life.

The train arrived in London in the steamy early hours and it was obvious that it was no time to begin my new career. On the other hand it was important, I realized, to start as soon as I could, otherwise my capital would be eroded.

When Dante and I had stayed in London on occasional visits, we had always taken a suite at Burridges in Mayfair and now, at this early solitary hour, I turned naturally towards the luxurious homeliness of that famous hotel. A suite, I reasoned, I could not afford, but a room was not beyond me. Burridges, with its chandeliers, its traditions, its fine courtesy and its almost family relationship with its special rich and regular customers. The thought suddenly caught me. What better place to set up a small whoring business!

The notion entranced me. All the way through the blank streets in the taxi it occupied my mind. When I arrived at those famous portals, the late, pale lamps shining through the panes and curtains, I could almost envisage a modest red light shining there too.

I was a guest who was known to them well, and they even turned some poor young under-manager out from whatever cubby-hole he was occupying to greet me. This familiarity could only be of help. Who would suspect Mrs Dante Sheridan of operating an illicit room in one of the finest hotels in the world?

The under-manager, once he had rubbed the sleep from his eyes and straightened his tails, accompanied me to my room and I must have mystified him not only by my lack of luggage (explained by my complaints of misfortune and mix-up) but my obvious and detailed examination of the bed and the bathroom facilities.

'Spendid,' I said, enthusiastically bouncing on the bed. 'It will do just fine.'

The young man stood red-faced while the porter who had carried the key observed me with astonishment. 'Er ... I hope you have a pleasant stay, Mrs Sheridan,' said the young man. They backed towards the door, still looking at me strangely. Before they went the under-manager said gravely: 'We were, of course, madam, terribly sorry to hear about Mr Dante. Please accept our deepest sympathy.'

I accepted it sadly and graciously and they went out, looking puzzled. Then I stripped naked and lay back on the large bed. I felt weary but free. Now, at last, I was back. Once more I could lead the life that came so naturally to me. The life to which I belonged.

The morning, naturally, brought a great many second thoughts, not concerned, needless to say, with the morality or properness of the plan but merely the mechanics. How to collect customers?

In a place like Burridges, it was obviously not the done thing to solicit in the foyer, standing provocatively swinging a door key. They would hardly have allowed that even from a guest of my standing. I could advertise discreetly, I thought, but it would not take long for that to be exposed. What I really needed was an agent. Someone to quietly point clients in my direction. Someone I could trust.

As a beginning I questioned the waiters who brought my breakfast trolley about the status of the guests at present staying at the hotel. There were the usual small princes, a maharajah and two or three sheikhs, but this was before sheikhs were fashionable. There were the usual English society names, some of whom I knew and I would need to avoid, and a lot of Americans. It was obviously a situation for a reconnaissance.

After breakfast I navigated the lounges and the foyer, attempting to look interesting but chaste. I sat elegantly in one room and then in another. Then I circled the entrance hall, made a foray up and down the street, and then returned to the foyer. The hall porter and some of the staff began to notice. Did madam require assistance?

I thanked them and declined with grace, backing towards the lift. As the doors closed I heard the porter say to the doorman 'Racked with grief, I've no doubt. Racked with it.'

I occupied the remainder of the morning trying to think how to begin my business. At lunchtime the answer was dropped neatly but quietly into my lap in that efficient way fate often has with those who need her.

My solitary lunch was taken in the grillroom and I found myself placed at the next table to a large and apparently lonely young man, plum-faced, who devastated his food with rural relish. We fell into conversation in a way which, I supposed, would have scandalized the older Burridges customers. He was a Yorkshire landowner in London to conclude a deal for beef. That much I understood. But he was one of those people who believe that everyone knows as much about, and is equally interested in, their business as they themselves. We were soon in a world of poundage and pedigree agricultural shows and artificial insemination. Somehow it seemed quite easy that we continued the conversation from the grillroom and up the stairs until we found ourselves, in the most natural way, outside my room. I then began a protracted point about horses and during the course of this I led him easily into the room.

Only inside the door did he react to the situation. He may have been from the country but he was no bumpkin. 'By Christ,

265

theres a nice bed!' he exclaimed. 'By God, you know I *do* fancy a lie down!'

'It's twenty pounds,' I said before I thought the better of it. Then not wanting to lose him. 'Fifteen in the afternoons.'

'Oh, right,' he nodded solemnly. 'You've got a little shagging business going 'ave you lass? I wondered what you were about chatting me up like that.' He sniffed like I suppose he sniffed when bidding at a cattle auction. 'Well,' he said, looking at the hefty watch around his huge, red-haired wrist. 'A've got an appointment at four, matter of some heifers, but it's only 'alf past two. Yes, why not, lass? Let's have one.'

It seemed like magic. I took his money and had my clothes off and was prostrate on the bed in only a moment. He gazed at me with slow appreciation. 'By Jesus, you've got some form on you,' he said. 'Beautiful. Aye, right gradely. Here I come.'

He was a grand-looking chap himself, though a bit carpeted in rough hair, not unlike that on some cattle. He climbed athletically above me, briefly kissed each of my nipples in the manner of an uncle greeting two neices, and then unerringly entered me.

He was not one to make a meal of it and within five minutes we were lying together, him smoking a large cigar, deep in post-coital conversation.

' 'Ow long have you been about this game then?' he inquired. 'In this hotel, I mean. It's not generally known for its shagging, you know. More for its roast beef.'

I had to tell him. 'You're the first one,' I confessed. But I want to set up a regular business if I can. The trouble is you can't be too obvious here. The staff watch everyone like vultures anyway. I've got to find a way of building up a clientele.'

'Well,' he said ponderously thinking. 'Ah know one or two who'd be only too pleased to come along and give you a fuck. And I know some cricketers too. The season starts at the end of the month. It's no bother to me, I like to see a lass trying to get on by her own efforts. There's too many sit at home. There'll be the word going around, don't worry, but discreet, like.'

I was so pleased, I offered him a refund of half the fee, but he waved it aside with the cigar. 'No lass,' he said kindly. 'It were not half a fuck, so I don't want half the money back. You keep it. Good luck to you.'

*

Two hours was all I had to wait for my next customer. He was in a hurry, banging urgently on the door and almost falling into the room when I opened it. He was a middle-aged man in a city grey suit, bowler and umbrella, red in the face from running, completely out of breath. Worried by the state of him I helped him to a chair, opened his winged collar and got him a glass of water. After a while he smiled through his sweat: 'Got in here in time, anyway. I ... I wasn't sure what time you closed.'

The young Yorkshireman had sent him with a warm recommendation. 'We've been doing some business,' he explained when his lungs were working normally again. 'I'm a solicitor.' He laughed throatily. 'We're both in the same line, in fact. Anyway I hear it's fifteen pounds, is that right?'

'Twenty after six o'clock,' I replied, thinking I ought to get these matters in order right from the beginning. We both looked at our watches. 'Is it time of arrival, or the time intercourse actually takes place?' he inquired, his solicitor's mind taking over. 'If it's the first then I got here with three minutes to spare, if it's the second then we're going to have to move terribly quickly.'

I had to laugh. 'We'll make it time of arrival,' I said.

'Oh good,' he replied. 'You have a sort of sliding scale, do you? I must say I think it's a grand idea doing it here at Burridges. Such comfort, such elegance, good beds. But don't they notice the customers coming up to you?'

'You're only the second,' I admitted. 'I only started today. I expect they will notice in time.'

'Only the second! Then my Yorkshire friend was the first! How marvellous.' He began to undress enthusiastically. There are some men who want to undress you (always the same types who cannot undo a button or a hook and eye) and others who want you to undress them, just like their mothers did, and a third sort who don't want the preliminaries. This man had his clothes off like somebody in a comic obstacle race. 'You ought to try the fire escape, you know,' he said thoughtfully. He sat down quietly, naked in the chair while I undressed, feeling a trifle disconcerted at his concern with the technicalities.

My breasts came from their covering, round and ripe. 'I worked on the fire regulations for this hotel,' he said, not seeming to notice. 'If I remember, there's a fire escape just along this corridor. You ought to bring your clients up that way, certainly

267

after dark. Let's see, you get to it by going along East Audley Street and turning right into a little alley. Yes, that's it. Remember the situation well.'

Patiently I sat down. We faced each other, both professionals, both clients. 'Even if they caught you at it,' he mused, 'I wonder which section of the act they could use. You're not keeping a disorderly house. You're not soliciting. Hmm, interesting. Listen if they *do* nab you, here's my card. Give me a call.' Automatically he reached for where his waistcoat pocket would normally be. His fingers touching his bare chest woke him up to the situation. 'Oh dear, sorry,' he smiled thinly. 'I do chatter on, don't I?'

'I was beginning to wonder who was consulting who about what,' I said.

'Yes, quite. Well I came here about *my* problem, not yours. Can we start right away? A few minutes with you will give me the fortitude to face my wife for another evening. Here's the money. Fifteen pounds, we said. Could you give me a receipt.'

'A receipt!'

'Er ... yes ... sorry. Unusual, I know, but I have to cover myself. Here, I've got some blank paper if I can find my briefcase, just jot down something like "Inquiries *re* fire escapes. Mayfair". That'll do. Scribble a signature underneath. They don't check very thoroughly. Good, thank you very much.'

I finished signing. I sat back and looked at him oddly. We had been naked for several minutes and nobody had laid a finger on anybody up to that time. 'Sorry,' he waffled. 'Taking up your precious time. Well, I'm pretty well ready now.' He tried putting the receipt into a pocket in his bare chest, blushed with embarrassment again and filed it in his briefcase. 'London,' he muttered. 'All rush. All bustle. No time to breathe.'

He fussed about for several more minutes, folding his trousers in their creases and arranging his stiff collar tidily on the dressing table. I waited, my patience diminishing. 'Is there anything else before we start?' I asked sarcastically. 'You wouldn't like some tea by any chance?'

'No time, no time,' he fluttered. Then he realized. 'Oh you're pulling my leg. Pull the other one.'

I reached out and pulled the middle one. I almost tugged him towards me, pushed him back on the bed and mounted him from above. He liked that. 'Ah yes, the dominance syndrome,' he murmured. 'Yes very unusual. Tried to get the wife to do this, but the silly bitch keeps falling off. Yes. Splendid. Most acceptable.'

He did not stop all the way through. In contrast to his fussing beforehand, he climaxed very quickly and efficiently, glancing at his watch immediately afterwards and noting: 'One minute forty-three seconds.'

After that I had to lie back and watch him. In a vivid series of jerks and jumps he got himself washed, dressed, collar fixed, bowler on, umbrella over arm, and then pointed like some greyhound towards the door, he again consulted his watch and said: 'Ten minutes to get the six-fifty. Cheery-bye.' And out he flew.

After that first day my business grew with gratifying speed. At all hours of the day and into the night gentlemen might have been observed – but fortunately were not – creeping up the fire escape of Burridges or coming with casual boldness through the main foyer and up to the third floor by the lift. The cocktail bar and even the grillroom took on the form of a waiting room, with clients drinking or sometimes having a meal, while they waited for an appointment. They came from a variety of sources, my fame, or infamy if you like, and my telephone extension being passed around quickly by word of mouth. Lunchtime became particularly busy with pin-striped men rushing across the city by taxi for a ten minute session before returning renewed to their bulls and their bears. One man regularly brought his sandwiches and a bottle of good wine which we always shared, the only disadvantage being that he invariably left crumbs in the sheets.

Late afternoon would bring the going-home brigade, coming in one after the other from their offices, their eyes on their watches and muttering about British Rail and London Transport. I became quite an expert on suburban timetables and certainly, with some of my regular clients, I knew to the very stroke when they would have to be finished and on their way to their homeward train. By heart I began to know the frequency of services to Tunbridge Wells, Horsham, Basingstoke and, appropriately, Effingham Junction.

Early evening would bring gentlemen in evening dress. One left the notes of a speech he was going to make at the Dorchester under my pillow and, very agitated, had to rush back for them at the last minute. Then midnight would bring the inevitable sequence of well-dined chaps, who had to be cautioned about making a noise in the corridors or on the fire escape, and there was an occasional early hours emergency call from some fellow who had missed his last train or had his car stolen or was in some way stranded.

Even the cricketers promised by my very first customer began to materialize as May grew longer. I was told that my activities had a profound effect on that year's matches, and one team had a brilliant, and as far as I was concerned profitable, arrangement whereby they sent to my room a particularly clever batsman or bowler who was due to play against them the following day. I undertook to make sure that his performance – on the field that is – was below expectations.

Naturally I found I was making money hand over fist (although that is hardly anatomically accurate), and my account at my Park Lane bank was healthier by the day. Unfortunately many men are not satisfied with what nature intended and requests for diversions were soon being made. I had to lay in a stock of costumes, ironmongery and implements of chastisement that faintly disgusted me. Indeed it was this aspect of the business that finally revealed me for what I was, and sent the general manager of Burridges to begin a new career as the publican of The Hanging Grapes on the Great West Road.

Three of my regular irregulars, as it were, the punishment addicts, always arrived together and underwent their session at the same time, never speaking a word nor even apparently recognizing each other even though they were all Members of Parliament (from different parties). This half an hour was probably the most sexless of the week, for it involved me doing nothing more than putting one in the pillory, which I had arranged to have smuggled into the hotel in kit form and which could be erected in a few minutes in the middle of the floor. He would take off his clothes and hang there, head and arms imprisoned like some pathetic pick-pocket from the Middle Ages. One of his companions demanded to be stood naked in a corner wearing a dunce's cap and boringly recited his multiplication tables, while the third required to be beaten with a stick of fresh, wet celery.

It was when this strange tri-partite activity was taking place, with me wearing my school matron's costume, that the management of Burridges decided to raid my room. Without even the courtesy of a knock on the door the general manager, the manager, the house detective and half a dozen staff who came out of curiosity flung themselves into the room. I was just raising the celery to deliver the first of the half dozen blows that the client required across his bent, bare bottom.

'Mrs Sheridan!' howled the manager. 'What in God's name is happening here?'

I remained cool. 'Let me see,' I ruminated. 'That man in the corner is a dunce saying his tables, this chap is a naughty boy in the pillory and I'm just about to give this one a crack with a stick of fresh, wet celery. That's all.'

The three clients all began to howl like children because they thought they would be recognized and I insisted that the management troops withdraw while the gentlemen regained their everyday clothes, attitudes and reputations, and were allowed to leave, unobserved, by the fire escape. I guessed rightly that Burridges wanted to make as little fuss as possible. A scandal like this must not be allowed to come to the ears of the newspapers.

For the same reason they waived my bill for the week and hurried me off the premises. They were shuddering around my room getting my luggage and my props shifted when a man appeared through the window of the fire escape, a tall, sallow man with grinning eyes and a small moustache. I attempted to wave him away, but he was not in the least put out by the obvious dismantling of my business. In front of the general manager, the manager and those who were fussing around, he bowed and said: 'Mrs Sheridan, I am delighted to meet you. This is my card. I hope I can be of some service to you in the near future.' Then he replaced his bowler hat, bowed and made his exit the same way as he had arrived – through the fire escape window. Entranced by the performance I looked at the card before the aghast faces of the hotel men. It said 'Pierre Arthur Bickerstaff', and beneath that modestly: 'First Rate Businessman.'

seventeen

Pierre Arthur Bickerstaff had attained the difficult distinction of being a rogue and a fraud without being a hypocrite. In my past and many dealings with dishonest persons, particularly in my Riviera days with Davie, they had, almost without exception, made excuses of ill-fortune and the cruelty of the world as the reasons of their thievery and worse. They were snivellers, moaners, cowerers, belly-ache bandits. Pierre Arthur Bickerstaff was a bastard without alibis.

I went to see him, in one of his offices in a financial house of the City of London, about a week after he had presented his card with such style in such strange circumstances. I had money and the ambition to make more. But I needed guidance.

He sat behind a desk only marginally less elegant and polished than he was, around him sombre panelled walls, decorated with paintings and photographs of shipwrecks, which was something of a hobby as well as a business interest with him. I sat opposite, set his card upon the desk, and said bluntly: 'Well, what do you do?'

His response was unforgettable. He leaned back in his black upholstered chair, put his thumbs in the armholes of his striped waistcoat (he also wore what he always described as his 'near-Old Etonian' tie) and recited, without appearing to pause for breath.

'Pierre Arthur Bickerstaff,' he intoned, 'was born, circa 1928 or thereabouts, at Buxton, the lovely Derbyshire spa, of a French mother, Madam Lisette Reynaud, of Alsace, and an English father, Arthur Bickerstaff, a roving dealer, sometime of Dingle, in the City of Liverpool. His schooling was of a desultory nature but through endeavour, cleverness and some artistic cheating, he rose quickly but steadily through the strata of business life, arriving in the City of London at the early age of eighteen. He was called to the army but served only three days before being honourably discharged with a pension, whereupon he returned to a relieved City to begin what has certainly been one of the most remarkable careers of this business century.

'Mrs Sheridan, you are now looking at that same Pierre

Arthur Bickerstaff. You ask what do I do? The answer is every-thing, but only a little of each. I am, you might say, a wheeler and a dealer who has been known to double-wheel and double-deal. I have been very rich and very poor, unkempt and kempt, but always with prospects ahead. I have dealt with shipbuilding and shipwrecking, the insurance aspects that is, I have moved in every sort of commodity in the share market and once I was almost admitted, through error I must confess, as a member of the Stock Exchange and of Lloyds. Since that disappointment I have preferred to play the part of an *éminence grise*, a pim-pernel, a flitting ghost of the financial alleys. Everyone thinks they know me, few actually do. But my touch is everywhere, Mrs Sheridan, I am the least well-known person in London and the best least-known.' He smiled conclusively. 'In fact nobody knows how famous I am.'

He then told me he could get me cheap groceries, petrol, collections of Green Shield Stamps or interests in Bolivian tin mines. He also had a friend who ran children's parties and owned his own cowboy suit.

I sat fascinated and amazed. 'None of that interests me,' I said, however. He remained blithe. 'I did not think it would,' he said. 'But it's entertaining isn't it? It's merely a patter I have learned by heart and I like to use on the occasional person.'

I applauded gently. 'Very nice too,' I said. 'Very entertain-ing. Now, what did you want with me?

'Well, frankly Nell, that particular afternoon when I appeared through the fire escape window, I had come for a fuck, but I quickly ascertained that your game was up and Burridges were hurrying you away. There was nothing in the gossip columns was there?'

'They were scared stiff of publicity,' I pointed out.

'Of course. You should have blackmailed them. That must have been worth a couple of thousand at least.'

'I didn't think of it.'

'*Exactement.* That's why you need Pierre Arthur Bickerstaff,' he said. He rose from the desk. He was very tall and slim, the pinstripes seeming to go on for miles, like railway tracks. 'Let's have a drink,' he suggested. 'I have just taken a rare consignment of Moroccan champagne, so much less fussy than the French variety I always think. Will you have a glass?'

I said I would and watched him lope around the room like a

giraffe until he opened a concealed wall cupboard and produced his Moroccan champagne. As he progressed, the photographs of the shipwrecks passed behind him like a cinematograph. 'Tragedies of the sea,' he said, sensing my look, pointing the long finger as he went by. 'Each one a ring on the Lutine Bell and a wringing of a hundred hearts. You were in a shipwreck once, I understand, Nelly.'

His knowledge shocked me. I was very impressed. 'How in the world did you know that?' I asked.

'Ah, newspaper cuttings, records, I have them all available. When I became interested in you I had a little research done and among the social chit-chat of the past few years, all worthless, appeared a photograph of you as a young lady being helped ashore in France after a vessel had foundered. You were very young at the time, I think.'

Dumbfounded I reached out and took the champagne from him. 'You certainly seem to know your business,' I said. 'But I'd still like to know . . .'

'Your good health, Nelly,' he said, raising his glass. 'I have a notion that this might be a propitious day for both of us.'

I raised the glass but said nothing. I couldn't take my eyes from him. Every movement was long and accomplished, every word, every expression an entertainment. 'Moroccan champagne,' he beamed over his glass. 'Not bad for a poor lad from Derbyshire, eh?'

Like a snake he suddenly curled and slid around the desk. Once more he was in his businesslike position, thumbs tucked into the waistcoat, confidence in every slim line of his face. His moustache twitched enticingly. 'I have two propositions to make,' he said eventually. 'I hope that you will find them both of interest. Firstly may I say that your setting up business in Burridges Hotel had a touch of genius about it, and being of that nature myself, I was quick to acknowledge it. Unfortunately that sort of traffic was bound to be discovered eventually. Did you know that the takings in the little bar downstairs were up thirty per cent? That was your customers waiting until you were free. Yes, a marvellous stroke, but one that could not be sustained.

'My suggestion is based on the fact that a great proportion of your fortunate clients came from the City of London. Indeed I first heard your name and game whispered in a tavern in

Leadenhall Street. If you now merely rented yourself the conventional flat in the Curzon Street area you would only be duplicating a service which is already overloaded. Your attraction was not only your undoubted beauty but the uniqueness of your bedroom.

'What I would now like to put forward is that you should transfer your business to the City of London itself, away from the traditional haunts of illicit pleasure. No one, as far as I am aware, has ever set up a knocking shop within the City. And yet it is crying out for it. There's money there, God knows, great pressures and the need to relax and unfold, and always the odd couple of hours in the day when the market gets a bit dull. The City has everything, banks, finance houses, legal institutions, even Fleet Street for God's sake, and they're randy enough down there, insurance, bustle and business. Every business in fact but yours.'

I sat feeling my mouth drop lower as he continued. He smiled at my fascination. 'Not bad, eh?' he said. 'And it could all be daytime business. By seven o'clock, apart from the odd dinner or reunion, the place is as dead as a fish's eye. Your evenings would be your own.'

'It's . . . it's never been done before?' I said.

'Not as far as I know. For diversions of that sort the frustrated financier and the steaming stockbroker either have to travel east to the lower confines of Aldgate Pump and thereabouts, which is not of great quality or salubriousness, or get in a taxi and make their way to the opposite side of London to the more usual places, as before mentioned. We must set you up in luxury, an apartment or a penthouse worthy of your beauty and desirability. It would not even be illegal, for a cat house only becomes a cat house in the eyes of the law when there is more than one cat using it. Neither would you need to solicit business. I will be your agent and send the right people your way. For this service I will charge a set fifteen per cent. All expenses to come from income.'

He smiled dazzlingly. His teeth were carnivorous. 'I think it sounds interesting,' I said at last.

'Good, good. Well done Nelly,' he enthused. 'Think – you could be the *Young* Lady of Threadneedle Street!'

'What was the other thing you mentioned? The other proposal?' I asked cautiously.

'Ah yes, that *other* proposal,' he mused. He looked down at the desk and then directly at me again. 'Well, it's simply this. The whole scheme would be a lot easier to handle if you married me.'

We were married a month later, very secretly, in the registrar's office at Bognor Regis, a very secret place, and we spent our honeymoon through a series of thunderstorms in the Commercial and Regent Hotel in that town. I was still supposedly in mourning for Dante Sheridan but Pierre's need for secrecy was even greater (for very good business reasons he did not want our union to be known), thus our resort to Bognor.

I wore white, as has been the custom at my weddings, but this time reduced it to a linen costume and a small white hat. Pierre wore his pinstripes – I can never remember seeing him in anything else – he even wore pinstriped pyjamas – and the only other people in attendance were the registrar and a council workman we invited in off the street to act as a witness, for a small fee.

If the wedding was unpretentious, the honeymoon was the most enjoyable I had ever had, which I suppose was not difficult. Pierre was a breezy companion, always talking or reciting or singing, which he did rather well in an old-fashioned Victorian manner. Our sexual union, which we saved for the wedding night, another old-fashioned touch, was easily and happily achieved since we had nothing to hope or fear from each other. During our three days in the Commercial and Regent Hotel he bought the hotel and resold it at a modest profit without ever using any money of his own. In many ways he was someone you could admire.

In between thunderstorms we would go out to get something to eat or to breathe some strong sea air and he would walk beside me telling a continuous stream of jokes. Most of them were very funny. But it was the way we staggered along, holding hands, in the gusty wind or began running when it started to rain again, all the time him keeping up a breathless commentary of funny stories. That was what was so enjoyable. In a strange way he began to make me feel young again. One afternoon we went to a tea-dance in a hall along the front and I found myself waltzing and tangoing with this lean, elegant and surprising husband, while powdery ladies and furtive men shared pots of tea and crumpets and the band played wheezily.

Before leaving London he had set about obtaining an apartment for me within the business bounds of the City and when we returned, by chauffeur-driven Bentley, it was ready to be visited. Pierre had been living in St John's Wood and we kept that house as our home. The other would be a workplace.

It was a sumptuous workplace, five rooms spread across the top floor of an office building, and soon carpeted and furnished with every need, including a circular bed with an oyster shell canopy. The City men, he said, were partial to a little fantasy.

We stood at the living-room window looking down at the scurrying heads of London. 'See them beetling about down there,' he said, not sarcastically but with a certain fondness. 'Rush from the brokers to the Stock Exchange, from the banks to the insurance houses, from the shipping offices to the financiers. Busy, busy, busy. But each pause at some time and each must have thoughts away from this turmoil of money. And you, Nelly, will provide the satisfactions they seek. Down there are your lovers.'

He discovered somewhere an old Japanese proverb which said : 'In the hustle and bustle of the market place there is much money to be made. But under the Cherry Tree there is rest.'

He had this printed on small but distinguished looking cards with merely a telephone number below. These were distributed to discreet customers; our apartment immediately became known as the Cherry Tree, and Nelly Luscombe was in its foliage.

On the first day of opening Pierre sent me a magnificent bunch of red roses. We had installed a tongue-tied Turkish housemaid who stood poised to answer the door while I lay at the centre of the oyster shell on my round bed, looking very fine in a pink nightgown. It took only half an hour for the first phone call, but the customer, when he arrived, was something of a surprise.

It was a heatwave in the street and he arrived, wet with perspiration, handing the astonished maid his briefcase and his jacket with one thrust as he came through the front door. He advanced on me in his shirt and braces, a large, excited man.

'It's going up!' he said. 'Up and up.'

'The Bank Rate?' I asked.

'No, the bloody temperature, dear. God, it's like Panama

down there. Be glad to get my togs off. How much is it?'

I must confess I felt a bit hurt by his attitude. After all my careful and romantic arranging of myself on the bed I had expected at least a compliment on how I looked. He dropped his trousers without ceremony. 'At least they're out at last,' he went on. 'The bloody Aussies. Bastards they are. England fielded well for once. Got their fingers out.'

All I could do was nod at this stream of uninteresting information. But I learned in time that the City Englishman would rather talk about anything other than what he was doing or about to do with me.

'Shallots!' cried one as he climbed across my bed. 'Can't grow shallots in my garden. Try as I may.' Others would tell me about their wives, usually their shortcomings, or the girls at the office who wore their skirts too high, or that their golf swing had gone to pieces (this, quite often, with a demonstration, standing there naked, erect and swishing an imaginary golf club).

Every whore gets used to it. She must be an actress and an athlete, a lover and a mother, a listener and occasionally an adviser. She is put-upon almost as frequently as she is laid-upon. She must never, except in the most outrageous circumstances, lose her temper. She must be able to turn on love as though it were a tap, but she must expect nothing in return except money. A woman who gives herself to love must never expect to receive it. One moment she is the object of every desire, high and frequently low, an oasis, a resting place, a comforter, and the next she is abandoned for the demands of the five-thirty to Sevenoaks. Two things she must have, understanding and a strong back.

The Cherry Tree was a great success from the first day. I remember Pierre calling me in the early evening. 'How much did we take?' he asked.

'Eighty-seven pounds,' I said.

'I'll come and pick you up,' he whispered fondly. 'Tonight we will go somewhere special for dinner.'

Our life together was surprisingly simple. At weekends we would go out from St John's Wood to Richmond and take a boat down the river and have tea in some place with a garden and trees crowding the water.

Or we would go down to the park on a Sunday and sit in the

chairs and listen to the band in the bandstand. Pierre would wear his white shirt open at the collar at weekends and he would lean back in his pinstriped suit and warble away to himself and to me while the band trumped out some overture or some music hall melody. It used to give me such pleasure just to see him enjoying himself. We would leave the music-makers and walk across the park to the public house where we would sit holding hands and drinking lemonade shandies and after that we would walk home to our house. With this unlikely man I was beginning to find peace.

We were never anything less than comfortable and occupied in each other's company. He always told me jokes, thousands of them, and I enjoyed his antics while he told them. On impulse, to amuse me, he would take a parked bicycle and ride it down the street, or he would take off his shoes and socks and paddle in a roadside puddle like a boy. We made love only on Saturday nights because he did not want to tire me for business commitments.

The week at the Cherry Tree would start quietly, but about midday those who had been running the matter over in their minds at the weekend would begin to telephone and sidle in. Monday afternoon was frequently the busiest few hours of the week and I would be quite glad when seven o'clock arrived and they all went home to their wives and the streets of the City were deserted and hushed. Usually I would walk to the taxi rank among the cats and town dogs sniffing around, with janitors going for their evening pint and charladies waiting for their buses home. It was so empty then it was like being in Devon again.

There were, of course, times when my customers were kind enough to give me information about financial matters that were to my considerable advantage. I remember one stockbroker who, riding me like a national hunt jockey, gasped between jumps, 'Tanlings, buy Tanlings, Nelly. There's a take-over bid.'

This was followed by other genuine information and I got myself a stockbroker and phoned him between assignations, frequently making ten times as much from the phone call as I had done from the performance which led to the whisper.

Some Members of Parliament who had been my customers at Burridges and who had dealings in the City continued as clients, but at the Cherry Tree I discontinued the satisfactions which required so much equipment and embarrassment. I simply could not get used to the idea that those who governed us should want to be governed themselves in such curious and elementary ways. The City customers, because they were for the most part fairly quickly in and out (sometimes in the space of a coffee break), had no time at all for shackles and such-like and I was glad to exclude it.

From my activities in the City I began to get invitations to travel with various gentlemen. At first I refused on the grounds that I, of all people, could not leave the business. Then fees of such enticement, plus the attraction of a visit to Paris, Zurich, Toronto or New York, were offered and I asked Pierre Arthur what I ought to do. To my amazement he was touchingly shocked at the very idea.

'Nelly, I am *not* permitting my wife to travel abroad with another man,' he announced with the logic that was his alone. 'It's quite scandalous.'

However when the amounts on offer began to look like three hundred pounds he regarded it more charitably and said it might be good for me. The change would broaden my outlook and there would be some social life for me to enjoy. Yes, I could go. But I had to be home by the weekend. We were going to Kew Gardens. The daffodils were out.

My role on these visits varied with the circumstances of my host or employer. Sometimes it would be a businessman who could openly enjoy having me with him at social functions and for dinner. Or perhaps it would be some hole-in-the-corner man who tucked me away in a room and then would sneak in when he could with an elaborate system of knocking on the door. One of these furtive fornicators did not pay me one visit throughout our trip to Washington and I discovered later that his wife had followed him unexpectedly and he had had to pay attention to her requirements. I spent the entire four days watching television and eating chocolates. Naturally he still had to pay.

Sir Courtney Bellow took me with him several times, a charming old fellow with a white moustache like a pair of horns. He was so busy and so absent-minded that he often forgot about me altogether and would return exhausted to the hotel after some trying session with the International Monetary Fund, and be amazed and delighted to find me waiting in bed.

'Good God! Nelly! Damned forgot you were here, dear. Had a nice day? Hope so. Absolute fucker myself. Be with you in a moment.' He would pour himself a gigantic scotch and take it into the bathroom with him. After some twenty minutes I would go in and find him fast asleep-in the bath, pushing furrows across the water like some benevolent old snoring walrus. I would have to get him out, dry him, dress him in his flowered pyjamas and roll him into bed. He was a lovely old fellow.

There was a Treasury official, a young ambitious man, determined to get his money's worth, who would tear back to the hotel to screw me between sessions of whatever conference he was attending. He would come in like a middle distance runner, taking his clothes off as he came through the door, slam himself on top of me, have it, then dash for the debating table again. By the end of the day it cannot have been much fun for the delegate sitting next to him.

After every foreign assignment, no matter where, I returned alone and Pierre would be at the airport to meet me with a slim but glad smile, a bunch of flowers and the latest limerick or joke. He would collect the money from me (half paid on leaving, half on return) and whisk us home to St John's Wood where I would rest before going out to the pub or the park on my husband's arm. It was becoming a fine life.

It was not always possible for me to take every telephone call that came for an appointment at the Cherry Tree, and the Turkish maid, who gradually became less tongue-tied, sometimes made these appointments for me.

It was as a result of one of her arrangements that one afternoon a diminutive telegram boy, bicycle clips, peaked cap and a deadly squint behind rimless spectacles, arrived at the door. He was shown in and I swayed out in a long blue silk negligée, expecting a client, to be confronted by those small wild eyes and hanging mouth.

'Oh,' I said, half covering up my front. 'Just leave it then.'

'Just leave wot?' he asked, his eyes even further askance.

'The telegram,' I said. 'You're a telegram boy aren't you?'

'This ain't the uniform of the Coldstream Guards, lady,' he sniffed. 'But there ain't no telegram. I came for the other.'

'The *other*?' I was sincerely shocked.

'Yeah, you know, the *other*, what you can get in 'ere. Is it you?'

I felt quite giddy. 'What? Who ... who sent you?'

He sniffed. 'I got sent. Let's leave it like that. Listen ... missus, I know this is where it is.'

I had sat down. Now I got up sternly. 'I think you'd better clear off, young man,' I ordered. 'Come on. Hop it.'

He looked so crushed I took my hand from his arm. 'Aw, hang about,' he said. 'I got the money. I was looking forward to it.'

I sat down heavily. The maid, who was hovering about like a thrush on a window sill, went to open the door, but I waved her away. I reached out and brought the boss-eyed boy closer. 'I really think you ought to go son,' I said. 'It's not right.'

'I got the money,' he said again. 'Look.' From his pocket he took four five-pound notes. 'I won the office sweep, see. For the most goals in the month. I can spend it on anything I want. And ... I want ... you know ... Don't kick me out, missus. It took all the guts I got to come 'ere in the first place.'

There was nothing I could say. I sat there and studied him. His face was bright with eagerness. 'I'm not sure it's not illegal,' I said half to myself. 'At your age.'

'Sixteen in March, I was. So it's all right. I found out for you. In fact lady, there ain't no such thing as under age for boys with women, only girls with dirty old men. I know a bloke in a solicitor's and he told me. It's true. But I want to undress myself.'

'Oh Christ,' I said.

'Here's the money,' he said, holding out two of the five pound notes. 'Ten quid. Or do I get half price?'

'I don't think you get anything,' I decided firmly. 'Come on. Off you go. Home to your mum.'

He looked stunned. 'No,' he whispered. 'Don't send me away. I'm old enough. And I won't tell anybody. Straight.'

To my own surprise I began to wonder whether he ought to keep his glasses on or take them off, whether that reckless squint would be too much to look at when it was roaming free. He smiled in a juvenile way. 'If I don't get it now I don't reckon I ever will,' he said, playing the card carefully. 'Girls don't like me because I'm so bleeding ugly.'

My heart and my hand went out to him simultaneously. He

grinned because he knew he had won. 'I'll get my fings off,' he said. 'Don't look.'

I went almost entranced to the bed. I lay back against the oyster shell and waited for him to appear. In less than a minute he had scampered around the bathroom door without his glasses and came laughing towards me. He stopped when he saw the bed. 'Blimey, that's somefink, that bed, innit?' he said. 'Like them fings wot you get jellied eels in dahn the Mile End Road.'

He was white and skinny as a stick. But he had plenty of confidence now. He climbed exuberantly on to the bed and pushed his small skinny head straight into my bosom. 'I like them,' he sighed, 'ever so.'

He knew where everything else was too, despite taking off his spectacles. I still could hardly believe this was happening and I almost leapt from the bed when he lifted my hem and made straight for me with his junior jumbo.

'My name's Fred,' he said before making another movement. His manner suggested he thought we ought to be introduced.

'I'm Nelly,' I said dazedly. 'Pleased to meet you.'

He was the sweetest lad ever, I swear. No expert lover could have been more kind, more gentle or more enjoyable. Every now and then he lifted those madly crossed eyes and smiled. 'Are you all right down there?'

'I thought you'd never done this before,' I found myself whispering. I had never felt so flattered in my life. 'That's what you said.'

'Not to a *lady*,' he said, pausing to pass on the information. 'I've done it with a couple of girls in our alley. One was my sister. She's cross-eyed as well.' He sighed and went into my woman's warmth again. 'This is the first time I've done it without taking the bleeding skin off my knees.'

Needless, perhaps, to say, at the conclusion when he was once more uniformed and ready to go on his messenger's way, I offered to toss him double or quits for the ten pounds. We did. He won.

The Cherry Tree blossomed, as you might say, for almost two years. It became a comfortable, unexciting existence, weekends in the park in summer or at the Science Museum or Madam Tussaud's waxworks in the winter, and weekdays on the round

283

bed. We, and I include Pierre Arthur because he handled all the contacts, built up a clientele that would have graced *Who's Who*, *The Directory of Directors*, *Debrett* and *Crockford's Clerical Directory*. I had regular assignations with a sly but jolly rural dean from Somerset who was most energetic between the sheets and who then talked to me of the error of my life for an hour afterwards. He had the full rounded voice of the West Country man and he reminded me of my long lost home.

One morning the same nostalgia, although more sudden and poignant, touched me when I received a letter with the postmark 'Upcoombe, Devon.' The handwriting was round and honest. It could only be from my sister Mary.

She wrote:

Dear Nell,
I am sending this to the last address I knew you were at, although we read in the papers that your poor husband had hung hisself. We also saw that he had lost all his money which was very bad luck for you.
This time I am writing to tell you that our Dad is dead too. He fell down in the street in Plymouth (drunk as usual) and was run over by a taxi. He never changed. Just before he died there on the road he got enough strength to punch the taxi driver in the face. The police said there was more blood from the taxi driver than there was from our poor Dad. They took him to hospital in the same ambulance as Dad, but Dad was dead by then. Anyhow he's dead for sure. He had two thousand pounds in the bank and the solicitor says that it's a thousand for each of us, though I don't expect you'll need yours. Dad was buried here, right alongside our Mum's grave (if you can remember where that is). They are back together anyway but Fred my husband says there's no cider where he is so he can't get drunk anymore. Fred's really witty sometimes.
I still work at the bakery and Fred is a pigman at Upcoombe · and we have five children, four boys and a girl who looks just like you did then.
I hope one day you will come in for a cup of tea and see your sister again.
Your sister, Mary

God knows why, but I sat on the bed and had a little cry for my father. Then I pictured the little old bastard lying in the Plymouth street and punching the taxi driver in the face before dying. It made me laugh and then remember all the terrible things he had always done, the bomb he made from his army mess-tins, the marching behind our mum's coffin with that shotgun and firing it across her grave, the terrible thing he did when he abducted me from my own wedding in France and sold me to pay his gambling debts. I wondered how he would fare on Judgement Day. He would probably get off with a caution.

Two months later I received a cheque from a solicitor in Plymouth for a thousand pounds. I sent the money to the person in charge of the old folks' home in the town to provide cider every day for the people there. I said it was from the Luscombe Cider Memorial Fund.

Towards the end of our second year of marriage and business I began to notice a marked decline in my number of daily appointments. At first they dropped to half a dozen and then to four, then two and after that I was glad to hear the doorbell ring as I sat disgruntled and watched afternoon television. I mentioned this to Pierre Arthur but he was quite airy and unworried about it. 'There's not the cash about, dear,' he said. 'Uncertainty in the City and suchlike. We are a country on the downward path.'

He seemed to take the matter so calmly that I began to be concerned. Takings had dropped by seventy per cent and I was finding it difficult to fill my time. I even considered taking a part-time position somewhere else.

One afternoon a nice, gentlemanly fellow, a solicitor from Lincoln's Inn, was sharing my round bed and I mentioned this slump to him. 'Yes, yes, Nell,' he replied. 'It's a great pity. You have always given such satisfaction, such good measure. I'm sure the new girl can't match you for that.'

I lay back against the oyster shell, feeling myself go pale all down my naked body. 'The new girl?' I muttered. 'There's a new girl?'

He looked professionally aghast at having given away a secret. 'Oh dear, Nell,' he said. 'You didn't know. Oh dear, oh dear.'

Even then I concluded, naturally, that this was some rival organization set up to take away the business. 'Just wait,' I muttered. 'Just wait until Pierre Arthur knows about this.'

'I think, my dear,' said the solicitor, 'I think you'll find he knows already.'

There was a fairground that weekend on Hampstead Heath and I knew that Pierre Arthur would want to go there. I said nothing to him about my discovery until, on the Saturday evening, we were sitting high above London at the top of the big wheel. It paused at the top and we could see the widespread lights of the city below and feel the thrill of being suspended in the air.

Pierre Arthur had been acting the card that evening, as he so often did, making quick jokes, singing a ditty about coming to the fair, and holding my hand. Within me my heart was like a piece of stone for, with that instinct formed by long experience, I knew that something was going to finish us that night. It would be our last few hours in each other's company. So I laughed with him for a final time. We rode on the dodgem cars and roundabouts, him like some eccentric teenager making zooming noises over the handlebars of a tin motorbike. I sat on a funny ostrich and watched him with tears just behind my eyes.

We fired at moving targets and bit into clouds of candyfloss. He seemed to be no different from the way he always was, the eternal boyish businessman. Then we took our ride on the wheel.

When we were stopped at the height of the great wheel with the fairground music gurgling up to us from the revolving lights below and then darkness stretching away across the open heath to the limpid lights of London, I pressed his hand and said in the most ordinary voice I could make: 'Pierre Arthur, who is the new girl you have working for you?'

For the only time since our first meeting I saw him shaken out of his composure. He climbed back quickly but the look had been there, rushing to his face.

'Girl? New girl?'

'You've opened a new apartment,' I said steadily, still holding his slim hand. 'All the customers have been going there.'

'Not all,' he protested. 'Only some, Nelly.'

'Who *is* she?' His admission, although I had been awaiting it, was crushing.

He let out a manic laugh which shrieked across the fairground night and even made people in the din below look up towards us. I could see their faces like coins. 'Well . . . she's just a girl, Nell. An apprentice. I thought I'd try her out to take some work off your shoulders . . . if that's the right thing to say.'

He tried to laugh again but he could see I was not joining in. The man controlling the big wheel began to let it down gently. 'Who is she?' I repeated. 'Come on.'

'Just a girl called Connie,' he said, almost blurting it out. 'Just a kid. A beginner.'

'How old?'

'Oh, I don't know . . . twenty-one, twenty-two, something like that.'

Just the mention of the age entered me like a chill. I was now in my thirties. The big wheel reached the bottom and Pierre Arthur helped me out, making an automatic joke to the attendant. I had released his hand now and we began to walk in the same direction but separately. In the two years we had known each other we had never once quarrelled.

'Look Nell,' he said pleadingly. 'It's time you gave it a rest, For your own sake. Let somebody else do it.'

'You didn't tell me,' I said quietly. 'You kept it from me.'

'I would have. Of course I would have. It was going to be a surprise.'

'It was a surprise. A nasty one.'

'Don't you think it's a good idea? Logically now? Honestly? When you're successful you open a branch office. This is all it is. Hah! That's a good one! A branch of the Cherry Tree! What about that Nell?'

'Bugger off,' I said briefly 'Go away from me.'

He looked around to the front of my face. He could see I was angry and crying. 'I suppose you had to . . . to try her out first,' I snivelled.

'Well, what's in that, it was just a . . .'

I didn't give him time to finish. 'Adulterer!' I bellowed. 'Dirty adulterer.'

People turned everywhere. Some smirked, some looked shocked and accusing. Pierre Arthur went red in the lights.

'What about you?' he blurted back at me. 'Ten times a day.'

Exclamations went up all around. People began to gather for a closer look. 'That's business,' I howled. '*Your* bloody business.'

287

'It's *all* business!' he shouted back, not caring now. 'All of it. She's just business. And so are *you*!'

It stunned me that he said it. But all at once I saw that it was true. He did not love me. And *now* I had found out after coming to care for him so much.

'Oh,' I bawled. 'Oh, now you've said it Pierre Arthur Bickerstaff!' I picked a coconut from a box standing by a stall and heaved it savagely at him. It actually bounced off his head and went on to shatter what was alleged to be a cut-glass flower vase on a shelf of prizes. Pierre Arthur fell down in the Hampstead mud and the two showmen, one short of a coconut and the other of a glass vase, started shouting. People gathered around my husband as if he were some sideshow himself. I ran away from the fairground lights and over the black heath, sobbing, running, running. Running again.

eighteen

That same night I went back to Weymouth. I did not know why; perhaps with some idea of escaping to youth, if not to innocence. After running down the slope of Hampstead Heath I reached a main road and from there took a taxi to Waterloo Station. At that moment I was running anywhere. Had my passport been in my handbag I would have gone to London Airport.

There was a melancholy lateness about Waterloo, the station concourse blowing with stray paper, most of the platform gates pulled and the damp night air lying over everything. There were some tramps huddled on the wooden seats bent almost double in sleep. I stood, isolated, looking at the indicator board. I would have gone to any place. Then I saw that at a quarter to two in the morning there was a train to Weymouth. I decided to return.

The tramps sat like a scruffy oasis in the station desert. There was nothing for me to do but sit in the waiting room or pace the concourse, and somehow I gravitated towards the tramps.

There was a space on one of the benches and I sat there, pulling my coat around my neck.

The bundle of rags to my left stirred and a cracked woman's voice came from it. She was speaking from the middle of the bundle and she did not look up.

'You on the road?' she asked.

'Yes,' I answered. 'I suppose I am.'

' 'Ow long you been on the road?'

'All my life.'

'It gets cold don't it?'

'Yes, it's cold.'

'And those church bleeders ain't come round with the soup tonight, neither. Can't trust nobody.'

'You going to Wimbledon this year, Eustace?' one of the other tramps suddenly inquired of the pile of rags at the far end of the benches.

'Course,' replied the rags. 'Never miss Wimbledon do I?'

'Same as me with Ascot and 'enley Regatta,' the first tramp called across. 'Never miss.'

'It gets cold on the road,' said the lady tramp next to me. 'Those church bleeders.'

I thought I ought to get them something to eat. Murmuring, 'Excuse me', I rose carefully from the bench and went through the station archway to where I could see a wan light in the café across the street. It was an Italian restaurant and they had just closed. There was a man wearily sweeping up but he opened the door when I banged on the glass. From him I purchased a large saucepan full of spaghetti which we reheated on the stove. I poured in all the Bolognaise sauce he had left, paid him and carried the saucepan back to the station benches.

The tramps, to my relief, all had their own spoons and forks and they crouched around the saucepan delving into the hot spaghetti and the thick sauce. The dark station air was warmed by the aroma. Then the lady tramp, my neighbour on the bench, paused and looked up, her spoon halfway to her ragged mouth. 'Mind you,' she said. 'For myself I like it with a sprinkling of Parmesan cheese, and a nice glass of good red wine.'

It was strange to be in Weymouth again. We change but some things never do. It could have been the same breath of wind, the same day of sunshine, the same clouds and the self-same sea that rolled and grumbled forever to the beach.

I went to the Eden Roc Hotel, a rich place, unheard of in my days in the town, and in the morning stood in the bowl of the bay window of my room to look out across the fine grey patterns of the Channel on that cloudy day. There were ships hugging the horizon and I saw a small rolling fishing boat working off-shore. Perhaps young Rainbow was still hauling out there in the sightless sea.

I did not hurry. I had risen late after the cold, stopping journey in the train carrying myself and the newspapers from London, and I had a quiet lunch in the almost vacant hotel dining room, and then walked down to the harbour. I felt like a ghost. The town that came to meet me was familiar enough, the buildings along the front, the clock and the flowers, for many things change less than we would have them change in our imagination.

But when I got to the quay and the place where Hal's Café ('always something hot') had been in those early days of my adventures, it had vanished and in its place was a tarty little coffee bar where three indolent teenagers lolled at a table and listened to music banging from a juke box. No one had ever heard of any people called Hal and Flossie. They had gone.

The wind pushed the clouds from the sky in the late afternoon and freed the sun. It splashed along the beach and the mounds of the waves and I remembered how many times I had walked that same sand in the icy winter of my girlhood there. There were some early visitors on the beach, making the best of the discomfiting wind, playing with children, lying with their faces to the sun. I walked among them, still in the clothes I had worn at the Hampstead fairground the previous night that now seemed very long ago.

This place of my past set me thinking that I must take stock and plan for my future. My tears for Pierre Arthur Bickerstaff were dry and almost forgotten, for I do not grieve for long; if nothing else, I am resilient. I felt a residue of anger towards him for his amateur (as distinct from my professional) infidelity and with this I firmly closed the door on him and the period we had known.

For once, though, I was not changing lives penniless. Thanks both to my efforts beneath the oyster shell canopy and the investments I had made from advice offered in that same situation I had £32,850 in my bank account. I was free and rich. I also felt a certain oldness.

Back in the hotel I lay down for an hour and thought of what future I might have. I had many acquaintances, but hardly a friend, an occupied past but an uncertain future. I took my clothes off to bathe and stood before the mirror, remembering, for some reason, how I had done so long ago in girlhood, in front of the cottage looking-glass when Davie and I were in our runaway days. Considering the use to which it had been put, the body of Nelly Luscombe had survived well. The curves were fuller, but still symmetrical, the skin touched with small pockets and wrinkles but I had looked after it, it remained creamy. It was the eyes and the mouth and the breasts where the tiredness showed. I sat on the bed and crossed my legs. My thighs bulged. In a few years I would be forty. It was time I did something else for a living.

In the night I dreamed there was a storm with tiny ships trembling in great seas. I was on the bridge of a trawler with the Commander and, in the logic of dreams, we were playing housey-housey while the tempest spilled around us.

'House!' he was calling in that hurt, croaky voice. 'House Nelly! House!'

The dream so stirred me that I almost fell out of bed in the waves and awoke on my knees in an attitude of prayer. I rose and stumbled to the window. It was the loveliest calm night, moon travelling high, the sea silver, the land smooth. I sat by the window for a while, watching it and following the lights of a few fishing boats a mile or two out. I wondered if some fruity, willing Weymouth girl was out there with the lusty crews. Perhaps not these nights.

Because the dream was still with me and it had disturbed me so much I was reluctant to return to bed. For a while I missed the attentive Pierre Arthur, but I thought that at that moment his attentions were most probably on his new apprentice lover and I dismissed his face from my mind. But the nameless restlessness, provoked by the sea perhaps, once familiar, now a new sensation again, would not go. I began to dress.

Outside among the silver and the shadows it was chilly and I tugged my coat against my body. The dozing hall porter had presumably seen odder things in his life and he had merely wished me a pleasant walk as he turned the large key in the door. I walked immediately towards the shoreline.

Every step, even across the grass, seemed to sound in the standing night. The air pressed cold against my eyes, the heaving of the Channel became more distinct. Then, almost at the beach, I saw the surprising sight of a Rolls-Royce parked on the grass with its headlights dipped. Walking towards it I saw that the door was open and there was a man sitting on the step looking down towards the beach. And on the beach, clear in the moon, was a young boy dancing to the sound of the sea. I looked towards the man, and he towards me, and we saw that we knew each other.

He was Derek Blane, a prominent Member of Parliament, who had been a business acquaintance of Dante. He had visited us and I had met him again, after Dante's death, at Zurich during one of my professional visits as the guest of a British delegate to a conference there.

We exchanged greetings as naturally as if it were the middle of the day not the night, and at his invitation I sat beside him on the doorstep of the Rolls. He was a dark, slender, sharp-faced man, then a good deal more good-humoured than he looked. I remembered thinking that about him before. The laugh would suddenly break from the serious and lined face, so quickly and easily that it came as a surprise.

'That's my son, Simon,' he said nodding at the lad making ballet movements on the beach. 'He wants to be a dancer.'

'He certainly seems to have the dedication,' I said, hardly knowing how to reply. 'Practising in the middle of the night.'

Derek sighed. 'I'm told that he is really very good,' he said. 'He is ten now and they say he could become an exceptional dancer. And he loves it. He has been going down to the beach in the day and dancing on the firm sand. People have been gathering around to laugh at him but he's taken no notice at all. His eyes just glaze over when he is dancing and he doesn't see anybody.'

'People are like that,' I agreed. 'It's ignorance.'

'But,' he added, 'suddenly even they become quiet and they watch him and they realize what he is doing and just how talented he is. And at the end they stand and applaud. Some people come back every day. It's very funny, actually, because when they clap it sort of wakes him up. He blinks at them as though he has just come out of a trance.'

I watched the shadowy boy on the beach. His movements were like a graceful ghost or perhaps a sprite. The moon lay over the white sea, caught his shadow and threw it across the sand.

'He doesn't even need music, does he?' I said quietly.

'Not at all. In fact he comes down here at this time of night because it is so silent and the waves and sometimes the wind make the noises he wants. The strange thing is, Nell, he is such a masculine kid. He's the best footballer I've seen in years at his age.'

'If he moves like that it's not so surprising,' I said. I waited, then added: 'Where's his mother, Derek?'

He looked directly ahead and said: 'At this moment I would think that she is in bed with one of my political opponents. That's what hurts. If it were one of our side then it would not seem as if you were defeated in every direction.'

'Oh dear,' I said inadequately.

'And you, Nell?'

I thought it was improbable that he would know about the Cherry Tree and my occupation there for, although Members of Parliament were among the regular climbers of those City stairs, the secret was only spread very carefully. He was not, I thought, the sort of man who might have heard it.

'I married again after Dante's death,' I said simply. 'But it seems as if that's finished now, too. Only just. That's why I came down to Weymouth. I spent some time here when I was a girl.'

'That's why I find you wandering abroad by moonlight then,' he nodded. 'Trying to think things out?'

'No,' I said certainly. 'I've done all that. All the thinking out. It's done, finished. But it happened rather suddenly and it's left me in space. At the moment I really have nothing to do in my life, nothing at all.'

'I imagine you'll soon repair the situation,' he smiled. 'I seem to remember thinking that, even as a wife of Dante, you had a good deal more potential than anyone gave you credit for.'

I smiled too. 'I was holding myself in,' I shrugged. 'Dante was not the sort of husband to let me *do* anything.'

The boy had completed his dance. He concluded with a marvellous bow to the moon and the sea. I began to applaud and his father, after a quick glance sideways at me, joined in.

It was as though he had never thought of it before. The boy jogged up from the beach. He was wearing a track suit and he looked like an athlete. He had his father's serious dark expression. He looked up at us from the rising shingle, surprised at the clapping and at my appearance there, but then grinned and came forward to be introduced.

'We will be leaving in a few hours, Nell,' said Derek. 'Are you staying down here in Weymouth for a while?'

'I expect so,' I said. 'I want to look up some old friends. You never know, I might even find myself.'

They got into the car. 'Goodbye,' he said shyly. 'Would you mind if I telephoned you at your hotel this evening?'

'Please do,' I said. 'I'd like that. It's the Eden Roc.'

He regarded me steadily for a moment and I returned the same look. Then he smiled and we all shook hands. He drove the large, silent car towards the moonlight, and I turned and walked up the slope away from the sea. I could hear it muttering knowingly behind my back.

That unusual, casual meeting was yet another hinge to my life, another entrance to another place. Derek Blane was exceptionally intelligent and stable for a Member of Parliament and despite his betraying wife and his own sharp good looks and his manner he had none of the reputation of womanizing that many of the less appealing men in the House had achieved. I think that our affair was his first for many years.

He had, however, heavy political ambitions and when we met he was on the verge of a seat in the Cabinet. We had to be secret. Discretion being the better part of my life, this was no trouble for me and his normally solemn face was as good a shield against pryers as I have known.

Royal Ascot week arrived within ten days of our meeting and we set out in our hats and finery for the course, but each day made a circuit before we arrived and went to a small beautiful hotel, where we made love all the afternoon. The first time I playfully kept my picture hat on my head while the rest of me was naked and he sat in the bed entranced, while I paraded as the Ascot ladies do (and were doing at the moment on our bedroom television set). 'And here is the Honourable Lady Nelly Luscombe,' he intoned from the sheet. 'A delightful hat of turquoise feathers, a fine shade of an exquisite face, skin like

294

porcelain, the finest pair of breasts in all the land, shapely waist, an intriguing little posy at the meeting of the legs ... and ... God knows what else.'

I went to him on the bed and, still arrayed in my wide hat, I lay above him and stroked his skin, finally letting him ease himself into me. He was a composed but deeply passionate lover and I found it difficult to keep my hat on my head.

We drank champagne and ate from a Fortnum's picnic basket. That morning I had gone to the bank and checked the sum of £32,850 in my account. Apart from the fun of a pound on the Grand National or the Derby, stretched perhaps to ten on the rare occasions I had been taken to a race meeting, I had no experience of betting. I told Derek nothing of it but I gambled away a thousand pounds on that first afternoon while we were making love. As we embraced in that warm hotel room, the horses carrying my faith were being beaten by varying distances on the course three miles away.

On the second day of Ascot we again dressed in our finery and with our champagne and pâté enjoyed the afternoon in naked privacy at the hotel. We made love between and during the races and talked and learned to like each other and enjoyed the novelty of our situation. 'What are you doing Henley Regatta week?' I asked him breathlessly as we lay panting against each other after a torrid period that lasted through the running of the Ascot Gold Cup. 'Those rowing races last a lot longer,' I pointed out.

'There's the Lord's Test Match too,' he grinned from beside me. 'Five days of it.'

It was intriguing matching our actions to the voice of the commentator ('And here's the favourite. He's coming again.') and we enjoyed the pantomime almost as much as the lovemaking. On that afternoon I lost another thousand pounds to the bookmakers.

Had Derek known of what the horses who laboured on the screen behind my back were costing me, I could not have given him any logic for my sudden plunge into such uncontrolled betting. It was partly, I suppose, that £30,000 seemed a rounder figure than £32,850. It seemed a flatter base from which I could restart my life.

On the third day of Ascot I put the remaining £850 on a treble wager, three horses called Devon Fields, Bedfellow and

Future Uncertain, all of which had to win their races. I still said nothing to Derek Blane and we smiled at our private joke as we met once more, he in topper and tails and me in an orange hat decorated with small ducks' eggs.

At the hotel they hardly gave us a glance. It was one of those London fringe hotels, a pretty, lawned place on the Thames where couples go not only to have sex but to be romantic as well. The staff was probably used to unusual situations.

Devon Fields won at four to one and I mentally rang up £4,250 while Derek was kissing my neck and I was stroking his loins (a whore achieves this facility of cashing-up while touching-up through long practice). I said nothing about the win or the wager, however, but when Bedfellow loped past the post two lengths ahead of the next horse, and at three to one, I began to take some heed of what was going on at the racecourse.

'What's the matter, Nelly?' asked Derek from the bed, seeing my attention wandering. 'What's upset you?'

I still didn't let him know. I kissed him and laughed and tried to keep my excitement still. Future Uncertain was running in the four-thirty and the hour between Bedfellow's win and then was the longest of my life. My lover could not understand what was worrying me.

At the start of the race we were sprawled across the bed and he was wanting me again (he was very healthy for an MP), his hands were rolling against my breasts and his tongue was pressed in my navel. But he could sense that my heart was not in it. My eyes were wandering around at the twenty-two inch screen.

'Ah,' he said knowingly. 'It's that that's annoying you. Right, let's turn it off.'

I raced him to the knob. 'No. No. It's not that darling! Truly. Leave it on please.'

'Then what is it?' he pleaded. 'You've suddenly changed.'

'Very shortly I'll tell you,' I said trembling.

'It's not me is it? You're not tired of me?'

I reached out for him, anything to take my mind off that bloody race, and turned him on to the bed. I heard the commentator shout 'They're off!' as we embraced. In all my life I've never had a few minutes like that. We were doing it and I kept hearing 'and third ... Future Uncertain ... and he's moving up ... he's in second place ... four furlongs to go.'

It was more than I could stand. Like a wrestler I rolled over front down on the bed, motioning that my surprised and interrupted lover should mount me from the rear. I had to watch that screen.

'God help me Nell!' he cried. 'What the hell's going on?'

'Derek,' I moaned. 'Oh Derek, darling.' I half turned my head backwards towards him riding my rear like a jockey himself. 'That horse – there – Future Uncertain. I've got a fortune on it!'

There never was a *coitus interruptus* like that. He rolled and slid from my back and we lay clutching each other while Future Uncertain fought it out, car by ear, with the favourite. 'How much?' he kept jabbering in my ear. 'For God's sake, how much?'

'Thousands,' I jabbered back. '£17,000. Oh Christ, I can't look! I can't!'

Future Uncertain won it by a sneeze. We lay like two dead people on the bed. 'Nelly,' he croaked. 'You've won a fortune. What ... what ... odds?'

'Something like four to one,' I said. My face was soaking with sweat and tears. We waited, prostrate. Then they announced it, Future Uncertain, at six to one. I moaned and lay close to him. 'There was seventeen thousand pounds riding on him,' I whispered. 'I had a treble. They all won. Oh darling ... sixty-one thousand two hundred pounds!'

The following week, on impulse, I went to Diana Seagram's house in Westminster and, after waiting for a moment to give myself the opportunity to change my mind, I walked to the door and rang the bell.

I arrived at the hour she was about to leave forever. I found her sitting sorrily among trunks and packing cases and she was delighted to see me. It was odd to visit her again after the interval of years, lines traced on the beautiful skin, the eyes tired but her figure still slim, her voice always soft. The voice can always stay beautiful.

'You find me at a melancholy moment, Nelly,' she said after we had embraced. 'After all these years I have decided to give up this house. I am retiring to Sevenoaks to join the senior citizens, the legion of the damned.'

'You're hardly ready for that,' I said. 'You look just the same.'

'And you have become a woman of the world,' she smiled. 'Just as we always knew you would.'

'How is he?' I asked tentatively. 'The Commander.'

'Oh just the same.' She laughed, I thought a shade guiltily. 'A trifle short on patience and temper.'

Her eyes came up slowly to me now for she knew what my next question would be. 'You . . . you didn't get married then?'

Diana shrugged. 'No. I decided against it. A merger is a big thing, bigger than marriage in it's way. As I told you at the time, that's all he proposed – well, *we* proposed really – a merger of souls. In the end we . . . we didn't do it. He is still stumping about up in Shropshire and I am here. At the moment.'

We sat down. She on a tin trunk, me on a chair. The years seemed to have reversed us. 'We have read something about your life, Nelly,' she said cautiously. 'It has not all been happy has it? We discussed whether one or the other of us should write to you but we decided against it. Sometimes one can fare better without sympathy.'

'Dante,' I sighed. 'My husband. Yes, it was very unpleasant. There have been other things, a lot, good and bad. Mine's just been one of those lives. All I can say is it hasn't been dull.'

I looked up at her as though expecting her to guess what I had done with those years, but if she did, she did not show it. 'You've escaped that dullness anyway,' she said. 'I've had more than enough, I think, chiefly brought upon my own head. Sometimes it does not pay to lead a life that is too comfortable, emotionally comfortable I mean,' she smiled wryly. 'I'm quite looking forward to playing fast and loose in Sevenoaks.'

As she spoke I was still looking around the room, remembering it from that first sun-filled day when I had walked into it, a rosy apprentice lover from the breezy seaside. Now she was leaving and I was looking for somewhere to live. 'Diana,' I said carefully, 'this house. What will it cost?'

'Nelly!' she almost cried out. 'Nelly . . . you think *you* might . . . ?'

I found myself blushing as though even the thought should

have been beyond me. 'Yes,' I nodded. 'I *did* think. Would it be . . .'

'Possible? Well of course, Nelly. How marvellous. There is only a short lease left, about five years, so if you would be willing to take it on for that period the landlord could hardly ask a fortune. It would be wonderful wouldn't it? A sort of passing on to a new generation of friends.'

My hands went involuntarily out to her and hers to mine. We were, as ever, comfortable with each other, like sisters. We both burst into laughter. She rose from the trunk. 'Do you remember it?' she said excitedly. 'All the rooms? Come on, let me remind you.'

She held out her hand like a girl and I gave her mine and we went through the house, as voluble as exploring children. It was a tall, slim house, elegant as a tall man may be elegant, with more rising rooms and corridors than I ever remembered. It was almost devoid of furniture now and our steps echoed as we went from one door to another. The bedrooms were large with the sun splashing through the vacant windows. And one of those windows, I saw, was filled with a vista of pointing towers and turrets and the great grey clock of the Houses of Parliament.

The house that became known, and indeed notorious, as Strangeways never had a name, only a number, 184, Westminster Terrace Gardens. The Members of Parliament who frequented it over the next few years, unofficially, The Strangeways Society. At the famous court case, of course, this was alleged, by my defence, to be a collection of MPs dedicated to prison reform.

None of this had been my intention when I took over the lease from Diana Seagram. I only thought of it as an indulgence. The grand London home of Nelly Luscombe from Devon, the completion of a neat circle begun many years before, and probably the place to entertain the occasional rich lover; perhaps, some time, another husband.

Poor Pierre Arthur had sent me telegrams and tea-roses, had phoned and pleaded and, once I moved in, walked up and down outside the house for so many days that it was rumoured among the neighbours that he was a special detective guarding an important new resident. But I was never good at retying knots and now I decided quite calmly and sharply that his part of my life was used up, finished. In one of his many tearstained letters to me (held, I suspected, for a few moments below a slow-dripping tap) he promised that he would disband the Cherry Tree and its branch and that we would regain our happy life in the parks and showgrounds and museums of London with me no longer required to work at all. But this I refused, my door to his life being firmly closed, and, eventually, as I guessed he would, he made the best of it and recruited another, younger lady to lie on the round bed framed by the oyster shell. Gradually he backed away and bowed out of my life and I was not to see him again until that New Year's Eve utterly ruined by his untimely death.

My affair with Derek Blane developed easily and steadily and when I moved into Strangeways he would frequently visit me when the House of Commons was sitting. Before long his friends came too, their lady friends and occasionally even their wives. There were dinner parties when wives and lady friends (the wives at least unknowing) sat at the same table. Derek was acknowledged as host on many of these occasions. His wife had asked for a divorce and it was generally and, by me, comfortably accepted that when this was over and my divorce from Pierre Arthur was complete, that – with my recent past miraculously hidden – we could marry. I had become a famous hostess, due to marry a man who might one day become Prime Minister.

One of the several troubles with Members of Parliament, of course, is that they talk, and they drink as well. They also fancy themselves with women. I was careful, naturally, to exclude from Strangeways any of the half a dozen or so who had engaged in dealings with me at the Cherry Tree or at Burridges, but I realize now that I must have been in a fool's dream to think that this would remain untold for long.

At the dinner table one evening I found my knee being fumbled below the cloth by a port-faced old bastard who had been fancied for high office years before, but had missed by a whisker and had taken his revenge on both the country and the party ever since. I made a joke of the incident at first, although the finger crawling like a fat caterpillar up my thigh filled me with distaste. It is different when you are pawed for money.

Eventually, when he ignored my whispered warnings, I stuck a fork firmly into his hand. He let out a boozy cry and pulled his hand away. It was late, a lot had been drunk around the table and few people noticed it. We confronted each other. His eyes became dull and nasty and he said: 'Come on Nelly Luscombe. You didn't mind when you had that little love spot in the City, did you? Nor at Burridges. I've heard all about that, Nelly. The goings on.'

He froze into hurt silence then and soon left, but I knew it would not be long before the shadows of my past came creeping along like an unwelcome evening to shroud me once more.

It took two weeks. The morning newspapers had said that Derek was to be invited into the Cabinet in a government reshuffle and at four in the afternoon he arrived himself. Standing at the window I watched him jump from a taxi and come hurrying up the steps. His face was like a hatchet.

I tried. 'Didn't they ask you to be Foreign Secretary after all?' I said when he came into the drawing room. 'You look so fierce, Derek.'

He stood immobilized at the door. The terrible thing was I knew that he loved me. He faltered, then walked forward and embraced me with genuine love for the final time. We kissed and he turned and went to the window, staring out towards Westminster and his future.

'Nelly, God, Nelly, I've got to ask you about something,' he said. 'I've got to ask you if something is true or not.'

'I promise – I cannot tell a lie,' I said, trying to ease it. 'Like George Washington.'

He turned to me and jumped at the phrase. 'Is that a saying from the Cherry Tree?' he asked bitterly. 'You remember the Cherry Tree, don't you?'

Within me I shivered. But I controlled my answer. 'I'm unlikely to forget it,' I said defiantly. 'But it's all over now.'

He seemed shattered by the answer even though he must have expected it. 'Christ,' he stumbled. 'How *could* you?'

That made me angry. 'How could I *what*? To make a sodding living, that's how Derek. How was I to know I was going to meet a better class of person?'

He backed away from the sarcasm. 'I could hardly believe it,' he whispered. 'You – doing that.'

'I've done it for you,' I pointed out. 'Many times.'

'There's a difference!' he shouted now. 'For God's sake, Nelly!'

'Because I got paid? I'll say there was. It kept me fed and clothed for a start.'

'Don't tell me that. That's rubbish. You . . . you of all people Nell Luscombe. You need never have done it for money. Never!' He bawled the word at me. He was in a scarcely controlled frenzy. I backed into the room and stood behind a chair. In that moment, however, I knew he was speaking the truth. I need never have done it. It was always easy. It was the most convenient of all professions.

'Well Derek I did.' I felt that I was going to cry. 'But . . . that's finished. It's all past.'

'If you think that you must be simple,' he retorted.

'I am.'

'For God's sake how can you imagine that something of that kind could be hidden? It's a bloody miracle that it didn't come out before.'

'Who told you?' I said, conversationally now. It was too late to save anything.

He looked up. His face was like a sheet. 'The Prime Minister,' he muttered. 'Who else?'

'I never screwed the Prime Minister,' I said callously.

'Nelly, don't make a joke of it. Don't you see. Everybody knew but me, it seems. Somebody put the poison in for me. If the news of this Cabinet job had not already leaked to the press, I doubt if I'd have got it. Anyway, he's told me to . . .'

'Get rid of me,' I suggested.

'Not in those words, but that's what he meant. Can't you see . . . ?'

'Very well indeed,' I said. 'But don't worry. You don't have to get rid of me Derek, because I'm getting rid of you. Go out of the door and point yourself towards Downing Street and keep going, boy. Don't look back or you won't be a pillar of society – you'll be a pillar of fucking salt!'

I left him standing ashen in the room. I went unhurriedly up the stairs and closed my bedroom door. He had some political books and files in there. I took them to the window and dropped them on his head as he left the house. He turned and shook his fist at me as he scrabbled around trying to pick them

302

up. I laughed at him and turned away from the casement.

That time I cried a bit longer than usual. Not just for him, not many of my tears are for men, but for myself again. The moment I went out in that fishing boat with Rainbow, all those years before, I had set the pattern of my life. There was no help nor cure for it. But I was running out of places to go.

It was six months later that I made the decision to turn my elegant house in Westminster Terrace Gardens into a luxury salon for Members of Parliament and others in need. The idea had been lingering ever since the disgraceful walkout of Derek Blane, bartering love for office, and had been willingly promoted by several of his fellow Members who had neither his scruples nor his hopes of glory.

The firm and final suggestion, in fact, came from one of Derek Blane's Cabinet colleagues, an older man, surer, and one who would never have put power before pleasure. His name was Sir Barthold Wick and even in his sixties he could live up to his singular boast of an erection tall enough to match a pile of thirty-three two-shilling pieces topped by an old fashioned threepenny bit. Towards the end of his time (he died in the bath tub while taking a dip with his wife's maid and his own faithful bull terrier), he found to his chagrin that he could not manage the threepenny bit.

He was a large, gentle, grey man, and once I had returned (so easily I'm afraid) to my old ways, we spent many a convivial hour together in my bed. Indeed he half seriously suggested, after cutting his return to the Commons rather finely on an important vote, that a division bell should be installed in my house. But he was without cant and even his necessary political hypocrisy was performed tongue-in-cheek. One day, speaking of a fellow minister, he sighed: 'That man my dear, would stay at a hotel, leave without paying *and* steal the Gideon Bible.'

'You know Nelly dear,' he murmured one afternoon while we were drinking gin in the drawing room. 'You're not using this fine house to the best of its capacity. You have all these rooms, why not turn it into a nice little brothel. Get some decent, honest tarts in. The boys in the House would love it.'

He took no heed of my half-hearted protestations, merely hooding his rheumy eyes and continuing speaking as so often he did when rudely interrupted in the Commons. 'You could have a room for this and a room for that. You know what varying degrees of interests Members have. You'd make a fortune, my dear.'

I went to Monte Carlo for a month and thought about it. It was running the risk of the law, for I had never managed other whores before, always working alone. But being on the Riviera again, thinking about the past years, L'Horizon, the distant Dante, the hopeless Davie, and standing outside the Hôtel de Paris from whence I was kidnapped in my wedding gown by my own father, I came to the conclusion that my life was never meant to run placidly.

Returning, fortuitously, on the day Her Majesty opened Parliament in the autumn, I decided, watching the ranked, blanked faces of the politicians assembled in the House to hear the Speech, that I should have a grand opening of Strangeways, as it became known, just before the Christmas Recess.

It began in a luxurious but conventional way, with carefully invited guests being entertained to cocktails by four engaging and easy-going girls who had been selected with equal care. Evening gowns with wide views, special grooming, cheerfulness, understanding, intelligence and physical fitness were required. Each evening a piano played.

There were five dim bedrooms on the first floor and two more above. In the basement was a dancing room with a mirrored floor and there were two other rooms below ground where some of the more exotic diversions were permitted and which, perhaps needless to say, proved in time to be the most popular in the house.

Amateur dramatics night was invariably crowded (during one Commons debate on the Future of the Isle of White Watercress Industry it was said that there were more Members to be seen at Strangeways than in the House itself). On these theatrical nights we arranged to put on various charades which excited individuals and groups in the most spectacular way and for this we had to keep a wardrobe of costumes including such bizarre items as Red Riding Hood's cloak, a Florence Nightingale outfit, two Rasputin costumes, various Roman and Greek robes and togas, some whips and nastier looking implements of punishment, chains, shackles, and other ironmongery, slave disguises, guardsman's uniforms and a small stuffed mule.

More girls were recruited and I was able to manage my establishment from a velvet chair in the main salon, spending my evenings drinking, eating and conversing with some of the country's most respected and responsible figures. Our champagne consumption became legendary. It was not necessary for me to take part in any of the sexual activities if I did not choose, although I quite liked to play the part of the Bleeding Nun of Lindenburg, in an occasional melodrama we produced. I could choose my bed partners as I wished and charge them twice as much as girls half my age.

Our door was knocked many times. Others came to hear of Strangeways and actors, actresses and that sort would join in by special invitation. It was amazing how after a night of devoted debauchery everyone emptied into the morning streets and became again the idols of society they were popularly seen to be.

Our operations continued for four years – spanning two Governments and many changes of fortune in individual power – and Strangeways became an estabished place of entertainment for officials and participants in Commonwealth Prime Ministers' Conferences, the casts of Broadway shows playing in London's West End, Church Conventions, reunions of senior officers and occasional exclusive groups from overseas, Japanese and Germans in particular. We also held a complimentary Police Night once every few months.

My young ladies were acknowledged as being the most attractive and kindest in London and the guests appreciated this. There was Molley Burtenshaw, a red-haired Yorkshire girl, who never sent an unsmiling man from her room. Members of Parliament would stalk into Strangeways, their teeth clenched after frustrating debates and political skullduggery, — and Molly would be summoned to be considerate to them. They would return to the rough-edged world calmed, satisfied, Mollified.

There was Angelica Brownjohn, who sang sweet ballads at the piano and the same songs, in lower, softer key, into her client's ear while he enjoyed her embrace. She wore leopard-skin tights and had raven hair. Her parents in Wiltshire knew nothing about her activities and imagined that she was unemployed. When she visited them they would give her groceries and second-hand garments to take back to London, believing she was in need. Once she returned aghast from a weekend at home with a consignment of headless plastic gnomes, obtained for her by her father. The heads, provided in a separate box, had to be screwed on to the bodies, and the manufacturers paid a pound for every five hundred of these completed monstrosities. She had to make some sort of show to please her father and she completed almost a thousand gnomes and earned nearly two hundred pounds before becoming exhausted. Encouraged by her industry he then provided a further cargo and she brought these despairingly to Strangeways where the upshot was the extraordinary spectacle of harlots and visiting Members of Parliament busily fixing plastic heads on to plastic gnomes. After this questions were asked in the House about the low rates paid to outworkers by exploiting manufacturers.

Cynthie Broad, one of our original hostesses, lived in a suburban house with her sister, who was a secretary and imagined Cynthie went off each night to work as a waitress in a nightclub. Eventually she discovered what her sister did and was dreadfully shocked until she discovered how much her sister earned and for what effort. A week later she was on the staff as well.

They were all marvellous girls. We had a West Indian hostess, Teresa Longmate, who had great influence on some of the immigration debates in the Commons, Lucy Wing, a Chinese girl whose oriental anatomy was a constant source of conjecture and interest. She did a marvellous act sliding naked down the banister of the main staircase. There were two French ladies of noble families who had been sent to London as *au pair* girls to learn how to make a coal fire and placate screaming children and scheming husbands.

It was, in its manner, rather like a luxurious harem, a comfortable, warm, secret place, where, at a price, even the most difficult ego, the most tormented soul could be provided for and even the most outrageous appetite, the most pathetic need, could be satisfied and the recipient sent out into the world cleansed and sane, lighter in spirit and, of course, in pocket.

It was eleven thirty on New Year's Eve and the festivities at Strangeways were developing towards the almost inevitable orgy which traditionally took place while Big Ben struck the year almost outside the window. There were a great many, stranded foreigners with us that night and a good gathering of people from Mayfair and the West End, but rather less Members of Parliament, due to their being reluctantly exiled to their constituencies for the Christmas Recess.

My comfortable duties over the past year and more had resulted in my putting on some nicely rounded poundage and I was astride the thick and happy legs of a handsome Teutonic industrialist who liked larger sizes. We were singing traditional German songs such as 'We March Against England' when the telephone rang almost at my elbow and from it came the terrible and lonely voice of Pierre Arthur Bickerstaff. He said he was dying.

I left the New Year to my guests and hurried out into the damp night. People were shouting good drunken wishes in the streets and there were party lights in many windows. A timely taxi came by and I took it and was in St John's Wood in fifteen minutes.

Oh God, what a night that was! It was bad enough going back to the house, our old familiar place, our dwelling shared in the days when we went to the park and the river. Nostalgia swamped me like nausea, a silent wave of it all the more poignant because the noises of celebration had now drifted away and the path and the trees were wet and dark and from the house came a solitary uncomfortable light. Trembling I walked to the front door. It was standing six inches open. I touched it and walked in.

He had been living there with some idiot girl chemist and the place stank of ether and ammonia and the other smelly pieces of her trade. As soon as I went through the door I could hear him coughing in the kitchen. The solitary light was in there. Shaking I walked in.

He was sitting on the floor, his back propped against a kitchen cupboard. His face was set in an awful mask. But even then he tried to smile when he saw me, the most terrible sight.

'Pierre Arthur,' I whispered, crouching down by him and taking his freezing hand. 'What have you done?'

'I'll tell you what he's done.' She came out of the other room, out of the shadows. It was his girl, a yawning creature scratching her own back. 'He mistook something very nasty for custard powder. He had a lot to drink and he tasted it. He likes custard you know.'

'Don't tell me, I'm his wife,' I snapped. 'I know he likes custard. Is the doctor coming?'

'I've just managed to reach him,' she said. 'He was out celebrating. There's nothing we can do anyway. I've given him an emetic, but it's too late. That stuff would go through steel.'

And with that, all delivered in tones of the utmost boredom, she pulled a scraggy blanket around her shoulders and walked out of the front door. I bent over poor Pierre Arthur and pulled him to my bosom. His hand still felt the same there, except it was rather more limp. Outside I heard the doctor's car pull up on the gravel and the man came in full of bonhomie and scotch, with a paper hat stuffed in his dinner jacket pocket.

He bent and briefly examined Pierre Arthur. He glanced at me and saw I was convivially dressed also and that I had my coat. 'You know him well?' he inquired.

'He's my husband,' I replied throatily.

'He's not now dear. I'm afraid he's dead.' He took out a pocket watch. 'Bang on midnight too. Fascinating. It's a toss-up which he died in.'

nineteen

For the next two years Strangeways entertained and prospered in Westminster. Some of the more healthy denizens of the House of Lords took to coming there and, since they always had to have things different from the members of the Commons, to them the house became known as Kinky Court.

It became necessary to take on other girls, and they were, of course, always of marked beauty, charm and great stamina. One, who acquired the name of Dirty Diedre, was a sweet redhead, the daughter of an earl, and she proved a great favourite with certain left-wing MPs who, I was gratified to see, had the same weaknesses and appetites as the most conservative Tory. She entertained regularly a notorious neo-communist who, astride this aristocratic beauty, would leap about with revolutionary fervour and cry: 'Forward the Oppressed!'

Who the spoilsport was I never did discover. It may have been one of the Socialists, riven by conscience, it may have been a sneaky Tory, aspiring to office, or it may have been a peer admonished for some outrageous perversion which endangered the well-being of the girl involved. Their Lordships, in fact, were far more difficult to accommodate than their colleagues in the Lower House whose demands were normally more humble. Whether it was the rot of aristocracy, the long shadow of the public schools, or some other flaw, I cannot tell, but I soon grew to know what the expression 'a belted earl' really meant. During those long, dozing sessions in the House, filled with lunch and wine, they dreamed unruly dreams that woke them grunting and brought them shuffling to my door in the hope and expectation of the dreams being gratified. Some of their abnormalities could be accommodated but others were so outrageous that I would not allow my girls to take part. I once found a terrified young lady, legs apart, stretched out on a bed with a titled man, old enough to be her grandfather, *and* in full ermine and red robes and coronet, ceremonially running an ornate sword between her thighs. He argued it was not sharp. Other activities emanating from that regal place included the use of chocolate spread, lemon curd, fire irons, dog collars, recordings of Melba, false moustaches (for the girl) and other oddities. A fee of one hundred and fifty pounds was offered by a Scots peer who wanted to ride a district nurse's bicycle over a tethered whore. This was never taken up.

My own sexual life had now reverted to an amateur basis. I no longer had to live by bed alone. Life was prosperous. In the Portobello Road antique market one Saturday I met a young man who sold bogus watches with a smile and he charmingly asked me to go and have a pint with him. His name was Albert Farthing, he was a Hackney Cockney, and his lovemaking was fierce and uncomplicated.

'Look at that, Nell,' he would say, stretched full on my bed, admiring what God had blessed him with. 'Ever seen the like of that? Like a lucky dog's bone, ain't it?'

When I first undressed for him and lay indolently, my breasts lolling, so that he could see me, he crouched at the foot of the bed like a lean alley cat, eyeing me along all my landscape. 'I reckon the look of you, Nell,' he said genuinely. 'I like a body what's been lived in.'

He was amazed, then scornful, of the idiosyncracies of those who were paying clients of the house. 'Disgusting,' he grunted when he realized some of the things that went on. 'This sort of thing gives fucking a bad name.' And he was particularly outraged when, one evening, I showed him the mirrored dance floor. A slow waltz was playing and four customers were dancing with my girls.

'They 'unchbacks or something?' asked Albert, nodding at the slowly revolving men, each one with his head bent forward.

'No,' I smiled and whispered. 'They're looking down into the mirror.'

'What they doing that for?' he asked innocently.

'Because the girls don't wear anything under their dresses.'

Even in the dim lights I could see the shock encompass Albert's face. 'Oh the dirty sods,' he breathed. 'The rotten, dirty old sods. And these are the buggers who keep putting up the income tax.'

However simple his outlook, Albert was an enduring lover and I enjoyed his energy, his hard Cockney body and his homespun filth. He loved to tell jokes and we would spend an hour or more, cooling off on the bed after making love, while he regaled me with the newest foul anecdotes, riddles and rhymes.

The raid by the police on Strangeways came, appropriately, on St Valentine's Night. We had organized a grand fancy dress orgy (strictly invitation only) and this was in progress when Albert rushed through the back door. 'Nelly!' he shouted across the room. 'The Law's everywhere!'

I turned angrily at first, for shouting was not allowed at Strangeways, but immediately I realized what he meant I sounded a pre-arranged alarm signal – three blasts on a coastguard's whistle. We had practised this drill regularly but had never needed to use it.

We always enjoyed good relations with individual police officers from Scotland Yard and the London police stations. We never paid protection money to anyone, but policemen were always welcome and were permitted trade discounts, as indeed were editors and other journalists. I never thought they would turn and bite the hand that caressed them. But they do and they did.

Fortunately the front and back doors were kept locked and

when the demanding banging began we were able to delay them for a few precious minutes, while the bolts were clumsily drawn, and rearrange the salon.

When the police were finally admitted, two dozen customers, half of them Members of Parliament, and a dozen of my girls were sitting primly watching Albert Farthing dropping into a spiritualist's trance. The lights were dim, the drinks hidden, the dress of everyone decently adjusted.

'What's going on here?' demanded the first police inspector through the door. 'What's this you're up to?'

Albert was superb. As the lights went up he went into an uncontrollable fit of shouting, rolling and raving, and had to be calmed and restrained before anything else could be done.

'Now you've done it,' I threatened the inspector. 'Now you've done it. Don't you know it can be fatal to disturb a medium in a trance.'

'Trance my arse,' he said rudely. 'We know what's going on here.'

'We were just trying to contact the other side,' I told him acidly. 'Now you've ruined it. We were just getting through, too.'

They were everywhere by now, of course, running through the building like spiders, every boudoir, every bathroom, every cupboard (except one which they somehow missed) and every chest. I always contended they found nothing incriminating (there is no law against having silk sheets on all the beds, mirrors on ceilings – not to mention one on the floor – and a full scale model of a slave galley in the conservatory) but they were satisfied enough for their purposes. They took everybody's name, although those of the Members of Parliament somehow floated out of the police car window on the way back from the road, and I was arrested and taken to their police station.

They kept me all night in their cheerless charge room, with questions and answers and cups of limp tea. My solicitor came down at four o'clock in the morning and told me I was in serious trouble. For that sort of advice I had to pay him.

I was released on bail of £5,000 after appearing at the magistrate's court the following morning, tired and drained and charged with keeping a brothel, living on the earnings of prostitution, and procuring for an immoral purpose.

In tatters I went out into the street and took a taxi back to my house. There were photographers and police everywhere. The police had been through everything, even lifting the paper from the walls, presumably to see if it concealed filthy drawings and writings. I got them out as soon as I could without going altogether mad and sat amid the debris of my life, drinking gin, alone again. Then, from far away it seemed, I heard an echoing banging.

'Christ! Lord Corwellian!' I almost shouted to myself.

I ran from the room and down to the basement to open a concealed cupboard which the police, for all their efforts, had failed to find. Inside, hanging by his hands, wearing only a' surgical support, was the Ninth Earl of Corwellian, an elderly man who derived his sensual enjoyment by being suspended thus in this secret cupboard. Hurriedly I cut him down. He collapsed in a thin naked heap on the floor.

'Oh Nelly,' he sighed. 'I thought you'd forgotten me hanging up here. I was kicking the door with my heels.' He looked up, poor old ravaged bugger, and smiled. 'But I've had a lovely time,' he sighed. 'It was a truly wonderful night.'

I dressed him and led him to the door where he waved happily and went hobbling off in the direction of the House of Lords. As I was about to close the door I saw a face looking at me from the gate. It was Diana Seagram. She was pale and uncomfortable but she appeared to know nothing of the events at her former house, although the newspapers with the episode were already on the streets, nor did she make any comment on the condition in which the house had been left by the police. Probably she knew everything but said nothing.

Instead she said: 'I have just had news that . . .' she hesitated '. . . that the Commander is very ill. They say he is dying.'

My face went cold. We regarded each other strangely, like rivals.

'He wants to see you,' she said. 'Will you go?'

'Oh of course. You are coming too?'

'No,' she shrugged with what was the first trace of bitterness I had ever seen in her. 'It's you he wants, Nell.'

It was very strange going to see him again. I went north at once that afternoon, weary though I was after my night with the police and their questions. Most of the way I dozed in the soft, deep back seat of the chauffeured car while rain melted against the windows and the February day darkened early.

Years had gone since I had last seen him. It was difficult to recall how many. The thought that I was only going to him again at what were the last few days of his life filled me with regret. I wondered why, in fact, I *had* kept away from him. Perhaps it was because I thought he might see how I had used my life, and I would want to hide that from him.

It was difficult to know what to expect. When the driver found the house, ten miles from Shrewsbury, it turned out that night to be an uncomfortable, grey Victorian place, in a few acres of anonymous parkland. Misgivings crowded in on me as we drove along the trees of the drive. Who would be there? His family? What would they think of me, a trollop arriving out of the night?

The door was opened by a lead-faced woman with already pursed lips. She knew who I was and indicated that this excluded the need for all the but the minimum of conversation. She led me through the uncared-for house to a large cold bedroom and said she would tell the Commander I had arrived. I would have liked a drink or a cup of tea but I was afraid to ask. I looked about the walls and then out into the weary landing. God, if I had been with him all these years he would not have had to die in a dismal place like this.

The ashen-faced woman returned and surprisingly jerked her thumb towards the outside corridor. 'He says he wants to see you now,' she muttered. 'He don't think he's going to last the night. For once in his life I reckon he's right.'

With this depressing forecast delivered, she turned and I nervously followed her down the passage. She paused at a large carved door and banged on it with her fist. A roar came from within. 'Come in! Come in, Nell.'

The wonderful thing about him was how his very presence, frail though it was now, lifted my spirits and my heart. There he was sitting quite jauntily in bed, his face like driftwood, but with a wonderful grin of greeting for me. 'Push off, Martha,' he amiably ordered the doleful woman. 'Let's have some smiles around here.' He opened his pyjama arms to me and I hurried forward, my heart glad, just as it had been when I had greeted him as a girl. We hugged each other, me falling on my knees by the bedside and burying my tearful face in his hard cheek and he patting and comforting me in the way he had always done. Dear God, what had I done with all those years?

He eased me away from the beside. 'Let's have a look at you, Nell,' he grinned. 'God, but you look fine. The beautiful little girl become the beautiful woman.'

I was attempting to calm myself. 'And you?' I eventually said. 'How do you feel?'

'Well they say I've had it,' he said in a matter-of-fact voice. 'But it's not the first occasion. I've had a good many death beds in my time, Nell.' His eyes, steady blue amongst the creases in his face, were alive. 'See over there, in the cabinet. There's a bottle of champagne on ice. They tried to stop me getting it. But I fooled them. I even hobbled down to purloin the ice when nobody was looking.'

I went to the cabinet and took the cold bucket and its bottle back to the bed. 'I think we deserve a drink,' he said strongly. His voice was less of a croak than it had been in the old days. 'Open it up, Nell. Let's have a toast.'

There were some glasses in the cabinet also and I returned with these. Despite his brave words he had no strength to open the bottle so I did. 'Performed like an expert,' he observed from his sheets. 'You've had a lot of champagne have you, Nell?'

'Some of it less than vintage,' I smiled.

'I've followed your fortunes occasionally in the newspapers and the gossip magazines,' he said seriously. 'You've used your time, had a full life.'

'Misfortunes too,' I pointed out. I had the cork free now and as the white tongue of the stuff came over the lip I poured it into our glasses. We lifted them together. 'To you Nell,' he said.

'And I drink to you,' I said, almost choking with the feeling of the moment.

When we had drunk I pulled a chair to the bedside and sat holding his firm but faded hand. 'The first time we met I was stuck in bed,' he remembered. 'And here I am again.'

'It suits you,' I smiled. 'Do you remember when we went on the Serpentine and I rowed you around in the boat? And the time when you came to the Manor when I was a kitchen maid, and the day you met me at Waterloo when I first came to London from Weymouth?'

I could not help it. I hung forward and buried my face and my thick hair in his neck and his cheek, against his old wounds. He put his hand tenderly around my hair and stroked it. 'It's not too difficult, is it,' he said. 'Remembering our joint past. There has not been a great deal of it.'

'I'm so sorry,' I sniffed. 'I should have come to see you before. It's just that ...' Whatever excuse or confession I was about to make was interrupted by a fist hammering on the door.

'It's old cheery,' said the Commander. 'Come in Mrs Modley.'

The glum woman entered bowed over a trolley on which I was glad to see, was set a meal for two. She managed to demonstrate her overwhelming disapproval of me by ignoring my polite appreciation and only speaking to him. 'I thought we might have dinner together,' he said when she had shuffled out. 'She's a miserable old boot isn't she? Been here years. Asked me the other day what I expected her to do when I've gone to glory. She'll be out of a job she said. She blames me for everything. Even for dying. But she's been here about a million years. Poor old thing.'

'Who else is in the house?' I asked, arranging the cutlery and the plates for us. We had another glass of champagne and there was a bottle of burgundy on the cloth, already opened. The meal was a beef casserole which was excellent. I was very hungry.

'I've got various relatives flitting in and out just to see if I'm still one of the living,' he joked. 'I wouldn't bore you with them Nell. It's bad enough having to bore myself with them. Dying's difficult enough without that crew all around. They all hope to get a million quid.'

'Who actually *says* you're dying?' I inquired. 'I mean, have you got any proof?'

'Good girl,' he laughed. 'That's my Nell. Well only what the damned doctor says and he's in his dotage. Probably beat me to it yet. Ha! Be quite funny to go downstairs and announce that the doctor had passed away wouldn't it! God, I'd enjoy that.'

'So really it's just a rumour,' I said. The food and the wine were warming us. I was glad this was how it had turned out. 'A wild rumour.'

'Not according to those that are supposed to know,' he

replied. 'According to these alleged specialists, all these bits of string and lumps of metal that have been holding this poor bloody frame together since the war are in a terrible state and I'm liable to disintegrate more than actually die. I mean, I'll end up a pile of random bits, all fallen apart. They'll be able to bury me in a brown paper parcel.'

It started from that point. I began to fill in the years, telling him about the days and adventures of my life, those of which I was not actually ashamed. I did not tell him I had been arrested and charged the previous night. He sat listening, his grin growing and receding on his handsome face, his eyes full of interest. Occasionally he would explode with laughter and I would laugh too while I went over some story again. It was while we were amused like this that Mrs Modley returned for the trolley and wheeled it out like a hearse, asking at the door, 'Is there anything else, sir?' There was not. And there would never be again.

We had finished the champagne and the wine. I had eaten most of the food. He found that too difficult. The rain brushed across the large ugly windows and the time grew late. He seemed smaller, exhausted. I arranged his pillows for him. He thought I was going. 'Can you stay a little longer, Nell?' he said.

'Much longer,' I said. I rose. 'I'll be back in a few minutes. Don't go away.'

'I won't,' he promised, now very subdued. He watched me go to the door as though fearful that I was really going to leave and not tell him. 'I'll be five minutes,' I promised again. 'I'll be back, then we can talk all night.'

'Good girl, Nell,' he said from the bed. He looked small and isolated there. I returned and kissed him firmly on the cheek and then left the room.

Going to my own room I undressed and put on my nightdress and my robe. Then I went back along the corridor and quietly opened his door. He was still propped up, waiting anxiously. When he saw me a strange smile cracked his lips. 'And not before time, either,' he said throatily.

I climbed into the bed beside him and after a while put out the light. I was conscious how vibrant, how alive my body was against his frailness. Lying against him softly I put my warm arms about him and cradled his head into the fullness of my breasts. My heart was so crowded I could hardly trust myself to speak and we only said a few words before we closed our eyes. I was overcome with the tiredness of my long night and long day and the emotion of these last hours.

Several times I awoke in the night and he was breathing peacefully, his hand against my thigh, his face still resting on my breast. Before I slept I wondered what might have been if our lives had been joined all those years before. The way I felt that night I was full of sorrow for those wasted years.

At four o'clock I thought I heard him snore but when I awoke in early daylight he was dead, still lying close to me. At least we had spent one night together.

My trial took place at the Central Criminal Court three months later, before Mr Justice Bonner. The very name of the place chilled me. Central Criminal Court meant Crippen, Christie and murderers of that type. I preferred to call it the Old Bailey which seemed less sordid and, indeed, had a touch of the theatrical about it.

It was, as all trials are, an entertainment for everyone but the accused in the dock. The public seats were filled as soon as the doors opened and there were crowds left outside to view me as I went in. On the first morning, not realizing the immensity of the attraction of such an occasion, I arrived at the court by taxi and fully believed that the moving throng held back by the police in front of the building must have been there to catch a glimpse of someone else. For a moment I thought perhaps even the Queen was making a visit to the court.

But the instant my head appeared from the taxi there was a rumble from them, as if a motor had been started, and they began to press against the policemen's arms. I looked out, still misunderstanding, and then, as I stepped to the pavement, I realized with a perverse thrill that they had come to see *me*. Nelly Luscombe was infamous.

As I stepped, as steadily as I could, to the door of the court, where my counsel, James Threadgold, waited in his robes and a little bib, the excitement gathered like a small wind blowing through streets. There was a growing buzz, the sucking in and blowing out of breath, the clucking of disapproving tongues, the little squeaks as lips were pursed, and over all that the comments.

I was wearing an olive velvet suit, a cream blouse and a curling hat. I felt smart. From behind the shopping baskets and the briefcases came the voices like darts.

'Don't look like a prossie, do she?'

'Brazen bitch.'

'Taking men from their wives and children.'

'Go back to your knocking shop!'

The choice British hypocrisy was counterbalanced by a call from some scaffolding clinging to a building across the road. From there a workman shouted through an improvised loud-hailer: 'Give the judge one, Nelly. He'll let you off with a caution!'

James Threadgold put his experienced arm on my shaking shoulder and led me into the merciful shadows of the court. I was shaking, a pint of tears ready to run. 'Those people,' I managed to say. 'God, talk about going to the guillotine. Do I have to come in that way every day?'

I felt him smile. 'Nell,' he said, 'by the end of the week they'll be cheering you.'

'I hope the jury isn't like that,' I said, walking with him.

'Oh God, so do I,' he said fervently.

'What could I get?' I had never asked him before and I was too frightened to make other inquiries.

'Five years,' he said stonily.

'Five. Oh God.'

'Keep calm, Nelly,' he said quietly. 'Especially in the witness box. I'll keep calm too. Let the others do the shouting. You never know, we might just win.'

There are few things, of course, that the public and the news-papers savour more than the brutal baring of people's morals. Alongside a sexual trial the most gross of murders becomes commonplace. There is a preference for beds even over blood.

Standing in the dock, my fingers resting on the ledge where many notorious hands had touched before, I felt as lonely as I had ever done in a life that has had its share of loneliness. The court reminded me of some form of animal auction room, with the shoulders and the faces of the bidders projecting from booths all around. It was an especially warm day for early summer and the sun hung through the windows like a series of banners. Five years. The two words revolved inside my head. Five years in a prison where you could not even feel it rain.

James Threadgold sat reassuringly just in front of my place in the dock. His assistant, a young fellow called Morton, was hopelessly in love with me. During the weeks before the trial, after the hearing at the magistrate's court, he had been overcome with what can only be described as a sickness for me although he had never uttered a word of it. I would catch him gazing at my full bosom and he would go scarlet and begin to stutter. 'Nelly,' he said dolefully that morning, before the opening of the trial. 'If they put you away, I will never rest until you are free once more.'

'Nor me,' I smiled at him.

The counsel for the Crown was Peter Crowburn QC, a hard and handsome man, tanned from April skiing in Europe, the edges of his gown in symmetrical lines, the papers in his hands used theatrically, his eyes full of menace for me, his voice clipping away like the clipping of scissors. On that first morning he sat below me and to my left, unmoving as wood, staring directly ahead, waiting for the judge. His papers were piled with tidy confidence before him, he did not whisper to his junior. He gave the appearance that the matter was cut and dried and I would soon be on my way to prison. Looking at him later from the witness box, I could not help but think that he would have made a fine lover.

There were so many reporters behind the press enclosure that it looked like an overcrowded lifeboat. They jostled and whispered snarls to each other as they tried to make their notes. The jury sat timidly in their pen. Everyone waited.

The chimes of the City outside the window marked ten thirty and as though he had been awaiting the cue Mr Justice Bonner materialized through a door which suddenly opened in the panelling behind his raised position. He looked sad but kind, weighed down by his robes and responsibilities. Everyone stood, counsel bowed, the judge bowed, I did a clumsy curtsy. The most important day in the full life of Nelly Luscombe was about to commence.

The Queen versus Nell Luscombe began with a voice. I still remember it better than almost any other thing in my life. It was very like someone calling through a hollow tube and it reached every rafter and every ear of that courtroom where I stood accused.

'Nell Luscombe, you are accused that on the fourteenth day of February this year and on divers other days you, being the householder of 184, Westminster Terrace Gardens, London, SW1, did cause those premises to be used for the purpose of prostitution. How do you plead? Guilty or not guilty?'

'Not guilty, sir.'

'Further, that on the fourteenth day of February this year and on divers other days you were a prostitute using these premises for the purposes of prostitution. How do you plead? Guilty or not guilty?'

'Not guilty, sir.'

'Further, that on the fourteenth of February this year and on divers other days at 184, Westminster Terrace Gardens, SW1, you did procure Lady Diedre Mountjoy, Molly Burtenshaw, Angelica Brownjohn, Cynthia Broad, Teresa Longmate, Lucy Wing and others to be prostitutes. How do you plead? Guilty or not guilty?'

'Not guilty.'

'Further, that on the fourteenth day of February this year and on divers other days at 184, Westminster Terrace Gardens, SW1, you did live on the earnings of prostitution. How do you plead? Guilty or not guilty?'

'Not guilty.'

I did not like to lie in that bold way but I could not let myself go to prison for five years.

For two days the healthy and handsome Mr Crowburn outlined the case for the prosecution and called his witnesses. The police had been watching the house for weeks and produced timetables of the comings and goings of many men. I had wondered why the gang repairing the gas-main across the street had been so long about it and had worked such unsocial hours into the night.

Some of the unusual finds at Strangeways, including an oar from the model slave galley, ropes, whips, canes, rubber things and a variety of beautifully photographed pornography, were trotted out in the solemn courtroom like an inventory of some ancient uncovered Egyptian tomb. Small museum-like men went into the witness box and read out their scientific analysis of stains found on beds and cushions. Watching them I wondered if they ever, beneath those frozen faces, secretly gloated over their finds; I wondered how their lovemaking was with their wives.

'A great deal of money was found at this house and you may think Miss Luscombe shows every sign of being a wealthy woman,' said the elegant counsel in his elegant tones. 'I will eventually put it to you, members of the jury, that here was a veritable harem, a place of available sin, a house of disgust and disgrace, in short a brothel, a bordello in the very heart of Westminster. And to keep a brothel is against the laws of England. It is a very serious offence and I ask you to believe that Miss Nell Luscombe is guilty of that offence. The observations of the police officers, the exotic and devilish implements of sexual depravity, the testimony of witnesses show that the very nature of this establishment is in no doubt.'

It sounded very damning to me. The timid eyes of the jury – with their fat, respectable foreman – turned one by one to me. I returned them a tired smile. They looked away.

Strange as it seems, and I did not realize it then, it was a trial I could never lose. Too many famous names were involved. The prosecution were hampered from the start and as the proceedings went on I began to sense the frustration of Peter Crowburn as he sought to condemn me on diminishing evidence.

Then, in the middle of the following night, itchy-eyed and sleepless, alone in my bed, I had a telephone call. It was my erstwhile lover, Derek Blane.

'Nell, I am speaking from New Zealand,' he whispered.

'Why are you whispering then?' I said dryly. 'Nobody will hear you from there.'

'Don't fool about Nelly,' he said. 'It's this damned trial. It's going to put a lot of people in jeopardy you realize.'

'I'm one of them,' I answered.

'God, they must have been fools to prosecute. I've been abroad for three months. I'd no idea ...'

'It could topple the Government,' I said. I sat up on the pillow with sudden hope. 'Names might be named.'

'That sounds like blackmail.'

'It's you who is telephoning me,' I pointed out.

'We both need help,' he rasped.

God, I thought, how different from those afternoons at Ascot.

'Listen Nell,' he went on, 'whatever you do – no names. I am going to take whatever action I can from here. Understand? It may be too late but I'll try. It's such a bloody mess.'

'It looks like that to me too,' I said.

'No names, then. I'll try and do something.'

I heard him slam down the phone all those miles away.

'Nelly,' said James Threadgold at the end of the second day and the prosecution case. 'They have not produced one witness – thank God MPs don't tell tales – nor one decent bit of evidence, which says that you took *money* from the people who visited your house. That is the one matter they must prove. I think if our case is tidy, and I will endeavour to make it so, and if our witnesses keep their heads under cross-examination, then we must have a chance. Above all it depends on you, Nelly. How you perform in the witness box. Your fate truly is in your own hands, dear girl.'

My cross-examinations began on the morning of the fourth day. Outside the court the spectators were just as numerous but, as James Threadgold had foretold, they had warmed to me as each day's proceedings were reported in the newspapers. Now, although there were still the individual insulters, others shouted encouragement and there was even a modest burst of applause – the sort you might hear at a village cricket match – as I left the taxi and made for the door of the court.

Within the courtroom there was now a familiarity also. It was like becoming accustomed to a fresh place of work. Ushers and policemen nodded to me and the jury seemed more at ease in their box. Peter Crowburn even smiled minutely at me from his robes. But I thought that it was his ploy. It was the tiger's smile.

Mr Justice Bonner made his entry to the City chimes. His robes seemed to get heavier for him each day and he smiled a trifle wearily as he sat down, his wig hanging like the ears of some doleful and unusual dog.

I went to the witness box immediately. I had stood there the previous afternoon while my counsel questioned me gently on my life and the events which had brought me to the court. That was an easy journey. Now came the moment for which the Old Bailey audience had been waiting. A woman who for days had been knitting in the public gallery stilled her needles to pay attention. Noses were blown. I stood in my wooden pen, calm at the top but feeling my knees were like wool. Counsel for the prosecution showed no sign of the difficulties and frustrations which, behind the scenes, were piling upon him. He took his time. He shuffled with his papers, sniffed, looked around, dropped his pen, and showed no general hurry to rise. Everyone watched him. The air of suspense thickened. I knew he had begun to play his weakened hand.

Then the judge, with the smallest lean forward, said: 'Mr Crowburn, are you intending to keep a lady waiting?' The words warmed me.

'I am sorry, my Lord,' Peter Crowburn said, hurrying to his feet. There was a small flush around the dark hair curling about his ears.

'Don't apologize to me,' murmured the judge.

'I do apologize, ma'am,' said the lawyer more grandly than was necessary. He bowed towards me, boxed in with the Bible and my fears.

'Your apology is accepted,' I returned quietly. My stomach was beginning to move. I must be calm, I must think every step. Five years under one roof would be a long time.

'Your true name is Mrs Nell Bickerstaff,' he began carefully. 'You are a widow.'

'That is correct,' I said. 'But I prefer to be called by my maiden name of Luscombe.'

'You are known by that name – Nell Luscombe,' he murmured. 'So be it. And you reside at 184, Westminster Terrace Gardens, London, SW1, the premises which are in fact the core of this case.'

'I do.'

'Would you like to tell us your age, Miss Luscombe?'

'No. Of course if the court thinks it is necessary, I will. But otherwise I would prefer not.'

'The court may well think it is necessary, indeed to have a definite bearing on one aspect of this matter,' he replied smugly. 'But, if you prefer it so, I will not press you at this time. You prefer to be called Miss Luscombe, although it is a fact, is it not, that you have been married a number of times?'

'Three times,' I answered. 'And three times widowed.'

A little sigh, like the smallest of breezes, came from the gallery. The judge glanced up disapprovingly.

'Could you tell us a little about your husbands. Their names for example.'

I saw an expression of alarm take root on my counsel's face. But James remained seated and waiting. He had his fists clenched white on the table before him.

'I have been Mrs Turnbull, Mrs Sheridan and Mrs Bickerstaff.'

'And Mr Turnbull, Mr Sheridan and Mr Bickerstaff are no longer with us? Would it be true to say that each of these gentlemen died in somewhat unusual circumstances, in a violent manner, and ...'

James was on his feet now. His face scarlet with anger. 'My Lord,' he said. 'I object most strongly to this manner of questioning the defendant. What difference does it make to these charges if Miss Luscombe had a dozen husbands and they all came to the most extraordinary ends? It matters nothing whatsoever.'

'I believe it does,' muttered Peter Crowburn as he sat down.

'Mr Crowburn,' observed the judge equably. 'That may be so, but I think at the moment all we really require to know is that Miss Luscombe has been married and widowed three times.'

The QC began a scowl but thought better of it, bowed his acknowledgement and then turned to me. 'So be it,' he said. 'Let us then go on to matters which I hope may be deemed to have more validity in the case. Miss Luscombe, would you say that you are and have been, an exceptionally sensual woman, or even a little stronger, a *sexual* woman.'

'Yes, I have had quite a lot to do with it.'

'Good. Yes. You have had not only husbands but many lovers also.'

'A great variety,' I answered.

'Variety also. Yes. Would you go perhaps further? Miss Luscombe, are you, have you ever been, a prostitute?'

'I have been. I am not now.'

'But you have been a prostitute?'

'I like to think of myself as a courtesan. I don't like the word prostitute.'

He arched his excessive eyebrows. 'You don't? Well I think it is a word acceptable to this court. We all know what it means. We are talking about a woman who sells, or hires anyway, her body for sexual purposes.'

'It sounds so much better when you put it like that,' I said tartly.

'Well that is the way I intended to put it. A prostitute. Now, could you tell the jury when this mode of life, this prostitution began. Can you remember that Miss Luscombe?'

'Very well. When I was about sixteen. I was without parents or home or friends. I was working in a café in Weymouth and I went out with a young fisherman in a boat. I had intercourse with him and his father gave me half-a-crown.'

'His father? Half-a-crown?'

'It seemed a lot then. The father had given me to his son as a sort of birthday present. His name was Rainbow. He had lovely dark hair, like yours Mr Crowburn.'

He went a dull red. There was a small rumble in the court and I thought I saw a small twitch at the edge of the mouth of Mr Justice Bonner.

'Thank you,' sniffed the QC. 'That's very flattering, I'm sure. What happened after that?'

'I used to oblige the fishermen. I made a few pounds.'

'And you've continued making more than a few pounds ever since?'

'Not at all. After that I went to France and on my return to England I met my first husband and we married. A good many years went by before I found the need to do it again.'

'The *need*?' He seized on the word. Although I did not realize it fully, I sensed there was something wrong, something desperate about him. The telephone voice of Derek Blane came to my mind : 'I'll try and do something.' In fact he had done something; people had to be protected. But Peter Crowburn's own integrity would not let him give up. His case against me became a personal one.

'What *need* is that, Miss Luscombe? A financial need or was it an emotional need, a need to have intercourse with as many men as possible, and to take money for that intercourse? In other words, the need of a *compulsive prostitute*, a person who becomes a harlot for other motives than just money. A woman who cannot resist the calling.'

God, I thought, he had put his finger on it right away. There it was. What I knew I had always been, a compulsive harlot.

He knew it too. He stood cooling. His experience would not allow him to leap yet. It was too early.

'With the court's permission,' he said, 'I will read the synonyms for prostitute as listed in Roget's *Thesaurus*. They are as follows: Prostitute, adultress, advoutress, courtesan, strumpet, tart, hustler, chippy, broad, harlot, whore, punk, fille de joie, woman of the street, street-walker, cyprian, miss, piece, frail sister, fallen woman, demirep, wench, trollop, trull, baggage, hussy, drab, bitch, jade, skit, wanton, fornicatress, Jezabel, Messalina, Delilah, Thais, Phryne, Aspasia, Lais, lorette, coquette, petite dame, grisette, demi-mondaine, white slave, doxy fancy woman, kept woman, chère amie, bona roba, mistress, pandar, bawd, mackerel, wittol.'

He paused and drew a stage breath.

'Hooker,' I pointed out quietly. 'You missed out hooker.'

'All right. Hooker too. Can you see yourself under those headings, Miss Luscombe?'

'Some of them,' I agreed. 'I don't like the sound of being a mackerel or a wittol.'

'Would you agree that you are a woman of ill-repute?'

'I am a woman of excellent repute, sir.'

'Perhaps you might like to tell us how you think a prostitute could be described. Since you are in the business.'

'Since I *was* in the business,' I corrected. I had no difficulty in framing the words. I had lain many a night hour running them through my mind. 'A prostitute,' I said patiently. 'Well she must be something of an actress and an athlete. She must be a mother, a daughter, a mistress. She must be able to switch on love and switch it off again. She must realize that she is a man's heart's desire at one moment and a cast-off the next. She must learn the art of loneliness and there is one thing she can never expect. She can never expect love.'

That staggered him. It staggered the court. I could see their new amazement all around me. 'Oh,' said Peter Crowburn hollowly. 'You sound as if you learned that off by heart.'

'I have, sir,' I said. 'I've had a long time to learn it.'

It must have taken two or three minutes for the atmosphere to clear. James Threadgold was staring at me in pleased disbelief, Morton was sitting at a crouch, his mouth agape. Mr Justice Bonner asked if I would like a glass of water. I accepted it and a blushing usher brought it on a neat tray. He came forward with it as if he were offering his heart.

Counsel for the prosecution would not allow the skirmish to become a battle. He skirted around like a prowling tiger for several minutes asking routine and innocuous questions about my purchase of the lease of 184, Westminster Terrace Gardens. Then he began steadily to move into the attack again.

'Surely,' he said. 'A house in that position, in that part of London, must have cost a great deal. Also it was furnished in great style. You must be a wealthy woman, Miss Luscombe.'

'I have money,' I said.

'How did you come by that money?'

'My own work,' I said. 'I saved. I had some good investments. In my profession not all the whispers were of passion. Some were tips for the Stock Exchange.'

'You must have had excellent information. The market has not been at its brightest. To have earned the sort of money you have would have kept yourself very busy. Are you sure it did not come from the sexual efforts of others? The young ladies who disported themselves in your house, for example?'

'The bulk of the money for the house and the furnishings came from one afternoon's racing at Ascot,' I told him simply, as though it was the most logical of matters. 'I won in excess of £100,000. On three horses.'

There was a sound like escaping gas around the courtroom. This time Mr Justice Bonner appeared to join in.

'You won £100,000 at Ascot?' queried Peter Crowburn. 'A hundred thousand?'

'I was not actually there, at Ascot. I was three miles from the course. In bed.'

'You can, I assume, prove this amazing piece of fortune?'

'The gentleman whose company I was keeping could corroborate my story,' I said. I laughed quietly inside as I pictured Derek Blane reading that in the newspaper. 'But I would not embarrass him by calling on him as proof. The bookmakers would confirm it. They remember it very well.'

He sniffed optimistically as if he expected no one to believe me. 'And with this pile of winnings and your fortunate investments, you purchased the house at Westminster Terrace Gardens?'

'I did. The lease, that is.'

'What, madam, was your object in taking that house?' He emphasized the 'madam'.

'For years it had been the home of a friend,' I told him. 'She was leaving it and I was looking for somewhere to live. It was one of those happy coincidences.'

'It was also a coincidence, was it not, that this house was so conveniently placed to the Houses of Parliament.'

'Yes, I have a great many friends in both Houses of Parliament and I enjoyed being a hostess to them. So many of the poor creatures are far from home, you know Mr Crowburn, and they have absolutely nowhere to go.'

'Oh, Miss Luscombe you will have me in tears,' he said sarcastically.

'It is very sad,' I replied. 'They are like lost souls.'

He said, abruptly blunt: 'I would like to put it to you that Members of Parliament and others visited your house for sexual activity with the prostitutes you housed there. *And for those services they paid in cash!*'

'That is not true,' I lied. 'They came there as friends.'

'Why then, tell me, was your house known as Strangeways? It was, was it not? Strangeways.'

'That was just a joke. Some Members interested in prison reform came there and they pulled my leg about the place being like a gaol. They said it was like Strangeways Prison, that's how it started.'

'The truth is, is it not,' his voice was much harder now, as if it had broken through a crust. 'The truth is that the joke referred to the sexual perversions that could be enjoyed, *at a price*, under *your* roof. Sexual services provided by *you*, Nell Luscombe.' Suddenly he shouted and frightened me. *'That is the truth, is it not?'*

'No it is *not*,' I cried back. Suddenly he had me trembling. I caught James Threadgold's worried eye. 'That's not true!'

'All the police observations, all the evidence of the sexual equipment found in that house, then, is wrong. How do you explain the whips then? Go on, Miss Luscombe, explain that.

'I like to be whipped!' I howled. It was not true of course. The tears were coursing down my face. 'I like those things. So do others. Or perhaps *you* cannot understand that.'

'Indeed I cannot,' he observed with personal menace. 'What

I do seem to understand though is that these activities did take place and that you enticed and procured the younger girls to perform these perversions and to receive payment for what we might call their pains. You, madam, say you had no need of the money. That may be true, but now we are back – are we not, madam – at the point where I suggested that you are a prostitute by compulsion, not by necessity.' His face had grown darker as if a bruise were coming out. He hurled the words at me. I could not stop trembling and crying. There was no respite, no breathing space, no mercy. Peter Crowburn, harried as he was from high places, was not going to stop now. He would pursue me if no one else would. I faced him. Now it was him and me. He came at me like a tiger.

'I put it to you and to the jury that you encouraged this *filth*, this *infamy*, for your own personal sexual satisfaction. Now madam, here we come to your age again – I said it was pertinent. I apologize for this impoliteness, but would you agree that getting beyond the bloom of youth, now you are feeling and knowing your age, even if you don't care to divulge it. Now you get *others* to work for you to give *you* satisfaction. So you can watch, observe and enjoy the sensations. So you can use the facilities offered by your ill-famed house. So that you, Nell Luscombe, a lifelong sexual addict, can squeeze the last ounce of pleasure out of the sexual life you know is slipping away. So you debauch young girls, make them perform these acts with men, and get *your* kicks, *kicks* madam I said, in that way. Is that not true? I put it to you plainly. You are a prostitute by proxy. Now – because it is *too late* for you, madam. Too late!' He shouted the final words at me.

Now I was on my emotional knees. Tears were splattering my cheeks and my chin, my whole being vibrated with a great, sorry, outrageous rage. I could feel my very bones trembling. All I remember is looking at him and seeing him in that very same state, furious, shaking, shouting. It was astonishing. We confronted each other like a pair of warring, wounded sealions. Then my own fury rose and engulfed me.

I do not remember clearly the next minute. I can still hear myself shouting 'Too late for me? Too late is it?' And then I was tearing at the buttons on the front of my blouse, pulling it open and with one movement breaking the clasp between the cups of my brassière. My proud and beautiful breasts tumbled out, large, creamy, superbly nippled, free! 'There!' I bawled at him. 'Now tell me it's too late!'

For seconds that seemed like years there was a stillness. The whole courtroom was petrified. I remember the expression on Peter Crowburn's face and the sagging mouth of James Threadgold and young Morton. Then uproar. Ushers, policemen, converged on my exposed person. I felt the room turning, quite slowly, around me and I fell in a faint in the bottom of the witness box.

In the circumstances it was the best thing I could have done.

'Nell,' said James Threadgold, squeezing my arm, 'something has happened. They've chucked it. I damn well know they've chucked it. Something has gone on somewhere. They're going to back down.'

I smiled confidently at him but he did not understand what I knew. He was still cautious however and he wanted to make sure.

'Nell,' he said coyly, 'as soon as the judge begins his summing up to the jury, stand on the left-hand side of the dock. See, where the beam of sunshine is. Stand in that sunbeam, Nell. Try to look like Joan of Arc.'

It was the last day of my trial. Nobody who had been present throughout would ever be quite the same again. I now faced not only the original accusations but a singular charge of Contempt of Court.

I walked two paces sideways – the dock being large enough to accommodate several prisoners at the same time – and stood where the streak of sunshine struck as it came through the clouds and the windows. It had faded temporarily and I stood, listening to the somnolent words of the judge as he directed the jury, like a father trying to give understanding to children. They were to forget everything that had taken place in that court, he said, apart from the facts that had been presented to them. That would have required a miracle.

'*You* and only you must decide whether this extraordinary lady operated her house as a place of ill-repute, for gain, for *money*, and whether she made herself available there, for *money*, and procured others to do likewise. But I emphasize that you must be satisfied that the prosecution have shown beyond doubt that whatever took place at Miss Luscombe's house was for money, for her financial gain.'

He turned towards me at this point and their twelve pairs of eyes followed him and, God bless me, at that moment the sun came out and streamed down through the big windows upon me. I could feel it lightening my hair. I tilted my chin. Like Joan of Arc.

They retired to think about their verdict. James sat quietly by me. I was still drained by it all. I felt at that moment that I would have welcomed a quiet five years in prison. Eventually I whispered, 'What do you think, James?'

'I think we will get an acquittal,' he said calmly. 'Poor Crowburn. Something shot his case from under him. They have not produced one little turd of evidence to show that any money changed hands. It's fortunate too that the gentlemen who were present in the house were all properly attired and, in any event, since they're what they are, politicians, were always highly unlikely to be caught as witnesses.'

He put the tips of his fingers together to his mouth as though considering a prayer, but thought again about it. 'I have never seen Peter Crowburn get into such a mess as that,' he said, a note of sympathy in his voice. 'I understand his wife left him last week. That may have been behind his outburst. Even Queen's Counsel are not immune from inner conflict. Also they gave him a shitty case to handle. I think he's been betrayed. I think we will win, Nell.'

I felt very grateful to him and I touched his hand. He smiled seriously. 'On the other hand, for your truly stupendous Contempt of Court, you could go to prison for six months,' he said. 'You can bare your heart, your soul or your conscience in the Old Bailey, but not your bosom.'

I stood facing them, judge and jury, my stomach shaking within me, my face burning, my hands wet. The four charges were read again and each time the judge leaned towards the jury and asked: 'Do you find the accused guilty or not guilty as charged?'

And four times the voice from the big-bellied foreman sounded surprisingly small. But how sweet.

'Not guilty,' he said.

I felt the relief engulf me. My legs wobbled, my view became fuzzy with tears. All around me the sound from the people came like the starting of a dynamo.

'Nell Luscombe, you have been found not guilty by this court of the four charges brought against you.' The judge's words came to me as though they were being sung by a baritone angel. His dogged face seemed many miles away up there at the end of the court. 'On those counts you will, therefore, be discharged.'

He wrinkled his expression. His wig wobbled. 'Miss Luscombe, do you think you could stand out of that fortuitous sunbeam? Yes, thank you. That is much less dramatic.'

I stood in the cool now, the rays gone from my hair. 'There is now the matter,' he said, 'of the very serious Contempt of Court. I have taken into account the extreme stress you found yourself under and also that there was no mean measure of provocation on the part of the counsel for the prosecution.'

Peter Crowburn stared ahead, not a finger moving. He had a fine strong back. I wondered why his wife had gone. 'On the other hand,' continued Mr Justice Bonner, 'it constitutes one of the gravest contempts I have ever witnessed in a court of law. I was very tempted to send you to gaol without any option. However I decided, in view of the other verdicts, that I shall impose upon you a fine of two thousands pounds with the added punishment of three months in prison . . .' There seemed a year until the next words. '. . . This to be in the form of a suspended sentence.' He leaned towards me in the distance. 'Miss Luscombe . . . you must *never, ever* do that sort of thing in the Central Criminal Court again.'

'No sir,' I whispered. 'I won't. I'm sorry.'

With James Threadgold and the adoring Morton I went out into the free London sunlight, my heart welling with emotion. Outside were my lovely girls, Dirty Diedre, Angelica, Suzy and the others, to surround me and kiss me for the photographers. They would be famous forever.

A furtive man appeared at my elbow. 'Miss Luscombe,' he said. 'I am Detective Sergeant Parry. I congratulate you on the verdict.'

'Thank you,' I said, surprised.

'I wondered if at some time I could have a few words with you about the late Mr Pierre Arthur Bickerstaff? Just routine, you understand.'

'You don't *think* ...'

'We never *think* anything Miss Luscombe. Just routine, nothing to fret about.'

I stood amazed. Then I laughed. I had just been proved innocent of a crime of which I was guilty. I was not afraid of their questions about poor Pierre Arthur although to this day they have pursued me.

'Any time,' I said lightly.

'Thank you Miss Luscombe,' he said, touching his pork pie hat. He sidled away.

There was an enormous turncoat crowd, cheering and happy now that I Nelly Luscombe had won the day – and with what sensations. Something made me turn and in the shadows of the door to the court I could see the solitary Peter Crowburn. I could not help it. I turned back, away from everyone, re-entered that now un-frightening place and confronted him. His face, and certainly his heart, were loaded.

'I suppose it's easy for me now,' I said to him. 'But I wanted to say I am sorry for that demonstration in the witness box.'

He smiled wanly and we shook hands. 'Don't apologize,' he said. 'I got what I deserved. You are a very beautiful woman, Nelly.' We smiled together and I wondered if we had planted a seed. He grinned boyishly now 'And the sunbeam trick was brilliant. I must remember it. Goodbye Nelly.'

'Goodbye Peter.' I did not return to the crowded front of the court, but went through its landings and corridors, guided by a pleased usher to a small back door. As we passed by the inner doors of each courtroom I knew that in every one justice was being done, or not, as the case was.

Outside again I was in a brief shadowed street. A taxi was idling at the kerb as if it had been waiting for me for days. I got in and sat, suddenly deflated and sad, on the long seat.

'Where to madam,' the driver asked. His 'madam' was different.

'Take me home, please,' I said wearily.

'Where's home?' he asked.

'Devon,' I said on impulse. 'Take me to Devon.'

It was an evening returned from childhood. May, with warm Devon air and an airy lightness, the day drifting only reluctantly towards the sea. The hamlet seemed empty of people, only voices calling from houses, gardens with flowers crammed behind their stone walls, birds in trees and cats on walls.

I had walked the mile from Hopewell, over the unchanging hill, drinking from a bottle of gin as I went. Tomorrow, I promised, I would go and see my sister Mary, her good husband, and her children, all the things she had gained. But now, empty once more, without substance, I needed to see if the ghosts of long ago were still lingering.

At the top of the hill, and how small it seemed now, as though it had shrivelled with its ageing, I looked down and saw my stream below still moving through green banks. Where our homely terrace had been was now a smart run of mews-like houses with bogus Georgian windows and coach lamps at the doors. I did not look at them. They had taken the old place away, foundations, earth, heart and all.

The gin was making me drunk and I had not eaten since breakfast that day. The taxi driver had declined to drive me to Devon but had taken me to Paddington in time for the train. I was still in my Old Bailey clothes, my hat awry, my shoes biting my feet. With another swig from the gin bottle I made the last few yards to the bank of the brook.

Miraculously it was just as it had always been. Just as solitary too. Midges, the descendants of those who whirled there long before, were dancing over the darkening water. The day had finally decided to go. Crying, inebriated, I sat on the damp bank and watched the water. I let my shoes and my stockings dangle down into it. I was alone there as I had so often been. The cold water embalmed my feet. I had to do it. Taking a large swig from the gin bottle I laid it on the bank and then undressed. I put all my clothes in a pile on the grass and, naked, stumbled drunkenly into the clear, cold, shallow current.

Then I sat down and let the water run about my middle-aged thighs. A sort of mad melancholy held me. I reached for the bottle, had another mouthful, and began to sing a little Devon song.

Bare Nell Luscombe was back.

Leslie Thomas
Dangerous Davies, The Last Detective 80p

When Dangerous gets a murder case, it's a twenty-five-year-old sex crime. His witnesses range from a veteran of the Zulu wars to a mad policeman who thinks he's Peter the Great ... and the mightily endowed Ena Lind, catsuit-wearer and crème-de-menthe drinker.

Exhibit A is the pair of pale green knickers that the victim wasn't wearing ...

'Cheerfully vulgar ... sharply observed' THE TIMES

His Lordship 75p

His Lordship was what the girls in a posh boarding school called William, their handsome tennis coach. They laid traps for him. They teased him. They were very fond of him. Very fond. That is why William is in a prison cell when the story opens ...

A girls' school that makes St Trinians sound like a nunnery' THE LISTENER

'High jinks and low jinks ... Ripe comedy, very funny and an ingenious pay-off' DAILY EXPRESS

Tropic of Ruislip 75p

'A romp among the adulteries, daydreams and nasty woodsheds of an executive housing estate ... there are Peeping Toms, clandestine couplings, miscegenation on the wrong side of the tracks, the spilling of gin and home truths on the G-Plan furniture and the steady susurrus of doffed knickers' THE GUARDIAN

'Extremely funny ... for sheer pace, invention, gusto and accuracy, Leslie Thomas takes some beating' SUNDAY TIMES

Tom Sharpe
Wilt 75p

'Henry Wilt works humbly at his Polytechnic dinning
Eng. Lit. into the unreceptive skulls of rude mechanicals, his
nights in fantasies of murdering his gargantuan, feather-
brained wife, half-consummated when he dumps a life-sized
inflatable doll in a building site hole, and is grilled by the police,
his wife being missing, stranded on a mud bank with a gruesome
American dyke' GUARDIAN

'Superb farce' TRIBUNE

'. . . triumphs by a slicing wit' DAILY MIRROR

Blott on the Landscape 75p

'Skulduggery at stately homes, dirty work at the planning inquiry,
and the villains falling satisfactorily up to their ears in the
minestrone . . . the heroine breakfasts on broken bottles, wears
barbed wire next to her skin and stops at nothing to protect her
ancestral seat from a motorway construction' THE TIMES

'Deliciously English comedy' GUARDIAN